Praise for Janelle Denison's
"hot [and] sexy" * *Wilde novels*

"Perfect ten — *Wilde Thing* is filled to bursting with scorching sensuality, red-hot and graphic sex scenes, and sexual tension that is off the charts . . . A perfect blending of sensuality, romance, and mystery."

— *Romance Reviews Today*

"Ms. Denison has the unbeatable ability to write a love story that is so erotic, so captivating, you just can't put down the book until you've read it in one sitting. Kudos to Ms. Denison for her fantastic, hot, steamy love stories and the heroes that leave you wishing you had one just like him!" — *A Romance Review*

"*Wilde Thing* is nothing less than divine. Fast-paced action, realistic dialogue, and unbelievably sexy situations all blend together for a definite keeper." — *Escape to Romance*

"Janelle Denison has done it again! *The Wilde Side* is a hot, sexy read that will keep you thinking about the characters long after the last page is read. Ms. Denison weaves a tale so intense that you can't help but get caught up in the character's world. This reviewer is anxiously awaiting the other stories of the Wilde family."

— **Fallen Angel Reviews*

"*The Wilde Side* is everything you've come to expect from Ms. Denison. Scott is sinfully sexy, and readers will find him as irresistible as Ashley does. Fans of Janelle Denison will not only love *The Wilde Side*, but they will be anxious to read the next installment of the sexy Wilde family!" — *The Best Reviews*

continued . . .

"Hotter than hot."

"This is a Wilde and delicious book! It will make you Wilde with desire . .̇. Get ready for a hot and bumpy ride into exquisite passion and desire."

"Ms. Denison knows how to make a story more than a romance. She makes it sensual, electric, and with a plot that keeps readers turning the pages. With a talent such as this, readers will agree that she'll be around for a long time to come!"

"Denison gives us another sensuous tale about the Wilde brothers that borders on erotic. Her men are sexy, charming, and gorgeous, and her heroines are strong yet vulnerable women who can hold their own with a Wilde man. *Wilde Thing* teases, entices, and seduces readers!"

"Janelle Denison is a master at creating the perfect bad boy . . . Passion sizzles with each and every erotic encounter, and there are plenty of erotic scenes guaranteed to heat the room."

Wild
for Him DEN

JANELLE DENISON

BERKLEY SENSATION, NEW YORK

THE BERKLEY PUBLISHING GROUP
Published by the Penguin Group
Penguin Group (USA) Inc.
375 Hudson Street, New York, New York 10014, USA
Penguin Group (Canada), 90 Eglinton Avenue East, Suite 700, Toronto, Ontario M4P 2Y3, Canada
(a division of Pearson Penguin Canada Inc.)
Penguin Books Ltd., 80 Strand, London WC2R 0RL, England
Penguin Group Ireland, 25 St. Stephen's Green, Dublin 2, Ireland (a division of Penguin Books Ltd.)
Penguin Group (Australia), 250 Camberwell Road, Camberwell, Victoria 3124, Australia
(a division of Pearson Australia Group Pty. Ltd.)
Penguin Books India Pvt. Ltd., 11 Community Centre, Panchsheel Park, New Delhi—110 017, India
Penguin Group (NZ), 67 Apollo Drive, Rosedale, North Shore 0632, New Zealand
(a division of Pearson New Zealand Ltd.)
Penguin Books (South Africa) (Pty.) Ltd., 24 Sturdee Avenue, Rosebank, Johannesburg 2196,
South Africa

Penguin Books Ltd., Registered Offices: 80 Strand, London WC2R 0RL, England

This is a work of fiction. Names, characters, places, and incidents either are the product of the author's imagination or are used fictitiously, and any resemblance to actual persons, living or dead, business establishments, events, or locales is entirely coincidental. The publisher does not have any control over and does not assume any responsibility for author or third-party websites or their content.

WILD FOR HIM

A Berkley Sensation Book / published by arrangement with the author

ISBN-13: 978-0-7394-9673-2

BERKLEY® SENSATION
Berkley Sensation Books are published by The Berkley Publishing Group,
a division of Penguin Group (USA) Inc.,
375 Hudson Street, New York, New York 10014.
BERKLEY SENSATION and the "B" design are trademarks of Penguin Group (USA) Inc.

PRINTED IN THE UNITED STATES OF AMERICA

Wild for Him

One

WITH a slight frown, Ben Cabrera glanced down at the formal place setting arranged in front of him, silently contemplating the array of forks, spoons, and knives laid out for him to use. Even for a casual lunch meeting for three, the large, long dining table had been lavishly decorated with painstaking perfection, with a white lace-edged tablecloth, three extravagant bouquets of fresh flowers, and unlit tapered candles in two matching silver candelabras flanking each end of the table. Then there was the expensive, gold-rimmed china he was supposed to eat off of, the cloth napkins that had been folded into a fancy, intricate design, and the delicate crystal glasses with stems that looked so fragile he was certain he'd snap them in two with his fingers if he wasn't careful.

The thought nearly made him wince. As an ex-Marine who'd fought in the Iraq War, he was more used to rowdy mess halls and MRE field rations. After his last tour of duty had ended and he'd returned to the States, he'd settled into a bachelor existence, preferring take-out or prepackaged food and paper plates that didn't require a whole lot of thought or cleanup. As a security agent, he'd honestly never been in a situation where his dining etiquette was called into question.

Until today.

Feeling way out of his element, Ben hoped like hell that he made it through the meal without making too much of a fool of himself in front of gubernatorial hopeful Nathan Delacroix and his daughter, Christine, when she arrived for the impromptu lunch. Maybe he could just watch to see what piece of silverware Christine used before picking up his own so he didn't make any high-society faux pas that pegged him for the simple, small-town guy he really was, and always would be.

"Don't let the elaborate place setting make you nervous," Nathan said, a bit of easygoing humor lacing his voice. "My wife insists that the table be formally set at all times, no matter the time of day or occasion."

Ben glanced at the other man, who was sitting beside him at the head of the grand table. For someone in his late fifties, Nathan was still an extremely good-looking man, the kind that voters were drawn to, with his sandy blond hair, dark, intelligent green eyes, and a distinguished appearance one would associate with a politician. Even on a Sunday afternoon, he was impeccably dressed in a collared polo shirt and pleated trousers.

"Was I that obvious, sir?"

With a grin tugging at the corners of his mouth, Nathan shrugged in answer. "I'm used to my wife's idiosyncracies, but I know others find all the formality and decorum a bit . . . overwhelming."

To say the least. There was just enough wryness in the other man's tone to let Ben know that he was also referring to the ostentatious elegance encompassing the entire house. The stately home located just out of the city limits of Chicago had been decorated in a way that was dramatically elegant and smacked of affluence and wealth, with expensive pieces of furniture; rare, collectible art and antiques; marble flooring; and imported rugs throughout the downstairs area.

Truly, there was nothing warm, welcoming, or inviting about the inside decor of the house, but having been in the same room with Audrey Delacroix more than a few times over the past year, Ben had to admit that everything about the furnishings was just like the woman herself—refined and polished, but also very cool and aloof. Quite the opposite of her husband, Nathan, who was warm, friendly, and an all-around nice guy.

Good thing *she* wasn't the one running for office, Ben thought dryly.

Then there was their only child and daughter, Christine, who'd luckily inherited her father's amicable disposition. Despite her rich and privileged upbringing, she was far from being spoiled or snobbish, and was nothing at all like her mother in terms of Audrey's standoffish personality and the aura of entitlement the other woman exuded.

"Christine should be here any minute." Nathan cast a quick look at his Rolex. "I sent a car to pick her up so she wouldn't be on the road alone, and my driver is pretty good about being on time."

"That's fine." Ben certainly wasn't going anywhere anytime soon. At least not until this current assignment of his was set up and put into action, all of which required Christine's presence and cooperation.

At Nathan's unexpected and insistent phone call earlier that morning requesting Ben's security services, he'd hurried out and arrived at the Delacroix home nearly an hour ago, more than a little curious as to what the other man needed him for so urgently. Ben was a partner of ESS, Elite Security Specialists, and Nathan Delacroix had become one of Ben's high-profile clients over the past year. The other man called on Ben whenever he needed extra security for campaign events, public speeches, or other political situations. And with the race for governor only three weeks away and things heating up for a big finale, Ben could only assume that Nathan was in need of extra security and backup for the duration of the campaign.

But instead of the simple, routine security detail he'd expected, Nathan had thrown him an unexpected curve by informing him that as of that morning, he was being hired to provide his daughter with round-the-clock protection. Nathan had gone on to tell him that he'd received an anonymous threat against himself that also put Christine's safety in jeopardy. The note that had arrived in an unmarked envelope instructed Nathan to drop out of the election, or risk losing what was most precious to him. And there was nothing, and no one, that Nathan adored more than his daughter. Ben had seen that for himself over the past year.

And now, Nathan was trusting Ben to keep Christine safe and out of any potential danger.

Earlier, Nathan had handed Ben a dossier on his daughter, which gave him important information—her newly formed business and job as an event planner, where she lived, and details about her recent past and breakup with her ex-fiancé, Jason Forrester, seven months ago. Including the fact that Christine had to have a restraining order issued against the man due to continual harassments and threats.

The elder Delacroix had no idea if her ex was behind the current blackmail attempt, but considering Jason had worked directly for Nathan as a political consultant before being fired and blacklisted in the political arena for his blatant indiscretions, along with the discovery that Jason had been embezzling money from the campaign contributions, Christine's ex had every reason to want to sabotage Nathan's campaign for governor. Delacroix had assured Ben that Jason would have no qualms about using Christine for leverage to ruin him, since Nathan had been the one who'd been responsible for sending Jason, and his shot at a political career, on a downward spiral.

At least that's how Jason had seen things. According to Nathan, the other man should have been far more considerate and faithful to Christine, as well as keeping his hands out of the campaign funds.

Thinking back on the security details they'd discussed in Nathan's study earlier, there was something Ben had meant to ask the other man, but he had been sidetracked by other more imperative issues. "Sir, is your daughter aware of the fact that you've hired me as her bodyguard, twenty-four/seven, until the election is over?"

"No, not yet. Which is why I've invited her to join us for lunch today, so I can break it to her gently." The older man laughed. Clearly he understood there would be nothing easy or *gentle* about informing his daughter she'd have a shadow for the foreseeable future.

Leaning back in his chair, Nathan's expression took on a firm and determined look. "My daughter has become very independent recently, but I can promise you she'll cooperate with this sudden change of plans. Having a private bodyguard, especially during election time, isn't something new for her. She might be a bit surprised at the live-in arrangements, but she'll understand that it's absolutely necessary and non-negotiable."

Ben nodded in agreement. Until they discovered who the culprit was that had sent the intimidating letter, he'd be glued to Christine's side.

Ben had to admit that the job of protecting Christine's body certainly wouldn't be a hardship, not when she had the kind of shapely curves that made him wonder, and imagine, what she'd look like naked, with nothing but moonlight painting her supple, creamy-looking skin. Then there was all that silky blond hair the color of rich honey, those bright blue eyes that were always so full of life and carefree laughter when she was around him, and that sweet mouth of hers that could smile so guilessly, yet also managed to fuel some hot, erotic fantasies of how those soft, sensual lips might feel sliding against his skin.

The front door slammed shut, the sound jarring Ben out of his inappropriate and too arousing thoughts. His job was to protect Christine Delacroix, not seduce her, no matter how much she'd made her interest in him clear. And she had, each and every time they'd run into one another over the past months of Ben working for her father.

But no matter how much she flirted and teased, or how much the mutual attraction simmering between them tempted him, Ben was a professional. He could daydream and fantasize about Christine all he wanted, but he'd never touch.

Not only was she about to become a client—and he didn't mix business with pleasure—but she was so out of his league, in so many ways. Socially and financially being at the top of the list. The only reason he was even a part of her affluent world was because he was a hired security agent. Other than that, there was nothing about her privileged lifestyle he could even begin to relate to.

"Speaking of the angel, here she is now," Nathan said fondly.

The sound of heels clicking on the marble entryway sounded seconds before Christine appeared in the dining room, dressed in a beige V-neck top, slim black jeans, and a pair of expensive-looking designer shoes that enhanced the length of her slender legs. Her dossier pegged her at five foot five, a good eight inches shorter than himself, but the confident way she carried herself, combined with those killer heels she always wore, made her appear much taller than she actually was. And they made her legs and her ass—his two favorite attributes on a woman—look sexier than hell.

But despite those four-inch heels strapped to her feet, there was a distinct and lively spring in her step that caused her loose hair to swirl around her shoulders. The brisk energy in her walk also made her small, firm breasts bounce with just enough motion to draw his gaze for a brief, appreciative moment before lifting back up to her lovely face once again.

He silently agreed with Nathan. Christine did look like an angel, but Ben's thoughts were anything but saintly or pure when it came to her.

As she entered the room, her gaze locked on her father first, since he was seated at the head of the table, and she headed toward Nathan with a sweet, genuinely-happy-to-see-you grin curving her lips.

"Hello, Daddy." Reaching his side, she leaned down and placed a kiss on his smooth-shaven cheek.

The warm, affectionate smile Nathan gave his daughter in return made him appear ten years younger than his true age. "Hi, sweetheart."

Ben pushed back his chair and stood up to greet Christine, finally bringing her attention to the fact that he was in the room, too. She glanced at him in startled surprise.

"You remember security agent Ben Cabrera, don't you?" Nathan asked his daughter.

Once her initial shock at seeing him there on a Sunday afternoon ebbed, she flashed him one of her effusive grins. "Of course I do. Hello, Ben."

He nodded politely in return. "Christine."

She rolled her eyes at all his formality, then waved a hand toward his chair, setting off a light, tinkling sound from the gold bangle bracelets circling her wrist. "Please, sit down. You don't need to stand when I enter the room. I'm hardly the Queen of England," she said, laughter in her voice. "And how many times have I told you to call me Christy?"

He settled back into his seat, doing his best to remain unaffected by that mischievous twinkle in her eyes that made her look too damned irresistible. "A few." He knew that her friends called her by the informal nickname, but for Ben, calling her Christy was too personal and intimate. Especially since he was about to become her private body guard for the next three weeks.

"Maybe someday you will." Her sexy wink and the playful lilt to her voice indicated that she wasn't done trying to sway him—no big shock there. Undoubtedly, she was used to getting her way. She also took great delight in provoking him, the minx.

She slid into the chair next to Nathan and across from where Ben sat, then glanced at her father. "Where's Mother? It's nearly one o'clock in the afternoon. Is she not joining us for lunch today?"

"She's still in her room, as far as I know." Nathan sighed, the sound barely concealing the frustration creeping into his tone. "According to Maggie, she woke up with a headache and claimed she wasn't feeling well this morning. Things haven't changed much since you moved out."

Ben shifted uncomfortably in his chair. Though he was used to people discussing their private lives in front of him, since he was supposed to be the invisible bodyguard, this intimate table discussion was more than he wanted, or needed, to know about this family's conflicts that centered around Audrey. Ben had no desire to get involved, and he figured if he was lucky, he wouldn't even have to see the woman for the next three weeks.

"I'm sorry." Christine went on as she shook her head,

apparently used to her mother's personal issues, too. "I'll be sure to stop by her room to say hello before I leave."

Nathan nodded. "I'm sure she'd like that."

Christine tipped her head toward her father. The diamond hoop earrings in her lobes caught the light from the overhead chandelier and sparkled brilliantly. "You don't have to fib on my account, Daddy. She hasn't even come close to forgiving me for calling off the wedding and embarrassing her in front of her high-society friends. Never mind *my* humiliation. She tolerates me right now because I'm her daughter and she has no choice."

Nathan grimaced, but didn't refute her claim. "Fair enough."

An elderly woman with graying brown hair and kind hazel eyes entered the dining room from an adjoining doorway, a glass pitcher in her hand. Judging by the apron tied around her small waist, and the way she began pouring iced tea into their crystal glasses, Ben guessed that she was part of the household help.

"Hi, Maggie," Christine said in cheerful greeting. "How are you doing?"

The other woman beamed at her as she finished filling Ben's glass with tea, then moved on to Nathan's. "Just wonderful, Sweet Pea. When your father mentioned that you were going to be here for lunch today, I decided to make one of your favorite meals."

Christine thought for a quick moment, that infectious gleam sparking to life in her eyes again. "You made peanut butter and jelly sandwiches?"

Maggie laughed. "You always did love those as a little girl, didn't you?"

She gave Maggie an impish grin. "Still do, actually."

Amusement softened Maggie's features. "I sure do miss having you here at the house every day," she said, an unmistakable hint of melancholy in her voice. "As for

lunch, I made wild mushroom ravioli with sweet ver-
mouth and cream sauce. And for dessert, bread pudding
with my special apricot sauce."

"Mmmm, you spoil me." The hunger and anticipation
reflecting across Christine's face made for an arousing
combination. "I can't wait."

Once Maggie retreated to the kitchen, Christine reached
for the sugar bowl, dropped a few of the crystallized cubes
into her tea, and met Ben's gaze from across the table as
she stirred her drink. "I didn't realize that lunch on a Sunday afternoon was such a security risk," she teased good-
naturedly. "Should I be concerned that you're here?"

It was clear that Christine was just kidding around and
making light of his presence, but Ben wasn't quite sure
how Nathan wanted to handle telling his daughter of his
purpose for being there. So, he glanced at the other man,
giving him the opportunity to handle the situation and
answer the question.

Nathan cleared his throat. "Actually, Ben's here at my
personal request."

"Oh." Christine picked up her napkin, unfolded the
piece of expensive cloth, and placed it on her lap.

Ben immediately followed her lead and did the same
thing.

"Are you going somewhere after lunch that requires
security?" she asked her father curiously.

Before Nathan could launch into an explanation, Maggie
arrived with three salads and set one of the plates in front
of Ben. "Thank you, ma'am," he said automatically, and
glanced up as the older woman finished serving Nathan and
Christine.

A sassy grin quirked one corner of Christine's mouth,
and she lifted a perfectly arched brow in amusement.
"*Ma'am?*" she mouthed to him, as if she couldn't believe
he'd used such a formal expression.

She was toying with him. Again. Because she could and obviously enjoyed the seductive game that tempted him to play along. God, if she was anyone else, he'd be flirting right back and wouldn't hesitate to act on the undeniable attraction between them. Wouldn't hesitate to drag her off to some dark, secluded spot so he could kiss her, slow and deep, and slake all the pent-up lust she'd been stirring in him over the past few months. If she was anyone else, he would have had her by now, in all the shockingly erotic ways he'd imagined for much too long.

Unfortunately, she wasn't anything like the easy, forgettable women he met at Nick's Sport Bar or The Electric Blue. A woman he could enjoy for a few weeks until he had his fill, then leave her behind. No, this beautiful, sensual woman came with too many complications, and he wasn't about to jeopardize his personal and working relationship with Nathan Delacroix by taking advantage of his daughter's interest. No matter how badly his sorely neglected libido wished otherwise.

So, instead, he had to sit there and struggle to remain completely unaffected when she knew damn well that she was causing him all kinds of discomfort. She was just waiting for him to react to her outrageous behavior, and when he didn't rise to the challenge, she finally glanced away.

He watched carefully as she ran her fingers across the three forks lined up on the left-hand side of her salad plate, and waited for her to choose the correct utensil. When she picked up the fork on the inside closest to her dish, he subtly copied her move.

She didn't start in on her salad right away. Instead, she held her fork just above her plate as she turned her attention to her father. "So, tell me, what's going on? Is everything okay?"

"Everything's fine, sweetheart," Nathan said reassuringly as he took a drink of his tea. "But with three weeks left until the election, I figured it never hurts to have extra security around."

She nodded. "I couldn't agree with you more."

Just as Ben was about to dig into his salad, Christine casually set her fork back down on the table and traded it for the one on the far left. Frowning in confusion, he placed his own utensil back where it had been and made the mistake of lifting his gaze to hers. She gave him a cute little *gotcha* smirk and winked at him, telling him without words that she was so on to his ploy.

The woman was something else, and he had to tamp the unexpected urge to laugh at being caught in the act. That bit of humor she evoked surprised him, because it had been much too long since a woman had amused him as much as Christine did. If anything, he knew they could at least be friends during the next few weeks.

Christine continued the conversation with her father without missing a beat. "There are so many fanatics and extremists out there, especially with the whole gentrification issue at stake, and your safety is definitely a priority."

Nathan ate a bite of his salad. "Actually, this is about *your* safety for the next few weeks, and that's why Ben is here."

Upon learning who her father had hired for her, Christine met Ben's gaze, her blue eyes bright with delighted pleasure and satisfaction, the kind that spelled pure, seductive trouble for Ben. "*You're* my bodyguard?"

"Yes, *ma'am*," Ben drawled, and gave her a good-ol'-boy grin before digging into his salad again.

She bit her bottom lip to keep from laughing out loud. "So, during the next few weeks, when I'm out at a public function, Ben will be with me?" Christine asked her father, to confirm exactly what to expect from Ben's services.

Finished with his salad, Nathan set his fork on his plate and looked at his daughter, his expression uncompromising, showing Ben the resolute opponent that Delacroix had the ability to be. "Actually, this security detail is a bit different. I've hired Ben to be your bodyguard twenty-four/seven, until the election is over. He'll be by your side at all times, day *and* night, which means he'll be living with you and staying in your guest room at your place."

Christine's jaw dropped open, then snapped shut again. For the first time since arriving, she was clearly shocked and speechless at her father's unpredicted bombshell and it took her a few moments to speak.

Finally, she glanced at Ben, then back to her father. "Is having Ben live with me really necessary?"

Nathan reached over to his daughter and clasped his larger hand over hers on the table and gave it a gentle squeeze. "I know it seems extreme, but right now, it's *absolutely* necessary."

"Why?" Christine's worried gaze searched her father's for answers. "What's going on that I'd need that kind of stringent, round-the-clock protection?"

Nathan moved his hand back as Maggie came through the dining room and cleared their salad plates. As if sensing the serious tone to the conversation, the other woman quickly and efficiently placed their main entrée dishes in front of each of them, then retreated back to the kitchen.

Ben inhaled the rich, redolent scent of pasta and cream sauce topped off with grated parmesean cheese, and his stomach rumbled hungrily in response. It wasn't often, if ever, that he ate something homemade and smelling as mouth-wateringly delicious as the wild mushroom ravioli that Maggie had prepared, and he was anxious to taste and enjoy the meal. But, at the moment, Christine was obviously too upset to feast on one of her favorite dishes, and Ben was trying to be a gentleman and not start without her.

"You know I'd hire security for you regardless since the election is so close," Nathan went on in an obvious attempt to alleviate his daughter's fears. "But this morning I received an anonymous letter demanding that I drop out of the election or face some kind of dire consequence. While the threat wasn't specific and I have notified the police, I'm not taking any chances with your safety or your mother's safety. I'm making sure that we *all* have round-the-clock protection."

It didn't escape Ben's notice how Nathan had cushioned the truth about the intimidating note he'd received, and knew he'd done so deliberately, to keep his daughter's panic at a minimum. Ben appreciated the gesture, since it was much easier to watch over someone who wasn't jittery and constantly looking over her shoulder for something to happen. He needed Christine calm and relaxed and cooperative, and her father had achieved that state of mind beautifully.

Christine drew a deep breath and let it out slowly, her initial trepidation fading beneath the small smile she gave her father. "You're right, of course. I'm sorry I overreacted. It's just that you've never employed a full-time bodyguard for me before."

Ben guessed that Nathan never had any reason to until now.

"It's strictly a precaution, okay?"

Seemingly reassured, she nodded. "Okay." She picked up one of her remaining forks and pierced a ravioli, her appetite restored. Before taking a bite, she asked, "Do you think the threat for you to drop out of the race for governor is related to the gentrification issue?"

Since Nathan Delacroix was one of ESS's clients, over the past year Ben had kept up on Nathan's campaign and political views, and what he'd learned had given him a healthy respect for the man.

Even though Nathan was very wealthy himself, he was a man who fought for the underdog and was a huge advocate for the poor. He believed in equality and nondiscrimination, and he also believed in preserving the integrity and historic quality of many of the inner-city neighborhoods, especially the lower west side of Chicago.

"It very well could be related," Nathan said with a shrug. "But as I said, there wasn't anything definitive stated in the letter, so it could be for any number of reasons, as well as just a hoax. The police will be checking into any leads they might find, but in the meantime I'll sleep much better at night knowing you've got Ben watching over you."

Christine nodded in understanding.

While Nathan and his daughter went on to discuss her father's political agenda, specifically his opposition to tearing down old, lower-income neighborhoods in Chicago to make way for luxury condos and commercial high-rises, Ben listened to their avid conversation and ate his lunch.

Ben made it a point to understand not only the people he watched over but the agendas around them. While Nathan was committed to restoring and revitalizing the rundown neighborhoods, he had political opposition to his views on gentrification. Charles Lambert, Nathan's opponent for governor, was pushing to tear down the deteriorating lower west side to make way for a chic and trendy locale that would bring in a substantial income for all involved.

But Lambert's way would also destroy the inner city and those who lived there. Long-time residents would be evicted and displaced in lieu of modern, state-of-the-art buildings and upscale businesses. And unfortunately for Nathan, Charles had the support and financial backing of major developers and many of the city's wealthy residents.

The three of them finished the delicious main course, and Maggie followed that up with a heavenly-looking bread pudding drenched in a rich, decadent apricot sauce.

Christine took a bite of the dessert, then closed her

eyes, a soft, appreciative moan escaping her lips as she savored the delectable taste. Ben wholeheartedly agreed that the confection was as close to ambrosia as he'd ever enjoyed, but it wasn't the dessert that captivated *his* attention. No, it was Christine's sensuous response that ensnared him and kept him riveted to the sated expression on her face. When she finally let her lashes drift back open, met his gaze, then *oh-so-slowly* swiped her bottom lip with her tongue, he felt his blood pump hard and fast in his veins.

She blinked at him, then smiled sweetly.

He dropped his gaze to his own dish and released a deep breath. Lord, she was brazen. Or maybe it was *his* overactive imagination putting a sexual slant to her enjoyment of the dessert, because her father seemed oblivious to his daughter's wanton display.

"There is absolutely *nothing* that compares to Maggie's bread pudding." She sighed, and ate another spoonful, and Ben was eternally grateful when she didn't launch into another moaning, groaning, orgasmiclike response again.

"I have to agree," Nathan said in between bites. "I think she outdid herself this time, if that's even possible."

"Absolutely." Christine wiped away a bit of sauce from the corner of her mouth. "By the way, Ben, since you've officially been hired as my bodyguard, I wanted to let you know ahead of time that I have plans tonight."

Ben swallowed hard, trying not to choke on the bread pudding he'd just eaten. "A date?" Jeesuz, was he about to be a tagalong chaperone while Christine went out with some guy? How awkward was that? He hadn't even considered *that* possibility, and for some odd reason the thought of her being with another man as he stood close by and watched made his stomach churn with something too close to jealousy.

And he was so *not* the jealous type.

"A date, an engagement, whatever you want to call it," she clarified with a wave of her hand, which sent off another melodious sound from her gold bracelets. "I'm meeting up with some friends at Envy. It's a nightclub in the city. Have you been there before?"

He shook his head. "No. I've heard of it, though." Envy was so not his type of place to hang out. It was like comparing sophisticated cosmopolitans and caviar to the cheap beer and pretzels he preferred. But it didn't matter what he liked, because he was being paid to remain by Christine's side, no matter what she did or where she went.

"As far as I'm concerned, Envy is a hedonistic place, and you don't belong there," a pretentious female voice interjected, the chastisement in her tone glaringly evident.

Ben immediately recognized the voice. It seemed that Audrey Delacroix had deigned to grace them with her presence.

Christine rolled her eyes at her mother's derogatory comment. Then, with a smile in place, she glanced toward where Audrey had just entered the dining room, dressed in a brown silk blouse and matching slacks. Her blond hair was pulled back into a complicated twist, and though her makeup had been impeccably applied, there was no mistaking the dark circles beneath both of her eyes.

"Hello, Mother," Christine said amicably.

Ben automatically stood up, not daring to look at Christine this time. His manners were ingrained, and he figured greeting Audrey formally might earn him a few points in his favor. "Good afternoon, Mrs. Delacroix."

Audrey spared him a brief, dismissive look that made him feel like pond scum and said nothing in reply. Ben sat back down. Clearly, she didn't appreciate him, *the hired help*, eating lunch in her fancy-schmancy dining room with her husband and daughter.

Nathan nodded toward his wife, his acknowledgment stiff and forced. "Audrey."

"Nathan." She gave him an insincere smile in return.

Oh, boy. The strain and tension in the room was suddenly thick enough to cut with a knife, and Ben decided his best course of action was to keep his mouth shut, finish his dessert, and try to blend in with the damask wallpaper behind him.

Audrey slid gracefully into the chair at the farthest end of the table, keeping herself separated from the three of them. She gave her daughter a pointed look, her blue eyes brimming with disapproval. "I don't understand why you feel the need to go to a place like Envy."

Christine straightened in her seat and didn't back down from her mother's criticism. "It's a nightclub, Mother. It's fun, I enjoy being with friends, and I've hosted events and parties there. I go for business as well as for pleasure."

Audrey opened her napkin and smoothed it onto her lap. "Then maybe you ought to reconsider your so-called job, as well as the people you choose to hang out with."

Christine stared at her mother, a glimmer of hurt passing over her features before firm conviction took its place. She opened her mouth to say something, but her father was much quicker.

"Leave her alone, Audrey," Nathan cut in brusquely. "She's not doing anything wrong or something that's going to sully the Delacroix name."

Audrey pursed her pink lips and glared at her husband, but remained quiet.

Maggie came out of the kitchen, and Audrey asked the other woman to bring her some dry toast and fresh fruit. Once she was gone, Nathan spoke.

"Just so you know, I've hired Ben here as security for Christine," he told his wife, "and Dominic has been assigned to you for the next few weeks."

Audrey appeared totally put out and annoyed. "I'll be glad when the election is over. The last thing I need is a bodyguard dogging my every move."

"I'm sorry it's such an inconvenience," Nathan replied, his apology genuine.

Instead of softening, Audrey's gaze darkened with resentment. "It's for the greater good, now isn't it?"

Ben nearly winced at the sarcasm in the woman's tone.

Nathan sighed heavily, almost with defeat. Placing his napkin on the table, he pushed back his chair and stood. "You'll have to excuse me. I have an appointment with my advisors at the office."

Audrey lifted an incredulous brow. "On a Sunday?"

"Yes, on a Sunday." Nathan met his wife's gaze, and Ben watched as something passed between the two, a battle of wills that had Audrey bristling. "I don't know how late I'll be home, so feel free to make other plans for the evening."

Before Audrey had a chance to respond, Nathan glanced at his daughter, his smile affectionate and warm. "As always, it was wonderful seeing you, sweetheart."

"You too, Daddy," she said softly.

Nathan turned toward Ben. "Make sure you take care of my girl," he said, his gaze speaking volumes.

Nodding, Ben shook the other man's hand, sealing the deal they'd made back in his study. "I will, sir," he promised.

And that meant keeping his eyes and ears open for trouble, and his hands *off* his client.

Two

CHRISTINE had never been so grateful to leave her parents' house, not to mention escape her mother's constant criticism of how she lived her life now that she was no longer engaged and living at home. And, as her new bodyguard had witnessed, Audrey Delacroix had no qualms about expressing her disapproval and disappointment over her daughter's choice of career, and single status, and she did so every chance she got. Even knowing how critical her mother could be, the digs were sharp and always cut deeper than Christine expected or anticipated.

As soon as they settled into Ben's vehicle—a new but basic Ford truck in pewter gray—he told her he needed to swing by his place to pick up some of his things before heading to her house, then he excused himself to make a phone call on his cell. At the moment, he was talking to someone named Kevin and letting him know about the sudden change to his work schedule, and that he'd be on this new assignment until the election was over.

As the two men discussed a few of the open cases Ben

had been working on and what needed to be done on each in his absence, Christine leaned her head back against her seat and attempted to relax after that awful, and embarrassing, confrontation with her mother. And she couldn't think of a better way to unwind and calm her frayed nerves than to listen to Ben's smooth, deep voice as she admired everything that made him so exceptionally male.

And there was plenty about him to appreciate and enjoy. From his thick, rich, brown hair, to those disarmingly seductive eyes that reminded Christine of her favorite Godiva chocolate. He possessed a full, sensual mouth that had inspired many shameless, wicked thoughts, and she liked that he smiled easily and often and didn't seem to take her, or life in general, too seriously.

The fact that he could indulge in a bit of humor, even while working, was a pleasant and welcome change from her ex-fiancé's oppressive personality.

His facial features were lean and defined, as was the rest of his body. Standing, he was much taller than her even when she wore her highest heels. His shoulders were broad and he had a firm, muscular chest that had made her wonder, more than once, what he looked like without a shirt on. No doubt, breathtakingly gorgeous. From the waist down, he was just as honed and well built . . . everywhere.

As an ex-Marine and professional bodyguard, he looked strong and capable of keeping her safe and protected. As a man, he looked just rough and tough enough around the edges to give him a bit of a bad boy image. But that rugged appearance and his lack of pretense was what made him real, solid as a rock, and oh-so-appealing to her. What you saw with Ben was exactly what you got, and it was such a refreshing, welcoming change. Those traits also made him stand out from the pack of polished, self-absorbed men she was used to being around.

No question about it, Ben Cabrera was hot, sinfully sexy, and he was exclusively hers for the next three weeks. *Imagine that,* she thought with a small, private smile.

Actually, imagining Ben any number of ways was extremely easy to do, considering how attracted she was to him. With just a slow, dark-eyed look or one of those half-smiles of his that tried to bank his own mutual interest—and failed—she felt as though she was melting inside. He made her pulse race, her skin tingle, and her stomach feel as though someone had released a dozen butterflies inside.

Her intense awareness and reaction to Ben was like nothing she'd ever experienced for another man. Her ex-fiancé included. And that said a lot about just how incompatible she and Jason had been from the beginning, on so many levels. But now, looking back at the entire scope of their relationship, it was easy to see Jason's hidden agenda as well as her mother's ulterior motives in pushing them together.

None of that mattered now. She was done living her life for anyone other than herself, and now she was going to do things *her* way. With her new event planning business taking off faster than she'd anticipated, and living out on her own for the first time in her life, she was in a great place emotionally and mentally. She loved her newfound freedom and independence, and she was going to enjoy both for a good long time before even contemplating settling down again—with the right man, of *her* choosing.

But in the meantime, there were certain things she was very open to exploring and experiencing. Like the undeniable sexual chemistry between her and Ben. Their situation and forced close proximity couldn't be a more perfect way to take advantage of all the smoldering heat and awareness they'd both been skirting for months now.

"I'll be in touch over the next few days," Ben told the

man on the other end of the line, effectively pulling Christine's attention back to the present. "And if you need anything from me regarding those cases, just give me a call on my cell. Talk to you later, Kev."

He snapped the unit closed and glanced at Christine to find her turned his way, since she'd been watching him during the entire phone discussion. After scrutinizing her expression for a quick moment, he returned his gaze to navigating the road.

"Are you all right?" he asked.

She wasn't sure why he was asking, and she wasn't about to give him an answer he might not be expecting. "Why shouldn't I be?"

Again, he looked at her, searching her features for what, she wasn't sure. "No reason," he said vaguely. "Just checking to make sure you're okay with everything."

For her, *everything* encompassed a whole lot after this afternoon's lunch meeting with her father, then her mother's theatrical entrance into the dining room. "If you're asking about *our* situation, I'm one hundred percent fine with you being my bodyguard, and I'll try to make your job as easy as possible for you." Although she wasn't frightened by the threats her father had received, she did take his concern seriously and would never argue the point of him hiring a security agent for her until the election was over.

"Don't worry about me," he said as he gave her a glimpse of one of those sexy, toe-curling smiles of his. "You do what you have to do and go about your life and business as usual, and you won't even know I'm around."

Ignoring his existence for the next three weeks was going to be virtually impossible, she knew. Even if he was invisible, everything that made her inherently female would sense whenever he was near, would feel his eyes wandering over her. He'd be close enough at all times, like now for instance, for her to inhale the warm, virile scent that was uniquely his—an arousing blend of heat, sex, and pure male temptation.

Feeling hot and bothered, she shifted in her seat and addressed the other issue Ben had been privy to when her mother had joined them for lunch. "I'm really sorry that you had to witness all that family drama back at the house."

"Hey, stuff happens." He shrugged casually as he eased the truck off an exit ramp just outside of the Chicago city limits. "I've learned to tune out conversations like that."

She shook her head, finding that hard to believe. "I don't know how that's possible. I mean, you were *right* there, and it's not easy to tune someone like my mother out. Believe me, I've tried."

He chuckled, the rich, warm sound sliding over her like a caress. "Okay, I'll give you that. Let's just say I hear more than I care to when it comes to my clients, but I don't judge or make assumptions. At least I *try* not to, anyway. It's not my place."

Which said a lot about his own moral compass. There had been too many instances in her life where people had judged her, based on something as simple as her last name, where she lived, and what her father did for a living. It was a refreshing change to find someone who didn't give a damn about those things.

"I'm glad to hear that you're not one to think the worst based on someone else's opinion, because what my mother had to say wasn't very flattering, or even very nice for that matter."

A familiar frustration reared its ugly head, and she sighed in an attempt to keep all that bottled up resentment from spilling out of her right here and now. Instead, she kept her voice calm and steady as she said, "I'm truly beginning to wonder if my mother is ever going to forgive me for calling off my engagement to Jason only months before the wedding."

Ben cast her a brief but incredulous look. "Are you kidding me? From what I've heard, the man is an ass and deserved what he had coming to him."

She lifted a brow and teased blithely, "Isn't that a bit . . . judgmental?"

"You and I are *participating* in a conversation, and in that case I'm entitled to express *my* opinion." His gaze scanned the area, then his rearview and side mirrors, an action he'd done routinely on the drive to his place. "I'm certain you saved yourself a boatload of future heartache by ending your relationship with him."

She silently agreed. Surprisingly, there had been no regrets when she'd broken up with Jason, just an immense, profound relief that she hadn't ended up marrying a man she didn't love. She'd known the truth deep inside even as he'd slipped a huge diamond solitaire on her finger, but her own feelings had been eclipsed by the overwhelming pressure from her mother to accept Jason's proposal. And once the word *yes* had slipped from her lips, she'd been swept into a maelstrom of engagement parties, bridal showers, and wedding plans.

She had Jason's careless actions to thank for stopping her from making the biggest mistake of her life.

"I just wish my mother would swallow her pride and let the whole entire fiasco die, instead of continually punishing me for something that was more awkward for me than it was for her."

"What's her problem?" he asked with a slight frown. "The guy *cheated* on you, and not just once. You had every right to call off the wedding."

She assumed Ben had learned from her father all about Jason's trysts with a number of call girls, along with the restraining order she'd had to issue against him shortly thereafter. "According to my mother, it was a few minor indiscretions and I should have looked the other way."

Just as Audrey had with her own husband's infidelity.

Ben made a sound of disgust. "Yeah, well, your father obviously felt differently."

True. Her father had gone so far as to not only fire Jason from his staff, but he had also dealt a huge blow to Jason's political career in Chicago—and rightly so since Jason had been siphoning campaign funds.

Unfortunately, the whole entire scenario with Jason had planted a few doubts and insecurities about her own desirability, and made her question what was lacking in her that Jason had turned to paid escorts to fulfill. Oh, sure, there had been the obvious differences between herself and the upscale prostitute she'd caught him with—such as the other woman's voluptuous breasts and centerfold curves and the provocative way she always dressed—but the things he'd been doing to and with that woman before Christine had interrupted them had been not only shocking, but so opposite of the tame, missionary-only style of sex Jason insisted on with her. There had been no passion between them, no burning desire, or even a whole lot of pleasure for her. A few quick touches, a couple of hard thrusts, and he was done.

Since she'd only had one other sexual experience to compare Jason's technique to—and that encounter had been as exciting as a gynecologist appointment, and just as memorable—she couldn't help but wonder, and fear, that maybe she shared her mother's dislike for sex and just didn't, and couldn't, enjoy the act. That like her mother, for her sex would always be more of a marital chore or duty rather than an unrelenting and provocative need to take and be taken in return—without hesitation or reserve.

She'd worried about those things a whole lot . . . until Ben. The lust and desire she experienced when she was around him was proof enough that she wasn't frigid, and she was more than ready to shed any and all inhibitions for a taste of what hot, demanding, explosive sex was like.

Minutes later, Ben made a left into a quiet middle-income neighborhood, drove down the street, then turned into a driveway leading to an apartment complex. The two-story structure looked as though it had been recently painted, and the landscaping around the building was well-kept. The place was modest and simple, just like the man.

He parked his truck beneath a carport, cut the engine, and they both got out of the vehicle. He came around to her side and they headed toward a pathway leading to the complex.

"It should only take me a few minutes to pack up what I need," he said, glancing at her.

"It's not a problem," she assured him, enjoying the way the afternoon sun glinted off his dark brown hair, streaking it with warm strands of gold. "I'm not in any hurry, so don't rush on my account."

A slow smile eased across his lips, and his eyes glimmered with animated concern. "What about your plans tonight? Don't you need to get back home so you can start getting ready?"

She rolled her eyes. "I'm not meeting my friends at Envy for another three and a half hours. Contrary to what you might think, I'm not that high maintenance."

He laughed. "I'll believe it when I see it."

They passed a chain-linked area where a small group of boys were playing basketball on a concrete court. As soon as they saw Ben, they ran for the open gate to greet him, then formed a semicircle around the two of them.

"Can you play a game of hoops with us, Ben?" One of the kids asked hopefully. He looked about twelve, as did

the three other boys who'd joined him, and it was obvious
by the bright expressions on all four of their faces that
they were very fond of Ben.

Ben reached out and affectionately ruffled the boy's
unruly brown hair. "Sorry, guys, not today."

"Awww, man." Clearly disappointed, he hung his head
and scuffed the ground with the toe of his well-worn Nikes.

"Who's your girlfriend?" one of the other boys asked
as he tucked the basketball beneath his arm.

"This is Christine, and she's a *friend*," Ben clarified,
then went on to introduce her to the boys, who also lived
in the apartment building.

"Well, she should be your girlfriend, because she's
hot," the one named Jimmy said, eyeing her much too
boldly for someone so young.

Ben cringed at the unexpected, and very suggestive
comment.

Unoffended, Christine laughed. It had been a very
long time since someone had referred to her as *hot*, and
she wasn't about to turn it down. "Why, thank you, Jimmy.
That's a lovely compliment."

Nick, another one of the boys, looked pointedly at her
outfit, her bangle bracelets, then her high-heeled shoes
before meeting her gaze. "We'd ask you to play hoops,
but you look *way* too girly for us."

There was an edge of sarcasm to the kid's voice, and
she arched a brow at him. "Just because I look like a girl
doesn't mean I play like a girl."

"Yes, it does," Samuel chimed in, backing his friend
with a succinct nod.

Smiling, she held her hand out to Andrew, the one who
was holding the basketball. "Let me have the ball," she
said in a friendly, easygoing tone.

Andrew frowned and took a small step back, unwilling

to give her the coveted ball that clearly defined them as "men" in their minds. "You're a *girl.*"

"Why, yes, I am," she agreed, and kept her hand stretched toward him.

Beside her, Ben sighed. "Christine—"

Ignoring her bodyguard, she kept her gaze locked with the boy's. "Come on, give me the ball, please? I'd like to show you something real quick, and then you can have it back. I promise."

Still skeptical, Andrew glanced toward Jimmy, establishing the other kid as the leader of their pack and the one who made all the crucial decisions in their circle of friendship.

After a few seconds, Jimmy gave him a nod and said, "Go ahead and give it to her, Andrew. Let's see what she can do."

Reluctantly, Andrew shot the ball her way, fast and hard, and she caught it with both hands without flinching, as he no doubt expected. She walked onto the basketball court and up to the three-point line, and her audience followed behind to watch.

She calculated the distance to the basketball hoop, bounced the ball a few times to get a feel for it, then glanced back at the small group of boys waiting with varying degrees of feigned boredom and subtle curiosity etching their expressions. Ben stood off to the side as well, his arms crossed casually over his chest, amusement flickering in his gaze.

"Okay, boys, and that includes you, too, Ben," she said, winking at him. "Pay close attention, because I'm about to show you what this *girl* can do."

She dribbled the ball a few more times, positioned herself, then concentrated on all the important elements of making a basket that her high school basketball coach had taught her. Visualizing the shot, she sent the ball sailing through the air, watching as it arched toward her target. The ball hit low on the backboard, and instead of bouncing back onto the court, it circled the rim of the basket before dropping through the net.

Yes, she thought in exhilaration as she suppressed the urge to do a victory dance of some sort. It wasn't the cleanest shot she'd ever made, but it was enough to prove that she was a girl with a few hoop skills of her own.

Nick ran out to fetch the ball as the other three stared at her in shock and blatant disbelief.

"Whoa," Samuel breathed in awe.

"That was awesome," Jimmy added, his eyes wide.

"Not bad for a girl," Andrew muttered beneath his breath.

"Nice shot," Ben said, the bland tone of his voice belying just how amazed she knew he really was beneath that indifferent facade of his.

Feeling a little cocky after mastering her shot, she strolled back toward the boys, her gaze on the biggest, sexiest one of the bunch. "Awww, come on, Ben. You were impressed. Admit it."

The corner of his mouth twitched with a smile, but he managed to keep his humor under wraps. "Maybe that was just beginner's luck."

"Hardly." She stopped in front of him and gave him a smug look. "I'll have you know that I was a guard on my high school varsity team."

That bit of news finally shook a surprised reaction out of him. "You played basketball in high school?"

He sounded as stunned as her mother had been when Christine had announced her choice of extracurricular activity at the all-girls boarding school she'd attended. Audrey had been pushing for ballet or something equally feminine and had been less than pleased to discover her daughter had chosen what she considered a boy's sport.

"I know it might be hard to believe, but it's true," she said to Ben, as well as the boys who were still gathered close by. "Of course, it's been a while since I've actually played a game, but I'm sure I can hold my own. How about a quick ten-point game with the boys?"

"Yeah!" the foursome cheered enthusiastically in response.

Ben's gaze narrowed. "You're kidding, right?"

She spread her hands wide. "Do I look like I'm kidding?"

His gaze took her in, all the way down to the red painted toe nails peeking from her open-toed shoes. Then he gave her a private, teasing smirk. "You'll break your neck in those stilts you're wearing."

Which was easily remedied. She kicked off her Jimmy Choos, pushed up the sleeves on her top, and glanced back up at Ben, now four additional inches shorter than him—and much closer to the boys' heights. "I'll go barefoot."

He shook his head, not the least bit moved by her efforts to sway him. "I don't think so."

He was in full bodyguard mode, obviously trying to protect her from something as simple as a game of basketball, which she found ridiculous. Sure, she was smaller than most girls, but she was far from being a delicate debutante, and she wasn't about to let him treat her like one.

"I'm not that fragile, Ben. I swear I won't break if I get bumped around a little bit."

He blinked lazily and rocked back on his heels. "Maybe not, but you'll definitely get all hot and sweaty."

Something about the low, husky tone of his voice and the too sensual way his gaze held hers gave his comment a whole different meaning and inspired tantalizing fantasies of hot, sweaty *sex* . . . with him. The sudden awareness flaring between them made her feel restless, and a bit daring, and she didn't hesitate to act on the impulsive moment.

Still mindful of their young spectators nearby, she leaned closer to Ben to give them a small measure of privacy, licked her bottom lip, and whispered, "That's what showers are for."

Ben experienced a swift kick of lust straight to his gut as Christine's less than innocent comeback flooded his mind with provocative, erotic images—of her joining him in his shower, a steady stream of water sluicing down her naked body and a come-hither smile on her lips as he lathered all her sleek, sensual curves.

He swallowed back a low groan and shoved those dangerously arousing thoughts of Christine right out of his head. But despite the disappearance of those risqué images, he still had to deal with the flesh-and-blood woman standing in front of him, who seemed so bound and determined to tempt him with what he couldn't have. *Her.*

Ever since they'd left her parents' house that afternoon, he'd noticed a distinct change in Christine. While she'd always teased and flirted with him in the past when their paths crossed, now that he'd been assigned as her bodyguard for the next three weeks, there was a stronger, more tangible seductive quality to her behavior he found way too inviting.

Like now. The irresistible dare in her sparkling blue eyes encompassed a slew of possibilities, and beckoned him to accept every single one of them. Then there was that beguiling curve to her lush mouth that captured his full attention, along with the fact that she was standing close enough for him to look down and watch the intriguing rise and fall of her small, firm breasts.

"Awww, come on, Ben," Jimmy said, effectively reminding him that he wasn't alone with Christine, as he suddenly wished he were.

"It's just one quick game," Nick added.

Christine batted her lashes, taunting him in that affable way of hers. "Yeah, come on, Ben," she cajoled, her tone sugar-sweet. "Or are you afraid I might whoop your butt?"

"Ooooo," the foursome chorused together, as if she'd just issued the ultimate challenge to his masculinity. Which she had.

He pointed a finger toward her pert little nose. "You're so on." After that bold, nervy statement, he wasn't about to say no. "And don't expect me to go easy on you because you're a girl."

She tossed her head back and laughed. "And don't whine like a little boy when you lose."

God, she was too much, though he had to admit that her confidence was a huge turn-on.

They divided up into teams, with two boys on each side. With a toss of the ball, the game began. Christine took the sport seriously, using exceptional skill when it came to playing with the kids, but she saved all her womanly wiles for when it came to dealing with him. Like when he came up behind her to steal the ball from her grasp, and she turned the move into a full, frontal body assault as she scooted back and pressed her curvy bottom against his groin, forcing him to retreat from the too-intimate position or risk embarrassing himself in front of the boys with a raging hard-on.

But putting distance between himself and Christine on the court didn't stop him from noticing how a gradual pink flush suffused her face, or enjoying the fun-loving laughter that pierced the air as she managed to outwit her opponents. She played aggressively, and she was in it to win. She passed the ball to her teammates when the opportunity presented itself, made a few shots of her own, and didn't mind getting down and dirty for fear of breaking a nail or messing up her hair.

Every time she got close to him, Ben caught a whiff of her signature scent—a warm, vanilla fragrance that made him want to take a big bite out of her. Or lick her skin to see if she tasted as good as she smelled. And the harder she played the game, the stronger the scent grew, combining with everything else about her to distract the hell out of him.

He couldn't focus on the game, couldn't make a shot if his life depended on it. Because when he tried, she was right there in front of him, trying to take the ball away—and using everything in her feminine arsenal to do it.

She didn't play fair, at least not with him.

By the time the game ended, with his team losing by four points, he was sweating and breathing too hard, and it had little to do with the October sun overhead, and was more a result of Christine's frisky moves.

As she celebrated with her teammates with high-fives and atta boys, all he could do was grin, shake his head, and take the loss like a man.

His teammates, Jimmy and Andrew, weren't as benevolent.

"I can't believe we lost to a *girl*," Jimmy grumbled.

"Yeah, that totally sucks," Andrew added with a frown.

"Come on, guys, don't be poor sports," Ben said as he clasped both Jimmy and Andrew on the shoulder in a small attempt to soothe their bruised egos. "They won fair and square, so let's go congratulate them."

With a little push from Ben in the right direction, the boys headed toward the champions and issued a "good game" compliment. The foursome went back to playing basketball on their own, and Christine picked up her shoes and strolled toward Ben, glowing from the exertion of playing the game, and from her recent victory.

She stopped in front of him and wrinkled her nose. "Well, well, well. It looks like *you're* the one who's all hot and sweaty."

He dragged his fingers through his damp hair and laughed. It figured that she'd turn that comment back around on him, and he did the same thing.

"It's nothing a quick shower can't take care of." But while he'd previously fantasized about her joining him, in reality he was all on his own.

Three

CHRISTINE followed Ben inside his apartment and waited as he locked and bolted the door after her. The extra bit of security was a direct reminder that it wasn't all fun and games between her and her bodyguard, even if she'd had a blast playing basketball and showing the boys, and Ben, that she wasn't the prissy girly-girl they'd thought she was.

"Go ahead and make yourself comfortable," Ben said, waving a hand toward the small living area of the apartment. "And help yourself to something to drink in the kitchen. I think there's some bottled water in the fridge, along with Gatorade and beer, if you feel like drinking and belching like one of the boys," he teased.

"No beer for me," she said with a shake of her head. "That's where I draw the line and prefer a froufrou drink, like an apple martini or piña colada."

His smile was slow, deliberate, and combined with his still tousled, sweaty outdoor appearance made him look sexy as hell. "Sorry, but I'm fresh out of fruity umbrella drinks."

"Ha-ha," she replied with a sassy grin of her own. "Go take your shower, smart aleck."

He placed his keys on the counter that separated the living room from the kitchen. "I only need about twenty minutes to shower, dress, and pack a bag, so I shouldn't be long."

"Ahhh, the joys of being a man." She sighed enviously. "A quick shower, no angsting over what to wear, and no preplanning what to pack for your stay."

"Being a man does have its perks," he agreed. "By the way, what do I need to wear tonight? Does the club have a specific dress code?"

"Jeans and a nice shirt are fine."

He looked relieved that she hadn't asked him to don a suit and tie. "Perfect. That's just my style."

She watched him head down the short hall and nearly groaned when he pulled his damp shirt off just before he turned into the bedroom. She caught a quick glimpse of his smooth, muscled back, and that was more than enough to make her stomach clench with the desire to see what all that hard, honed flesh felt like sliding against her fingertips.

He didn't close the bedroom door, but a moment later she heard a different door shut, then the sound of running water, indicating he was about to get into the shower . . . completely naked.

Realizing just how dry her mouth had become, she walked into the kitchen and opened the refrigerator. There wasn't a whole lot inside—mainly take-out containers, a carton of milk, and the drinks he'd mentioned earlier. Definitely a sign of a bachelor. Bypassing the beer and Gatorade, she grabbed a bottle of water. Strolling back into the living room, she twisted the cap off the bottle and swallowed a good amount of the cool water as she took in his sparse furnishings.

A single reclining chair in a dark brown leather material, worn from plenty of use, occupied one side of the room. An old, scarred wooden side table was situated nearby with a few *Soldier of Fortune* magazines stacked neatly on top. Against the opposite wall was what appeared to be Ben's one main indulgence—a large, flat-screen TV tucked inside a basic entertainment center.

The apartment looked like he'd just moved in but hadn't had the time, or the inclination, to decorate or give the place any special touches of his own. The off-white walls were completely bare, and except for a clock on the wall there weren't any knickknacks anywhere to be seen. The only things she saw that she'd even consider remotely personal were two small framed photographs set on one of the shelves in the wall unit.

She found herself gravitating toward those pictures to take a better, closer look. Surprisingly, they weren't snapshots of family. The first photo was a group of men standing together, surrounded by canvas tents in a desolate desert setting. All of them were dressed in military fatigues and sporting short buzz cuts, Ben included. The men looked tired and weary, but the comradery between them was a visible thing.

She assumed the picture had been taken a few years ago, when he'd been in the service. She remembered her father mentioning that Ben was an ex-Marine who'd served in the Iraq War but she didn't know anything about his time in the military, or what his duties had entailed.

Taking another drink of her water, she glanced at the second photograph of Ben and a pretty, dark-haired woman, completely unprepared for the depth of emotion so evident between the couple. Both of them were dressed in fatigues, with the same dry, barren stretch of desert as their background. The woman was hugging Ben around the waist, a wide smile on her lips as she looked up at him with a wealth of love and adoration shining in her eyes. Ben was laughing at something she must have said or done, but there was no denying that he was equally as smitten with her.

"Oh, wow," Christine breathed, shocked at the realization that Ben might have a steady girlfriend. One who might even be living with him, though she doubted that by the lack of feminine presence in the apartment. But the fact that Ben openly displayed such an intimate picture of himself and the woman said a lot about his feelings for her.

Not sure what to think, she dragged her fingers through her hair, wincing as a few tangled strands tugged on her scalp. All she knew was that if Ben was in a serious relationship, then she had absolutely no business flirting with him the way she had been, and vice versa.

"You're awfully quiet out there," Ben called from the other room. "Are you doing okay?"

He was obviously done with his shower. "I'm good." She glanced at the clock on the wall. "And you're down to about twelve minutes. Are you still on schedule?"

He chuckled, and she felt a slice of guilt for enjoying the low, husky sound when there was a chance of him having a girlfriend.

"I'm *way* ahead of schedule," he said as she heard a shuffling sound coming from the bedroom. "All I have to do is finish getting dressed and pack a few things, and I'll be ready to go."

Still troubled by that picture, she finished her water, tossed the bottle in the kitchen trash, and gave Ben another two full minutes before wandering down the hallway to his bedroom. She had to know if he had a significant other in his life, and if he did, she needed to change her behavior toward him drastically. She'd never poached on another woman's territory, and she wasn't about to start now. She'd been on the other side of that scenario, and it hadn't felt good at all.

She stopped in the bedroom doorway and leaned a shoulder against the frame. As good as her intentions were, she wasn't prepared to find Ben looking so gorgeous and sexy. He had his back to her as he stuffed a few items into a duffle bag, giving her a few quick moments to take in his appearance. Fresh from his shower, his hair was still damp, though he had run a comb through the strands. He'd pulled on a pair of new looking jeans, but he hadn't gotten around to putting on a shirt yet, and tearing her gaze away from the mesmerizing ripple and flow of his incredible muscles as he moved was a difficult thing to do.

He zipped up his bag, then reached for a blue chambray shirt he'd laid out on the bed. As he shrugged into the garment, he turned around, saw her standing in the doorway, and gave her a half-grin.

"Did you come to check up on me?" he asked as he strolled toward the only dresser in the room.

He'd left the shirt open and unbuttoned, treating her to a delectable view of his abs, which were just as toned as the rest of his body. "I just wanted to make sure you weren't wasting time."

"Trust me, I'm a very efficient, no fuss kind of guy."

She watched him open a drawer and withdraw a semiautomatic and a black holster. Even though she didn't like the thought of him carrying a weapon, she knew and understood that it was all part of the job. She was also grateful that he *preferred* to dress casually, rather than wear what seemed like the prerequisite suit and tie that most of the security agents in her father's employ wore while on duty—which also made their presence as bodyguards openly known.

As Ben clipped the holster onto the waistband of his

jeans and tucked the actual holder just inside his pants to conceal the fact that he was armed and dangerous despite his laid-back appearance, she cast a quick glance around his bedroom. The furnishings were just as meager as the rest of the apartment, with a bed and the single dresser, leading her to believe, once again, that he'd just recently moved in. It was the only explanation that made sense for the lack of all those personal, intimate trappings that made a house a real home.

She brought her gaze back to Ben, both disappointed and relieved to find him buttoning up his shirt and covering up that magnificent chest of his so she was no longer tempted to stare at all that bare, naked flesh.

"I take it you haven't lived here long," she commented.

He lifted a dark brown brow. "What makes you say that?"

She shrugged. "The place looks deserted, like you just moved in."

"Actually, I've lived in this apartment for almost two years." Leaving the tails of his shirt untucked, he sat on the edge of his bed, pulled on a pair of socks, then slid his feet into brown leather loafers. "As for the place looking deserted, I've never needed much. That, and the military has a way of making your life as compact as possible. Most of the time, all your personal effects are what you can fit into a duffle or backpack, and I guess I just got used to living that way."

That made sense, yet in a way it made him seem so detached and a bit of a loner, as though he could pick up and move at any time with little effort. "Does your family live nearby?"

He hesitated, his jaw tightening ever so slightly. "No."

His tone of voice didn't encourage further questions, but there was something about the sudden change in his entire demeanor that prompted Christine to ask, "Where does the rest of your family live?"

"Like you, I'm an only child," he said, his tone holding a shade of impatience. "My father passed away just before I joined the military, and as for my mother . . . I have no idea where she is, nor do I care."

He was so matter-of-fact about his parents, and while she was curious to know more about his past and what had caused that twinge of bitterness she'd detected toward his mother, he stood up, grabbed his duffle and what appeared to be a computer carry case, then glanced at his wristwatch.

"I'm ready to go with four minutes to spare," he said. "Even *after* your little interrogation."

There was just enough humor in his voice to let her know that he wasn't upset with her, even if her questions had brought back what seemed like some unpleasant memories for him.

He passed by her on the way out the bedroom door to the living room, smelling like soap and warm male essence. She followed behind, then waited as he checked the answering machine on the kitchen counter for messages. Again, her gaze strayed to the pictures in the wall unit, specifically the one with Ben and the smiling, happy brunette.

God, she was such a glutton for punishment today. After their exchange in the bedroom about his parents, she ought to leave well enough alone, but she just couldn't walk out of his apartment without knowing about the woman in the photo.

"Ben?"

He grabbed his car keys from the counter and turned toward her, clearly ready to leave. "Yeah?"

She bit her bottom lip, her stomach suddenly churning with a bout of nerves. "I'm sorry, but I really need to ask you something."

Shifting his stance, he adjusted the strap of the computer case over his shoulder. "Okay."

She exhaled a deep breath and let the words out before her fortitude deserted her. "That woman in the picture with you," she said, indicating the shelf with the two separate photographs, "is she your girlfriend?"

His gaze slid past her to the framed print, a distinct pang of sadness etching his features. "She was my fiancée."

His answer, said in the past tense, confused her. If he was no longer engaged, then why did he have such a loving, affectionate photo of the two of them so openly displayed? "*Was* your fiancée?"

Those golden brown eyes, when they met hers again, were filled with a barely perceptible grief that made him appear, for the very briefest of seconds, raw and exposed. "She died in the Iraq War four years ago."

Startled by such an unexpected reply, her eyes widened and it took her a moment to shake off her shock and respond. "I'm so sorry, Ben," she breathed, her heart hurting for him.

"Yeah, me, too," he said gruffly.

He glanced away, but not before she caught a glimpse of a deeper torment and guilt she didn't fully understand. In the span of just a half an hour, she'd seen a whole different side to Ben, a man with many facets and a past devastated with loss on many levels. Beneath his charming smiles and easygoing nature, there was a wealth of personal pain and secrets he kept to himself, and was very reluctant to share. Not that she could blame him.

She wondered what had happened in Iraq, and how his fiancée had died, but didn't dare ask.

He started toward the door. "Come on," he said, sounding tired and worn out, as if she'd put him through an emotional wringer in a very short span of time. "Let's hit the road. We wouldn't want you to be late for your date tonight."

He was back to teasing her, and she smiled, grateful that he hadn't held her inquisitive questions against her.

CHRISTINE was nearly finished getting dressed to leave for her evening out when her cell phone rang. Still in her bedroom with Ben waiting for her out in the living room, she dug her BlackBerry from her purse. Recognizing the name on the ID display as Craig Crosby, the owner of Envy, she answered the call.

"Hey, Craig," she said as she padded over to her dresser in her bare feet. She still had a few more things to do before she was completely ready, and they were easy enough to finish while she talked on the phone.

"Hi, Christy." His greeting was, as always, spoken in a low, husky tone that made her all too aware of his interest in her. "I'm just calling to see if you're still planning on coming to Envy tonight?"

"Absolutely." She rummaged through her jewelry box until she found the pair of gold chandelier earrings she wanted to wear with her outfit. "I'm meeting Ronnie and Madison for drinks in about an hour," she said of her two best friends.

"Great. I'll make sure to let the bartender know that I'll be picking up the tab for you and your friends for the evening."

She pushed one of the French wire earrings into her lobes, then switched the phone to the other ear to repeat the process. The gold, shimmering links brushed her bared shoulders in a cool, sensual caress that made her feel sexy and flirty.

"Craig, that *really* isn't necessary." In fact, she preferred that he *didn't* pay for her drinks, because he did it way too often and it was beginning to make her feel a bit awkward.

"I know, but I want to," he said, dismissing her attempt to refuse his generous offer. "Consider it a perk of being good friends with the owner."

A *friend* who'd given her enough signals to let her know he was more than willing to take their amicable relationship to a more personal level—despite the numerous times she'd gently turned down his request to go on a date. The man didn't give up easily, and even though she'd tried to let him know by her words and actions that she didn't have any romantic feelings for him, he continued to try to persuade her in little, subtle ways. And his persistence made for an uncomfortable situation for her, considering how essential he'd been in helping her to build her new business.

Keeping things cordial but warm and friendly between them was a fine line that was becoming more difficult for her to walk.

"You've done more than enough for me, Craig," she said, truly grateful for all his referrals and contacts and the way he'd given her business such a huge boost. "I wouldn't have half my clientele without your recommendations. You've been more effective than any ad I could have placed."

He chuckled at the compliment. "It's nothing, Christy. I want to see you succeed. And so far, judging by the comments and feedback I've heard around town, you're creating quite a name for yourself in Chicago as an exceptional event planner."

Smiling, she slipped a wide gold bracelet onto her wrist. "I'm working on it." Thanks to him, she was booked for some very upscale events that would put her name and business in front of a lot more influential people.

"In fact, The Big Event is doing so well that you're making Leanne Baker green with envy."

Cringing at the mention of her rival's name, Christine sat down on one of the plush chairs in her room and reached for the pair of black, suede Manolo Blahnik boots she'd left nearby. She'd known Leanne for years since they'd grown up in the same social circles. Christine had learned very quickly that while Leanne had perfected a sugar-sweet persona on the outside, beneath that I-want-to-be-your-best-friend facade lurked a bitter, spiteful woman who had mastered the fine art of backstabbing or sabotaging anyone who threatened her standing as one of Chicago's premier night club event promoters.

Leanne currently had Christine in her evil sights.

Christine didn't consider herself, or her flourishing business, a direct threat to Leanne's chosen profession, but the other woman clearly did. Christine had heard through the ever-present grapevine that Leanne resented the fact that Craig had taken Christine under his wings in terms of supplying her with all the right contacts to help build her business, when Leanne had been attempting for years to get Craig's attention, along with his support—with only a few second-rate referrals to show for her efforts.

"Speaking of Leanne, she'll be at Envy tonight," Craig said. "She's hosting a bachelorette gig at the club."

"Thanks for the heads-up," she replied ruefully as she pushed her foot into one of the soft suede boots, then zipped up the side all the way to just below her knee. "I'll be sure to keep my distance."

He laughed again, obviously amused by the rift and clash of personalities between herself and Leanne. "By the way, since you'll be at the club tonight I was hoping to steal a few moments alone with you to discuss some of the details for your birthday bash here at Envy."

His request to meet with her alone caused her to hesitate

before answering, because when it was just the two of them, without anyone else around, that's when he poured on all the charm and tried to finagle a date out of her—even if it was in the guise of having a drink together.

Tucking the phone between her ear and shoulder, she pulled on the other heeled boot. Since Craig was hosting her twenty-seventh birthday party at Envy the day after the election, and he was inviting a few high-profile contacts for her to meet, she couldn't very well tell him no. "Umm, sure."

"Great," he said enthusiastically. "I'll see you tonight, then."

After saying good-bye, she disconnected the call and sighed, not quite sure what to do about Craig. He really was a nice guy and he'd been a great friend over the past few months, but she had no idea how to handle his growing interest in her, especially when he'd been so integral to making her event planning business such a quick success. At forty-one years old, not only was Craig much older than her, but she just wasn't attracted to him in that sort of way.

Most important, she wasn't looking to jump into another serious relationship after what had happened with Jason. She was experiencing her first taste of real freedom and independence, and enjoying both—she wasn't ready to give up the life that was finally her own for any man.

Standing, she walked back to the bed and dropped her BlackBerry into her purse, then headed over to the vanity and selected a rosy pink lip gloss to use for the evening. Dealing with Craig would be so much simpler and easier if she was casually dating someone, a guy who could accompany her to Envy, and one she could use as a decoy to make Craig believe she was involved with someone else so he wouldn't continue to ask her out.

She swiped the shimmering gloss across her lips, her

mind immediately thinking of the gorgeous, sexy man sitting out in her living room who was all hers for the next three weeks. Sure, he'd been hired as her bodyguard, but she couldn't think of a better guy to act as her boyfriend, which would also eliminate him trailing beside her and *looking* like a security agent, which she hated. As a bonus, they wouldn't have to pretend that they were attracted to one another—the awareness and desire between them spoke for itself.

She lightly spritzed her neck and shoulders with her favorite vanilla fragrance, then gave her appearance one last check in the long mirror on the wall.

Using Ben to put an end to Craig's pursuit was the perfect plan. Now she just had to convince her bodyguard to play along.

FIGURING he had time to kill while Christine was getting ready, Ben set up his laptop computer on her coffee table in the living room and decided to get a head start on typing up his daily security report, which would then be uploaded to the Delacroix case file for Nathan, or any of Elite's partners, to review at any time. Today's report was all basic information so far, mainly outlining his meeting with Nathan, what the assignment entailed, and later he'd follow up with anything interesting or pertinent that happened tonight at Envy.

There was no reason to mention this afternoon's basketball game where Christine showed off her impressive skills and kicked his ass, or the discussion they'd had at his place about his parents and his fiancée, Kim. None of that mattered in the context of his security report, yet it was the too-personal conversations at his place that he couldn't get out of his head.

Out of the handful of women he'd been with since

moving to Chicago a few years ago, he'd never brought
any of them to his apartment, and now he knew why—
because women were inquisitive, emotional creatures who
needed too many explanations on why he lived his life the
way he did. They wanted to know about his family and
his past and everything else in between, and he'd made it
a point since leaving the military to keep his private life
private, and that meant keeping his place off-limits.

His personal tactics worked well for him and he managed to keep his own emotions untouched. He'd purposefully kept his affairs with women brief and all about
physical pleasure. He never let them get close enough to
care, to ask about his parents, his mother, or the fiancée he
hadn't been able to save from a roadside ambush in Iraq.

Ben scrubbed a hand along his jaw and exhaled a deep
breath. Four years after Kim's death, the pain of losing her
had dulled, but the guilt had not abated one bit. No, he
feared that deep, painful remorse would be something
he'd bear on his conscience for the rest of his life.

How was it that in just the span of half an hour Christine had hit on all those hot topics that no other woman
had even come close to realizing about him? And why had
he given up as much information as he had to Christine?
True, he'd kept much of the ugly truths to himself, but
she'd still managed to extract way too much out of him.

He had no answers that made sense, and he refused to
dwell on that conversation with Christine any longer. Sav-
ing the security report in his Word file, he shut down the
laptop computer and leaned back on the wide, comfortable
couch. Clasping his hands behind his head, he forced
himself to relax and rerouted his thoughts to something
more mundane, like the contrast of his basic, barely furnished apartment with Christine's beautifully decorated
house.

When they'd arrived at her place, he'd been pleasantly

surprised by the modest size of the house in an upscale neighborhood that boasted two-story monstrosities and enormous, custom-built homes. In comparison, Christine's house was a small, three-bedroom structure that was perfect for someone who was single and lived alone.

Since he needed to know the exact layout of the place for security reasons, she'd given him a tour of each and every room, as well as showing him the guest bedroom where he'd be staying for the next several weeks. Her master bedroom, he noted, was just down the hall from where he'd be sleeping.

In the two years he'd lived in his apartment, he hadn't bothered to do anything to really make the place his own. To him, it was just a place to eat and sleep and shower, and occasionally on the weekends enjoy a few games on the big-screen TV. Christine, on the other hand, had completely transformed her new house in just the few months since moving in. Decorated in neutral tones and accented with brighter shades of deep reds, burnished oranges, and forest greens, the place was warm and inviting in every way, and so much the opposite of her parents' lavish home.

He found himself smiling as he recalled the proud way in which she'd told him that she'd bought the place on her own, without her father cosigning on the loan. She'd used part of a trust fund left to her by her grandparents on her mother's side to make a deposit that would leave her with a monthly payment she could afford, and kept the rest of that money untouched. She was determined to do it all on her own for the first time in her life, without depending on anyone to help her out, and he couldn't help but be impressed by her fortitude.

"Okay, so I'm not nearly as quick as you when it comes to getting ready," he heard Christine say. "But I did get a phone call that put me about ten minutes behind schedule, if that counts for anything."

Ben shifted his gaze from the contemporary framed art that he'd been staring at to the woman walking toward him, looking like a temptress in the purest form of the word. Stunned by the transformation, and unable to help himself because he was a man, after all, he took in her jaw-dropping outfit, along with that sensual gleam in her bluer than blue eyes and the blond hair that now fell to her shoulders in a sexy, disheveled mass of curls, and felt his mouth go dry and his groin tighten with an unequivocal heated awareness.

He immediately sat up straight before his reaction to her became obvious.

If that teal, off-the-shoulder sweater molding to her breasts and outlining the enticing curve of her waist and hips wasn't enough to make a man do a double take, then those black suede knee-high boots with a four-inch heel and that thigh-skimming miniskirt would render a guy brainless.

He knew this because he suddenly couldn't speak or think beyond imagining her strolling over to him, straddling his lap, and living up to the bad girl image that outfit of hers portrayed.

Good God, he was certain he was going to have to beat back half of the male population at Envy tonight, because somewhere along the way Christine had transformed from a wholesome girl-next-door into a sultry vixen.

As the silence stretched between them, she tipped her head to the side and regarded him with a good amount of amusement. "I take it you like the outfit?"

He shrugged his stiff shoulders and attempted a nonchalant facade, unwilling to admit just how much her ensemble affected him. "It's okay."

A half-smile lifted the corner of those glossy pink lips that made him think of sweet cotton candy. "You're such a liar."

"And you're looking for trouble in a short skirt like that," he retorted bluntly. *Not to mention those fuck-me boots you're wearing.*

She looked momentarily taken aback by his reply, and he was grateful that he'd kept the latter part of his comment to himself.

"Trust me, it's not *that* short compared to what some of the women wear to Envy," she said, her hands on her hips and her stance full of sass and attitude. "Besides, that's what I've got you for, to protect me from trouble."

Knowing just how unruly guys could be when it came to a woman who looked as hot as Christine did tonight, he narrowed his gaze. "You're not making my job very easy on me, now are you?"

"We're going to a nightclub, Ben," she said with a long-suffering sigh. "This outfit is completely and totally appropriate."

"And sexy as hell," he said gruffly, realizing too late that he'd spoken his thoughts out loud.

A confident, Cheshire cat grin curved her too kissable mouth and her eyes lit up with silent mirth. "Ahhh, so you *do* like it, then."

"That was just an impartial observation on my part."

Her light laughter was infused with delight and too much satisfaction. "Sure it was."

He didn't say a word, figuring it was his smartest, safest bet in keeping the rest of his dignity intact.

She set her small purse down on a nearby chair. "Look, before we go, I have a huge favor to ask."

Grateful for the change in topic, he gave her his undivided attention. "Sure. What do you need?"

She started pacing in front of the coffee table, distracting him all over again with the provocative sway of her hips as she walked. "I know having you by my side for the next three weeks isn't an option," she began, giving him a smile that didn't quite erase the nervousness that had suddenly crept into her voice. "If my father hadn't hired you as my bodyguard, it would have been some other security agent in your place."

"True enough." He was beyond curious as to what she was getting at. "What's the favor, Christine?"

Her pacing came to a halt and she met his gaze. She bit her lower lip anxiously. "Do you think that maybe, possibly, when we're out in public together I can introduce you as the guy I'm dating?"

He blinked at her, not sure what to make of her unusual request. "You mean, as your boyfriend?"

She nodded, looking relieved that he hadn't outright refused her. "Sure, that works for me."

He settled back against the couch cushions, trying to analyze her proposal, but unable to figure out her motive for making such a suggestion. "And just why does that work for you, Christine?" he prompted. "Why the charade?"

Again, she started that restless back and forth walk in front of him. "Two reasons, actually. First, I hate having the typical, obvious security agent walking three feet behind me and *looking* like a bodyguard."

A grin twitched the corners of his mouth. "Cramps your style, huh?"

"That's not how I meant it." A small frown marred her delicate brows and she shook her head. "I honestly hate the fact that everyone knows that I have a bodyguard, because in the scheme of things I'm just not all that important. The whole setup just seems so . . . pretentious, and I don't like bringing that kind of attention to myself."

So far, he was finding her explanation pretty darn convincing, and he truly believed that flaunting a bodyguard was so *not* her style. She might have always lived a privileged life, but she'd never given him the impression that she was a spoiled, pampered princess.

She slanted him a quick glance to gauge his reaction so far, and when he said nothing, she went on. "If I could introduce you as my boyfriend, everything would be much more casual and relaxed when we're together, instead of so awkward, stiff, and formal with you lurking in the background."

He didn't disagree with her rationale, but he wasn't ready to concede to her plan just yet. "And the second reason?"

"I have to admit that this one is a bit more self-serving." Her cheeks turned pink at that admission and she went back to nibbling on her bottom lip again. "The owner of Envy, Craig Crosby, has a thing for me, but I'm just not interested in him in a romantic way. He's forty-one, and no matter how many times I've gently turned him down for a date, or dinner and drinks, he knows I'm single and he keeps asking me out in hopes that I'll change my mind, which I won't." She sighed in frustration.

The name Craig Crosby sounded very familiar, and Ben mulled it over in his head until he realized where he'd heard it before now. "Is Craig Crosby related to the developer Jonathan Crosby in any way?"

Surprise lit her features as her pacing came to an abrupt stop. "How do you know Jonathan Crosby?"

"I don't know him personally. I just know *of* him from what's been written in the papers recently about the gentrification issue surrounding the upcoming election." Jonathan Crosby was a big-time developer, and it was no secret that he was also a huge supporter of Charles Lambert, Nathan's opponent in the race for governor. "In fact, it's been hinted at that Crosby is tucked firmly into Lambert's pocket and is guaranteed to head up the new construction on the lower west side if Lambert wins."

Christine nodded, causing her silky soft waves to brush her bare shoulders. "Unfortunately, that's all true."

"So, is Craig Crosby related to Jonathan in any way?" Ben asked again.

"Actually, Craig is his son."

He lifted a brow. "So, you're socializing with the enemy?"

"He's not the enemy," she said with a wave of her hand. "At least, *we're* not enemies, despite our fathers' differing political views. Believe it or not, it's never been an issue between Craig and I. I do know that Craig doesn't have the greatest relationship with his father because he opted to open a nightclub instead of going into the development business like his dad, but I'm sure he supports his father, just as I support mine. People can be friends but not be on the same side of the fence politically."

True enough, but it still made for an odd situation, especially if Craig wanted to date Christine. "Isn't Craig kind of old for you, anyway?"

She rolled her eyes. "Okay, yeah, he's almost fifteen years older than me, but his age aside, he's actually a very nice, decent guy."

He sat forward and clasped his hands between his widespread legs, his gaze on hers. "You just don't want to go out with him."

"Exactly," she said, her tone exasperated. "I've tried to be nice about telling him I'm not interested, but he's very persistent."

Ben's jaw clenched. He hadn't even met the guy yet and already he didn't like him. Then again, maybe his annoyance had more to do with his own attraction toward Christine. "So why not try the direct approach and just flat out tell him thanks, but no thanks, and make your feelings clear so he doesn't ask again?"

She winced. "You're such a typical guy and that's such a harsh way of handling things. Besides, men don't take that kind of blatant, in-your-face rejection lightly."

"So?" Ben didn't see what the big issue was in that. "He'll get over it. We all do."

Exhaling a deep breath, she crossed her arms over her chest, which effectively caused the creamy, upper swells of her breasts to peek out from the low, scoop neck of her sweater. "The problem is, the situation with Craig is different."

"How so?" he asked curiously.

"When I first started my business, Craig was essential in getting my name in front of a lot of influential people, who in turn hired me to plan an event or a party for them. With Craig being a club owner, he has a lot of prominent contacts and he's been very generous in putting me in touch with some amazing people who have put me way ahead of my competition in the area. I'm very grateful for everything he's done for me, which makes this whole issue of him asking me out something I need to handle delicately. Does that makes sense?"

"Actually, it does." To Ben, it sounded like Craig had the ability to make or break her newfound career, and that was a precarious situation in his estimation. "But despite how nice he's been, you don't owe him anything, Christine."

"I know that." She rubbed the tips of her fingers along her forehead. "But I don't want to be rude to him, either. I also don't believe in burning bridges. It's just not good business practice."

Realizing they needed to leave because they were already running late, Ben stood up and went around the coffee table toward her. "How about putting some distance between yourself and Craig?" he suggested. "Maybe not spend so much time at the club?"

"I've already thought about that, but I'm sort of in a position where I have to deal with Craig for at least three more weeks." She hesitated for a moment, then reluctantly continued. "He's insisting on throwing a birthday bash for me at Envy, which is another way of getting my name in front of potential clients, and he's already started to plan the entire thing. I just need to get past that party, and then I can make a clean break with Craig."

He nodded in understanding. "So, in the meantime, you want a pretend boyfriend to make him back off and quit asking you out."

She gave him an impish look. "That just about sums it all up."

Ben scrubbed a hand along his jaw, wondering what her father would think about his daughter's ploy to waylay another man's interest with the bodyguard he'd hired for her. "Christine, as sympathetic as I am to your situation, I wasn't hired on to be your boyfriend."

"*Pretend* boyfriend," she clarified, and smiled oh-so-sweetly at him. "What I'm asking you to do doesn't really affect your job as a security agent. If anything, it'll keep you close to my side and a part of everything I do."

Ben thought about all the things that being her boyfriend would entail in order to convince everyone, and Craig especially, that they were a couple. Seductive glances, affectionate touches, and private smiles meant to tempt and tease. Jesus, such an intimate scenario was bound to test the attraction between them and push not only his restraint, but his libido, to the limit.

As if sensing his indecision, she took a step toward him and placed one of her hands on his chest, her eyes soft and imploring. "Please, Ben?" she whispered. "You're in the perfect position to do this for me, and the last thing I want to do is have to find someone else to help me out."

He didn't doubt for a moment that she'd attempt to recruit someone else for the job, and the unsettling thought of watching another guy getting up close and personal with her, even if it was just for show, caused a burning, churning sensation deep in his gut.

Bringing in a third party just wasn't going to happen, he decided. Not on his watch. And that meant agreeing to Christine's ploy and everything it entailed so Craig would finally back off.

Ben figured that standing in as a pretend boyfriend wouldn't interfere with the job he'd been hired to do. If anything, it would enable him to get a better insight to all the people she hung out with without them knowing he was a security agent. Bottom line, his job was to protect Christine, and he could do that just as easily impersonating a guy who was smitten with her.

He exhaled a deep breath and took the plunge. "Okay. Fine. I'll do it."

Christine's eyes widened, and before he realized her intent she wrapped her arms around his neck and enveloped him in a tight, appreciative hug. "Thank you, thank you, thank you!"

With Christine's soft, lush body plastered so guilelessly against his, Ben's pulse skipped a beat and he wasn't sure what to do—return the embrace, or gently push her away before she realized the kind of effect she was having on him. Her warm breath caressed his neck, her smooth cheek pressed against his, and the seductive scent of vanilla infused his senses. Acute awareness, and a hard kick of lust, flooded south in a rush of heat.

One thing was for certain—faking an attraction wasn't going to be an issue at all. Settling his hands on her hips, he eased her back so he could breathe without thinking about skimming his hands along her curves and other places they didn't belong.

She looked up at him, her eyes shining gratefully. "I can't tell you how much I appreciate this," she said, still caught up in the fact that he'd agreed to help her out. "Just knowing that I won't have to deal with Craig's subtle advances for the next three weeks is a *huge* relief."

He smiled, enjoying her enthusiasm. "Good."

Despite those four-inch heels of hers, there was a bounce to her step as she walked over to the chair and grabbed her purse. When she spun back around, she was grinning effusively. "You know what this means, don't you?"

He didn't quite trust the mischievous gleam in her eyes. "Umm, no." But he was positive she was about to enlighten him.

She strolled back toward him and trailed a pink painted fingernail down the center of his chest. "This means, as my boyfriend, you're gonna have to call me Christy."

His deep groan rolled into a laugh, and he shook his head at her impudence. Leave it to Christine to revel in that small bit of victory.

Four

BY the time Christine arrived with Ben at Envy, her friends were already there and had claimed a table in the downstairs lounge where it was much quieter than upstairs near the dance floor and circular bar. Instead of stiff, uncomfortable bar stools, the lounge area was sectioned off with velvet armchairs, couches, and love seats in vibrant shades of purples, greens, and reds. Despite how crowded the place already was, the overall atmosphere was warm and inviting, which made for an enjoyable nightclub experience.

Wanting to make sure she established Ben as her boyfriend to anyone who might be watching her, especially Craig, she clasped his hand in hers as she led the way to Madison, Ronnie, and her boyfriend, Mark. Ben automatically wove his fingers through hers, bringing her attention to just how large his hand was as it closed around hers. She thought about how it would feel to have his heated palm and long fingers stroking across her bare, sensitive flesh, and shivered.

As she neared the group, she noticed Ronnie's curious expression as her long-time friend's gaze zeroed in on Ben. Then there was Madison. They'd been sorority sisters in college and had remained close friends even after graduation. Since Madison was also Christine's assistant at The Big Event and they spent days and hours together, she was the friend that knew her best, and was like the sister Christine never had. The two of them talked about the most intimate details of their lives, and shared just about everything, and that was why Madison was staring at Ben in shocked surprise, because to her best friend's knowledge, Christine hadn't been dating anyone.

Christine had already decided that she'd explain the situation to Madison and tell her the truth about her new boyfriend who was really her bodyguard—as well as their twenty-four/seven living arrangement. But in the meantime, she had a new beau to announce to everyone.

"Hi, gang," she said brightly, and launched right into the introductions. "I'd like you all to meet my boyfriend, Ben. Ben, these are my good friends Ronnie and Madison, who is also my assistant at The Big Event. And this here is Mark, Ronnie's boyfriend."

Ben stepped in front of her and greeted the two women in that polite, gentlemanly way of his, then shook hands with Mark. Compared to most of the guys at Envy who were wearing the latest designer styles for men, Ben definitely looked dressed down in his jeans and his untucked chambray shirt. He was also so opposite of the polished men she'd dated in the past. But there was no denying that with his thick brown hair tousled in a no-fuss style, those dark, seductive brown eyes, and a hard, gorgeous body made for sin, he was sexier than most of the men in the place in an earthy, rugged way.

And Ronnie was definitely taking notice of all those little details that made Ben so uniquely male, while

Madison was much more reserved in her speculation of who Ben *really* was.

"We didn't know you were bringing someone," Ronnie said, still checking out Ben. "So, we only grabbed one extra chair."

Christine shifted on her feet. Ronnie and Mark had claimed the love seat, Madison was sitting in one of the plush armchairs, and there was one left free, obviously for her. She glanced around for a vacant seat for Ben, but there wasn't one to be found in the lounge.

"That's not a problem," Ben said, taking matters into his own hands. "There's plenty of room for two in this chair right here."

Before Christine realized what Ben meant to do, he sat down in the plush armchair, then grabbed her hand and pulled her toward him, until she was draped across his lap with her hip pressed against the gun he'd holstered just inside the waistband of his jeans—which he'd told her he had a license to carry in public. She gasped in surprise and caught the wicked glint in Ben's gaze that told her he was taking his role as her boyfriend very seriously.

"My, my, my. Such a resourceful kind of guy," Ronnie said, seemingly impressed with Ben's take-charge approach. "I like that in a man." She took a sip of her cosmopolitan.

Ben slid one arm around Christine's waist, and rested the palm of his other hand on the bare skin of her thigh right below where the hem of her miniskirt ended, his touch undeniably possessive. And hot. *Very hot*.

"I'd rather keep Christy nice and close, anyways," he replied with a grin.

From across the way, Madison was sending her a *What the hell is going on?* look, and all Christine could do was smile at her best friend for now and keep up the charade that was of her own making.

One of the bar's cocktail waitresses came up to their group. Since Christine frequented Envy, she immediately recognized the pretty auburn-haired woman as Jodie.

"What can I get you two to drink?" she asked, eyeing Ben with too much interest.

"I'll take an apple martini," Christine said, needing something with a bit of a kick to help her get through the next few hours.

"Sam Adams for me," Ben told the other woman, once again establishing himself as someone who didn't give a damn about social pretenses. In an upscale club where most men ordered hard liquor over cheap beer, he was an anomaly.

Once the cocktail waitress headed back to the bar, Ronnie snuggled up to Mark's side and turned her green-eyed sights back on Ben. "So, Christy, where have you been hiding this fine specimen of a man?"

Forcing herself to relax against the hard, muscular thighs beneath her bottom, she slipped an arm around his broad shoulders and leaned into his chest. "We've been dating quietly for the past few weeks, and I thought it was time to take things to the next level and introduce Ben to my closest friends."

"He's definitely your best-kept secret," Madison murmured wryly, and followed that comment with a sip of her strawberry margarita.

"Well, I, for one, am glad to see you back in the game after you-know-who did you-know-what." Ronnie lifted her cosmopolitan in a mock toast, then finished off the rest of the drink.

As much as Christine adored Ronnie, her friend didn't know the meaning of subtlety. She was bold and brazen, and usually said whatever was on her mind. She'd never liked Jason, and couldn't have been happier when Christine had ended their engagement.

At least Ben knew what she was talking about, and it wasn't something she'd have to explain later.

Jodie arrived with their drinks and set them both on the table. "By the way, the bartender just told me that Craig is picking up your tab tonight."

Before Christine could issue a reply, Ben beat her to it. "Thank you, but *I'll* pay for the drinks," he said firmly, playing his role with a believable amount of authority.

Taken aback by his firm tone, Jodie's eyes widened. "Oh. Okay. I'll let Craig know."

Well, that was certainly one way to bring Craig's attention to the fact that she had a boyfriend, Christine thought.

"So, what do you do for a living, Ben?" Ronnie, the inquisitive one, asked.

"I work for a security firm," he said smoothly. Before Ronnie could drill him about what, exactly, his work entailed, he added, "Prior to that, I was in the military."

That bit of information caught Mark's attention. "Which branch?"

"The Marine Corps." Ben handed Christine her apple martini, but didn't touch his bottle of beer.

Mark's gaze lit up with interest. "My younger brother, Tim, is in the Marines. He was just recently deployed to Iraq. He says the conditions there are pretty deplorable."

Ben nodded in agreement. "It can be a tough assignment."

Christine knew that Ben spoke that statement from the heart. Having lost someone he cared deeply for as a direct result of the combat zone in Iraq, he had firsthand experience of just how harsh and unforgiving the war could be.

The two men continued to talk about the military and discuss their opinions on the war. Ronnie rolled her eyes in boredom, and signaled Jodie for another cocktail, then launched into a more girl-appropriate discussion about an incident that happened at the exclusive boutique she managed. While Christine listened to Ronnie's animated story about a woman who'd attempted to shoplift a designer purse by stuffing it down her stretch pants and concealing the bulge with a loose blouse, she sipped her drink and tried to keep her mind off the way Ben's deep, husky voice was so close to her ear as he talked, and the sensual feel of those hands still on her body.

She failed miserably. Sitting on his lap, she was so keenly aware of him, in every way. His thumb absently stroked the inside of her knee as he continued his conversation with Mark, and at some point the hand at her back had glided up her spine and slid beneath the fall of her hair. His strong fingers gently kneaded the nape of her neck, and she had to swallow back a moan of pure pleasure.

Everything about the man, about his touch, was so seductively mesmerizing. So arousing and exciting, made more so by the fact that everything he did seemed so natural and unrehearsed. And while he appeared to be completely relaxed and unaffected by her close-enough-to-kiss presence, she on the other hand couldn't stop her long deprived body from reacting to each and every sensation. Her pulse quickened, something deep in her stomach fluttered, and her breasts felt tight and sensitive against her lacy bra.

Inhaling a slow, even breath, she shifted her gaze from Ronnie to Madison as they continued to chat and laugh about something her friend said, and Christine smiled and pretended to join in on the amusement. She took another long drink of her martini and was grateful when the liquid slid down her throat much more smoothly than the first few sips had.

Over the next hour and a half, the five of them talked about inconsequential things and laughed like old friends. One drink turned into two, then a third that she didn't quite finish, and Christine decided it was just what she needed to relax, enjoy herself, and have a good time.

"Uh-oh," Ronnie said, her suddenly narrowed gaze honing in on something beyond Christine's shoulder. "You'll never guess whose working the room behind you."

Christine didn't turn around to look. She didn't have to. Craig had warned her that her nemesis would be at Envy tonight, and that's the only person she knew that could shift Ronnie's easygoing personality into protective mode on Christine's behalf.

"It's Leanne, I'm sure," Christine said.

Madison, who'd taken a peek at the people mingling behind them as soon as Ronnie made her comment, now stared at Christine in surprise. "How did you know?"

"I have great radar when it comes to her." Feeling carefree and lighter than air, Christine grinned. "Maybe if I hide she won't notice *I'm* here."

Without thinking her actions through, not that she was thinking all that logically at the moment, Christine buried her face against Ben's neck to shield herself from Leanne's predatory gaze that always seemed to pick her out in a crowd. One deep breath later, she realized her mistake. The warm, heady male scent of him curled through her senses like a hypnotic drug. She grazed his neck with her lips, touched her tongue to his skin, and the broad hand still on her thigh tightened in reaction.

Ben's fingers tangled gently in her hair, and he tipped her head back so that she was looking into his dark, intense eyes. Forgetting everything but the two of them and the undeniable desire wrapping around her, teasing her with something so deliciously forbidden she licked her bottom lip in anticipation. She wanted to kiss him so badly, ached to see if all the heat and chemistry between them was everything she'd fantasized it would be.

He smiled at her—a sexy, bad boy grin that added to

the chaos smoldering within her. "I think three drinks is right about your limit," he murmured huskily, seemingly sensing the direction her thoughts had traveled. "Who's Leanne, Christy?"

His gaze was curious, but she was sober enough to realize he'd switched to bodyguard mode. With the threat hanging over her family, his job was to make sure he knew everyone around her.

"She's just the most miserable, spiteful bitch you'd ever want to meet," Ronnic said before Christy could offer a polite, diluted version of Leanne's character. "Don't let the smile fool ya. Once you turn away from her she'll stab you in the back and give the knife an extra twist while she's at it."

Ben casually glanced over his shoulder to check out the woman they were talking about, and Ronnie was once again quick to pipe in with her own helpful description of Leanne.

"You can't miss her," Ronnie said. "She's the bleached blonde in the tight pink dress and big, in-your-face breasts."

Madison choked on her own laughter. "Geez, Ronnie, tell it like it is, why don't you?"

Mark smirked. "You should know by now that Ronnie isn't one to sugarcoat the truth. Besides, Leanne's reputation precedes her."

Ben glanced back at Christine, raising a dark, inquiring brow. "And you know her, how?"

"She's sort of a business rival," she said with a shrug. "She's a club promoter who is trying to expand her contacts, and she resents the fact that Craig has helped me so much in getting my event planning business off to such a great start." Seeing the concern in his gaze, she added, "I know who and what I'm dealing with, Ben."

He nodded, but she knew he'd just added Leanne to a

mental list in his mind of people he needed to keep a close eye on.

"I need to go to the ladies' room." Madison stood and glanced at Christine. "Anybody else care to join me?"

"I'm good," Ronnie said with a wave of her hand.

Christine really didn't have to go, but there was no mistaking, or ignoring, the direct look Madison was giving her. "I'll go with you."

Easing off of Ben's lap, Christine stood and smoothed the hem of her skirt down, then reached for the purse that Ben had tucked between himself and the chair cushion. "We'll be right back." She walked away with Madison and did her best to keep out of Leanne's line of sight.

The restroom wasn't far from where they were sitting, and Ben had a clear view of the entrance and exit.

As soon as they were in the women's lounge area of the bathroom, Madison finally asked all the questions that Christine had expected from her good friend and assistant.

"Okay, what's the real deal with Ben?" Madison demanded, her hazel eyes flashing with exasperation. "Who is he, and why are you introducing him as your boyfriend and getting all cozy with him when I know damn well you haven't so much as dated anyone since Jason."

Christine headed over to the large vanity area that spanned one long wall of the room, where a few women were fixing their makeup and fussing with their outfits or hair. Setting her purse on the counter, she rummaged through the contents and pulled out her lip gloss.

She met Madison's gaze in the mirror. "He's not really my boyfriend," she said in a low tone of voice, so that only her friend could hear.

"No kidding." Madison crossed her arms over her chest and waited for Christine to explain.

"He's my bodyguard for the next three weeks, until the

election is over." She went on to tell Madison the more private details of the threat her father had received, and how her dad had insisted on twenty-four-hour protection for her.

"I've never seen you get so up close and personal with your other bodyguards in the past." A small smile curved Madison's lips. "Though I do have to say, Ben is a whole lot hotter than those security agents your father normally hires for you."

Christine couldn't argue with that. "You know how Craig has been so persistent in asking me out?"

Madison nodded, causing her straight, smooth bob to brush across her shoulders. "Yes."

"Well, Ben has agreed to act as my pretend boyfriend in order to hopefully make Craig back off until I can get past the birthday party he's throwing for me here at Envy."

"Yeah, well, if the guy could take a nice, gentle rejection, he would have already backed off by now," her friend pointed out.

"He obviously can't, and I just need to be careful about how I handle things with him." Christine swiped her bottom lip with the pink gloss, noticing how flushed her cheeks looked, and how bright her eyes were. She knew her rosy glow was due to all that sensual awareness between her and Ben rather than any of the drinks she'd consumed. "So, if you can just play along, I'd really appreciate it."

"Sure, I can do that." Madison's gaze narrowed just a bit as she studied Christine's reflection. "But why do I get the feeling that there's a little more than just *pretending* going on between the two of you?"

"The attraction is real. It's been there between us for months," Christine admitted. Tucking her lip gloss back into her purse, she snapped it shut and sighed. "Unfortunately, Ben is all business."

Madison tipped her head. "Unfortunately?"

Christine shrugged and grinned. "What can I say? The guys turns me on like no one else ever has, and I'd love to see where all that sexual tension between us might lead, but he's been real good about not crossing any of those ethical lines, if you know what I mean."

"Maybe you ought to give him a little shove," Madison suggested, a shameless gleam in her eyes. "I mean, you'll be spending a whole lot of alone time at your place. It's definitely something to think about."

With that brazen comment hanging in the air, Madison left her to take care of personal business.

Christine ran her fingers through her wavy hair to give it more of a tousled look while she thought about Madison's parting remark. The big flaw in her friend's scenario was the fact that Christine had never, ever, been aggressive when it came to men, and Madison's idea to seduce Ben would definitely require someone far more bold and daring than she'd ever been. But the notion did intrigue her—more than was probably wise or prudent.

When Madison returned, they headed out of the restroom together and made their way through the growing crowd of people filling the lounge and bar area. Halfway to where they'd been sitting, Leanne seemingly appeared out of nowhere, stepping in front of them and blocking their path. Christine was forced to come to an abrupt stop or risk colliding with those thrust-out breasts of hers.

The other woman was holding a fresh cocktail and sported an insincere smile. "I heard Craig gave you the O'Keefe Annual Corporate Dinner Cruise account." Her tone was more accusatory than friendly.

Such a nice, typical greeting for Leanne, Christine thought sarcastically. "Craig didn't *give* me anything, Leanne," she replied, determined to put Leanne firmly in her place with the facts. "He passed my name on to Lance

O'Keefe, who called me to discuss the possibility of me handling the dinner cruise this year. I gave him an estimate, as did a few other event planning companies, and he liked my ideas enough to hire The Big Event for the job. It was all very legitimate."

From behind Leanne, Christine watched as Ben strode purposefully toward her, arriving by her side before Leanne could launch into some kind of rebuttal.

"There you are, sweetheart," Ben said affectionately, and wrapped a strong, protective arm around her waist. "Everything okay?"

Christine smiled at Ben, eternally grateful for his timely interruption. "I'm fine," she told him, then glanced back at Leanne. "Excuse us. My friends are waiting."

Madison, who hated any kind of drama, made a quick beeline back toward where Ronnie and Mark were watching the scene with Leanne unfold from their cozy love seat. Christine started to follow her friend, but Leanne stepped in front of her once again, her gaze roaming with blatant interest down the length of Ben's body.

When the other woman's eyes finally found their way back up to his face, there was no mistaking the predatory smile on her bright pink, painted lips. "Aren't you going to introduce me to whoever this good-looking guy is?" Leanne purred like a cat in heat.

"I'm Ben," he said, taking charge of the situation. "Christine's boyfriend."

Leanne's eyes widened, and her expression took on an incredulous look. "Really? What a surprise. You're so *not* Christine's type at all." She soothed that insulting remark with a smile meant to be coy and sweet. "Regardless, it's very nice to meet you. I'm Leanne Baker."

"Yes, I know." Ben's tone was bland and completely disinterested. "Ronnie was kind enough to tell me all about you."

Obviously knowing how Ronnie felt about her, and nothing Christine's friend said would have been complimentary, Leanne's too-confident demeanor faltered. Face flushed, she took a drink of her cocktail.

"Christy! I've been looking for you."

Christine heard Craig's deep voice penetrate the noise in the lounge seconds before he joined their small group, overwhelming her with his presence on top of Leanne's personal attack. Standing next to her, on the opposite side of Ben, Craig touched her elbow and stroked his thumb along the inside of her arm much too intimately.

With his pitch-black hair combed neatly away from his handsome face, and dressed in an expensive designer suit, Craig gave her a gently chastising look. "Jodie told me that you brought a friend tonight who was very insistent about paying your tab."

"That would be *me*," Ben replied possessively as his fingers tightened at Christine's waist.

"Christine's *boyfriend*," Leanne was quick to inform Craig, knowing how that bit of information would likely stir up some trouble for Christine, and would hopefully, finally, turn Craig's attention her way now that Christine was off the market, so to speak.

That jolt of unexpected news caused Craig's fingers to drop abruptly from her arm. "Oh." Something dark and angry flared in the depths of his eyes, then he blinked, and it was gone. "I didn't realize that Christine was dating anyone." His voice was as tight as his clenched jaw.

Craig had definitely backed off, just as Christine had hoped he would, and she was relieved that her ploy had worked. "We were keeping things quiet, but once we made the decision to date exclusively, we figured it was time to make our relationship public."

A tight frown creased Craig's forehead. "Well, before

you leave tonight, I still need to talk to you about your birthday bash here at Envy."

Christine nodded and smiled, glad to see that she hadn't sabotaged her working relationship with Craig in any way. "Sure."

Leanne shifted on her stilettos, looking annoyed that nobody was paying any attention to her. She glanced around the lounge, then met Christine's gaze with a devious glint in her eyes. "Did you happen to see your *ex* sitting over there at the bar?"

Leanne's announcement caused both Christine and Ben to look over at the bar at the same time. Sure enough, Jason was sitting on a bar stool, tossing back a shot of liquor that the bartender had just set in front of him. He signaled for another shot, gulped that down as well, then turned and stared at her, his eyes narrowed into dark, angry slits.

A foreboding chill shivered down her spine. She'd never seen Jason look so unkempt. His shirt was wrinkled, and his hair, normally cropped short, was long, shaggy, and uncombed. But it was the unbridled rage that she sensed from where she stood that had her stomach churning with uncertainty and dread.

Ben glanced back at Craig. "Christine has a restraining order against Jason, and he's in violation of those terms just by being in the same place as her. Would you mind summoning your security to take care of the problem and escort him out of here?"

"Of course." Retrieving a cell phone from the breast pocket of his suit jacket, Craig pressed a speed dial number. As soon as someone picked up on the other end of the line, he explained the situation, but before his guys could arrive on scene, Jason was sliding off the bar stool and heading toward Christine.

Her heart started a hard, fast pounding in her chest, the rush of fear making it difficult for her to breath.

Ben cursed vividly. "Looks like I'll be taking care of things," he muttered, then gave Christine a quick, but adamant look. *"Stay put."*

Nodding, Christine touched her fingertips to the sharp stab of pain in her temples, hating that Jason was about to cause a scene in a very public place. Already, people were starting to take notice of the confrontation and were gathering around to see what happened.

"I'm sorry about this, Craig," she said, hoping that Ben could take care of her ex without things getting too out of hand. "Jason shouldn't be here, and he knows it."

"You don't need to apologize." Craig stepped in front of her, as if to shield her from potential harm. "I'll make sure he doesn't get anywhere near you."

Christine opened her mouth to thank Craig, but the words got caught in her throat as a splash of chilled liquid and bits of ice hit her in the chest area. *Someone had just spilled a drink on her!*

She sucked in a startled gasp and glanced back around to discover that Leanne was the culprit. The other woman stood in front of her, the drink glass in her hand now completely empty. As something cold, wet, and sticky trickled its way between her breasts and continued to spread downward, Christine's fear was suddenly eclipsed by a strong flash of fury that had her seriously considering ripping every last strand of hair from Leanne's head.

Hearing the commotion, Craig turned back around, his gaze shifting from Christine's soaked top to Leanne's feigned surprised expression. "Jesus, Leanne, what happened?"

Leanne batted her eyes innocently at him. "I'm so sorry. Someone just bumped into me and jostled my arm and my drink went flying."

Since most everyone had moved into the bar area in anticipation of a brawl, there was no one even near them now. Christine bit back a scathing remark, refusing to stoop to Leanne's childish level—or engage in the altercation she seemed to anticipate.

Leanne gave her a smile that was just as deceptive as the woman herself. "You might want to go to the restroom and use some paper towels to dry off," she suggested oh-so-helpfully.

Christine couldn't believe this was happening to her, and all at once. Between Jason belligerently challenging his restraining order, and now being soaked to the skin by Leanne's drink, Christine couldn't imagine the night getting any worse.

She knew she couldn't just stand there and drip all over the floor, but neither did she relish the thought of heading into the women's restroom where a gaggle of women would undoubtedly watch her sop up the drink another woman had spilled on her—and whisper about it behind her back. She'd much prefer a private, secure place where she could take her top off and wipe off the sticky residue on her skin.

She glanced at Craig, who was looking at her in concern, and didn't hesitate to ask a huge favor. "Would you mind if I used your private bathroom in your office, where there are clean, dry towels I can use?" And where she'd be far away from prying eyes and gossipy women.

"Of course," he said without hesitating, and gently grabbed her arm, which earned Christine an envious glare from Leanne.

Hearing a shuffling coming from the bar area, along with something crashing to the floor, Christine bit her bottom lip and tried to search through the throng of customers for Ben, and to see what was going on. Whatever was happening, it didn't sound good.

"Come on. Let's get you out of here," Craig said as he escorted her toward the back of the nightclub and away from the sudden mayhem going on at the bar. "Until the situation with Jason has been taken care of, it'll be much safer for you in my office, anyways."

Christine nodded gratefully. As more of the crowd swarmed toward the bar in hopes of getting a glimpse of some action, she decided that leaving with Craig was the safest, and smartest bet, until Jason was out of the club and back under the restraining order restrictions.

And in the meantime, she could clean up the mess that Leanne had made in the privacy of Craig's office bathroom.

Five

BEN strode determinedly toward Jason to put a stop to his progress toward Christine. Adrenaline pumped through his veins as it always did whenever he was about to face some kind of combat, and he rolled his shoulders to ease the tension settling there. As he closed in on her ex, he could see that the other man's bloodshot eyes were brimming with a maelstrom of emotion, and most of it wasn't of the warm, fuzzy variety. The fury and bitterness emanating from Jason was almost violent in its intensity.

Jason was so intent on getting to Christine that when Ben stepped right in front of him and put his hand out to stop him, the other man didn't even see it coming. Jason stumbled back a step from the force of colliding with Ben's unyielding arm, and caught his footing before he fell back on his ass.

Once Jason recovered from that unforeseen impediment, he glared up at Ben. "Get the hell out of my way, asshole," he sneered, fully expecting Ben to comply.

Ben didn't so much as budge. Instead, he widened his

stance and crossed his arms over his chest. "I suggest you stop right where you are, turn around, and leave the nightclub before you get yourself in a whole lot of trouble."

Jason stared at Ben with disdain. "Who the fuck are you?"

"I'm your worst nightmare," Ben said, borrowing the famous line from his good friend Joel Wilde. Noticing how the crowd around them was closing in and looking for a scuffle of some sort, he knew he needed to put an end to the confrontation, and quickly, before it spun out of control.

Calmly, he said, "If I have to tell you to leave twice, Christine will be pressing charges and *I'll* be the one escorting you out of here."

"Fuck you!"

Ben was normally a very patient man, but not when it came to people who did incredibly stupid things, and Jason, at the moment, ranked pretty high up on the list. Security was finally starting to make their way through the crowd and close in, and Jason noticed, too, which made him way too unpredictable in Ben's estimation. As soon as Jason tried to shove him out of the way, Ben reacted with lightning quick speed. He caught the other man's wrist before it made contact with his chest, then twisted until Jason was forced to turn around and Ben could jam his arm up against the middle of his back to restrain him.

A struggle ensued, and as Jason tried to break free of Ben's unrelenting hold, the other man tripped and fell against a nearby table, causing bottles and glasses to crash to the floor. With the table now cleared, Ben took the opportunity to pin him there, facedown, while security put him in cuffs.

One of the guards grabbed the back of Jason's shirt and pulled him upright. "Do you want us to call the cops so you can press charges?"

Ben shook his head. "No, not this time." He actually

felt sorry for the man and what he'd become—a pitiful drunk. "However, you come near Christine again, and all bets are off."

Security led Jason away, and with the other man taken care of and no longer a threat, Ben headed back to where he'd left Christine, only to find her gone, as was Craig. He glanced over at where Christine's friends had been, but they weren't there, either.

Un-freakin'-believable! Where in the hell did she go? He'd given her one simple order and she'd ignored it.

He jammed his fingers through his hair in frustration. Catching sight of Leanne, he headed in her direction, figuring she'd been the last to see Christine and would most likely know what happened to her. As he approached the buxom blonde, she eyed him like a fresh piece of meat she wanted to sink her teeth into.

"Hi there," she said, gracing him with a slow, provocative smile that hinted at a more indecent proposition—if he was willing.

Annoyed by the other woman's flirtatious attempts, and needing to find Christine ASAP, he got right down to business. "Where did Christine go?" he asked.

"She took off with Craig, and considering he's had the hots for her for some time now, who knows what they're doing," she said, clearly attempting to make him jealous. She stepped closer and ran her fingers along the collar of his shirt. "You know, since you're more my type than hers anyways, maybe you and I can hook up and have some fun."

"Not interested." He so did not have time for this shit. "Now where did they go?" he demanded, more forcefully this time. Every second that passed was a second more that something could happen to Christine, and he was starting to feel anxious and edgy.

"Calm down." His rejection must have stung, because

her lower lip puffed out in a pout. "They went to his private office," she admitted reluctantly. "It's right up those stairs."

She pointed across the lounge area, and Ben took off in that direction, his long-legged stride getting him there in less than a minute. He took the steps two at a time, walked down a short hallway, and came to a door marked "Private Office." He tried to turn the knob, but it was locked, and his stomach twisted with the worst kind of apprehension.

The door was solid and secure, and not one he could break open with one swift kick. So, he used his fist and pounded insistently on the surface with enough force to rattle the walls, until the door finally swung open and Craig stood on the other side with an irritable scowl on his face.

"Jesus, what the hell is wrong with you!" he bellowed.

Immediately, Ben noticed that Craig had taken off his suit jacket and tie, and his crisp white dress shirt was unbuttoned halfway down his chest. The knot in Ben's belly squeezed tighter.

Ben pushed his way inside, giving the other man no option but to let him in. "Where is Christine?" He'd already checked and she wasn't in this first room that was set up more like a mini lavish suite than an office, with a comfortable couch, a minibar, and big-screen TV.

"She's fine." Antagonism radiated off of Craig in palpable waves. "With Jason out of control downstairs, I thought she'd be much safer up here until he was taken care of."

His answer wasn't the one Ben was looking for. Standing in the middle of the room, he turned around and met the other man's stare, his own expression dark and dangerous and threatening. *"Where the hell is she?"*

This time, with Ben at his most foreboding, Craig didn't dick around with his reply. "She's right in there," he said, waving a hand toward an adjoining closed door. "She's using my private restroom, and she should be out in a few minutes."

Ben didn't have a few minutes to wait. He had to know that she was okay *now*. He strode toward the door with an irate Craig hot on his heels.

"Look, you can't just come in here and take charge like you own the place!"

"I believe I just did," Ben stated succinctly. He turned the knob and was grateful when it opened, even though he'd been fully prepared to bust this one down if it had been locked.

He stepped into the large, very plush and decadent bathroom, complete with marble flooring, an enclosed shower, and a large Jacuzzi tub. Christine, who'd been standing at the vanity in just a black lacy bra, skimpy panties, and black suede boots, sucked in a startled breath and jumped back upon his bold entrance. Her eyes widened as he shut and locked the door, then closed the distance between them.

Between Craig having shed some of his clothing, and now Christine, he automatically thought the worst—that Craig had somehow managed to take advantage of her. "Why are you undressed?" His throat felt raw.

She frowned at him and tried to cover herself with the small, damp hand towel she'd been holding. "Because I'm covered in sticky mai tai, from my chest to my thighs, and I'm trying to wash most of it off. Do you think maybe next time you can knock instead of just barging in like Conan the Barbarian?"

Covered in sticky mai tai? He shook his head in confusion, because he had no idea what the hell she was talking about. "Considering I'm in charge of making sure you're safe at all times, I'll barge in whenever the situation warrants," he said in a low, harsh whisper, just in case the walls were paper-thin and Craig could hear their conversation. "Like right now."

She lifted her chin defiantly. "Oh, really?"

"Yes, *really*." He was so damned relieved that she was okay, because he never would have forgiven himself if she'd been harmed in any way, but he was still more than a little pissed off at her for disobeying his orders.

Wanting her to know just how serious he was, he stepped closer, backed her up against the sink, and braced his hands on either side of her hips on the counter. His face was very close to hers, and he could smell something sweet and fruity, with a hint of rum . . . like a mai tai.

"I thought I told you to stay put while I handled Jason." She opened her mouth to say something, but he was quicker. "I can't do my job effectively if I don't know where the hell you are. When I tell you to wait somewhere, it means you don't leave the area. With anyone. Especially Craig."

"*Jason* was the threat," she said, keeping her voice hushed. "Not Craig!"

"I don't like him," he snapped. Ben knew his aversion to the man was irrational and based more on the fact that Craig wanted Christine for his own, but at the moment he didn't care.

"I asked to use his private bathroom after Leanne deliberately dumped her drink on me, which is why I'm standing here half-naked." She held her arms out to her sides, giving him a delicious glimpse of all that creamy flesh being plumped up by her push-up bra. "I'm trying to clean up the sticky mess, and I didn't anticipate an interruption!"

So that explained why she smelled like a fruity drink he wanted to taste. And it didn't surprise him at all to discover that Leanne was behind such a juvenile stunt.

He tipped his head, the beginning of a grin chasing

away the brunt of his anger. "Is your life always filled with this much drama?"

"Not until you became a part of it." She smiled sweetly.

Now that he'd gotten all that tension off his chest, he straightened and stepped away from her. He kept his gaze on her face, but his peripheral vision, and his vivid imagination, had no problem conjuring her figure from the neck down. A sexy black bra encasing her small, firm breasts. A smooth, flat belly. Skimpy lace panties. Slim, sleek thighs . . . and those damned dominatrix, high-heeled boots.

He swallowed hard and hoped her gaze didn't stray any lower than his waist, or she was bound to find more than she bargained for. "You have to remember that first and foremost, I'm your bodyguard. There is a viable threat against your father, and your family, and that includes you, as well." *Especially her.* "My job is to keep you safe, and it will go so much more smoothly with your cooperation. Got it?"

She nodded. "Yes, sir."

"Good." Grabbing her top and skirt off the counter, he thrust both at her, covering as much of her bared body as he could. "Put your clothes back on. You can shower at home. I've had enough excitement for one night. As soon as you're dressed, we're getting the hell out of here."

STANDING in her dark, quiet kitchen, Christine stared out the window over the sink to the moonlit backyard and took a sip of the hot chamomile tea she'd made. Closing her eyes, she savored the soothing, relaxing warmth as it spread its way down to her stomach.

Regardless of the late hour that was way past her normal bedtime, and despite feeling utterly exhausted after everything that had transpired at Envy earlier, she hadn't been able to fall asleep. She'd spent an hour tossing and turning in her bed with a myriad of thoughts running through her mind, and when the clock on her nightstand hit one A.M., she decided to resort to her good ole standby of tea to help her unwind and hopefully enable her to sleep. She had a busy day at the office tomorrow and couldn't afford to have her mind fogged by lack of slumber.

She sighed, still unable to believe how her evening had turned out. What had begun as a fun outing with friends had ended up being a night she wouldn't soon forget.

After leaving Envy, the drive home with Ben had been quiet, and once they'd arrived at her place, he'd conducted a whole house search even though her security alarm had still been on and untripped. That didn't matter to Ben, who insisted that until he was no longer in charge of her, this would be his routine whenever they arrived home. She had to admit, the man was thorough and efficient when it came to her safety.

Since her damp clothes had been clinging to her, she'd headed straight for her bedroom, stripped her clothes back off, and took a long, hot shower. By the time she was done and went in search of Ben, he'd already retreated to the guest bedroom and had shut the door.

She took another drink of her warm tea. Other than the incident with Jason, then with Craig in his private office, she'd had a great time with Ben. He'd meshed well with her friends, and he played the part of her steady beau exceptionally well. Almost *too* well, considering how comfortable she'd been sitting on his lap, how sensual his touch felt on her bare thigh, and especially how territorial he'd been when he'd found her seminude in Craig's bathroom.

Remembering the simmering heat in his gaze when he'd noticed her standing there in her bra and panty ensemble, then again when he'd crowded her against the vanity, a shiver rippled through her and tightened the tips of her breasts against her cotton camisole.

Her overwhelming reaction to Ben no longer surprised her at all. He made her burn with need, made her think about all the things she wanted to do to him, and with him. Sinful, shameless things she'd never done with any other man before.

She wasn't a virgin, but since her breakup with Jason she'd come to realize that she was far too inexperienced when it came to all that sexual foreplay a couple usually enjoyed before the main course. For that matter, she was pretty damned innocent when it came to positions, too. The only one she was intimately familiar with was missionary style, and there was so much more she wanted to know, learn, and experience.

As she finished her tea and set her cup in the sink, she thought about what Madison had said to her earlier tonight, about giving Ben a bit of a shove in the right direction. But in order to do that, it meant she'd have to shed all those rules of propriety her mother had drilled into her head for so many years. Being a demure good girl and suppressing her own desires hadn't gotten her much in terms of sexual gratification, and the thought of being a little wicked and wanton now held a whole lot of appeal.

But embracing that sexually assertive woman within her meant being bolder in her pursuit. More daring in her quest to please herself, instead of doing what everyone else expected of her. It also meant not settling for less than what *she* wanted.

And what she wanted was Ben Cabrera.

"You can't sleep either, huh?"

As if her thoughts had conjured him, Ben's deep, husky voice sounded from somewhere behind her. Turning around, she found him across the kitchen, standing in the doorway, the moonlight streaming through the window, illuminating him like a dark, fallen angel. Leaning casually against the frame, his corded arms were crossed over his bare chest, and he wore a pair of gray sweatpants that rode precariously low on his hips and revealed a good amount of his taut, rigid belly. Lower, the soft cotton emphasized everything that made him so heart-stoppingly virile.

Her mouth went dry, and she swallowed hard as she slowly, leisurely dragged her gaze back up the length of his gorgeous, well-built body, until she finally reached his face. Already, a light stubble had formed on his lean jaw, and his hair had been finger-combed into a wildly disheveled style that flaunted that sexy, bad boy image of his.

Lust, strong and undeniable, licked through her like a live flame. She knew her shot at seduction was now or never, that there was no better time than the present moment to go full force after the man who'd inspired some of her most erotic fantasies over the past few months.

"No, I couldn't sleep either," she said, her voice soft and low.

Gathering her confidence, she strolled across the kitchen toward him, wishing she was wearing a pair of her high-heeled shoes that gave her a bit more of a height advantage. Without them, and because Ben was so big and tall, she felt incredibly delicate and feminine when she finally came to a stop in front of him.

"It's all your fault, you know," she said, blaming him for the time she'd spent tossing and turning in her bed.

He arched a dark brown brow in amusement. "And just how am I to blame?"

"Because you make me feel hot and restless, and that isn't conducive to sleep." Smiling, she reached up and touched the tips of her fingers to his unshaven cheek, watching as his gaze darkened with awareness. "You feel it, too, don't you?" she whispered.

"Feel what?" he replied, his gruff tone giving away his attempt at nonchalance.

"This attraction between us." Stepping even closer, she skimmed the pad of her thumb across his full bottom lip, aching to kiss him. "Tell me you feel it, too."

Encircling his long fingers around her wrist, he gently drew her hand away from his face and let her arm drop back to her side. "It doesn't matter if I do, Christine. Nothing's going to happen beyond being your pretend boyfriend."

God, she hated that he'd reverted back to calling her Christine, which was his way of keeping things all business between them, she knew. But now that she'd come this far, she wasn't about to let him dissuade her from her ultimate goal. In fact, she was all-out determined to crack that steadfast control of his, because what she was beginning to feel for him was as honest and real as it got.

"You make me realize everything that was missing from my other relationships, not that I've had many." Drawn to the broad expanse of his bare chest, she splayed both hands on all that hard muscle and hot skin and experienced a thrilling jolt of triumph when he sucked in a sharp breath. "But even with the men I've dated in my past, I've never, ever, felt this kind of intense attraction before."

He didn't remove her hands this time, but neither did he touch her in return. Instead, his fingers curled into tight fists, and the muscles beneath her hand flexed oh-so-enticingly, revealing just how tense he'd become. "Don't go there, Christine," he said, his voice a rasp of sound in the shadowed kitchen.

"Oh, but I *do* want to go there. Badly." Letting her lashes fall to half-mast, she slid her arms around his neck, stood up on tiptoe, and brushed her mouth across his. "I want to know how real desire feels," she whispered, teasing the seam of his lips with her tongue. "I want to know what real passion tastes like."

The rumbling of a groan vibrated against her mouth, encouraging her to forge ahead while she still had the chance. "Kiss me, Ben." She nibbled on his bottom lip and gently tugged it between her teeth. *"Please."*

Like a man pushed to the brink, he finally fell over the edge and Christine knew she was about to reap the benefits of all that raw, powerful masculinity he exuded. With a rough growl, he wrapped the fingers of one hand in her hair, encircled his other arm around her waist, and hauled her up against his body as his mouth came down on hers.

Hot.

Hard.

And deliciously demanding.

There was no sweetness in his kiss, but slow and romantic wasn't what she'd been after tonight. This all-consuming embrace was exactly what she wanted from Ben, and for the first time in her adult life she discovered that desire felt like the most exciting thrill-ride she'd ever taken. And passion . . . oh, Lord, passion tasted like searing heat, ravenous hunger, and insatiable lust all rolled into one.

The hand at the nape of her neck tightened, then he shifted and moved, turning her slightly, backing her up, until her shoulders hit the kitchen wall and he trapped her there with the insistent press of his thighs and hips against hers. The solid length of his erection branded her with a need so primal, she ached to feel every inch of him inside of her.

With her head now pinned against the flat surface, he slanted his mouth across hers and deepened the kiss further, if that was at all possible. His tongue stroked across hers, and his big, strong hands wandered into more forbidden territory.

One palm glided down over the curve of her waist and around to her bottom while his other hand skimmed beneath the hem of her camisole. His thumb caressed the skin of her stomach, and she trembled in anticipation. Unrelenting fingers swept upward, until he finally enveloped her breast in his big, callused hand and squeezed the firm flesh.

She moaned against his mouth, and arousal, liquid and warm, spiraled its way down to her belly, then between her thighs. He rolled her taut nipple between his fingers and she automatically arched into him as a soft, mewling sound escaped her throat. Everything the man did, every illicit stroke and erotic caress, sent her soaring to a higher level of sensation, until she felt drenched in the most decadent pleasure of her life.

She wanted to touch him in return . . . everywhere. Wanted to make him burn with the same intoxicating fever spreading through her. As she smoothed both of her hands down his chest to his abdomen, then teased her fingers along the waistband of his sweatpants, his big body shuddered. Before she had the chance to pull on the drawstring that would give her access to his jutting erection, he abruptly ended the kiss. He jerked back, his breathing ragged.

Christine was disappointed, but not surprised by Ben's sudden retreat, especially when she witnessed the self-condemnation gradually filling his gaze. He had absolutely nothing to feel guilty about, not when she'd been the one who'd instigated the kiss, and she opened her mouth to tell him so.

"Don't," he ordered through clenched teeth as he pushed away from her. "Don't say a damned thing. You got what you wanted, so let's just leave it at that." He

walked out of the kitchen without looking back, and a moment later she heard his bedroom door slam shut.

She winced, and had to resist the urge to follow after him and demand that they hash out this attraction between them right then and there. But it was painfully obvious to her that he was in no mood to talk about what had just happened, and she'd be stupid to push the issue when he wasn't in the right frame of mind to admit that their kiss had rocked his world, as much as it had hers.

And that was okay with her. Just knowing she'd been able to penetrate a few of Ben's stringent barriers was more than enough for her. For now.

Six

BEN knew he was in trouble. *Big* trouble. Four days had passed since he'd given in to temptation and kissed Christine, and he knew it was just a matter of time before something else happened. He could feel it in the air whenever Christine was near him. Could sense the subtle changes in her since that night—a sensual self-assurance that kept Ben on edge, waiting and wondering what her next plan of attack would be.

It didn't help matters that he was keenly aware of the woman, in every way. She walked by him, and that warm, vanilla scent clinging to her skin sent a shot of arousal straight to his groin. She laughed, and the sound captivated him. She'd always been flirtatious with him, but now when she sent a smile his way, it was filled with a sultry feminine knowledge and womanly confidence that didn't bode well for him and his good intentions.

So far, she'd behaved herself, but he suspected that was because of how busy she'd been with work. This week she'd spent a good twelve hours a day at the office, mostly preparing for an upscale charity gala for the Children's AIDS Foundation, which was scheduled for this upcoming Saturday and was being held at the St. Claire Hotel in downtown Chicago. From what she'd told him, Christine had been hired to handle the sponsors and silent auction portion of the social affair.

Now, as he relaxed on a very comfortable couch in the reception area of Christine's office where he could keep a close eye on her as she worked, Ben found it hard to believe that he was getting paid five figures to spend most of his days playing FreeCell on his laptop to pass the time. But there wasn't a whole lot to do while Christine and Madison fielded phone calls, accepted various deliveries that arrived for the silent auction, and spent hours discussing the best way to raise the most money for the Children's AIDS Foundation.

In all honesty, with nothing productive to do other than ensuring Christine's safety, he had far too much time on his hands to think about things he had no business dwelling on. Like how great her ass looked in the brown slim skirt she'd worn today, and how incredibly sexy her legs were in yet another pair of designer heels. Then there was that hot, mind-blowing kiss they'd shared that kept replaying over and over in his head. Except in his mind, instead of pulling away and ending the carnal embrace, he gave into the untamed need to strip off her clothes, bury himself deep inside her soft body, and forget the long list of reasons why getting involved with her was a very bad idea.

She'd told him she wanted to feel desire, and taste passion, and that was another thing he mulled over much too often, as well. How could she have been engaged and not have experienced desire or passion? It didn't seem possible, yet the vulnerable glimpse of emotion he'd seen in her gaze just before she'd kissed him wasn't something she could have faked.

Shaking his head clear of those too interesting thoughts, he started another game of FreeCell. A few moments later, something out of the corner of his eye caught his attention, and he glanced out the office's glass-enclosed window-front to see a black Town Car with dark-tinted windows pulling up in front of The Big Event. As always, whenever someone parked near the business he went straight into security mode—taking in the car description, memorizing the license plate, and making a mental note of whoever exited the vehicle. If they entered the office, the scrutiny continued, but on a more personal level to make sure the visit was legitimate.

The driver, dressed in a uniformed suit, stepped out of the car and opened the back door. Ben groaned as Craig Crosby emerged, looking like the pretentious son of a bitch that he was in his dark blue, knit-collared shirt, tan trousers, and with his dark, glossy hair combed back from his face. He said something to his driver, then headed toward the shop with a portfolio folder in hand.

He pushed open the door, and a buzzer rang in the back rooms to let Madison and Christine know that someone had come inside. Looking straight ahead, Craig didn't notice him sitting on the couch off to the side, giving Ben the advantage. As the other man continued walking farther into the office as if he planned on going in search of Christine himself, Ben decided to squash his presumptuous stride.

"Hey, Crosby."

Craig jolted to a stop, and his head snapped to the left. As soon as he saw Ben, the suave grin he'd been wearing to greet Christine fell flat and animosity etched his features. "What a surprise seeing you here," he said dryly.

"I'm sure it is." Leaning back into the couch cushions, Ben folded his arms behind his head and smiled, liking that he had the upper hand over this guy.

"Especially at this time of the day," Craig said, the insinuation of Ben being a bum reflecting in his voice. "Don't you have a job?"

Ben shrugged. "I make my own hours. Do you have an appointment to see Christine?" Each morning he went over the day's agenda with her, and Crosby had not been listed for a meeting today. That's something he wouldn't have forgotten.

Craig visibly bristled with annoyance. "What are you, her receptionist now?"

"No. Just a very jealous boyfriend."

The other man's gaze flared with a mix of anger and frustration, and Ben had to admit that provoking Craig was the most fun he'd had in days.

Craig didn't bother hiding the look of disdain he gave Ben as he took in the casual USMC cotton T-shirt and well-worn jeans he was wearing today. "I don't understand what she sees in you."

"I can't really say." Ben mulled that one over as he compared himself to Craig and the biggest difference between them. "Maybe it's the fact that I'm just a normal, average Joe."

Craig smirked. "Well, that novelty will wear off in time, I'm sure."

No doubt, Crosby was hoping that was true, but Ben was well aware that even after he was out of Christine's life, she had no intentions of ever getting involved with Craig.

Thank God.

"Craig?" Christine came around the corner, a half-smile on her lips and a curious look in her eyes. "What are you doing here?"

"Hi, Christy." Crosby's smarmy smile reappeared as he turned all his attention on Christine. "We never did get the chance to discuss some of the details for your party on Sunday since you left so abruptly, so I thought I'd stop by and we could go over a few things. Do you have any spare time right now?"

She glanced at her watch, then nodded. "Sure."

"Great." He cast a quick, telling glance at Ben. "Do you mind if we go somewhere a bit more private?"

"How about the conference room?" she suggested.

"Perfect," he said, an unmistakable note of satisfaction in his voice.

Christine met Ben's gaze. "I'm sure this won't take long. I'll be done in just a while, then we can head over to Starbucks for a drink." She then smiled at Craig. "Ben knows all the long hours I've been working this week, so he dropped in to make sure I took a break today."

Ahhh, a good call on Christine's part to explain his presence.

She headed to the conference room, and Craig fell into step beside her. When he placed his hand at the small of her back as she preceded him inside the room, Christine stiffened and stepped away from Craig. Ben's blood boiled in his veins and it took every ounce of control he possessed not to charge in there and break the man's arm in a couple of different places so he'd keep his hands off Christine in the future.

Ben shifted restlessly on the couch and swore beneath his breath, unable to believe how this one guy could get to him in such an elemental way. Craig closed the door behind them, but the conference room was glass-enclosed, and while Ben wasn't able to hear their conversation, he was able to watch every move that slimy bastard made.

He shut down his computer, set it aside, and kept his gaze glued to the conference room and the pair inside. An eternity seemed to pass as he watched the two interact. Craig casually touched her arm as he pointed to something in his portfolio folder, and Ben's jaw clenched. The other man said something to make Christine smile and laugh, and Ben's stomach churned with an emotion he refused to exam too closely.

By the time they came out of the conference room, Ben was feeling more than a little surly.

Christine walked Craig to the door, said good-bye, then strolled back toward Ben with an amused smile curving her lips. She was wearing a button-up beige silk blouse with her brown skirt and killer high heels, and the expensive material shimmered across her chest as she moved, reminding him of how soft her breast had felt in his hand, how tight and hard her nipple had peaked against his fingers. At the time, he'd ached to pull off her pajama top and take one of those firm mounds of flesh into his mouth so he could taste her.

She sat down beside him on the couch. "Did I hear you right earlier when you said you're a jealous boyfriend?" She looked immensely pleased at the notion.

So, she'd overheard part of his exchange with Craig. "A jealous *pretend* boyfriend," he corrected her. "I'm just acting the part for your benefit."

She tipped her head, causing the ends of her hair to brush across her shoulder like expensive skeins of blond silk. "Are you sure about that?"

No way was he going to admit that his jealousy was real, and judging by her sweet, knowing smile, he didn't have to. The woman read him way too easily, and it was an unnerving feeling to realize she could get into his head that way.

"Even knowing you have a boyfriend, the man can't keep his hands off you," he said bluntly.

"I don't encourage it, as you've seen," she said, absently smoothing a hand down the front of her skirt.

"I don't like him."

She laughed lightly. "So you've said before. Not that you're jealous or anything." She made a face at him.

He held back a grin, because she just looked so damned cute and irresistible. "My dislike of Craig is all based on my professional assessment of the guy," he said gruffly.

With a sudden look of concern, she reached out and placed a hand on his forehead.

"What are you doing?" he asked.

"You're a little warm," she said, appearing completely serious. "I think you're experiencing office fever from being cooped up in here for so many days. And you seem to have all the symptoms of office fever, too."

He frowned in confusion. "And what would those be?"

A playful smile flirted at the corners of her mouth. "You're grouchy and irritable, which are the two most common ailments of office fever."

"Oh, you're funny," he replied.

"Luckily, I know just what you need. A change of scenery and some fresh air does wonders to alleviate office fever." She stood back up. "Give me another hour to wrap up a few things and make sure Madison has everything under control, then you and I can leave the office early this afternoon."

"To do what?"

"I have some errands to run, and then I was thinking you and I could grab a bite to eat afterward. I've had a craving for pizza lately. How does that sound?"

He grinned. His day had just taken a turn for the better. "Are you kidding me? Pizza and beer is my idea of a gourmet meal."

"You're very easy to please." She touched her fingertips to his jaw, and the lighthearted moment between them shifted and changed, as did the nuance of her comment.

He pulled back so that her fingers fell away, but the slight distance between them did nothing to dissipate the sensual awareness she'd kindled between them with just a simple caress.

And considering the desire warming her gaze as she stared at him, she knew exactly what she'd done, too.

As she walked away, he groaned beneath his breath. Oh, yeah, he was definitely in deep trouble when it came to Christine.

CHRISTINE opened her day planner and scratched off another item on her to-do list for the afternoon. "Only one more errand to go, and we're done for the day," she said, and glanced over at Ben, who was driving her around the city in his truck.

Over the past few stops they'd made, she'd noticed a gradual change in Ben whenever they came back to his vehicle and started for their next destination. He'd grown quiet and pensive, his gaze continually checking his rearview mirror as he navigated the streets of downtown Chicago.

"Is something wrong?" she asked.

"I'm not sure," he said, a frown furrowing his brow as he headed toward their next stop. "Do you know anyone who drives a white car?"

She automatically glanced over her shoulder and out the back window of the truck, her gaze searching the traffic behind them. It was close to rush hour, and all she saw was a sea of cars of various makes, models, and colors. "Why, is someone following us?" she asked anxiously.

"Well, that was nice and subtle," he said of her obvious rubbernecking.

"I'm sorry." She cringed, realizing her mistake too late. "It was just an instinctive response. What's going on?"

"It could be nothing, but I'm not one to take chances."
He looked into his rearview mirror again. "There's a
white car that seems to be following us from a distance,
and has been since we left the office. I can't get a good
feel for the make or model of the vehicle because it's too
far away, but my guess is that it's a smaller, sporty
model."

She thought for a moment, and it didn't take her long
to realize who owned a white vehicle. "The last I knew,
Jason drove a white BMW Coupe. I don't know if he still
has it, though."

Without warning, Ben eased his truck over to the curb
and came to a stop while the rest of the traffic kept driving by.

She glanced up at the tall building next to them in confusion, because it was nowhere near where they needed
to go next. "What are you doing?"

He kept his gaze riveted on the mirror on his wind-
shield. "I'm going to wait for the car to drive by and see
who it is."

The man certainly knew his business. Curious as all
heck to see the car's driver for herself, she sat there and
waited not so patiently for the white vehicle in question to
pass them. She didn't dare glance out the back window
again, though she wanted to.

Less than a minute later he slammed his fist against
the steering wheel and cursed beneath his breath, his
frustration palpable.

Startled by his outburst, she jumped in her seat.
"What's wrong?"

"The car turned down a side street before I could get a
good look at anything worthwhile." He put the truck back
into gear and segued back into traffic. "That leads me to
believe it was someone who didn't want to drive by us,
though I could be wrong."

Somehow, Christine didn't think that was the case, and the whole incident left her feeling uneasy and grateful to have Ben with her. She gave him the rest of the directions to their last errand, and they arrived across town in less than five minutes. This time, with no one following them.

"You need to pull into this upcoming parking structure," she said, and slid her date book back into her purse.

He did as she instructed, found a parking slot, and brought the truck to a stop. "Where do we need to go?"

She bit her bottom lip, unsure how Ben was going to take this next bit of news. "There's a men's clothing shop around the corner that you and I need to go to." It was an exclusive men's store her father frequented, where they also rented high-end formal attire.

That definitely grabbed his attention. "What for?"

She waited until they were both out of the vehicle and walking toward the men's store before explaining. "Did I happen to mention that the charity event this weekend is a black-tie affair? You know, the one you'll be escorting me to?"

A looming sense of dread swept across his features. "Uh, no."

"You wouldn't happen to have a tuxedo hanging in your closet at home, would you?" She already knew the answer to that question. Most likely the only suit he'd ever worn was his Marine dress blues.

He laughed, but the sound didn't hold much humor. "You're kidding, right?"

She held back a grin. "I didn't think so. Which means we need to get you one for this weekend."

"Why?"

Stopping in front of the shop, she faced Ben, who didn't look at all happy with the current turn of events. "Because this is a formal party, and bodyguard or pretend boyfriend, a nice suit is required."

He groaned like a man being taken to the gallows.

This time, she let a throaty laugh escape. "Don't worry. There's a fabulous tailor who works here, and I promise he'll be gentle in taking your measurements and getting you properly fitted. We'll be done in no time."

Ben grunted in reply, then held open the door for her in resignation. "Fine. Let's get this over with."

AN hour later, they were seated at Santori's, an old-world Italian restaurant known for their delicious deep-dish pizza and other authentic dishes. After ordering a pizza to share, a beer for Ben, and a soda for her, Christine smoothed a napkin onto her lap and glanced across the booth at Ben.

"Getting fitted for a tuxedo was relatively painless, don't you think?" She'd ordered him a Hugo Boss ensemble, and she just knew he was going to look gorgeous come Saturday evening.

He leaned back in his seat and crossed his arms over his chest. "Having a guy with a feminine lilt to his voice measuring anywhere near my crotch is *not* my idea of fun."

She burst out laughing, because he truly seemed miffed. "Paul was just making sure he had the right measurements for your inseam so your pants would fit properly."

"If you say so," he muttered. "He just seemed to enjoy his job way too much."

"Take it as a compliment," she said, trying to bolster his male ego, though she was certain there was no way that Ben felt flattered by having a man all but fondle his crotch.

Their waitress came by to deliver her drink and Ben's beer. Once she was gone, Christine closed her eyes and inhaled the delicious scent of rich tomato sauce and spices. When she blinked her lashes open again, she found Ben watching her in a way that made her stomach stir with awareness.

"God, I've missed this place." She glanced around, taking in the casual atmosphere and old-world charm surrounding them. "I haven't been here in forever, and I've forgotten how good pizza can smell."

"I take it you don't do pizza often." He took a drink of his beer. "It's a weekly must for me."

"That's because it's the perfect bachelor food."

He grinned, the first one since they'd left the men's shop. "I won't argue with that."

"Normally I'm eating for one, so buying an entire pizza just doesn't make sense because most of it would go bad before I could enjoy it." She fiddled with her fork and knife, just to give her hands something to do. "And whenever I go out to eat with my parents, well, my mother doesn't *do* pizza, and would be mortified to be seen in a place like this."

"What about Jason?" he asked unexpectedly. "Did the two of you ever come here when you were engaged?"

The switch of topic to Jason was a little startling, but not something she had an issue talking about with Ben. "Jason had this whole image thing he worried about, so he always insisted on going to the upscale restaurants where he could see and be seen, if you know what I mean."

He studied her much too intently. "From what I've read about him, and what I know about you, I just don't get what attracted you to the guy."

"Initially, his charm and my mother's insistence that he was quite a catch and great marriage material. We all know how *that* turned out."

"It turned out for the best, Christine," he said, his

voice softening with understanding. "You could have married the guy and *then* found out what a pig he was."

"You're right," she said, and sighed. "I just feel foolish that I didn't see his true colors until I was slapped in the face with it." She shuddered when she thought about the evening she'd caught Jason with his pants down—literally.

Ben's long fingers absently stroked the condensation off the bottle of his beer, the interest in his gaze genuine. "How did you meet Jason, anyway?"

"He was at a political party for my father, which my mother and I were attending as well." She shrugged, opting for an indifferent attitude on the subject. "It was fairly well known that Jason came from a very wealthy, respectable family back East, and as soon as he showed the slightest bit of interest in me, my mother was all over getting us together as a couple, and insisted that my father hire him on as a political consultant, which he did. We started dating, and within six months my mother was pushing for an engagement."

"It sounds like you were more pressured into the relationship than anything."

Looking back and analyzing the situation, Christine knew that had been exactly the case, and she hated that she'd fallen right into her mother's grand scheme to match her daughter up with an affluent family that would increase Audrey's social standing in the community. As for Jason, he'd obviously seen the opportunity to use Christine and her family's connections to further his own political career.

"Unfortunately, at the time, my mother was a huge influence over me and a lot of the decisions I made." And back then, she'd still been intent on trying to please her controlling mother, because that's all she'd ever known.

"All my life, my mother did everything she could to

groom me to be the perfect wife for someone prominent," she went on to explain. "She sent me off to an all-girls' boarding school, she signed me up for various pageants, enrolled me in etiquette classes, and I did the whole debutante thing, which thrilled my mother, as you can imagine."

All those scenarios had been Audrey's way of molding her into a polite, demure woman who would marry at a young age, have a family, support her husband's political aspirations, and look the other way when it came to her spouse's indiscretions.

Just as Audrey, herself, always had.

Christine shuddered to think that she'd almost ended up just like her mother in that regard.

Their pizza arrived, and while they both dug into a slice of the deep-dish pie, Ben was still reeling over this huge, revealing insight to Christine's past. Audrey, he decided, was a real piece of work, and it was amazing that Christine hadn't ended up more like her mother. Then again, from what Christine had just told him, there had been glimpses of her true personality trying to break free from Audrey's restrictive pressures and demands.

After enjoying a big bite of his pizza, he pointed out one of them to her now. "You being on the girls' basketball team in high school is quite a contradiction to all those formal, ladylike lessons your mother foisted on you."

She laughed, her eyes sparkling with humor. "I had to rebel where I could. My mother wanted me to take a dance or ballet class, and she wasn't at all happy about my choice of an extracurricular activity."

He chuckled, too. "I can just imagine."

She licked away the pizza sauce on her thumb, her expression more reflective now. "You know, looking back, I really should have learned to make more decisions for myself, rather than letting my mother dictate my life."

He shook his head. "You were just a kid, Christine. A good one who did as she was told, and you certainly can't be faulted for that."

"Maybe," she said, not sounding entirely convinced as she wound a long string of cheese around her finger. "But I'd like to think I've changed since ending my engagement to Jason. That I'm now one hundred percent in control of my life and every decision I make."

He grinned at her. "Well, if it's any consolation, I do have to say that during lunch last Sunday with your mother, you were quite impressive in the way you stood up to her about your job and going to Envy."

"I was impressive, wasn't I?" Her tone was sweet and teasing, and not at all conceited. "That's the new and improved me. And I don't think my mother is too happy about all the changes I've made lately."

"It's all about making the decisions that make *you* happy," he said, and reached for another slice of pizza. "That's all that matters at the end of the day."

"I *am* happy. With my life. My new career. Being independent and living on my own. And especially going after what I want without worrying about what my mother will do or think." Pride and contentment mingled in the tone of her voice. "What about you, Ben? Are you happy with your life?"

"Sure," he replied automatically. He had a great job and few responsibilities other than to the security company he was a part of, and the assignments he took on. But at the end of the day, there was definitely a sense of emptiness deep inside of him that he hadn't been able to fill, along with a host of regrets for things he'd once hoped for, but had lost back in Iraq. The woman he loved. A wife to come home to and share things with. And eventually, a family of his own.

Every single one of those things had slipped through

his fingers in one horrifying, life-changing moment that would haunt him forever.

Not wanting to launch into a conversation about his dark past, he instead watched as Christine finished off a second slice of pizza. The woman had a great appetite and didn't hesitate to feed it well.

When she was done, she sat back in her seat, placed a hand over her still flat stomach, and sighed. "That pizza was amazingly good."

He couldn't have agreed more. "So, did you leave any room for dessert?"

Her eyes lit up at the mention of something sweet. "Absolutely. They make the most fabulous tiramisu here, but don't expect me to share." She grinned impishly.

He shook his head and chuckled. "I wouldn't dream of it."

Seven

BEN sat out in the dark, quiet living room, skipping through the cable channels on Christine's TV in search of something worthwhile to watch at one o'clock in the morning. He stopped on an infomercial for some kind of car cleaner, then watched the ending of a cop chase on Court TV before jumping to a music video on MTV. Once that was over, he skipped to another paid program for Ginsu knives and decided that was about as good as it was going to get.

With a bored sigh, he tossed the channel changer onto the cushion beside him, then leaned back against the couch to make himself comfortable. Before the host could slice and dice through a tomato, Ben heard a door open, then the sound of feet padding across the carpet to the kitchen. He glanced in that direction and saw Christine's silhouette as she came to a stop in the distance, then changed course and started toward him in the living room.

She emerged from the shadows, looking sleep-tousled

and wearing what he'd normally refer to as a modest nightgown, but on Christine it was anything but demure. The straps holding up the gown were thin, and the front V-neck was trimmed in lace, with a tighter bodice that molded to her small, firm breasts. The hem fluttered around her knees as she walked toward him, drawing his attention to her slender, bare legs.

Ignoring his body's instantaneous response to her irresistible, sensual allure, he lifted his gaze back to hers. "What are you doing up?"

"With the charity auction tomorrow night, I've got a lot of things going through my head," she said, and sat down on the couch a respectable distance away from him. "I was just going to make myself some chamomile tea when I saw that you were up, too. Is everything okay?"

Her concern warmed him. "Actually, this is pretty normal for me."

She tipped her head, causing soft, disheveled waves to fall across her bare shoulder. "What, not being able to sleep?"

He nodded. Sleep meant dreams, and not all of them were pleasant. Not since Iraq. "I'm used to getting by with very little sleep. A few hours, and I'm good to go." He smiled at her.

"I can't even imagine. Normally, I have to have my eight hours or I'm not functional the next day." She brought her legs up to the side and covered them with the skirt of her gown. "Have you always been that way? Only needing a few hours of sleep?"

"No, just since being in the service. Specifically, when I was sent to Iraq." He glanced back at the TV just as the host cut through an aluminum can with one of the Ginsu knives. "Hearing IEDs and gunshots going off in the distance has a way of making you sleep with one eye open at all times."

"That couldn't have been easy," she said softly.

"You get used to it." He shrugged, not wanting to get melancholy about his time in the military. "So, most nights, like tonight, are spent watching old reruns of *I Love Lucy*, or cheesy infomercials, like this one."

"Ginsu knives?" She laughed and reached for the channel changer between them. "There has got to be something better than this on with all the cable channels I have."

Pointing the remote at the TV, she began flipping through the channels in search of something interesting to watch. The images on the screen blurred as she quickly jumped from one show to the next. She passed what appeared to be a couple in a heated embrace, and in the next instant she was hitting the reverse button and stopping on the Playboy channel and the soft porn movie in progress.

The man and woman were slowly stripping off each other's clothing as they indulged in deep, tongue-tangling kisses and provocative caresses as more and more skin was bared, until the pair was completely naked. It was evident to Ben exactly where this seductive scenario was heading . . . toward some hot and steamy sex.

Unsure why Christine had stopped on an adult skin-flick—possibly to torment him and remind him what he couldn't have when it came to her?—he slanted a covert glance toward the woman sitting on the opposite side of the couch. Her gaze was riveted to the TV, and she looked totally enthralled by the action unfolding on the big screen in front of them.

"What are you doing?" he asked, trying to sound casual about the whole situation, when he was anything but.

"Just watching," she said, never taking her eyes off the couple, who were now moving on to more erotic pleasures.

Ooookkkaay. If she could watch a porn movie with such composure and without getting flustered, then so could he. Except like most guys, the whole visual thing made his dick sit up and take notice—and wearing only a pair of sweatpants made it extremely difficult to conceal his growing hard-on.

The foreplay between the pair grew hotter, and more carnal as the woman in the movie dropped to her knees and focused her attention on her partner's jutting shaft. She parted her lips and took him deep inside her mouth, her cheeks hallowing as she slowly withdrew, sucking hard. The guy groaned and thrust in time to the woman's rhythmic strokes.

Christine shifted restlessly on the couch, her legs sliding against one another beneath her nightgown. "Now there's something I've always been curious about," she said huskily.

Her comment made no sense to him whatsoever. Being *curious* meant she wasn't all that familiar with what that woman in the film was currently doing to that guy. "Excuse me?"

"Oral sex," she said just as vaguely, her gaze still transfixed on the X-rated movie.

He still didn't get her point. But what he *was* beginning to realize was that watching the couple in the throes of foreplay was arousing her. He could see it in the way she was biting her lower lip, and especially how her nipples had stiffened into tight, hard peaks against the thin, cotton material of her gown.

Too damned intrigued by the direction their conversation was heading, he prompted her for a bit more information. "What, exactly, about oral sex has piqued your interest?"

"Everything about it." She finally tore her gaze away

from the adventurous pair to look at him. "What it's like. How it feels to have an orgasm when a guy returns the favor."

Jesus. Her blue eyes were dark and dilated with excitement and fascination, but in a completely guileless, naive way. She wasn't trying to act innocent or sucker him in with feminine wiles like he'd known some women to do. Her curiosity was honest and real, and that put a whole different spin on the sultry, entranced way she was currently staring at him.

It was time to change the channel before this situation escalated to a more risqué level. "Give me the remote." He stretched his hand toward her.

"I don't think so." She set the remote on the end table beside her, way out of Ben's reach. "This is just starting to get good. Maybe I'll learn a thing or two about oral sex and finally figure out what's so great about it."

Stunned by her comment, he had to ask the question foremost in his mind. "Are you saying that you've never had a guy go down on you before?"

Her cheeks turned pink at his frank, explicit description, and she shook her head.

The heat simmering in his gut kicked up a notch, because if Christine had been his, that would have been one of his all-time favorite ways of pleasuring her. "And you've never given a guy a blow job?"

Again, she shook her head.

His already hard shaft twitched at the thought of sliding deep into that warm, wet mouth of hers that had never taken a man's cock before.

Disbelief coursed through him. Christine was twenty-six, soon to be twenty-seven. How in the world had she gone her entire adult life without experiencing either intimacy? Unless . . . *Oh, shit.*

"Are you a *virgin*?" His voice sounded strangled.

A small smile touched the corner of her lips. "I might as well be, but no, I'm not. I've had sex before."

He remembered her comment the other night about wanting to feel desire and taste passion, and felt more confused than ever. "So let me get this straight. You were engaged to be married, you even had sex, but the two of you never . . ."

". . . did anything beyond your basic missionary position," she quietly finished for him. "It was always a quick, no fuss event. No hot and heavy foreplay. No oral sex. I wanted to, but Jason always got right down to business and it was all over with before I could get excited enough to have an orgasm. I guess he saved all the good stuff for those other women he was with." She drew a deep breath and released it just as slowly. "The best I can guess is that he just didn't see me as a sexy, sensual woman. And compared to the woman I'd caught him with, well, I certainly felt inadequate in comparison."

Her ex was a certified jackass, no doubt about it. "That's such bullshit, Christine. The fault wasn't, and *isn't*, yours."

A woman's breathy moan drew Christine's gaze back to the TV. At some point, the guy had laid his lover back on the big bed and he was kissing his way down her body, until he finally settled his broad shoulders between her widespread thighs, then lowered his head and slid his tongue through the woman's soft, dewy flesh. She gasped, arched against the man's mouth, then let out a long, unraveling groan.

The uninhibited display was hot and provocative and downright titillating, physically and mentally. But it wasn't the action happening on the TV screen that captivated Ben, but rather Christine's response to what the guy was doing to the woman that turned him on like no porn movie ever had.

He felt like a voyeur, but didn't care.

She was watching the scene intently, her skin flushed with arousal, the tips of her fingers touching the base of her throat. Her lips were parted, her breathing deep and shallow, and when the woman in the movie started to come with a high-pitched cry, Christine let out a small choked sound of her own.

That sexy little sound she made, combined with the look of longing on her face and the slow, sensual way those fingers of hers trailed down to her breasts, was enough to ignite a strong dose of heated lust in his veins, and elsewhere. God, he was so fucking hard, his entire body strung so tight he knew he'd never get any sleep tonight without some kind of relief. And a cold shower just wasn't going to cut it.

Christine turned her head and glanced at him, her eyes dark and glazed with the kind of desire that could bring a man to his knees. And, oh, Lord, was he ever tempted to do just that and make her come undone, then scream from the sheer pleasure and strength of her first orally induced orgasm.

"That's what I want to know and feel," she said, as if she'd been reading his mind when in reality she was referring to what had just transpired between the couple, which was pretty much the same thing. "I've fantasized about what it would be like . . . with *you.*"

He swallowed back a groan. She was literally killing him. With her candid words. With her soft, blue eyes. With her honesty and trust. He could only take so much, and he was nearly at his breaking point.

"Do not look at me like *that,*" he said, forcing a deep warning note to his voice.

She blinked at him, but the need shimmering in her gaze didn't dissipate one bit. "Like what?"

A wave of frustration crashed over him. "Like you

want *me* to be the one to teach you all about sex. *Good sex*," he clarified.

She glanced down at his lap and the fierce erection he couldn't even begin to hide, and a beguiling smile slowly eased up one corner of her mouth. "Maybe I do," she murmured huskily, and licked her bottom lip in a way that heated his blood even more. "Would that be so bad?"

He swore beneath his breath and resisted the overwhelming urge to give Christine exactly what she wanted, and so much more. He couldn't remember ever wanting anything as much as what she dangled in front of him right now, and after struggling between right and wrong, he managed, just barely, to do the ethical thing.

"It's not going to happen, Christine," he said, knowing he was trying to convince himself as much as her.

She sighed, her disappointment at his decision nearly tangible. She stood, and as she strolled past him she lightly skimmed her fingers along his jawline and brazenly stroked her thumb across his bottom lip, branding him with her oh-so-tempting touch.

"Okay, but if you change your mind, you know where to find me," she said, and started to walk away.

Ben didn't know what possessed him to reach out and grab her wrist, then tug her back so that she fell across his thighs. Because once he had her in his lap, all soft and warm and aroused, he knew that stopping her had been a very bad, bad idea.

Still holding her wrist, he stared into her eyes, torn between the multitude of emotions swirling inside him. Of course there was lust and need rising to the forefront, but it was the other more complex feelings that threw him off-kilter and had his heart beating hard and fast in his chest.

Affection and caring. Tenderness and longing. All the types of emotions that scared the shit out of him.

Christine shifted restlessly against his thighs, drawing his attention back to her and the unavoidable temptation she presented. "Either do something, like kiss me or touch me, or let me go so I can take care of this ache on my own," she whispered.

The seductive image of Christine bringing herself to orgasm zapped the last of his control, and his sanity. Refusing to think of consequences, regrets, or anything else other than giving this woman every pleasure she'd been denied, Ben tumbled her back onto the couch and stretched his body over hers.

She gasped and looked up at him with wide, shocked eyes that gradually glowed with excitement. Plowing all ten fingers into her silky hair, he shoved a knee between her thighs to align them more intimately, then dropped his mouth over hers, possessing her with the ravenous assault of his lips slanting across hers. He thrust his tongue inside, delved deep into all that silken warmth, and lost himself in the hunger and need inflaming him, heating him from the inside out.

She kissed him back just as passionately as her cool hands came around to his sides, glided in a sensual caress to the base of his spine, then skimmed up the slope of his tense, muscled back. Her fingers dug into his flesh, trying to pull him impossibly closer while she arched wantonly beneath him.

Even through the fabric of her nightgown, he could feel her stiff nipples rubbing against his chest. Aching to touch more of her, wanting skin on skin contact, he slid his fingers beneath those thin straps on her shoulders and dragged them down both of her arms, until the front of her gown was bunched around her waist and her breasts were freed.

With a soft, unraveling moan, he buried his face against her neck, nuzzling that warm, inviting spot and breathing in the heady scent of vanilla. She moaned, too, as he scattered hot, moist, open-mouthed kisses down her throat and along her collarbone, then lower still.

Shifting to the side, he settled a hand over one of her breasts and swept his thumb across the pebble-hard tip. She shivered and exhaled a breathy sound that shot straight to his already rigid cock. Dipping his head, he curled his tongue around her other nipple—licking, nipping, laving, until the peak was swollen and damp from his ministrations and she was writhing wildly beneath him. Finally, he took her breast into the wet heat of his mouth, and at the first suctioning pull of his lips she clutched his head and pressed him harder, closer, forcing him to take her deeper.

Her thighs tightened against the one he'd nudged between her legs, and she began to breathe hard and fast. "Touch me, Ben," she begged, without inhibition, or the faintest ounce of modesty or reserve. "Oh, God, I need . . . I need to come so badly."

Now that he knew just how selfish her ex had been when it came to foreplay and Christine's pleasure, Ben wanted to show her how good it could be, how it *should* be when it came to a woman's gratification during sex.

With his mouth still on her breast, he slipped a hand beneath the hem of her gown and smoothed his palm up her thigh, until he reached the drenched fabric of her panties. She was so wet and aroused, from the X-rated movie still playing in the background and their hot and heavy kissing, and he didn't hesitate to work his fingers beneath the elastic band so he could touch her intimately.

Instantly, his thumb glided through slick folds of flesh and found her clit, and he caressed her with slow, unhurried strokes meant to tease and build the tension cresting higher and higher, hotter and hotter. One finger, then two, pushed deep inside of her and that quickly, that easily, he felt the tremors within her begin.

She whimpered helplessly, and moaned incoherently. Her hands clutched at his back as her hips began to move in time to the circling pressure of his thumb, and the driving force of his fingers impaling her.

Giving in to the unstoppable urge to watch Christine as she climaxed, he lifted his head and stared down at her face. Her eyes were dark and filled with carnal need, her skin flushed with excitement all the way down to her heaving breasts. Her inner muscles fluttered around his fingers, and she tossed her head back in utter abandon, her lips parting on a shocked gasp of breath as the force of her orgasm sent her soaring. With his name tumbling from her lips, she shattered completely, blissfully.

When it was over, she slowly looked up at him, licked her bottom lip, and whispered, "I want more."

Her words shot liquid fire straight to his groin, unleashing his own lust, making him delirious with need. She was temptation personified, and having her became a live thing, something uncontrollable and inevitable, and suddenly jacking off all alone to ease his own ache held no appeal whatsoever.

He didn't have a condom, but he didn't need one for what he had in mind. Shoving his sweatpants down to his thighs, he released his heavy, throbbing erection and rubbed the sensitive head along the wet, gossamer stretch of panties covering her mound, saturating the length of his cock with the evidence of her own desire.

He settled his weigh more fully over her, pushing her thighs farther apart to make room for him between. He lifted her knees higher, parting them around his hips, then wrapping those slender legs tight around him. He slid every part of his body flush against her, hating the barriers between them, wishing they had nothing separating skin from skin. Meeting her heavy-lidded gaze, he thrust against her, the friction sending a warning shiver straight up his spine.

His self-discipline vanished. His control shattered. Knowing he wasn't going to last long, he crushed his mouth to hers, devouring her with the demanding pressure of his lips and aggressive invasion of his tongue. The hard ridge of his erection nudged her clit as he rocked against all that silky wet heat, again and again.

It was the next best thing to being inside of her, and he went a little wild at the thought.

Her moan vibrated deep inside him and she strained against him, ramping up his own urgency to let go. His hips pumped against hers in long, frantic strokes, and amazingly, he felt her shudder beneath him as another orgasm took her by surprise. And that was all it took for him to come right along with her in a hot, pulsing rush of unrestrained ecstacy.

When it was over, he burrowed his face against her damp neck, a raspy groan escaping him. Christine threaded her fingers through his hair, so sweet and affectionate, while her heart beat rapidly against his chest. Then she turned her head and pressed her lips near his ear.

"Thank you," she whispered, and he heard the lazy smile in her voice as she stroked her fingers along his nape. "That was *amazing*."

Amazing didn't even come close to describing what he'd just experienced, even without the luxury of being inside her. How in the hell was that possible?

He squeezed his eyes shut, unable to believe what he'd just done. Unable to believe he'd let things go this far when he knew better. His body was drained, depleted of every ounce of energy and months worth of all the sexual tension that had been building between them. His explosive orgasm had nearly slayed him, and the very worst of it was, he wasn't done wanting her. Not by a long shot.

And he had a feeling she was going to use every bit of that knowledge to her advantage.

WITH a whole lot to do before the elaborate charity ball that evening, Christine was up early Saturday morning and working in her office at home. She spent a couple of hours printing out bidding sheets and item descriptions for the silent auction, as well as organizing gold-embossed place cards to coincide with each donation. She checked and double-checked her master list against all the goods she had on hand to make sure everything matched and nothing was missing, then polished up her speech and made sure she had a copy of that, too.

By the time she was done, it was nearly noon and her stomach growled hungrily. She'd eaten breakfast hours before and had been running on pure caffeine since. She needed protein to keep her going for the rest of the afternoon.

Shutting down her computer, she picked up her empty coffee mug and headed down the hall toward the kitchen. She passed the guest bedroom, and for the first time that morning the door was open and no one was inside. It appeared that Ben had decided he could no longer avoid her after their hot and heavy make-out session the evening before, and had finally ventured out.

Smiling, she continued on, and when she walked into the kitchen she found him sitting at her small dinette table eating a big bowl of the Froot Loops he'd bought when they'd gone grocery shopping together earlier that week. He must have recently taken a shower because his hair was still damp. He didn't look up at her, and he didn't say a word.

Refusing to cater to his mood swing, she acted as though nothing was different between them. "Good morning," she greeted cheerfully.

"Morning," he muttered, and shoveled another spoon-ful of cereal into his mouth.

She retrieved sliced turkey breast, Dijon mustard, tomato, and lettuce from the refrigerator and set the items on the counter, along with a loaf of fresh honey wheat bread. "Did you sleep well last night?"

"Just fine."

She started putting together her sandwich, waiting for him to return the polite question. When he said nothing more, she took it upon herself to reply. "I slept great, too. Thanks for asking." She cast a grin over her shoulder, but it was lost on Ben, who was still concentrating on inhal-ing his Froot Loops.

Wanting to get some kind of reaction from him, she poured herself a glass of iced tea and went on. "In fact, I can't remember the last time I had such a good night's rest. It's incredible how a good orgasm can make a person relax, unwind, and sleep like a baby, huh?"

He merely grunted in response.

She carried her sandwich and drink to the table and sat across from him. Frustrated beyond reason by his cool composure and his refusal to acknowledge their hot, sexual encounter the evening before, she decided to shake things up a bit. "Do you think we can do it again some-time? Because I'd really like to." She picked up half of her sandwich and took a bite.

That snagged his attention and his head jerked up. His dark gaze, filled with stunned disbelief, met hers. She'd asked the shameless question purely for shock value, and she had to admit her ploy had worked in terms of snapping Ben out of his aloof attitude, but she couldn't deny that the idea of being with him again held immense appeal.

His gaze bore into hers, clearly trying to gauge if she was serious or not.

She exhaled an impatient sigh and opted for the direct

approach. "Are we ever going to talk about what happened last night?"

"I would prefer not to." Reaching for the box of Froot Loops, he refilled his bowl with the colorful cereal and added more milk.

"That's what I figured," she said, and summoned the confidence and determination to get through this conversation with Ben—and hopefully come out the other end with exactly what she wanted. "So, I'm just going to put it all out there and get everything out in the open."

Needing more food in her stomach, she ate another bite of her turkey sandwich, and washed it down with a drink of cold tea. "First of all, last night was not a fluke or something that happened in the heat of the moment. The attraction has been building between us for months, and I *wanted* to be with you because I knew it would be so good, and I was right."

He didn't argue or try to stop her, and that gave her an added boost of fortitude to continue.

"Last night, with you, was the first time a guy has ever given me an orgasm of any kind," she admitted, finding it much easier to open up to Ben the more she talked to him, and the more he listened. "And it was much better than any orgasm I've given myself."

"That's the way it should be," he replied gruffly.

"Yeah, well, tell that to my two exes," she said wryly, and finished off the first half of her sandwich.

He lifted a brow, silently prompting her to tell him more. Last night she'd given him some insight into her relationship with Jason, but now she was about to reveal a part of her past that not even Madison knew about.

"Besides Jason, I only had one other boyfriend that I slept with. I think I told you that I attended an all-girls' boarding school, and there wasn't a whole lot of opportunity to date or interact with guys. So, by the time I was in college, having a guy interested in me was new and exciting, and especially the hot quarterback on the football team."

She felt her face grow hot, because even now she could remember how infatuated she'd been with Brian, and how all his flirting and attention had made her feel special—only to realize much too late that it was all a ploy to get into her pants. Just like every other girl he'd dated before her.

Pushing her embarrassment aside, she forged ahead with her story. "The first time he took me out, we went to dinner and a movie, and afterward he walked me to my dorm and gave me my first French kiss. The second time we picked up fast food, ate it in the car, then he parked in a place that was dark and secluded and we made out. One thing led to another, and before long we were in the backseat of his Honda Accord doing the deed and it was over before I could get used to having a guy inside of me for the first time. He never called me again after that last night, so ultimately I'd given my virginity to a guy who didn't care about anything but getting laid."

"Jesus." Ben shook his head, his expression irate on her behalf as he pushed his empty bowl aside. "The guy was a prick, Christine."

She gave him a half-smile. "I can't argue with that, but at the time I couldn't help but wonder what *I* did wrong. That whole first experience, combined with Jason's preference for trampy *escorts* over the woman he was engaged to marry, left me feeling sexually inadequate." She drew a deep breath, and finished before she lost her nerve. "In fact, after Jason I couldn't help but wonder if I was frigid like my mother."

He stared at her incredulously. *"What?"*

She cringed, realizing she'd unintentionally opened a

can of worms. "That's a whole other story that we don't have time for right now," she said, dismissing her comment with a wave of her hand. "Suffice it to say, I had plenty of reason to believe that I just didn't have what it took to be sexy and seductive and arouse a man's interest sexually. Not to mention have an orgasm when I was with him."

He leaned back in his chair and crossed his arms over his chest, which was covered in a screen print T-shirt. "I think we dispelled that notion last night."

"Twice," she corrected him, and shivered when she thought about how hot and erotic their tryst had been, and how she'd love a repeat performance. "And it was great. *Better* than great. Even though I know it would have been even better if you'd been inside of me, the pretending was pretty damned exciting. Enough so to make me come that second time."

He groaned and scrubbed a hand along his jaw. "I really don't think we should be having this conversation."

She knew he'd eventually start resisting, especially when the subject became more intimate and personal between the two of them, and she was prepared to see this through.

"Why not? I'm just being honest, and I think last night proved that we'd be great together." Despite her outward bravado, inside her nerves were jumping. Never had she been so open and frank with a man before, but she had to admit it was a wonderful, liberating feeling. "With you, I feel desire and passion and lust. And that's more than I've ever had with either Brian or Jason. And I'd like to think that I aroused you a little bit, too."

"Yeah, a little bit," he replied, a sarcastic edge to his voice. "That's why I'm sitting across from you with a goddamn hard-on straining the front of my jeans. Because just thinking of how responsive you are when I kiss you or touch you makes me want to pull you across this table and have my way with you right here and now."

A potent thrill shot through her, searing a path straight down to her stomach. "If we weren't on a time constraint, I'd let you," she said, her voice taking on a low, husky quality.

He cursed heatedly and abruptly stood up. "You just don't get it, do you, Christine?"

Calmly, she stared up at him. "No, I guess I don't."

"Then let me explain things in a way that you'll better understand. Yeah, I'm attracted to you. I can't deny that." Placing his palms flat on the table, he leaned toward her, his eyes blazing with intimidation. "And yeah, I'd like to fuck you every way imaginable that would make your traditional missionary position look tame in comparison. But your father hired me to protect you, not to have sex with you."

He was trying to make her back off, but she was so done being the kind of good girl who in the past would have dropped the subject and retreated. Hell, a year ago she never would have been bold enough to discuss sex and orgasms with a guy. But most important, she was done doing what everyone else wanted or expected her to do.

"My father has nothing to do with my attraction to you," she said easily. "I'm a big girl and if I want to indulge in an affair, that's none of my father's, or anybody else's business."

He didn't look one bit convinced. "When the guy you want to have the affair with is me, your security agent, it complicates everything. And because of that, I don't ever mix business and pleasure."

"You did last night," she pointed out oh-so-sweetly.

He didn't seem to appreciate the reminder. He

straightened from the table, but he didn't say a word or move from where he was standing.

Pushing her own chair back, she picked up her plate and the empty glass of iced tea, and carried both to the sink. Then she turned around to face her bodyguard again.

"Look, Ben, I understand that you have a job to do, and I'm not asking you to compromise my safety in any way. Out in public, you can do what you need to do to ensure I'm protected, but here, in my house, there is no threat and I couldn't be more secure with an alarm system on at all times."

She strolled toward him, and he watched her approach through narrowed eyes. "With that said, why can't we enjoy each other like we did last night?"

Again, no reply, but that didn't dissuade her in the least. He hadn't flat out refused her, and if anything, his silence gave her hope that he was actually considering her proposal.

She came to a stop just a few feet away from him. "I'm not asking for any kind of commitment," she said, just in case that fear was running through his head. "I've had enough of that for a while and I want to enjoy my freedom and independence before getting serious with anyone again."

"So, all you want is sex," he said, his bland tone belying the heat flickering in his gaze. "No strings attached."

"Not just sex. Good sex. *Great* sex," she clarified, but she already knew that wasn't an issue when it came to Ben and her as a couple. "We have two more weeks together before the election is over, and I'm thinking that's more than enough time to enjoy this mutual attraction and get it out of our systems. And when your job is done, we part ways as friends."

For all her daring, determination, and no-nonsense approach to an affair with Ben, she already knew it wouldn't be so easy to let him go in the end. This was a man who didn't try to be something he wasn't, and accepted her for who she was, as well. That in itself was a novelty for her when it came to the men she dated. He was charming when he wanted to be, and he made her feel alive and sexy and desirable, too. And if a few weeks was all they had with one another, she wanted to make the most of their time together, to take everything he was willing to give.

The rules she'd just laid out between them had been all for Ben. To make it easy on him when the affair was over, so he could walk away without worrying about any expectations or pressures from her. She already knew by previous conversations they'd had, combined with the compact way he lived his life, that he wasn't a man looking to settle down with any one woman anytime soon. She supposed losing the woman you loved and adored in a country torn apart by war had a way of making a person more averse to emotional attachments—and more disposed to a single, solitary lifestyle.

"You're awfully quiet." She could only imagine what was going through that head of his, and knew there was nothing left to do but ask him one last question. The most important one of them all. "So, are you interested in a short-term affair?"

His jaw worked back and forth, and just when she thought he was going to give her an unequivocal no, he instead shocked her with his answer.

"I'll think about it," he said.

She realized that he was attempting to placate her with an answer that wasn't really an answer, but at least he hadn't flat out refused her, and that's all she cared about right now. Sure, she'd give him time to think about it, and then she was going to take matters into her own hands.

Starting tonight after the charity ball.

Eight

ARE you interested in a short-term affair?

He'd told Christine he'd think about it, and he hadn't lied. For the rest of the afternoon that question buzzed through Ben's mind like the greatest of temptations, seducing his body and senses with a dozen different erotic scenarios. At the most inappropriate times he thought about what it would be like to *really* make love to Christine, to be deep inside of her when she climaxed, to feel all those tight, rippling contractions around his cock as she came undone just for him.

On the drive over to the St. Claire Hotel to set up for the charity's silent auction, she kept up a steady stream of conversation, but instead of hearing what she had to say all he could do was watch her mouth move and remember how soft and sweet her lips tasted beneath his—and how badly he wanted to kiss her again.

Deeply.

Hungrily.

Greedily.

They arrived at the hotel, and since he refused to let her out of his sight she cheerfully put him to work setting up tables for the auction items while she and Madison draped them elegantly in panels of beige silk fabric. Christine leaned across the table to smooth out wrinkles in the material before pinning it in place, and her blouse pulled tight across her chest, outlining her perfect breasts and teasing him with a glimpse of those hard nipples he'd plied with his thumb and sampled with his tongue.

She'd bend down to pick something up, and her heart-shaped ass had him fantasizing about one of his favorite sexual positions.

She purposefully flirted and teased and sent him covert glances that kept him keenly aware of her all day long, and made him want her with each seductive smile and throaty laugh she sent his way. He'd spent their hours together in a stranglehold of desire, lust, and yearning for all the things Christine had offered him with one simple question:

Are you interested in a short-term affair?

After their work in the ballroom was done and the auction items displayed, they went back to Christine's place to take showers and get ready for the evening ahead. Standing beneath the hot spray of water and feeling the sleek caress of water and soap sluicing down his naked frame, it was Christine's hands he imagined were stroking across his chest, down his abdomen, and along his straining erection.

All he could think about was having an affair with her, and it was close to driving him insane. She'd planted the seed and all day she'd nurtured the idea, until resisting her, and everything she was suggesting, was nearly impossible for him to do.

Now, as he finished getting dressed, he suspected that tonight wasn't going to be any different than today—

except this evening he needed all his instincts clear and on target, his attention sharp and unclouded by all Christine's sultry attempts to seduce him. Being completely aware of their surroundings and keeping her safe during the charity event was his number-one priority until he had her home again tonight.

But before they could leave, he had to wrangle a long strip of silk into something that resembled a bow tie to go with the designer tuxedo he was wearing, and he wasn't having much luck with the task. He scowled at his reflection in the mirror when he ended up with a tangle of knotted material around his neck, and with an impatient growl he gave it a hard tug to unravel the mess so he could start the frustrating process all over again.

"Well, well, well" came a soft feminine drawl from behind him in the guest bedroom. "Don't you look nice."

"Except for this stupid bow tie," he grumbled irritably. "Who invented this contraption of material, anyway? And why couldn't you have gotten me one of those easy, pre-tied bows?"

"Because that would be cheating," she said, amusement in her voice. "You can't wear a cheap clip-on bow with a Hugo Boss tuxedo. It would ruin the entire look."

He rolled his eyes in disbelief. "Who would even know the difference?" Certainly not him.

"Oh, you'd be surprised."

He turned around to tell her that it was ridiculous that anyone would even care about a bow tie, but as soon as he saw Christine and what she was wearing his mouth went as dry as dust.

The black evening gown she had on for tonight's ball was an exquisite one-shoulder design, accented all over in beads that sparkled like brilliant jewels with the slightest move she made. The silky, shimmering fabric molded to her breasts, but from there the material lightly skimmed along her curves all the way down to the floor, gently emphasizing her womanly figure, rather than clinging to it. Of course, peeking out from the hem of her dress was a pair of black, open-toed, strappy high heels.

She'd swept her blond hair up into an elegant style of soft loose curls that left her shoulders completely bare, and her makeup had been applied in a way that made her blue eyes stand out and drew his gaze to her full, pink-glossed lips. Since the gown itself was so intricate, she'd kept her jewelry very simple—just a pair of diamond stud earrings that rivaled the lustrous shine of her eyes.

Somehow, he found his voice. "Wow. You look absolutely stunning." And she was so out of his league socially he felt like a fraud wearing such a high-dollar, designer tuxedo.

"Thank you." She smiled, her expression glowing from his compliment. "Now let's see what we can do about your bow tie."

"We can always throw it in the trash," he suggested with a grin.

"Sorry, but that's not an option." She turned him around so that he was facing the dresser mirror again and she was standing behind him. "Even in my high heels, you're too tall for what I need to do," she said, and moved away from him.

She returned a moment later, dragging the straight-backed chair that had been in the corner of the guest bedroom. She parked it behind him, then told him to sit down. Curious as to what she intended, he did as she ordered and lowered himself to the chair. She positioned herself behind him, the back of his head now resting gently against the soft cushion of her breasts—which wasn't a bad place to be, he decided.

She reached around him and took the two long ends of the strip of silk in her hands. "Tying a formal bow is just like tying your shoes," she said as she wrapped one end of the material around the other and made a loose knot at the base of his throat.

Her cool fingers brushed beneath his chin as she made some kind of loop with the fabric. "And you learned this how?"

"I did it for my father when I was growing up." She tilted her head ever-so-slightly as she continued manipulating the strips of silk. "Just yet another thing my mother insisted I learn for future reference. See, it did come in handy after all." She met his gaze in the mirror and grinned as she made one last adjustment to the immaculate bow she'd created.

"I hardly think your mother planned for you to use your bow-tying skills on your bodyguard," he pointed out wryly.

Finished with the bow, she smoothed her hands along the shoulders of his tuxedo jacket and bent low so her lips were close to his ear. "Then we won't tell her, now will we?"

She was teasing and flirting with him again, but Ben didn't disillusion himself that if Audrey ever found out that her daughter was fraternizing with the hired help, especially *him*, she'd come unglued and all hell would break loose.

"It looks like we're ready to go," she said, stepping away as he stood up. "I just need to get through the auction speech tonight without getting nauseous or sick, and I'll be happy." She absently placed a hand on her stomach.

He wasn't used to seeing Christine insecure about anything, and this unguarded revelation of hers surprised him and made him see a whole different side to her. "Not much of a public speaker, huh?"

"No, not really," she said with a shake of her head. "I've even tried hiring a public-speaking coach to help with my nerves, but I still get that churning anxiety in the pit of my stomach as soon as I'm standing at the podium and I'm the center of everyone's attention."

"You'll do fine." Without thinking, he reached out and caressed the backs of his fingers along her cheek, and her gaze softened in response. "It's a quick speech and I'll be nearby. It'll be done and over with before you know it."

"I hope so." She summoned a brave, determined smile. "We'd better get going. I'd like to get to the hotel a bit earlier than everyone else to double-check the auction display."

"Okay." He followed her out of his room, his gaze taking in the bare nape of her neck and all the smooth, silky skin revealed by the one-shoulder design of her gown. He glanced lower, to the alluring sway of her hips and the tantalizing way the fabric skimmed over her bottom as she walked. As he inhaled, he realized that she wasn't wearing her normal vanilla scent tonight, but instead he breathed in a richer fragrance that was as mysterious as it was provocative.

Feeling that familiar buzz of arousal kick in, he forced his attention elsewhere. "By the way, I went through the guest list for the charity event tonight, and both Craig and Leanne are going to be there."

"Yes, as are over two hundred other people." She picked up a black shawl from the coffee table in the living room, draped it over her shoulders, then turned around to face him. "We all run in the same social circles, so it's inevitable that our paths will cross."

He pushed his hands into the front pockets of his black trousers. "I want you to stay away from both of them. Especially Craig."

She laughed as she grabbed a black beaded purse that matched her gown. "You play the jealous boyfriend so well, not that I mind."

Okay, that did sound way more possessive than he'd intended, and he tried to backpedal so he didn't sound like a Neanderthal. "I just think tonight will be less stressful if you keep your distance from those two."

She opened her small purse and looked through the contents. "You're probably right, but I'll be mingling with everyone, so I can't deliberately ignore them if they come up to me. It would be rude, and since I'm in charge of the silent auction tonight, I don't want to make a bad impression on anyone."

He nodded in understanding. "Fair enough," he said, though he just didn't like the thought of Craig anywhere near Christine, which meant he'd have to find creative ways to steer them both clear of the guy.

THE ballroom of the St. Claire Hotel had been transformed into an elegant and festive affair for the glitzy charity event raising money for the Children's AIDS Foundation. Everyone was dressed in black formal wear, with most of the women in the room wearing their most glamorous gowns and equally stunning jewelry reserved just for special occasions such as this.

Sitting at their assigned dining table enjoying a succulent chateaubriand with béarnaise sauce and fresh steamed vegetables, Christine cast a surreptitious glance at Ben, who was sitting to her left, to see how he was faring. For a man who swore on the drive over to the hotel that he had absolutely nothing in common with anyone at the gala and would likely stick out like a greenhorn, she had to say that he'd managed to fit in with the upper crust of Chicago quite nicely.

They'd spent the first hour and a half of the evening enjoying cocktails and hors d'oeuvres while mingling with her friends and other people she was acquainted

with. When she introduced Ben, he shook hands with the
men, and acknowledged the women with a charming
smile and polite greeting that showcased him for the gentleman he was and made her feel proud to have a man like
him on her arm.

Of course they ran into Craig and Leanne during the
cocktail party and politely said hello to both, but didn't
linger to chat. Christine noticed that Ben was quick to
avert their attention elsewhere, but that hadn't dissuaded
Leanne from issuing her cutting stares from across the
room, or stopped Craig from watching them from a distance with a look of irritation on his face.

By eight P.M. they were asked to be seated at their designated tables while the president of the Children's AIDS
Foundation stepped up to the podium and gave a heartfelt
speech about the organization, AIDS statistics, and how
everyone's donation to attend the gala would help fund
pediatric research and raise awareness about the children's fight against HIV.

Then came the beginning of a five-course gourmet
meal, and when Ben furtively watched from the corner
of his eye which utensil she used and when, this time
she didn't try to trick him. While Christine found that
she was only able to skim from each plate due to her increasing nerves for her upcoming speech, Ben didn't
seem to have any lack of appetite. He finished each item
that was set in front of him, and in between courses he
kept up a steady stream of conversation with the men at
the table, which included a doctor, a lawyer, and a local
newscaster. All seemed fascinated by Ben's stint in the
military, as well as his current occupation in a security
firm.

As for the women at the table, well, they seemed very
captivated by Ben's easy charm and his handsome good
looks, not that Christine could blame any of them.

"Can I have one of those, please?" Madison, who was sitting to her right at their dinner table, said.

Christine glanced to the left as her friend indicated, and the only thing she found that Madison might want was the bread basket. "You want another roll?" she asked, just to be sure, since both of their main entree plates had just been cleared away.

"No, I want a hot guy like Ben," Madison clarified, grinning effusively. "He's been amazing tonight, and you'd never know that he wasn't a part of this crowd. Nice eye candy to have on your arm when you need it, too. Do you know if he has a brother?"

Christine held back a smile and shook her head. "Sorry, but he's an only child."

Madison sighed in feigned disappointment. "That's really too bad, because he's starting to grow on me."

He was growing on Christine, too—in a big way that went beyond just being hot for him. She really did love her newfound freedom and independence after spending years under her mother's overbearing influence, then Jason's controlling personality, but she had to admit that she truly liked having Ben around. She enjoyed his company and their verbal exchanges, and even their arguments sent a zing of excitement through her.

Their mutual attraction was a big bonus and one she had every intention of taking advantage of. Tonight. She couldn't wait to get him home, and she wasn't taking no for an answer, not when she knew how much he wanted her, too. And as exceedingly gorgeous as he looked in his tuxedo, she couldn't wait to get him out of it and see him completely naked so she could touch him everywhere.

A waiter came by and delivered their final course of the evening—dessert—a light, flaky pastry filled with Chantilly cream and drizzled with a caramel and orange sauce. Normally, Christine would dig right in and enjoy every bite, but again, her anxious stomach wasn't cooperating and she didn't even touch the delicious-looking confection.

Instead, she watched Ben eat his dessert, and when he finished he glanced at her uneaten pastry, then at her, his expression etched with concern. He stretched an arm across the back of her chair and leaned in close to her.

"Are you doing okay?" he asked, his voice a low, husky murmur.

She shivered as his thumb stroked down the nape of her neck in a soothing, but equally sensual, caress. "I'm just getting a little restless. I'll be fine once I'm done with my speech."

He glanced at his wristwatch. "You've got about another half an hour before it's time to face the crowd, so in the meantime why don't we walk around and try to calm your nerves?"

She appreciated his suggestion, and decided that his idea had merit. If she sat there at the table she'd do nothing but think about standing up at the podium and how not to panic while over two hundred people watched her speak.

Ben got up from his seat, pulled her chair back, and she stood, too. Hooking her arm through his, she strolled around the ballroom, as other men and women were beginning to do now that the meal portion of the party was over. The hired band began to play upbeat music, and some couples headed toward the dance floor, while others went over to where the silent auction was set up to see what kind of items there were to bid on.

Ben placed his large, warm palm over the hand she'd rested on his arm, the touch subtly possessive and inherently intimate, making them look like the couple they were posing to be. "Would you believe I actually see someone I know here?"

"Really?" She glanced around, trying to figure out who he might be acquainted with at a swanky charity event such as this one. "And who is that?"

"My good friend's brother. Come on and I'll introduce you."

Grateful for the distraction, she let him escort her toward two couples who were engaged in a conversation. One of the women, who was pregnant, looked vaguely familiar, but Christine couldn't place where she'd seen her before. As they approached, one of the men glanced toward them, his blue eyes first widening in shock. Then a big, friendly smile transformed his striking features.

"Hey, Ben." The good-looking man reached out and shook Ben's hand in a firm grip. "What a surprise to see you here."

Ben grinned. "You, too, Scott, though I did see your name on the guest list. I just didn't think this was your kind of thing."

The other man gave a slight wince. "Trust me, I could do without all the formal attire and hoopla, but Ashley is a big supporter of the foundation, so what's a husband to do but tag along?"

"I completely understand. My date is involved in the charity auction portion of the event," Ben said, then went on to introduce her. "This is Christine Delacroix. Christine, meet Scott Wilde and his wife, Ashley St. Claire-Wilde. Joel Wilde, my partner at ESS, is Scott's brother."

"It's nice to meet both of you," Christine said with a smile.

Now Christine knew how she'd recognized Ashley St. Claire, heiress of the St. Claire Hotel that was hosting tonight's gala. She'd met the woman a few years ago at another event, but hadn't seen her since, though she'd heard that she'd gotten married. Judging by the adoration on Ashley's face as she gazed up at her husband, and the soft pink glow of her complexion that complemented her pregnancy, it appeared that the two were still in the throes of wedded bliss.

Ashley indicated the other couple standing with them. "These are my good friends, Matthew Carlton and his wife, Faith. Matthew is a pediatric surgeon at Children's Memorial, so this foundation is very important to him, as well."

Matthew tipped his head as he studied Christine curiously. "Is your father Nathan Delacroix?"

She nodded. "Yes, he is." The question was always a loaded one that usually led to some kind of political statement. Whether the comment was a positive or negative one, she never knew. It all depended on which candidate the person supported.

"Well, he certainly has our vote for governor," Matthew said sincerely as he wrapped an arm around his wife and drew her close to his side. "Faith and I really respect what he's doing with the whole gentrification issue. It's nice to see a politician stand up for the less fortunate and push for inner-city rejuvenation, rather than destroying so many people's lives to make a quick buck," he said, obviously referring to Charles Lambert, Nathan's opponent.

"Delacroix has our vote, too," Scott added for himself and his wife, Ashley.

Christine was glad to have the positive feedback. "Thank you, I appreciate your support, and I know my father will, too."

Ashley placed a hand on her rounded belly, which was draped in black silk. "Ben mentioned that you're in charge of the charity auction for tonight. Scott's sister, Mia, donated one of her stained glass designs for the auction."

"Yes, she did." What a small world it was to discover how everyone was related. "Mia was incredibly generous and offered up a custom-made design of the winner's choice. Considering the beautiful work she does, I'm sure it will be one of the more popular items that people bid on."

"Excuse me, ladies and gentlemen." A female voice came over the ballroom's speakers. "In about five minutes, Christine Delacroix will be coming up to the podium to talk about the silent auction, so if she could have everyone's attention to give you all an explanation of how it works, that would be great."

Christine smiled. "Well, that would be me." She drew a deep breath to calm the flutters already hatching in her belly. "I'd better go ahead and make my way to the front of the room."

Right after the announcement, the guests in the ballroom started shifting toward the small staging area, and she let Ben guide her in that direction. It was difficult at times to get past the crush of people, but eventually they made their way to the raised dais, where a few people were milling around—including Leanne and Craig.

The event coordinator ushered the guests away from the platform, then came up to Christine. "Your notes are on the podium as you requested, and there's a glass of water on the shelf beneath if you need it."

Her mouth was already dry and she knew she'd need that water to moisten her lips and throat. "That's perfect. Thank you."

"I'll be right over here," Ben pointed out, and stepped off to the right side—far enough away so that he wasn't hovering over her, yet close enough to make her feel secure.

Lifting the hem of her dress so she didn't trip on her way up to the stand, she maneuvered the two steps and crossed the short stage without any problems, if she didn't count the rush of anxiety that swept over her. Before addressing the room, she took a big gulp of the cool water beneath the podium and took a moment to gather her composure.

As soon as she spoke into the microphone to welcome everyone to the gala, the entire ballroom fell silent and all eyes focused on her, and her aversion to public speaking immediately kicked in. Her heart beat faster in her chest, and she glanced down at her notes to keep her speech on track. Otherwise, she knew she'd babble and wouldn't remember a thing she'd written.

She began her presentation by praising the Children's AIDS Foundation and their cause, as well as how far they'd come over the years thanks to the selfless and altruistic donations that went toward research, grants, and advocacy programs. A little more than five minutes into her talk, she felt her skin flush warmly, and her arms and legs began to tingle.

Pausing between the points she'd outlined—as her speech coach had taught her if she needed a quick break—she took another drink of her water, letting the cool liquid soothe her throat and hopefully settle her queasy stomach.

She continued, first thanking all the various businesses for their gracious contributions to the silent auction, which included signed artwork, designer jewelry, autographed sports memorabilia, and a plethora of other coveted items. She assured the crowd that there was something for everyone, and encouraged them to bid generously, and often, since every dollar they spent went directly toward the foundation.

Her head began to spin, as did the room and the occupants, and when she glanced back down at her notes the words on the page were blurred and disjointed. She blinked to clear her vision, took another drink of her water that finished it off, and tried not to panic.

Clutching the edge of the podium so that she didn't sway, or God forbid pass out from the light-headed sensation enveloping her, she explained the bid sheet that accompanied each donated item, and how each person interested in an item would be assigned a bid number so as to keep their identity private. As she went over the rules for the silent auction, her dizziness increased as did the heart palpitations, adding to the growing pressure in her chest.

A wave of nausea churned in her stomach, and knowing she wasn't going to last up at the podium for much longer without embarrassing herself, she wrapped up her speech sooner than she'd intended, then tried to remember where Ben said he'd be waiting for her, but couldn't think beyond the desperate need for fresh air.

The crowd around her started to disperse, which only added to her confusion and her feeling of disorientation. She couldn't breathe. She only knew she had to get out of the room before she either collapsed or threw up.

Where was Ben?

She stumbled off the platform to the left, and somehow Craig was there, his expression filled with concern. Suddenly, the room started to spin in earnest.

"I've got to get out of here," she rasped, and nearly lost her balance as her legs seemed to grow weak. She felt so lethargic, her mind so muddled—like no other anxiety attack she'd ever had. "I need fresh air."

"Come," he said, and with his arm supporting her around her waist, he guided her through the throng of people and toward the double doors leading outside.

"Where's Ben?" she asked.

Craig didn't answer.

She looked around for Ben, but her vision was so unfocused and everything around her seemed to be moving in slow motion, and she hated the helpless sensation sweeping over her. She felt so tired. So sluggish as she tried to put one foot in front of the other. Craig was talking to her, but she couldn't decipher what he was saying because his voice was so garbled.

And then she felt a rush of cold air on her bare skin as they stepped outside to the front of the hotel, but it wasn't enough to snap her out of her stupor. It was as if she were drunk, yet she'd only consumed one cocktail a few hours ago. Was she still walking? Or was she standing still and everything around her was moving? She no longer could tell.

She wanted Ben. She *needed* Ben. But when she opened her mouth to tell Craig to go and get him, only a soft moan escaped. And somewhere in the back of her fading thoughts she knew that when Ben did find her he was going to give her hell for not staying put.

Nine

AS Ben stood off to the side and kept an eye on Christine up at the podium during her presentation, he instinctively knew that something was wrong. She'd explained how nervous she was about public speaking, but she wasn't showing the typical signs of anxiety. Rather, she seemed increasingly out of sorts and confused, as if she couldn't think clearly even though she had an outline right in front of her.

He watched her take another drink of her water, emptying the glass of the clear liquid, and then try to finish her spiel on the silent auction. Her breathing grew labored, and a frown furrowed her brow as she stared out at the crowd with a dazed look on her face. Abruptly, she finished her speech and headed down the platform away from him.

He called out her name, but she didn't seem to hear him.

"Son of a bitch," Ben bit out furiously and moved fast, but as the thick crowd around him started to separate and head in different directions, men and women inadvertently cut him off in his attempt to get to Christine. It was like swimming upstream through a sea of mud, and it was all he could do not to push and shove his way through the mass of people getting in his way.

Ben's gaze never left Christine as a man he realized was Craig ushered her toward the exit. He swore again, and once they disappeared through the double doors and Ben could no longer see them, a swift kick of adrenaline surged through his entire body. As he ran out of the ballroom, he resisted the urge to grab the semiautomatic he'd holstered beneath his jacket, because he knew that would cause a huge scene and chaos, and until he saw an actual threat he had to keep his weapon secured.

He burst through the main doors of the hotel that led outside, and he immediately caught sight of Craig guiding a wobbling-on-her-high-heels Christine along a path leading around to the far side of the building—where it was dark and very secluded.

Ben reached Craig before the other man had a chance to realize he was even nearby. He stepped in front of him and Christine, bringing them both to a stop. Craig looked startled by his sudden appearance, while Christine appeared bewildered and confused.

Instantly, Ben gently took Christine's arm and pulled her away from Craig. Once he had her safely by his side, the fury that had been building within Ben exploded in a blast of outrage. "Stay the *fuck* away from her, Crosby!"

"What the hell, man!" Craig retorted just as angrily. "She was obviously dizzy and sick, and I was just taking her to the courtyard right over there so she could sit down and get some fresh air!" He waved toward an area sectioned off by plants and trees, with benches to sit on.

Ben clenched his jaw. While Craig's story was completely plausible and most likely true, Ben wasn't about to back down from his stance. "Stay away from her," he said, enunciating each word.

Craig narrowed his gaze. "I don't know who the hell you think you are, but I'm getting damn tired of your continual harassment."

Before Ben could respond with a scathing remark, Christine fell against his chest, and he caught her around the waist to help keep her upright. She looked up at him, her eyes glassy and a semblance of a smile on her lips.

"Ben," she sighed, drawing out his name on a slur of sound.

It was as though she was drunk, yet Ben knew for a fact that she'd only had one cocktail, and that had been before dinner. The only other explanation for her uncharacteristic behavior was that she'd been drugged somehow. Had someone put something in her food or her soda at their table? And what about the water at the podium? It could have easily been tampered with before she'd arrived to make her speech.

Ben was beginning to suspect the latter, and he automatically glared at Craig. "What did you do to her?"

Craig visibly bristled. "I didn't do a damn thing to her, and I don't appreciate your accusations!"

He didn't give a shit what Craig did or didn't like. But ultimately, Ben didn't have proof of anything, let alone that Crosby was responsible for Christine's current state. Or Leanne, who was easily Ben's second suspect.

However, with over two hundred people attending the charity event, there was no way to nail any one person. Not only were there supporters of Nathan Delacroix at the party, but undoubtedly there were others who might hold a grudge against the man for his political views. Someone angry enough to issue threats against Delacroix to drop out of the race for governor, and bold enough to slip something to Christine to let Nathan know just how serious they were about his daughter's safety.

The possibility made Ben feel physically ill.

"Ben!" a deep male voice called out.

Ben glanced toward the hotel entrance to see Matthew Carlton, the man that he and Christine had met through Scott Wilde just before her speech. The other man was striding toward the three of them, his expression speculative.

"I noticed that Christine wasn't doing so well up at the podium," Matthew said as he came up to them. "Is she okay?"

She was still leaning heavily against Ben, her face buried in the crook of his neck. "I don't know," he admitted.

Christine shivered against him and burrowed closer, her arms sliding around his waist beneath his jacket. "It's cold and you're so warm," she whispered languidly.

Matthew pushed his hands into his pants pockets, his concerned gaze still on Christine. "Would you like me to take a look at her and make sure she's all right?"

Nothing about this situation felt good, but remembering that Matthew Carlton was some kind of doctor, not to mention a friend of Scott's, Ben chose to trust the other man. "That would be great. Let's get her back inside so she can sit down."

They started back toward the hotel entrance, and when Craig followed, Ben shot him a dark look. "*I'll* handle this," he said, leaving no doubt in Crosby's mind that he needed to get lost. "And like I said before, stay away from her."

Craig gave him a smug glance. "We'll see what Christine says about that."

Ben's temper spiked to an all-time high. If he didn't have his hands full trying to support Christine as they entered the hotel lobby, he would have beat the shit out of the self-righteous bastard right then and there.

Being a somewhat smart man, Craig didn't push the issue any further, and while Ben and Matthew led Christine toward a vacant group of couches and chairs set up in the lobby, Crosby veered toward the ballroom to return to the charity gala.

After gently maneuvering Christine so that she was sitting in the center of the couch, Ben removed his tuxedo jacket and settled it over Christine's bare shoulders. He knelt in front of her while Matthew sat to her right on the couch and immediately grabbed her wrist to check her pulse and heart rate. Christine's head fell forward drowsily, and Ben lifted her chin to try to keep her awake.

"Open your eyes and look at me, sweetheart," he cajoled in a low, soothing voice.

He watched her struggle to lift her lashes, and when she finally managed the feat and saw him, she smiled slow and sweet. "Ben," she murmured on a wisp of breath. "I'm soooo tired and sleepy."

He cupped her face in his hands. "I know you are, honey, but I need you to stay awake, okay?"

She licked her lips and tried to nod. "Mmmm-hmmm."

While Ben proceeded to talk to Christine to keep her alert, Matthew continued his examination. He looked into her eyes and checked her pupils and vision, then went on to monitor her breathing. He even pressed his ear to her chest so he could listen to the rhythm of her heartbeat. Matthew asked how much she'd had to drink, if she was on any type of medication, or had recently taken any kind of drugs.

The last question Ben couldn't answer, and when Matthew repeated the inquiry to Christine, she responded with an indignant, but sluggish, "I don't do drugs!"

Christine's spirited reply despite her lethargic condition *almost* made Ben smile. Instead, he glanced back at Matthew and decided to level with him on the situation.

"Look, I've been hired by Christine's father as her bodyguard, and I'd really prefer *not* to have to take her to the ER and have her exposed to the public for hours there, if it can be helped."

Ben could just imagine the field day reporters would have with that kind of story. Undoubtedly, someone in Lambert's camp would turn it into some kind of drug scandal against Nathan's daughter, and ultimately smear Delacroix's great reputation and his campaign.

"I don't have any proof, but judging by what happened up at the podium, and Christine's behavior now, I think someone slipped her something," Ben said, giving Matthew his gut feeling on what might have transpired. "I've never seen her act like this before."

Matthew checked her pulse rate again. "From what I see, she does exhibit many of the symptoms of ingesting Rohypnol," he said, referring to the street drug roofie. "Her motor skills are definitely impaired, and she's responding as if she's had a lot more to drink than she did. The good thing is, she only consumed one cocktail hours ago, so that does reduce the effects of the drug."

Ben nodded, grateful for that much, at least. "What do I need to do?"

"Take her home and watch her throughout the night to make sure there isn't any change in her breathing or any extreme drop in her pulse rate," Matthew instructed. "Her reaction is something she's just going to have to sleep off, and most likely she won't remember any of this in the morning."

Anxious to get her out of the hotel and safe at home, Ben stood, fished a ticket stub from his pants' pocket and glanced back at Matthew. "Would you mind getting our car from valet while I carry Christine out of here? I don't think she can walk or stand very well on her own and I don't want to risk her falling."

"Absolutely. I'm glad to help." Matthew took the stub and headed out of the lobby to the circular drive in front of the hotel to retrieve their vehicle.

Ten minutes later, Ben had Christine secured in the passenger seat of her Lexus, with the seat reclined so she could sleep on the drive home. He shut the door, then turned back to the good doctor, who withdrew a business card from his wallet and handed it to Ben.

"These are my emergency numbers where I can be reached twenty-four/seven," Matthew said. "Call me if you have any questions or need anything at all."

"Thanks, man." Ben shook Matthew's hand, thankful to have the backup if he needed it. "I appreciate it."

GETTING Christine inside the house and carrying her to the guest bedroom where he was staying was easy. Getting her out of her long, elegant dress when she was as limp as a wet noodle was going to be a bit more tricky. He laid her down on one side of the double bed, and she woke up long enough to reach for him, her hands sliding along the front of his dress shirt as she tried to unfasten the buttons with clumsy, fumbling fingers.

Her blue eyes were glassy, her lips oh-so-tempting as she murmured in a seductively drowsy voice, "Come 'ere . . . I want you."

A pained smile touched his lips. "I know you do, sweetheart. You've already made that very clear. Numerous times." Knowing one of the effects of Rohypnol was a lack of inhibition, he grasped her slender wrists and gently pulled her hands away from his shirt. "But first things first. Let's get you out of this dress."

"Yeah," she sighed as she looked up at him with a soft, come-hither look in her eyes. "Let's get naked."

Her head fell back against the pillow, and in the next instant she was asleep again, which would make his next task of stripping off her dress so much easier. Because of the one-shoulder design of her gown, the zipper was located beneath her arm and he pulled the tab all the way down to her hip. Slipping the material off her shoulder, he dragged the dress down her lithe body and off, leaving her scantily clad in a strapless bra, skimpy black lace panties, and a pair of black, sexy designer heels.

Those were the first to go. Then, keeping his gaze on her face, he unhooked her bra and added it to the gown he'd draped over the chair next to the bed. Thankfully, she remained unconscious, even when he pulled one of his T-shirts over her head, pushed her arms through the sleeves, then yanked the soft cotton material down to her thighs. Once she was sufficiently covered, he put her beneath the blankets, then took off his holster and stripped off his own formal attire.

Wearing just a pair of boxer briefs, he turned off the lights, slid into bed beside her, and pulled her close to his side with his fingers pressing gently against the pulse in her neck so he could monitor the beat of her heart.

He'd made the decision to bring her to the guest bedroom because it was less personal and intimate than crawling into her feminine bed, but as she snuggled up to him and her soft body curled so sweet and trusting against his, he realized that it didn't matter where the two of them slept tonight. His awareness of her was so acute, so undeniable, that they could have been in an igloo in the North Pole and his body still would have been as hot as a furnace.

Before that swift kick of lust could settle in his groin and keep him hard for the entire night, he rerouted his thoughts to something less arousing. Like the phone call Ben needed to make to Christine's father in the morning to let him know what had happened.

That definitely dissolved any last, lingering bit of desire. He didn't relish informing Nathan that someone had tried to drug his daughter at the gala, especially under his watch. He'd been hired specifically to protect Christine, yet someone had still been able to get to her in a way that he'd never anticipated. The results could have been far more tragic if he hadn't been around, but that notion did little to soothe his conscience.

Instead, it brought up haunting memories of his fiancée, Kim, and the brutal, unexpected way she, and most of her unit, had been murdered by a roadside bomb in Iraq—and how he'd been unable to keep her safe during a mission that had gone so horribly wrong.

Now, he lived with the guilt, the remorse, the vivid images of how he'd held her lifeless body in his arms and wished that it had been he who had died, instead of her.

A familiar lump formed in his throat and he squeezed his eyes shut to block the painful recollections. He'd failed to keep Kim safe, but he wasn't going to make that same mistake with Christine.

CHRISTINE cuddled closer to the hard, warm body next to hers. Still caught somewhere between sleep and sublime awareness, she grasped at the nebulous images and feelings floating through her mind, embracing the decadent sensations that could only be a wonderfully sensual dream. She breathed in the scent of earthy male, and her flattened palm skimmed over ridges of hot skin sprinkled with a trail of coarse hair that led to an elastic barrier.

Undeterred, and wanting to see where this delicious

fantasy led, she boldly slipped her hand beneath the waistband. Finding what she sought, she smiled and released a little hum of approval as she wrapped her fingers around an impressive erection. She squeezed the hard shaft, then stroked the hot, silky length of flesh in a tight fist—from the thick base all the way up to a broad, swollen head, which seeped with a slick moisture.

A deep groan rumbled beneath her ear, which was pressed against a warm, solid chest, the sound so vivid and real she felt her stomach curl with an answering need. Her breasts swelled, her nipples tightened, and between her thighs she throbbed for release. She turned more fully toward the temptation beckoning to her, aching for a deeper contact, to feel all that pulsing flesh filling her full.

Instead, strong fingers pulled her hand away from the erection she still held in her grasp, and she moaned in protest. This was not how her fantasy was supposed to end.

"Christine, sweetheart, wake up."

The deep, masculine voice and a gentle shake penetrated the fog that seemed to surround her. Forcing her eyes open, she blinked a few times, trying to clear not only her vision, but also the haze clouding her mind. It was as if she was dealing with a hangover, and after that one time in college when she'd woken up ill from a night of drinking too much alcohol at a sorority party, she'd never overindulged again.

Feeling confused and disoriented, she lifted her head and glanced down at the man lying half-naked beside her. Daylight streamed through the slats in the wooden blinds covering the windows, providing more than enough illumination to see Ben staring at her with dark eyes that were hot with the same desire burning through her. The stubble on his jaw told her that it was most likely morning, yet she had no idea where they were or what had happened.

"Ben," she said, her voice raspy and just as bewildered as she felt.

A lazy smile curved his lips. "Morning," he murmured. He brushed away stray strands of hair that had fallen against her cheek as his gaze searched her face with concern. "How are you doing?"

With a frown, she glanced around, recognizing the guest bedroom where Ben had been sleeping for the past week. She was wearing one of his T-shirts, and her hair was falling in a disheveled mess from where it had been pinned atop her head. She couldn't remember how she'd gotten here in his bed, and if they'd enjoyed any in-between-the-sheets kind of activity she had no recollection of that, either.

She supposed there was only one way to find out. "Did we sleep together?"

"Sleep was all we did in this bed," he said as he continued to watch her. "Well, actually, you slept and I kept a close eye on you all night long."

She sat up and pressed a hand to her cool forehead. "I don't understand," she whispered, trying to recall something, *anything*, that led to her waking up beside Ben.

He turned onto his side and propped himself up on his elbow. "What, exactly, do you remember about last night?" he asked.

Last night . . . She struggled to grasp some kind of flashback to give her a clue, but all she could come up with was odd, disjointed images that didn't make a whole lot of sense and only made her more frustrated. She caught sight of her black beaded gown draped over the chair beside the bed, and that, thankfully, helped to jog her memory.

"We went to the charity event together," she said,

meeting Ben's gaze once again as events starting meshing into a cohesive thought. "I remember the cocktail party, and our dinner, and meeting your friends. I even remember getting up on stage to make my presentation for the silent auction and being nervous about speaking in front of everyone . . ." And shortly thereafter that's when everything had gone fuzzy and vague and then completely nonexistent in her mind.

Those were the missing pieces of the puzzle she needed to fill in. "What happened? Did I pass out?"

Ben shook his head. "Not at first, no." Then he went on to explain everything that had happened, along with his suspicions that she'd been drugged at some point—either at the dinner table, or her water at the podium.

She listened as he told her about Craig's part in last night's escapade and how he'd been quick to take her outside for some fresh air. While Ben's loathing toward Craig was a tangible thing, Ben had no proof that Craig was responsible for what had happened.

"Wow," she said once Ben finished telling her everything, right up to the point where he'd taken off her dress and tucked her into bed—and spent the entire night watching over her, making sure she didn't have any kind of adverse reaction to whatever she'd been slipped.

"I can't believe all that happened," she said with an incredulous shake of her head, then winced when a dull pain jabbed at her temples.

Once the discomfort subsided, she smiled at Ben and reached out to trail the tips of her fingers along the rough stubble on his jaw. "I do have to say that my first thought when I woke up this morning was that you and I had finally done the deed, and I would have been pretty upset if we had sex and I had no recollection of any of it. Because when that *does* happen, I want to remember every single detail of the experience."

Chuckling, he slid from the bed, grabbed a pair of worn jeans, and pulled them on over the boxer briefs that molded to all those yummy, masculine parts of him. "Why don't you go and take a nice long, hot shower to clear your head? I need to call your father and let him know what happened, then I'll make you something to eat."

"Okay," she said with a nod of her head. "I should check in with Madison and make sure that the auction did well, despite my quick exit."

"Actually, Madison called your cell phone when I was driving you home last night, and I answered the call and let her know what happened," he told her. "She promised that she would handle everything for you, and she'd call you today to see how you were doing."

That said, he started for the door, but she stopped him before he could leave. "Ben?"

He turned back around. "Yeah?"

She was momentarily distracted by his bare chest and somehow managed to lift her gaze back to his. "Thank you for taking care of me last night and keeping me safe."

He gave her a slight, imperceptible nod. "That's my job," he said, then disappeared from her view.

Yes, she knew she was a job to him, an assignment he took very seriously, and she understood and respected his position as her bodyguard. But it was her own myriad of emotions that she wasn't sure she had a complete handle on. When it came to Ben, there was a wealth of want, need, and desire most definitely. Affection and caring was right up there, too. But it was the deeper, unexpected feelings wrapping around her heart that made her realize that she was falling for Ben in ways she'd never, ever, anticipated.

And she wasn't altogether sure what she was going to do about her growing feelings for him, especially when her life was finally her own and everything she'd wanted it to be.

Or so she thought.

FRESH from her shower and dressed in a comfortable sweat outfit for a lazy, restful Sunday at home, Christine walked into the kitchen to find Ben standing at the stove cooking up something that smelled so good it made her stomach grumble hungrily.

She came up beside him as he sprinkled grated cheese on what looked like an omelette sauteing in a pan. "Can I help you with anything?"

"Nope." He wiped his hands on a terry towel, then dropped two slices of bread into the toaster. "I made a fresh pot of coffee if you want a cup, and I'll be done with your breakfast in just a few minutes."

"Thank you." Pouring the hot brew into a mug, she added creamer and a spoonful of sugar, and stirred.

He cast her a quick look as he transferred the delicious-looking omelette to a plate and started in on another. "How are you feeling?"

"Okay." She took a sip of her coffee and let the warm liquid make its way down to her empty stomach. "That shower definitely helped to clear the cobwebs in my head, but I hate the fact that part of my memory of last night is gone."

He added fresh sliced mushrooms and chopped ham to the eggs, then started buttering the toast that had just popped up in the toaster. "Trust me, you're not missing anything worth remembering. Now go sit down so I can feed you."

Smiling, she obeyed his order and took a seat at the table, while he set a plate of fragrant food in front of her. "Wow, this is impressive," she said, taking in the fluffy omelette he'd made for her. "For a bachelor, that is."

He returned to the stove to finish his own breakfast. "Hey, I might love pizza, but I can't live on that alone," he said with one of his sexy grins. "You had all the ingredients for an omelette, so I took advantage."

Suddenly ravenous, she dug into her eggs, which were absolutely delicious with the mushrooms, ham, and cheese. "Where did you learn to make such a light, fluffy omelette? In the military?" she teased.

"No." With his own plate and coffee in hand, he joined her at the table. "This is a gourmet meal compared to what I ate for breakfast while serving in Iraq."

"Which was?" she asked curiously.

"MRE rations, a protein bar, or mushy scrambled eggs," he said, then ate a big bite of his omelette. "Learning to cook something decent to eat came from a lot of years of being on my own."

The comment was said ambiguously, but it made Christine think about how this man lived his life—alone, in a sparsely furnished apartment, and without any family to call his own. "You were on your own long before joining the military, weren't you?"

He'd just taken a bite of his toast, and he glanced up at her, his gaze suddenly dark and shadowed. "What makes you say that?" he asked gruffly.

Judging by his guarded reaction, she knew she was tiptoeing into personal territory he considered off-limits, but there was so much about this man she wanted to know and understand, and she didn't let his brusque demeanor dissuade her, as it had when she'd been at his apartment a week ago.

"I'm just going off of the conversation we had at your place when you mentioned that your father had passed away a few years ago, and that you had no idea where your mother was . . . nor did you care to know." She took a drink of her coffee, watching as a muscle in his clenched jaw twitched. "What was your childhood like, Ben?"

"It's not something I want to discuss," he said succinctly.

She rolled her eyes, unwilling to let the subject go. "Come on, Ben. We all have a past of some sort. You should know by now that I'm not one to judge, especially considering my own less-than-ideal childhood with a mother who was so intent on molding me into this perfectly demure lady and obedient wife to some man she approved of."

"At least you had a mother around." The barest hint of a smile made an appearance, lightening the moment between them. "Even if she was overbearing and controlling."

"That's putting things mildly and you know it," she said, and playfully pointed her fork at him. "My mother pretty much had my entire life planned out for me, including being a politician's wife. But you already know all that so stop trying to change the subject. We're talking about *your* mother, not mine."

"It's a long, depressing story that'll probably put you to sleep." He shrugged and continued eating his omelette.

"Luckily I had plenty of rest last night and we have the entire day ahead of us," she countered easily. "Time is not an issue."

He sighed, and surprisingly he didn't attempt to evade the topic any longer. "Honestly, I haven't thought about my mother and what happened with her in a very long time, and I'm not sure where to start."

"The beginning is always a good place," she said, trying to keep things light. "How did your parents meet?"

"They both lived in Perry, a small town in West Virginia. My father, Neil, was twenty at the time and worked in a local coal mine along with my grandpa, which is pretty much what all the men in that town did for a living and to support their families. It wasn't a glamorous life by any stretch of the imagination."

"I'm sure it was very hard, dangerous work," she said, going off what she'd heard on the news over the years about coal mines and the hazards of working in one. "But it's still a respectable job."

"My father and grandpa thought so," he said and smiled fondly, telling her that he'd at least had good memories of those two men who'd been a part of his life. "From what I've heard through town gossip, my mother is the one who pursued my father, and she was eighteen when she got pregnant with me as a way out of her own abusive family life. Of course my father married her, not only because it was the right thing to do, but apparently he truly did love her, too."

Finished with his breakfast, he pushed his empty plate aside. "After I was born, my mother started pushing my father for them to move to the city where he could get a better paying job. She hated living in a small town and the little two-bedroom house my father bought, which was all he could afford with what he made. She wanted to live in Charleston, but my father refused to move. He'd been born and raised in Perry and coal mining was all he knew."

Standing, she collected their dishes and carried them to the sink. "And that's where your father's parents lived, too, right?"

"Actually, my grandmother, who was a wonderful woman, passed away when I was about five, and a few years after that my grandpa died from black lung disease. So, really, there was nothing familywise tying my father to that town, but he was a simple man who didn't need or want anything more than what he had."

Picking up the carafe of hot coffee, she headed back to

the table and refilled his mug with the steaming brew. "Sounds like you take after your father."

"I suppose I do," he said with an easygoing smile.

She returned the coffeepot to the counter and remained there, leaning against the kitchen cabinets across from where Ben was sitting. "So, what happened?" she asked, knowing there was so much more to the story.

"By the time I was ten, it was obvious that my parents' marriage was strained." He absently traced a finger along the rim of his coffee cup. "Over the years, my mother's anger and bitterness toward my father increased, and she even grew to resent me, as well."

"What?" she exclaimed incredulously, unable to believe that a mother could blame a child for her unhappiness. "You were just a little boy!"

"One who kept her tied to a man and town that she no longer wanted to be a part of," he said matter-of-factly.

Christine's jaw dropped open. "She told you that?"

"Not directly, no." He hesitated for a moment, then meeting her gaze from across the room, he continued, "I was in bed one night when my mother and father were fighting in the living room. She didn't bother to keep her voice down, and after informing my father that she was filing for a divorce, she went on to tell him that she was tired of being a small-town wife, that she wanted something more exciting than being married to a coal miner and being a PTA mother. By the next morning, she'd packed up her things and she was gone. She didn't even wake me up to say good-bye, and I haven't seen or heard from her since, and I don't care if I ever do."

His tone was so blasé, as if he were relaying someone else's past and not his own horrible memories of a mother who'd turned her back on him without a second thought. But it was the raw pain she detected in the depths of his eyes that told another tale, about a young boy who most likely believed his own mother didn't love him enough to stay, or even fight to take him when she left town.

A lump formed in her throat and it felt as if her own heart were being torn in two. She closed the distance between them, and because he was sitting she didn't hesitate to straddle his lap, her only thought to get as close to him as possible, to let him know that someone cared for the hurt and confused little boy he'd been, and even the man he'd grown to be.

Their position was intimate, but was meant to be more comforting than sexual. She framed his face in her hands, his skin still rough with morning stubble. "I'm so sorry, Ben," she whispered, the ache in her voice real.

Instead of pushing her away or refusing the tenderness she was offering, he placed his hands on her hips, his gaze searching hers. "What for?" he murmured.

"For you and the little boy inside who endured a mother's cruel words and abandonment." She swallowed hard, her anger toward a woman she'd never met a palpable thing. "What kind of mother does that to her only child?"

"A selfish one," he said, meaning it, the harsh tone of his voice leaving no doubt about how he felt toward the woman who'd been his mother for only ten years of his life. "My father couldn't live up to her expectations, and I was more of a nuisance than anything else, so she bailed. The unfortunate part was that my father never stopped loving her, and in order to forget the pain of her walking out on us, he turned to the bottle."

Gently removing her hands from his face, Ben placed her palms on his chest and exhaled a deep breath. "My father was a good, decent man, but my mother completely destroyed him because he wasn't able to give her the kind of life she insisted on. After high school, I took a job in the coal mines, too, but when my father passed away a year later, I decided that there was nothing left for me in the small town of Perry, and I joined the Marines."

And his time in the military, she knew, was a whole other story rife with more pain and heartache. "You've done well with your life," she said, focusing on what he'd accomplished. "Your father would have been proud."

"Thanks." He gingerly eased her off his lap, and she straightened as he stood up, too, obviously ready to put an end to the personal conversation that had dredged up a whole lot of deeply buried and painful emotions for him.

Picking up his coffee mug, he carried it to the sink, then turned around to face her, his expression all serious business. "By the way, I did speak to your father while you were in the shower to let him know what, exactly, happened at the charity event, and he let me know that he received another threat today to drop out of the election, which also made reference to last night's drugging incident with you."

"He better not give in to those ultimatums," she said adamantly. As a family, they'd been in similar situations with his political career, and this campaign for governor was too important for her father to drop out over someone's blackmail attempt.

Ben leaned against the counter and crossed his arms over his chest. "He's going forward with the election, but he's definitely concerned about your safety, first and foremost, and we both decided that until the election is over you need to keep a low profile."

She didn't like the way that sounded. "Don't tell me that I have to stay cooped up in this house for the next week and a half. I know I had a close call this time, but I have a business to run and I'm not about to give this jerk the satisfaction of thinking he's scared me off."

Ben chuckled. "Yeah, your father said you'd react just like that, so we came to a compromise. No more public appearances until after the election, and that includes hanging out at Envy with your friends."

She lifted a brow, not at all surprised that he'd made Envy off-limits, which made her wonder if that was due more to the nightclub's crowded atmosphere, or Craig's presence there. "Whose decision was that?" she asked with a tip of her head. "Yours or my father's?"

"It was a mutual decision."

His expression gave nothing away, but she suspected that Ben was immensely pleased that she'd be keeping her distance from Craig. And honestly, she was fine with that. "I don't have anything scheduled until my birthday party at Envy, but that's *after* the election. So, until then, I'll keep things low-key."

"Perfect." He nodded his head in satisfaction and pushed away from the counter. "You've had a rough night, so you really should rest and take it easy today. As for me, I have some reports and paperwork to get done."

She recognized his comment as an excuse for him to put some distance between them. She wasn't sure if it was because of their intense conversation about his mother, or something else. But she understood his need to be alone, to think about everything he'd just shared, and for the rest of the day she'd give him the space that he seemed to need.

But come tonight, he was all hers.

Ten

STANDING in front of Ben's closed bedroom door at quarter after nine in the evening, Christine figured she had two choices. One, to heed all the subtle signals Ben had been giving off all day long to keep things nice and platonic between them, or two, to walk through the door separating her from the man she wanted in more ways than one and proceed to seduce him, and indulge in what surely would be the greatest pleasure she'd ever experienced.

Knowing her time with Ben was limited, her choice didn't require a whole lot of thought or debate. Embracing the latter option, along with her inner vixen, she opened the door and stepped inside the guest bedroom where Ben was reclining on his bed wearing just a pair of boxer briefs and reading a hardback spy novel.

As soon as she entered the room, he immediately sat up and placed his book on the nightstand, his entire body going taut in alert mode. "Is everything okay?"

"Everything is fine," she quickly assured him, and watched as he relaxed somewhat—except for the tentative look in his eyes as he took in what she was wearing. At the moment, all he could see was a bright red silk robe and her absolute favorite Christian Louboutin shoes—a pair of leopard print platform pumps that were lined in red and had a four-inch spiked heel.

"Nice outfit," he said, a hint of wry amusement underscoring his husky voice. "Are you going somewhere?"

She laughed at his attempt to keep things light and humorous when it was so obvious why she was there in his room. Slowly, she strolled toward where he was sitting on the edge of the mattress, and came to a stop in front of him within touching distance.

"The only place I'm going is wherever you take me tonight," she said, and tugged on the sash around her waist. She let the material unravel her like a gift, then let the thin strip of fabric drop to the floor. A sultry shrug of her shoulders, and the coverup slithered down her arms and fell to her feet in a pool of red silk. What she wore beneath—a red, sheer lace bra and matching panties—made Ben groan deep in his throat.

Retrieving the foil packets she'd tucked into her bra for safekeeping, she tossed the trio of condoms onto the bed beside Ben. "I'm yours to do with as you please," she said, daring him to take what she was offering.

His Adam's apple bobbed as he swallowed hard, and his hands curled into tight fists on his thighs. "Christine . . ."

Hearing the beginnings of a rejection starting to form, she pressed her fingers against his lips to stop the words she refused to let him speak. "I want this, and you, so badly, Ben," she whispered achingly. "Please don't tell me no. Not tonight."

Gently, he pulled her hand away from his mouth, his gaze dark with lust and something much more poignant that made her heart skip a beat. "I *should* tell you no and make you leave, but I can't." His hands slid to her hips, and he pulled her closer, between his spread legs. "I want you too much."

"I'm right where I want to be, Ben." There was so much truth to that statement, and the intensity of emotion she felt in that moment almost frightened her.

He said nothing more. Didn't bother to fight what they both so obviously wanted. In a quick, lithe move, he twisted toward the bed behind him and pulled her with him, lifting her slightly and tumbling her back so that she was sprawled in the middle of the mattress, his for the taking. He moved up next to her, his gaze devouring the soft swells of her breasts nearly spilling from the demi-cups of her bra, the dip and curve of her waist, and the flimsy scrap of lace covering her sex.

"You are so incredibly beautiful and sexy," he murmured as he traced an enticing trail between her breasts, then down her flat belly to the waistband of her panties. "I want to touch you, and kiss you, and taste you . . . everywhere." That same finger followed the patch of lace between her legs and pressed against the fabric that was already damp with desire. "Especially right here."

His gaze was hot with erotic intent and promises, and a shiver of anticipation coursed through her. "You can do anything you want to me, except one thing."

He stroked the inside of her thigh with his fingers, easing them apart so he could move his knee in between and move closer to her. "And that would be?"

She ran the tip of her tongue across her bottom lip. "No missionary position." It was all she knew, and this time with Ben was all about pleasure, excitement, and new, thrilling adventures.

"You don't have to worry about that," he said with a slow, wicked smile. "There are about a dozen other ways to get deep inside of you, and I want to try every single one of them."

His provocative words made her hot and eager, and anxious to experience it all. "Sounds like we're on the same page, then."

"Perfect," he said, then settled his mouth over hers.

With an unraveling sigh, she parted her lips for the caress of his tongue, and lost herself in a cloud of luxurious bliss. He seduced her with slow, deep, drugging kisses, the kind that gradually increased in heat and tempo, until he was claiming her mouth with a fierce, hungry demand that made her melt. One of his hands glided down her throat, across her shoulder, and pulled her bra strap down her arm, until she felt cool air brush across her bared breast.

She shivered, then moaned when he cupped the mound of flesh and caressed the taut peak with his thumb. He pulled the lace cup away from her other breast and plucked at her other nipple until it, too, was hard and aching. Feeling impatient for more, a soft, needy sound escaped her, but he took his own sweet time in arousing her and building the anticipation of what was to come, which only served to heighten her desire—and she was pretty sure he knew it, as well.

After a while his lips trailed along her jaw, and he nuzzled her neck before spreading more lazy, spine-tingling kisses down to her breast. He took her nipple into his warm, wet mouth, and sucked gently, over and over, drawing a gasp from her. Threading her fingers through his hair, she gripped his head and guided him to her other waiting breast. At his own leisure, he laved the plump flesh with his tongue—stroking, licking, swirling around and over the hard, sensitive crest, until she was panting and arching restlessly against the heat of his mouth.

Chuckling in pure amusement, he finally parted his lips and drew her deep into all that decadent, silky, wet heat. He sucked once again, and she felt that tantalizing pull all the way down to her weeping sex. Groaning, she clenched her thighs tight around the leg he'd wedged in between hers, and she could feel the steel length of his erection pressing against her hip. He was huge and hard and that's exactly what she wanted. Him. Deep inside of her. Filling her completely and giving her the orgasm building inside of her.

She reached down and cupped his shaft in her hand, stroking him through his boxer briefs. This time, it was he who groaned, deep and low. Releasing her breast, he grabbed her wrist and pinned her arm on the mattress beside her, then lifted his head to look down at her face.

"You keep doing that, and I'm not going to last very long," he drawled in a husky, lust-filled voice.

At the moment, she didn't care. "I want you inside of me."

"Don't be so impatient," he chided playfully as a sinfully sexy smile curved his lips. "I promise we're getting there, but I'm not done with you yet."

A moan of frustration slipped out of her. She was already burning up, her body already primed for his. "You're driving me crazy on purpose, aren't you?"

"It's called *foreplay*, sweetheart." He brought his hand back to her breast and lightly pinched the stiff peak, then soothed the sting with a featherlike brush of his thumb over the velvety crest. "I'm just getting you nice and ready for the good stuff."

"I thought this *was* the good stuff," she said, unsure of just how much more she could take of his sensual torment—or whatever else he had planned.

His fingers swept downward, tickling and teasing her belly with delicate, barely-there caresses that only served to electrify every nerve ending she possessed. "When it comes to sex, it's *all* good stuff, but the best is yet to come."

That made her laugh, which was something she'd never done in the bedroom with another guy. With Ben, it just felt so natural and right. "Pun intended?"

"Oh, most definitely." Quick and agile, he moved over her, straddling her thighs with his legs so that she couldn't move. He lowered his upper body to hers until they were face to face and his long fingers were tangled in her hair.

She felt deliciously trapped beneath him, unable to do anything but let him have his way with her. It was a little bit dangerous, and a whole lot arousing. The dark, hungry look in his eyes excited her even more, and she relished the heat and strength of his body pressing into hers, and the rasp of his lightly hair-covered chest against her smooth breasts.

With a gentle tug on her hair, he pulled her head back and skimmed his lips along the arch of her throat. "You're about to get your first lesson in oral sex," he murmured as he scattered tender love bites along her neck to her ear, rendering her breathless with not only his brazen words, but the feel of his mouth on her skin. "I'm going to go down on you and lick and suck your clit, and push my tongue deep inside of you until you come for me. Are you ready for that?"

She was already trembling inside, and because she trusted Ben so explicitly, she surrendered to him without hesitation. *"Yes."*

His lips captured hers again, and what began as a soulful and deep connection, eventually gave way to hot and primitive mating of their lips and tongues. His hands slid beneath her back, deftly unfastened her bra, and tossed the piece of lingerie aside. A moment later, his mouth paid homage to both of her breasts, bringing them alive with sensation once again before he continued his downward trek to her quivering belly. From there, he spread an agonizingly slow, damp trail of kisses around her navel, then hooked his fingers into the elastic band of her panties at her hips and started tugging the flimsy scrap of material down her thighs.

In order to remove them completely, he sat up so he

could slide the panties down her legs and carefully maneuver them around her heeled pumps so they didn't get tangled. He dropped the bit of lace to the floor, then smoothed
his hands up along the backs of her calves, gradually easing her legs wider and wider apart to make room for him in
between.

Being completely naked in front of Ben for the first
time, with the nightstand lamp leaving nothing to the
imagination—and especially with him still wearing his
boxer briefs!—she felt a small bout of modesty surge
through her. Grasping for any kind of distraction, she
caught sight of her red and leopard print heels and used
them to divert his attention away from the fact that she
was literally sprawled on the bed in front of him like an
offering.

Not that *he* seemed to mind.

"Aren't you going to take off my shoes?" she asked on
a ragged breath.

"Nope." He pressed a kiss on the inside of her bent
knee, his breath fanning hot and moist against her skin.
"They're sexy as hell and they're staying on."

Oh, God. Her heartbeat quickened as he licked and
nibbled his way up the inside of her thigh, leaving a damp
imprint behind with each lingering kiss, a reminder that
he'd tasted that part of her body and was moving on to
more carnal pleasures. When he reached the apex of her
thighs, he draped her legs over his shoulders, brought his
hands around so that he could splay them on her stomach
to hold her down, and settled in for a more thorough
exploration.

She wasn't quite sure what to expect, but when his velvety tongue slid along the soft folds of flesh, then flicked
across her clitoris, she gasped sharply at the shock of
sensation that shot through her. Liquid heat pooled at her
center as he slowly, leisurely stroked her cleft, as he

licked and laved and used his tongue in illicit, wicked ways that made her entire body flush in wanton need.

He controlled her every response with his clever mouth, meting out her pleasure a tiny bit at a time until she was whimpering and begging him for more. Still, he continued to tease and seduce every one of her senses, taking his cues from her soft moans and her quickened breathing. He knew exactly how to make her tremble and ache, how to bring her to the edge of release and then just stop short. And when he added a mind-blowing suctioning swirl to his arsenal of erotic play, along with a deep, endless stroke of his tongue inside of her, she cried out, her back arching off the bed and her fingers clutching the covers in a futile attempt to keep her grounded.

It was no use. The things he was doing to her with his mouth guaranteed that her climax was imminent. Ecstacy, pure and white hot, gathered inside her until there was nothing left for her to do but let go and enjoy the wild ride. Her body shuddered hard, then dissolved into a deluge of exquisite spasms that seemed to go on forever.

She'd never felt anything quite so incredible, so amazingly powerful than the orgasm Ben had just given her. The force and intensity of it all stole her breath, consuming her in a way she'd never experienced before. When the last of those heavenly contractions subsided, he pressed his damp mouth to her belly, nuzzling against her, his breathing just as ragged as her own.

After a while, he lifted his head and looked up at her, his gaze gleaming with unadulterated male satisfaction. "Are you okay?"

She laughed and furrowed her fingers through his thick, tousled hair. "Are you kidding me? I'm better than okay. That was like an out-of-body experience."

He chuckled, obviously pleased that he'd been the one

to provide such immense pleasure. "Good. That was just an appetizer. Are you ready for the main course?"

She gasped as he dipped his tongue into her navel, reminding her of how he'd used that decadent tongue on her elsewhere. "If the main course is anything like what you just did to me, I'm going to be one *very* hungry woman," she said shamelessly.

"I can handle it." Grinning with just enough arrogance to make him look sexy, he moved to the edge of the bed and stood up, then stripped off his boxer briefs. His erection jutted out from between his thighs, hard and thick and more than enough to fill her full, and then some.

A renewed surge of lust spiraled through her. This was the first time she'd seen him completely naked, and just the sight of his fine masculine form was enough to arouse her all over again. He was made up of just the right amount of muscle, lean and powerful and so mouth-wateringly gorgeous she wanted to spend the next hour just touching him, stroking him, and exploring everything that made him so virile and potently male.

He didn't give her the chance. Reaching for one of the foil packets she'd brought with her, he tore it open with his teeth and rolled the condom down the length of his shaft. Then he gently eased her onto her stomach, grabbed her hips, and pulled her downward, toward the edge of the bed where he was standing. Her heels hit the floor, and when she started to straighten, he splayed a hand against her back to keep her upper body pressed flat to the mattress.

"Stay just like you are," he murmured, then caressed both of his hands up the slope of her back, with his thumbs gliding over each notch in her vertebrae, all the way up to her neck, then back down again.

His impromptu massage felt so good, and she stretched sinuously, telling him with soft sighs and deep groans just how much she appreciated his TLC.

His heated palms skimmed lower, over her smooth buttocks, while those wicked thumbs of his traced along the cleft separating each cheek. "You have the sweetest ass," he said huskily, then aligned his hips against hers from behind.

With her high-heeled pumps on, she was the perfect height for this position. His erection was nestled between her thighs, the tip of his shaft gliding through the slick moisture coating her female flesh. Grasping her waist, he moved his hips, mimicking the act of sex, which caused the head of his cock to rub oh-so-enticingly against still-sensitive tissues. With each caress, nerve endings came to life all over again, tingling, tightening, making her toss her head back and moan with the agonizing need for him to be inside of her.

She must have gotten her point across, because with the next pump of his hips he sank into her, much too slow for her liking when she wanted to be taken completely. He pulled out slightly, then surged forward again, teasing her with the promise of another orgasm that he kept just out of her reach.

She was used to quick, lackluster sex that ended after a few hasty strokes, yet despite the tension she could feel radiating off of Ben, he took his time with her, building her hunger all over again. As for him, somehow, some-way, he maintained a controlled pace—one that made her desperate for a more frantic mating.

She looked over her shoulder at Ben, and swallowed hard at the sight of them together in such a primitive, uninhibited way that she'd only fantasized about. The dark, hot look in his eyes, and the barely leashed flex of his muscles in his arms and belly as he moved against her, made her shiver.

"Ben, *please*," she begged softly, when she'd never, ever, pleaded for anything sexual in her previous relationships. "I need you . . . harder, deeper, inside me."

With a ragged groan, he leaned over her from behind, his chest and abdomen pressing against the slope of her back. Bracing himself with one forearm on the bed beside her and tangling the fingers of his other hand in her hair at the nape of her neck, he gently pulled her head back so that his lips grazed her cheek. She felt completely surrounded by him, a part of him in so many ways—her body, her heart, her soul all his for the taking.

He withdrew and thrust back in to the hilt, finally filling her the way she longed to be filled—beyond what she believed was possible for her to take. And he didn't stop there. He increased the tempo of his strokes, each one a little faster, harder, deeper, than the one before.

"Oh, God," he rasped against her ear between quick pants for breath. "You're so wet. So hot . . . so fucking tight."

She closed her eyes and shuddered. His words were just as urgent as the unbearable pressure building between her legs and setting her aflame once again, as reckless as the demanding, aggressive way he plunged into her again, and again, and again. He overwhelmed her with desire and need, showed her what it was like to experience passion in its rawest form, and ultimately ravished her senses with the kind of emotion that was so dangerous to her heart.

A heart that was falling in love with Ben Cabrera.

Still, she accepted it all, savoring each moment, each feeling that was directly connected to this man.

He continued plunging into her with devastating effect, and incredibly, she could feel another climax rippling through her. A soft, mewling sound escaped her lips as her inner muscles contracted, squeezing hard around his shaft.

Her spontaneous response was all it took to trigger his own orgasm, and he came with a low, hoarse growl that reverberated through her entire body.

Eleven

THREE days later on the following Wednesday, Ben was sitting in the reception area of The Big Event, attempting to keep his focus on the same spy novel he'd been reading when Christine had ambushed him with her plan to seduce him on Sunday night. He kept reading the same paragraph over and over, because his mind just couldn't concentrate on the story line.

From one of the back rooms, he heard Christine and Madison talking, their animated conversation punctuated with an occasional burst of laughter. So far, since the night at the charity event, everything had been quiet in terms of anything happening to Christine, for which Ben was immensely grateful. Then again, he wasn't making it easy on anyone he didn't know to get close to her without a thorough interrogation. He was glued to her side when they were out in public, his instincts razor sharp at all times as he shuffled her from the car to her office, or wherever else she needed to go.

For now, she was keeping her outside errands to a minimum and only attending to things that were urgent. Weeding out the unimportant stuff would help to keep her as secluded as possible for the next week, until the election was finally over.

They spent their days at The Big Event, and went straight home at night and ate dinner at her place. That gave them a whole lot of alone time together, and Christine was quick to make good use of their long evenings—with sex, in lots of adventurous, daring, uninhibited positions. As if her inner seductress had been unleashed during their first time together, she'd become this insatiable, frisky, and zealous lover, eager to make up for lost time and the mediocre experiences that had left her physically unsatisfied in the past.

And even knowing they'd be parting ways in less than a week, he was so damned helpless to resist her sexy, tempting allure. Or anything else about her, for that matter.

The front door to The Big Event swung open, and Ben glanced up to see Kevin—a good friend and coworker at ESS—entering the place. Wearing one of his carefree grins, the other man strolled toward where Ben was sitting on the couch in the reception area with his feet propped up.

"Working hard as always, I see," Kevin wisecracked. "How is it that you always seem to get the cushy jobs?"

"It's all about charm and good looks, both of which you lack," Ben ribbed right back, glad to see a familiar, friendly face to break up the monotony of his day.

Kevin smirked as he dropped into the comfortable chair next to the couch. "I'm sure the hot babe I was with this weekend would disagree."

"It only takes a woman a few drinks to turn what looks like a frog into a prince." Grinning, Ben closed his book and regarded his friend curiously. "Other than busting my chops, what brings you by my neck of the woods?"

Kevin tossed the file folder he'd been holding on to the table in front of Ben. "I had the day off and I thought you might want to take a look at your next assignment, and get familiar with the logistics of the case before starting the job next week."

"Thanks. I appreciate that." Reaching for the folder, Ben flipped it open and quickly scanned the cover sheet, which contained an overview of the assignment. "Surveillance on an insurance fraud case. Those are always a load of fun," he said dryly.

"I'm sure it will be much more exciting than my security detail at the Art Institute watching over the Van Gogh exhibit for a week."

"You might be right about that," Ben said, and chuckled. Closing the folder, he set it aside and reclined back on the couch. "So, what's been going on at the office while I've been out?"

Kevin spent the next forty minutes bringing Ben up to speed on the latest happenings at ESS, including the new cases that had come in during his absence, and ending with an update on Joel Wilde's upcoming nuptials to Lora Marshall, which were set for that weekend. During that time, Madison left the office to run some errands, leaving Christine alone in one of the back rooms.

"It sure is a drag that you won't be able to join us boys for Joel's bachelor party this Thursday night at Leather and Lace," Kevin said, sounding bummed on Ben's behalf.

Surprisingly, Ben didn't even feel a glimmer of disappointment about missing out on an evening of watching various women strip down to skimpy G-strings, and that was enough to tell him just how far, and how deeply, he'd fallen for Christine in such a short span of time.

He tried not to think about that right now, because his feelings for Christine, no matter how strong and intense, made no difference to his future. After this next week, he'd still be spending it alone. "I'm sure you all will have enough fun to make up for me not being there."

"Yeah, you're probably right." Grinning, Kevin sat forward and rubbed his hands together in anticipation. "In fact, I feel so bad about you not being able to go that I'll even buy an extra lap dance in your honor."

Ben laughed. "Now that's a real friend for you."

Kevin held his hands up, palms out. "Hey, you should know by now that I'm the kind of friend who'll take one for the team, if need be." After a moment, he inclined his head. "Are we at least going to see you at the wedding on Saturday?"

He shook his head, his regret genuine. Joel was the first of their tight group of Marine friends to get married, and as much as Ben wanted to be at the wedding, he had a job to do that took precedence. "I really hate to miss it, but I'll still be on this assignment and I can't leave Christine alone."

"Of course you can't," Kevin agreed easily. "So, bring her with you."

Ben sighed. After what happened at the charity event, he was trying to keep her as secluded as possible. That, and taking her to a wedding where he'd be surrounded by his best friends, and Joel's family, seemed way too intimate. "It's not that easy."

"Sure it is," Kevin refuted, completely oblivious to Ben's inner turmoil. "All you have to do is *ask* Christine. I'm betting she'll say yes."

"Ask me what?" Christine asked as she walked into the reception area. Instead of heading toward the front desk to collect the recent mail delivery that had arrived right before Kevin, she veered toward the two of them, curiosity brightening her blue eyes.

Ben groaned beneath his breath, knowing just how persistent she could be. Before he could respond to her question, Kevin stood up and extended his hand toward Christine in greeting.

"Hi there. I'm Kevin," he said, introducing himself. Being the consummate playboy, Kevin's appreciative gaze took in Christine's blond hair, her black sweater, the red pleated skirt that showed way too much leg, and yet another pair of those head-turning high heels of hers. "I work with Ben at ESS."

Christine shook his hand, seemingly unaffected by Kevin's not-so-subtle interest that had Ben clenching his teeth in annoyance. "It's nice to meet one of the guys Ben works with," she replied with a smile, then returned her attention back to Ben. "What did you want to ask me?"

"Nothing," he replied gruffly, and cast a quick keep-your-mouth-shut glare at Kevin—a warning that his friend didn't bother to heed.

"Actually, he wanted to know if you'd accompany him to a wedding this Saturday," Kevin said with a persuasive grin as he sat back down in his chair. "Our good friend, Joel Wilde, is getting married—"

"Jesus, Kevin," Ben said, cutting him off midstream. "I already told you that I'm on assignment, and I'm sure Joel will understand why I'm not there."

Christine placed her hands on her hips, looking very determined—and sexy as hell. "You shouldn't have to miss a friend's wedding because of me. I don't have any plans for this weekend, so there's no reason why the two of us can't go together."

Ben crossed his arms over his chest and narrowed his gaze in a stern attempt to get her to back down. "We already talked about keeping your public appearances to a minimum."

She wasn't the least bit intimidated by his authoritative tone or demeanor. "Where is the wedding and reception being held?" she asked.

"That doesn't matter."

"It's a backyard ceremony at Joel's parents' place," Kevin said, providing the details that Ben was so reluctant to share. "Very small and low-key. Mostly family, a few good friends, and a slew of security agents to keep an eye on you and keep you safe." He winked at Christine, letting her know that she could count on him to watch over her, too.

Christine grinned broadly. "Perfect. We'll be there," she said to Kevin, then turned that sassy, confident attitude Ben's way and pointed her finger at him. "And no arguments from you about it."

And that was the end of that, Ben realized as he watched Christine walk away with a seductive sashay of her hips and her cute little pleated skirt flirting around those smooth thighs of hers. She collected the small box and the rest of the packages and letters that mail delivery had dropped off a while ago, then disappeared into one of the back offices.

Once she was gone, Kevin glanced back at Ben, and didn't bother to contain his amusement. "That one has a lot of spunk. I like her. And obviously, so do you," he added much too perceptively.

"She's a client," Ben replied, his tone brusque and to the point.

Kevin shrugged. "Doesn't change the fact that you have a thing for her."

This time, Ben scowled at his friend—as if that would make a difference to someone he'd fought side by side with in the Iraq War. He knew it would take a helluva lot more than just a glare to make Kevin back off.

"Just leave it alone, okay?" The last thing Ben wanted was to discuss his relationship with Christine with Kevin, or anyone else for that matter—mainly, because there was nothing to talk about. Another week, and this assignment, and his affair with her, would be a thing of the past. End of story.

A shrill, hair-raising shriek, straight out of some horror flick, erupted from one of the back rooms. Even before the bloodcurdling scream had a chance to ebb, Ben was on his feet and racing toward the sound with his weapon drawn, and Kevin right on his heels as backup. He turned the corner to the office, prepared to fire a shot at the person attacking Christine . . . except as his gaze scanned the entire room, he realized that there was no one in there but her. At least that he could see.

Oddly enough, she was kneeling on top of a nearby desk, with her arms wrapped around her stomach. Her whole body shook with fear, her face was drained of color, and she was muttering, "Oh God, oh God, oh God," over and over again.

Still unsure of the situation, he kept his gun firmly in hand. "What happened?" Ben barked out, hating the way his own stomach twisted with that awful sense of foreboding. Something was wrong, and he had no idea what had put that look of terror in her eyes.

"Sssssnakes," she said, her panic a tangible thing as she pointed a trembling finger at the floor behind the desk. "Get them out of here, *please*."

Ben rounded the desk, and sure enough there were three decent-sized snakes slithering across the carpet—all of them black with a yellow stripe and red markings. "What the hell?" he muttered in confusion as he holstered his weapon. Then he caught sight of the open box on the floor. "Did someone send them to you?"

She nodded jerkily. "Why would someone do that?" she asked, her voice breaking on a sob.

Obviously, to scare the crap out of her, Ben thought.

And the ploy had worked. He could only assume that this was yet another threat toward Christine to make Nathan drop out of the upcoming election.

But the more important question was, *who* had sent the box of snakes? Someone who knew she was deathly afraid of them, and as soon as he was able to calm her down, he'd find out that information.

Kevin stepped around him, then crouched down in front of one of the long snakes. "Honey, they're just common garter snakes," he said in an attempt to soothe her fears. "I used to play with these snakes all the time when I was a boy. They're completely harmless and won't hurt you. In fact, they look just as frightened as you are."

"I . . . don't . . . care!" Her voice rose hysterically, pushing her to the verge of hyperventilating. "Get rid of them!"

Realizing just how real Christine's phobia was, Kevin's gaze softened with compassion. "Take her out of here and I'll round up these guys and put them back into the box," he told Ben.

"Thanks." Ben moved out of the way of a snake heading toward his shoe. The last thing he needed was to have the damn thing slither its way up his pant leg. "If you could take them with you when you leave and see if you can trace the return address on the box, I'd appreciate it."

"You got it," Kevin said as he reached for one of the snake's tails, gently lifted it off the ground, then guided the reptile toward the box it had arrived in.

Ben held a hand toward Christine to help her step down from the desk. "Come on, let's go sit in the reception area while Kevin does his thing."

She glanced at the floor skeptically, then shook her head, her loose hair flying wildly around her face. "I . . . can't."

Her fright was so genuine, and he felt something in his

chest tighten with the kind of tenderness he hadn't experienced in a very long time. Understanding that she wasn't quite ready to place her feet on the ground, not when a few of the snakes were still on the loose, he scooped her into his arms and carried her out of the room and to the reception area. He placed her on the couch, and she immediately curled her legs beneath her on the cushion.

She ran still-shaking fingers through her hair. "I can't believe that someone sent me a box of snakes. I must have really pissed someone off," she said in an attempt to make light of the situation.

Ben didn't laugh, because he knew just how serious this newest threat was. "I'm pretty sure that it's all tied into your father's race for governor."

"I don't get it," she said as she smoothed the hem of her skirt over her thighs. "If someone wants my father to drop out of the election, then why did they send *me* the snakes?" She shuddered as she said the word.

Initially, Ben and Nathan had agreed to keep the details of those blackmail letters to themselves, but now that the intimidation tactics were escalating, Ben knew it was time to apprise Christine of the whole truth.

He looked at her, meeting her wide-eyed gaze. "The notes that your father received are demanding that he drop out of the election or risk losing what's most precious to him . . . and that would be you."

"Me?" she asked incredulously. "This person is using me as leverage, and as a target?"

He nodded, glad to see her fear being replaced by a more productive emotion like anger. "It appears that they're letting your father know that they're serious about their threats. How many people know about your aversion to snakes?" he asked, hoping for some kind of insight as to who might be behind this latest hoax.

"Not many, really. It's not something I bring up in casual conversation." She thought for a moment, her expression slowly reflecting a noticeable level of disdain. "The one person who is *very* aware of my fear of snakes is Jason. He was with me when I was bitten by one."

He couldn't even begin to imagine the scenario that had led to such an incident. "How did that happen?"

"Jason was an outdoorsy guy, and about a month after we were engaged, he took me hiking for a day on some trails at a state park in Antioch," she said, a slight frown marring her brow as she remembered, and explained. "We came across a snake, which I almost stepped on because of the way it blended in with the foliage. I thought it was a rattlesnake at first because it was shaking its tail and hissing at us, and of course I freaked out. Jason laughed and told me it was a gopher snake and insisted that it wouldn't hurt me. He thought it was funny that I was so frightened, and he deliberately pushed me toward the snake. I screamed, and the snake struck out and bit my calf." She absently rubbed at that spot on her bare leg.

"Jesus." Ben scrubbed a hand along his jaw as a slow-burning fury coursed through him. Her ex was a certified asshole, and Ben wished he would have beat the shit out of him when he'd had the chance that first ni   t Envy.

"We immediately went to the state park's first-aid station, where they cleaned and bandaged the bite." She crossed her arms over her chest and rubbed at her arms through the sweater she was wearing. "And I was fine since the snake wasn't poisonous, but Jason never let me forget what a big baby I was about the whole thing."

Ben's hands curled into tight fists as anger and contempt for Jason seethed inside him. Luckily, they were interrupted by Kevin, who walked into the reception area, the box of snakes in hand with the top folded down.

"I got all three of them," he said to Ben, keeping his

distance for Christine's sake. "Someone poked some small holes into the box, which is why they survived being mailed. I'll release the snakes somewhere safe and see what I can find out about the return address."

Ben gave his friend a grateful nod. "I appreciate that."

Kevin turned his attention toward Christine. His expression was grim, but his gaze conveyed kindness and sympathy for her situation. "I'm really sorry about all this, and I hope we catch the bastard who sent the damn things."

"Thank you," she said softly. "I know I overreacted back there, and I apologize for being so hysterical about the snakes."

Ben grabbed her hand and gave it a gentle squeeze. "You had good reason," he assured her.

"I'll contact you when I know something," Kevin said, his comment directed at Ben.

"Thanks, man."

Then Kevin grinned at Christine—one of those flirtatious smiles that could persuade a woman to do just about anything he asked. "I'll see you at the wedding on Saturday." Kevin winked at her, then headed out the front door to the truck parked in front of her business.

When Ben glanced back at Christine, she wore a half-smile on her face, the kind that told him that Kevin's charm had woven its spell on yet another female. Ben highly suspected that Kevin had done so to provoke him and force him to face the feelings Ben swore he didn't have for this woman. Judging by the annoyance gripping him, his friend's scheme had worked.

"Back to business," Ben said, redirecting Christine's gaze, and attention, back to him. "Is there anybody else you might have mentioned your fear of snakes to?"

She thought for a moment, and then a startling realization flashed across her features. "Craig knows, and so does Leanne."

Ben frowned. "How would they know about your aversion to snakes?"

"Normally, they wouldn't, but a few months ago Craig asked me to plan and put together a party night at Envy for a client. The guy wanted a *Snakes on a Plane* theme, like the movie, and I just couldn't do it because it entailed hanging rubber snakes from the rafters, and other snake paraphernalia." She visibly shivered. "Even fake snakes are enough to send me into a panic, so I explained to Craig why I couldn't take the job, and he had Leanne do it instead. Of course, she wanted to know why I refused the event, and gloated over the fact that I had to turn it down because I was afraid of snakes."

So, that left them with three key people who knew about Christine's phobia. At the moment, Jason was the most likely suspect for sending the snakes. The man held a huge grudge against Nathan Delacroix for ruining his career, and he obviously still had a lot of unresolved anger toward Christine. Jason had every reason for wanting to sabotage Nathan's campaign, and had no qualms about using Christine's fears to let Delacroix know just how serious he was about threatening his daughter.

Now, Ben just had to find some kind of proof that Jason was behind this latest effort to scare Christine. If Kevin could link her ex to the box of snakes, they'd have what they needed to nail Jason and put an end to the blackmail attempts.

Madison came back from running her errands, and as soon as she took one look at Christine her entire demeanor changed into best friend mode as she sensed that something was wrong. She approached where the two of them were still sitting on the couch, and she dropped her purse onto the empty seat beside the sofa and glanced from Ben to Christine.

"You don't look well. What happened?" Madison asked, her brow creased with concern.

Instead of making Christine relive the entire incident, Ben gave Madison all the gory details. Her friend blanched, obviously not a fan of slithering reptiles, either.

"Good God!" Madison said with a shake of her head as she tried to process it all. "I'm glad you're okay. Why don't you take the rest of the afternoon off? I'll get those party favors ordered for the bridal shower next month and take care of everything else that needs to get done today."

"That would be great." Christine smiled gratefully at her friend. "I think I've had enough excitement for today."

Ben couldn't agree more.

Twelve

CHRISTINE was quiet on the drive home, and Ben cast a few surreptitious glances toward her just to make sure she was doing okay. She looked tired, as though the events of the past week and a half were finally taking a toll on her psyche. Yet despite all she'd been through, she'd remained strong and tough on the outside, but it was how she was doing emotionally and mentally that concerned him the most.

They entered her house from the garage, which connected directly into the kitchen. He punched in the security code to disable the alarm, then locked and secured the door behind them. He switched on the overhead light, headed to the refrigerator, and took a look at what there was to drink.

He glanced back at Christine, who set her purse on the wooden table in the nook area. "Would you like a glass of wine?" If anything, he figured it would help to soothe what was left of her anxiety from the earlier incident with the snakes.

She shook her head and smiled at him. "No, I'm fine."

She really wasn't. He could see the weariness in her eyes, could sense how troubled she truly was by her latest attack, and he wanted to do whatever it took to chase away her distress.

Closing the refrigerator, he walked over to where she was leaning against the counter. Reaching out, he gently brushed a wisp of hair away from her cheek. "Tell you what. Why don't you go and take a hot shower, put on something comfortable like a pair of sweats, and just relax while I make you something to eat?"

"I'm not hungry," she said, her voice suddenly soft and husky. "Actually, there's only one thing I want right now."

He instantly recognized that look in her eyes. The undisguised wanting. The unabashed yearning. The blatant desire. She wore her need for him so openly and honestly, without any pretenses, and that was one of the things he loved about her.

He swallowed hard, refusing to analyze that last thought too closely. Instead, he decided to let Christine lure him in at her own pace, allow her to set the mood, and let tonight be all about her and what she needed the most.

"What is it that you want?" he asked, holding her gaze.

"You. I want *you*, Ben." The intense emotion etched in her features nearly stole his breath. "You're the only stable, reliable thing in my life right now. The one person who understands what I'm going through, and accepts me for who I am—without demands or expectations, or anything else." She stepped in front of him and placed a hand on his chest, right over his rapidly beating heart. "You make me feel sexy, and desirable, and that's what I need right now. I don't want to think about what happened today, or anything else but the two of us and how good you make me feel. Can you do that for me?"

Normally, she was so sultry and seductive, flirtatious even, when it came to wanting him. Now, she was just a woman who needed that physical connection, and that raw, mindless, no-frills pleasure that came with good, hot sex. It was a fascinating side to her that he'd never seen before, and it totally turned him on.

"Yeah, I can do that for you." He'd give her whatever she wanted. Whatever she needed.

"Good," she whispered. Moving closer to him, she slid her hand around to the nape of his neck and brought his mouth down to hers. Her lashes fluttered and her eyes closed; she sighed when his lips touched hers.

He let her control the kiss, which was at first warm and sweet, then gradually grew bolder and more daring, as did her actions. She pushed him up against the wall near the table at the same time she parted her lips and drew him into a deep, tongue-tangling French kiss he returned with an equal amount of heat and aggression.

He didn't bother asking her if she wanted to go into the bedroom to finish this tryst, knowing she'd refuse. Since their first time together, she'd embraced the adventurous side to sex, and he wasn't about to tame anything about the uninhibited, sexually confident woman she was becoming with him. Instead, he followed her lead and enjoyed everything about her enthusiasm and impulsive, sensual energy.

As her mouth continued to plunder his, she impatiently pulled the hem of his chambray shirt from his jeans, quickly unfastened the buttons, then shoved the material over his shoulders and down his arms. The shirt fell to the floor, and she skimmed her hands down his bared chest, until her fingers reached the snap of his jeans.

He caught her wrists to stop her, and a sound of protest rumbled up from her throat. He lifted his head and gave her a slow, sinful smile. "Give me a sec, sweetheart. I've got a loaded weapon on me and we wouldn't want it to accidentally discharge, now would we?" he teased.

She laughed breathlessly, giving him the moment he needed to remove the holster and the gun he kept concealed in the waistband of his pants, and place them safely out of their way. Then, before she had the chance to go back to stripping him out of his jeans, he reached for the hem of her black sweater and pulled it up and over her head.

"You're a little overdressed compared to me," he said, and tossed the garment aside. She was wearing a sexy, lacy, push-up bra that plumped her breasts oh-so-enticingly. He could see her hard, tight nipples through the sheer material, and he wanted to touch and taste and suck them deep into his mouth.

Slipping his fingers beneath the straps of her bra, he dragged them down her arms, his goal to uncover those luscious mounds of flesh so he could feast on them, but she pushed his hands away before he could accomplish his mission.

"Keep your hands to yourself," she said, as she playfully bit his bottom lip and plucked at his rigid nipples with her fingers before heading south. "You're distracting me, and I'm not done with you yet."

"Sorry," he murmured. He leaned back against the wall and relinquished control back to her.

No hardship there, he thought, not when those soft hands of hers caressed their way down his abdomen, released the snap and buttons on the fly of his jeans, then brazenly slid inside his boxer briefs to stroke the hard length of his erection in her palm.

Feeling his cock swell and thicken in her grasp, he groaned deep in his throat.

Emboldened by his response, she leaned into him,

pressing her covered breasts against his chest and nuzzling her warm, damp lips along his neck as her hand delved deeper between his thighs, until she was gently squeezing and fondling his balls.

Jesus. His gut clenched, and unable to help himself, he splayed his palms on the backs of her bare thighs and slid them up beneath the pleated skirt she was still wearing. Reaching the frustrating barrier of her panties, he slipped his fingers beneath the elastic band around her leg so he could cup her smooth, bare ass in his hands.

She released a hot gust of breath in his ear at the same time she grazed the head of his shaft with her thumb. Lust and need ripped through him, and it took every ounce of restraint he possessed not to spread her out on the table behind her and take her hard and fast and deep.

She nibbled on the lobe of his ear, then touched her wet tongue to the sensitive shell. "I want to go down on you," she whispered, repeating those similar words he'd said to her the first night they'd made love. "I want to lick you, and taste you, and take you deep inside my mouth."

Hearing those arousing words spill from her lips was almost enough to make him come right then and there, in the palm of her hand. *"Yes,"* he rasped, barely recognizing that scratchy voice as his own.

She kissed him again, a seductive preliminary of what else she was about to do with that lush, willing mouth of hers . . . and she took her slow, sweet time getting there. She stopped on the way to lave his nipples with her tongue, then kissed and nibbled her way down his taut abdomen, until she was kneeling in front of him. She gripped the waistband of his jeans and briefs and pulled them both down his thighs, completely freeing his throbbing shaft.

She stared at his erection in awe and fascination, her fingers caressing his length with a light brush, a tantalizing tease that had him gritting his teeth. She licked her lips, wetting them, reminding him that she'd never done this before, that he was her *first* when it came to this particular intimacy, and his cock swelled even more at the thought, growing hard to the point of pain.

Leaning forward, she slowly swept her tongue from the base of his shaft all the way up to the sensitive tip, tasting him in what felt like a long, endless, velvet stroke. She lapped the moisture that had seeped from the head, made a soft, eager sound for more, then took him, *all of him*, into the silken heat of that incredibly sweet mouth of hers.

White-hot sensations jolted through him at the erotic sight of her pleasuring him with such unbridled enthusiasm, with such shameless abandon. She pulled him in deep, then withdrew with a delicate swirl of her tongue and just enough suction to make him break out in a cold sweat. She repeated the process, once, twice, wrenching a guttural moan from him as every muscle in his body tensed.

She'd obviously paid closer attention to that porn flick than he'd realized, because he never would have known that she'd never given a guy a blow job before. Her sensual mouth was a man's wet dream come to life, a carnal fantasy that made him weak in the knees. Her lips continued to slide up and down his length, each time taking him a little deeper, sucking him a little harder, stroking him a little faster, and ultimately driving him straight to the edge of insanity.

Knowing he was on the verge of coming, and wanting to be inside of her when he did, he gently grasped her elbows and pulled her back up. Her beautiful face was flushed, her eyes a dark, arousing shade of blue, her soft, smiling mouth reflecting a feminine satisfaction that sent a renewed rush of heat spiraling down to his groin.

With a low, needy growl, he backed her up a few steps, grasped her around the waist, and lifted her so she was sitting on the table behind her. Her eyes widened in surprise at his unexpected and dominant move, and before she could object he dropped his mouth over hers and thrust his tongue deep. In response, she slid her hands up his chest to his shoulders, tracing the sinewy contours of his arms, the biceps that were taut from restraint.

A sense of urgency spurred him on. Pushing his hand beneath her skirt, he latched on to the sides of her panties and impatiently yanked them down and off. Still kissing her, he pressed his hands to her knees, shoved her legs wide apart, and skimmed his hand up her supple thigh.

He wanted to make sure she was ready for him. Wanted to make sure she was just as ramped up as he was. But as he reached the core of her, he realized that her own arousal wasn't an issue. She was already soft and slick with moisture, already turned on from giving him head, and that thought inflamed him even more.

Without hesitation, he pushed a finger deep inside of her and stroked his thumb over her clitoris, and she moaned against his mouth. A second finger followed, and her hips arched against his hand and her legs curled around the backs of his thighs in a desperate attempt to pull him closer. He increased the friction of his fingers— sliding, gliding, stroking, inside and out, letting the pleasure build until her entire body tensed, then shuddered as she climaxed.

He lifted his mouth from hers, breathing hard and fast. "I need a condom," he rasped.

She reached behind her on the table and found her purse. She rummaged through the contents and seconds later handed him a foil packet with an impish grin. "I figured it doesn't hurt to be prepared at all times."

He chuckled as he ripped open the package then rolled

the latex down his straining dick. Pushing his jeans farther down his thighs to get them out of the way, he moved back between her spread legs, fully intending to take her just the way she was on the table.

She stopped him with a splayed hand on his chest, and a sexy gleam in her eyes. "Sit down on the chair behind you."

Giving in to her request, he stepped back and lowered his bare ass to the chair, while she jumped down from the table, hitched her skirt up, then straddled his lap. He guided his cock between her thighs, holding it in place as she slowly, inch by excruciating inch, lowered herself onto his shaft, until he was buried inside of her to the hilt. She grabbed onto the back of the chair, dropped her head back, closed her eyes, and groaned in pure, unadulterated pleasure.

He soughed a ragged breath at the erotic sight of Christine half-naked and so shameless in taking what she wanted. The fit of their bodies was tight and deep, the position leaving both of his hands free to caress and explore while she rode him at her own seductive pace. He pressed his mouth to her neck, scattering damp kisses along her throat and to her chest as he tugged the lacy cups of her bra down, exposing her breasts and the swollen, hard tips that rose up and begged for his touch.

She leaned back, giving him better access to her breasts as he lowered his head and laved a nipple before taking it deep inside his mouth. She clutched at his head and arched, offering herself up to him while gyrating her hips harder, faster, against his.

Despite how close to the edge he was, he tried to hang on just a little bit longer, waiting for her to catch back up. He curled his tongue around her other nipple, giving it equal attention as he sucked and nipped and teased the tender peak. She continued to rock against him, creating the most delicious friction, her insides slick and hot, clenching and unclenching around him until he felt the bubbling heat of his climax fast approaching.

Desperate to come, he lifted his head and fitted his mouth to hers, his tongue claiming hers in a deep, wet kiss. Taking charge, he gripped her hips with his hands, giving him the leverage he needed to meld their bodies in a way that allowed him to pull her down while he thrust into her harder, pumped faster, deeper. The heat inside grew hotter, like liquid fire doused with lust and passion and desire.

He felt her thighs tense against the building pressure of her orgasm, her inner muscles tightening spasmodically around his shaft as she embraced the climax rushing through her. She whimpered against his lips and he finally let go of his restraint, allowing his own scalding release to send him into the realm of complete ecstacy and utter bliss.

When his tremors subsided, he wrapped his arms around her and buried his face against her damp neck, his emotions in a tangled mess. *"Christy,"* he whispered, her name a soft litany as it escaped his lips.

She wound her fingers in his hair and gently tugged his head back, an enchanting smile on her lips. "Did you say what I think you just did?"

She looked so beautiful with her face flushed with satisfaction and her eyes shining with adoration—*for him*, he realized. "I have no idea what you're talking about," he teased.

"Oh, I think you do." She kissed him softly, her lips so sweet and coaxing. "Say it again."

He was beginning to think he couldn't deny this woman anything, and he didn't even try. "Christy," he murmured against the tender press of her mouth on his.

"Mmmm," she purred as she nibbled on his bottom

lip. "I love the way that sounds, so sexy and husky." Sighing contentedly, their bodies still joined, she pulled back so she could look into his eyes. "You can't go back to calling me Christine. You know that, don't you?"

Her sassy, confident tone amused him. "We'll see about that."

She laughed and gave him one last affectionate kiss on his lips. "I could use a nice hot shower. Care to join me?"

"You scrub my back, I scrub yours?" he asked, lifting a brow.

"Yeah, something like that," she said with all kinds of sexy innuendo in her voice, the earlier incident with the snakes now completely forgotten. "I've never had a shower buddy before, and I'm thinking it could be fun."

He grinned, more than willing to give her another first. "Count me in."

CHRISTINE decided that taking a shower with Ben was a luxurious, not-to-be-missed experience. The stall enclosure, finished in beige granite, was roomy enough for two, with dual his-and-hers showerheads on opposite sides of the walls and a small bench seat. She didn't normally use both spigots, but then again, she'd never had company in the shower, either.

At the moment, she was standing face-to-face with Ben, with the spray of water hitting them both in the shoulders and back, massaging muscles and sluicing their skin with moisture. Between slow, lazy kisses, Ben gently scrubbed her chest, arms, and stomach with a soapy bath sponge fragranced with her favorite vanilla body wash, while she ran her palms over his muscled chest. The more sensitive areas of her body were treated to the slick caress of his hands and fingers, and he was very thorough in making sure she was clean everywhere.

She sighed and enjoyed the relaxing, arousing process, knowing she'd get her turn to do the same to him very soon. She kissed him again, then looked into his dark, seductive brown eyes as a slow, contented smile curved her lips.

He returned her smile with one of his own as his hand glided over her breast, spreading the soap over the plump flesh and her tight nipple. "You're looking awfully . . . satisfied."

"For now," she replied impudently, knowing it wouldn't take much for her to want him again, even after those two amazing orgasms she'd had in the kitchen.

He chuckled, the deep, male sound echoing in the cubicle. "You're determined to wear me out, aren't you?"

She lifted a brow. "Are you complaining?"

"Not at all, sweetheart." He crouched down in front of her, letting the water drench him completely as he trailed the sponge down her legs, then back up again, his hands and fingers following the same path. "I aim to please."

Nudging her knees apart, he leaned forward and slid his tongue along the folds of her sex, delving deep. She gasped and tangled her hands in his hair, pulling his mouth closer, opening her legs wider. "And, oh, do you ever please me," she murmured, then groaned as he added just the right amount of pressure and gentle suction to that taut bud of flesh still tender from previous climaxes.

Heat flashed through her, along with a liquid desire that spiraled straight down to her core. Just that quickly, just that effortlessly, he kindled an intense, wanton need within her.

God, she was so easy when it came to this man.

And she embraced every single minute of it.

Ever since her first sexual experience in college, she'd blamed herself for her lack of any physical response when it came to intercourse. She thought things would be different with Jason, but when she'd failed to derive any real pleasure from their quick encounters, it had only reinforced her belief that she was frigid. Then, when she'd discovered the intimacy issues between her mother and father and how it had affected her parents relationship, she'd seriously begun to wonder if she just wasn't destined to follow in her mother's path and would forever settle for mediocre sex.

Now she knew better. Ben had shown her that she wasn't the one with the problem, but that the men in her previous relationships had been all wrong for her when it came to physical intimacy. It was all about compatibility, chemistry, a strong attraction, and equal parts give and take. Especially that. She'd come to learn that her former partners had been much too selfish, and she'd been far too passive.

Not anymore. Now she knew what hot, mind-blowing sex was like, and she'd never settle for less again.

Those thoughts disintegrated from her mind as Ben's mouth continued to tease and torment her, his tongue gliding rhythmically within her soft, swollen flesh along with the trickle of water from their shower. His touch sizzled like lightning over her nerve endings, and when her legs began to tremble with the onset of her climax, he curved his big hands around to the backs of her thighs to help keep her upright as she gave herself over to the lust and ecstacy rushing through her body, pushing her higher, then higher still before letting her free-fall back down to earth.

When she opened her eyes again, it was to find that he'd risen to his full height, his eyes blazing with pure male arrogance and his long, thick erection prodding insistently against her belly. He layered his warm, pliable lips overs hers, and she tasted herself in his sweet, soulful kiss.

When he finally lifted his head moments later, she released a soft, sensual sigh. "Mmmm, that was nice. *Very* nice." Reaching between his thighs, she wrapped her hand around his shaft and nipped at his bottom lip. "I have to say that it's a huge relief to know that I'm nothing like my mother when it comes to sex."

He blinked at her, his expression suddenly wary. "Excuse me?"

Okay, that had just slipped right out without her really thinking through the impact of her comment. Judging by the uncertain look in Ben's eyes he obviously had no desire to think about her mother and sex in the same sentence. Yet, there was just enough curiosity lingering in the depth of his gaze to give her the fortitude she needed to explain, to divulge the secret she'd kept for so long to the one person she trusted the most. *Ben.*

That in itself was a huge revelation, and she exhaled a deep breath to settle her suddenly racing heart. "My mother isn't very fond of sex."

He digested that for a second, then asked, "And you know this how?"

"Because I had the unfortunate luck of overhearing a very heated argument between my mother and father." Needing something to keep her hands busy while she talked, she took the sponge from his hands, reapplied a generous amount of liquid body wash, and began scrubbing his shoulders and arms.

"I'd just graduated from boarding school, and when I moved back home for the summer before starting college, I realized that my parents were sleeping in separate rooms, which I found odd, but of course I didn't say anything." As she ran the sponge over his broad chest, the warm water from his showerhead rinsed the suds down the length of his body.

She concentrated on his taut abdomen, keeping her

gaze cast downward while she took her trip back into the past. "But one day I came home early from visiting a friend and heard loud voices coming from the master bedroom. My mother was accusing my father of having an affair, which he openly admitted to, and I remember him saying to her, 'Can you blame me? You won't let me touch you and we haven't had sex in over fifteen years. There's no intimacy between us, yet you've made it clear that if I file for divorce you'll make sure I can kiss my political career good-bye.' Then he stormed out of the bedroom and literally ran into me. Both my mother and father knew I'd heard everything, and that's when my mother decided I was old enough to know the truth."

Ben tucked his fingers beneath her chin and lifted her gaze back to his. "And that was?"

Touched by the tenderness in Ben's eyes, she went on. "My father left the house and my mother sat me down and told me that three years after I was born she got pregnant again, but five months into the pregnancy she miscarried. She ended up hemorrhaging so badly that she had to have a hysterectomy and couldn't have any more kids. After that, she said she had no interest in sex. She didn't want it, didn't need it, and she had no desire for it. And judging from what I heard, that translated into her not sleeping with my father anymore."

Ben visibly winced. "I can't even imagine. I'm not one to condone affairs outside of a marriage, but a part of me can understand why your father did it."

She nodded in agreement. "Me, too. Physically and emotionally, he wasn't getting what he needed from my mother. So, since my mother didn't want a divorce because she liked the social aspect of being married to a politician, and my father didn't want to tarnish his reputation with a nasty separation, they came to a compromise. They would stay married for my mother's sake and my father's career, and out in public they'd pretend they were a happy couple. Since my mother didn't want sex, she allowed my father to maintain his affair so long as he kept things discreet, which he has."

Ben looked completely taken aback by her parents' elaborate cover-up. "That's quite an arrangement."

"I suppose it works for them for whatever reason, but it's obvious to me that neither one of them is happy. My father has been with the same woman all these years, a paralegal at a law firm here in Chicago who understands the rules, and somehow accepts them to be with my father." She slid the soapy sponge down his thighs, then automatically worked her way back up to his chest. "As for my mother . . . now that I'm no longer the main focus of her life because I have one of my own, she spends her days with her rich, affluent friends, and drinks way too much at night when she's alone. She'd never admit that she has a drinking problem, but even I can see that she's abusing alcohol in order to deal with other issues in her life. I've tried to talk to her about it, and so has my father, but she refuses to get any help."

Reaching out, he tucked a wet strand of hair behind her ear, his touch as gentle and reverent as the look in his eyes. "I'm sorry you've had to deal with all that."

"It's okay." She shrugged as she rinsed the sponge. "I refuse to let my mother's issues become my own. I've learned to stand up to her, and live my life for myself, instead of what *she* envisioned for me. Now turn around so I can scrub your back."

He did as she asked, and just when she thought they'd exhausted the topic of her mother's and father's issues, he said, "I find it interesting that your dad was so angry about Jason's infidelity when he, himself, is having an affair."

Adding more soap to the sponge, she started in on his

shoulders and followed the strong line of his back down to the base of his spine, then up again. "I know it seems hypocritical, but my father has always been very protective of me, and while he knows that having an affair is morally wrong, he made sure I knew that he didn't want his daughter to marry someone that wasn't one hundred percent devoted to her."

"As it should be," Ben replied gruffly, apparently a strong advocate of monogamy.

"My mother, on the other hand, felt quite the opposite about the whole infidelity issue, as you well know," she added wryly. "She told me that was just the way men were and sex wasn't important, that they could get sex anywhere, anytime, and that being a good wife was what mattered in a marriage, especially when you married a prominent man, which she fully expected me to do."

Ben's only reply to that was a grunt of disgust.

She smiled as she stroked the sponge over the tight, muscular curve of his butt and the crevice in between that led to the crux of his thighs. "At the time, a part of me couldn't help but wonder if she was right about sex not being important, and considering how all my sexual experiences up to that point had left me cold, I was beginning to think that I was just like my mother in that regard. That sex would never be that thrilling, exciting encounter I'd always hoped it would be."

He turned back around to look at her, his expression sinfully sexy as water streamed over his shoulders and down his amazing body. "Now you know differently, don't you?"

"Yeah, thanks to you," she said as she trailed a finger down the firm line bisecting his abdomen.

"You've always been a sensual woman, Christy," he said, then grinned much too arrogantly. "It just took the right man to bring it out in you."

She laughed, then sobered, her feelings for Ben suddenly overwhelming her. "I'm glad that man was you."

He grew just as serious. "Me, too."

She stared into his gorgeous eyes, wondering if he felt even a glimmer of the same emotion for her that she did for him. She knew without a doubt he cared about her, but there was something that seemed to hold him back emotionally, and she wondered if it was the loss of his fiancée in the war that kept his feelings for her insulated, unable to give himself to another woman. Then there was the fact that she was just a client he was having an affair with until their time together was over.

Wasn't that exactly what she'd asked for? A hot, temporary tryst that didn't interfere with her newfound independence and freedom. So why was she beginning to want so much more with Ben? And why did her heart feel more involved than she'd ever intended?

Unsure whether or not she was ready to face the answer to those questions when she had no idea where she stood with Ben, she instead gave him a crooked smile and teased, "And here you thought you were the only one with a dysfunctional family and past."

He chuckled at that and ran his thumb over her rigid nipple, making her forget everything but him and the exquisite way he made her feel. "The water is starting to get cool. What do you say we take this party into the bedroom?"

"Mmmm," she purred deep in her throat as she took ahold of his shaft and gave him a slow, firm stroke that made him growl like a tempted tiger. "That all depends on what you have in mind."

"How about making you scream with pleasure?" he suggested, looking completely, deliciously depraved.

Knowing he was a man of his word, Christine wasn't about to turn down his wicked offer. "Oh, yeah, that definitely works for me."

Thirteen

THE shrill sound of the phone ringing woke Ben immediately. His first instinct was to reach for the receiver to answer the call, until he realized that he was in Christine's bed and *she* needed to pick up the phone. A quick glance at the digital clock on her nightstand told him it was almost twenty after eleven in the evening, and calls that came that late at night usually tended to be emergencies of some sort.

Another ring, and Christine stirred beside him and sat up, momentarily disoriented from being in such a deep sleep. She pushed her disheveled hair out of her face, reached for the receiver, and answered the call with a husky, drowsy, "Hello?"

She was quiet for a moment, then replied, "Yes, this is she," and grew silent once again as whoever was on the other end of the line continued to talk.

Concerned and curious, Ben came up on his arm and watched as Christine's expression gradually changed from sleepy to awake as she listened to the one-way conversation and answered with "yes" and "that's correct" and other short sentences that didn't give Ben any clue as to what was going on. The only thing he knew for certain was that the person she was speaking to wasn't family, which alleviated some of his worry.

Finally, she hung up the phone, switched on the bedside light, and turned toward him with a frown creasing her brows and a stunned look on her face. "Wow," she said with a shake of her head.

As far as explanations went, it didn't give him much to go on. "Is everything okay?" he prompted.

She shivered, and realizing that the upper half of her body was naked, she pulled the covers up to her chest. "You're not going to believe this. That was the Chicago P.D. and they have Jason in custody."

"Really?" he asked, equally surprised, then wondered if Christine had been Jason's "one call" that he'd most likely been granted. "Why did they call you?"

"A few hours ago one of the girls that I'm friendly with at the coffee shop across from The Big Event witnessed someone spray painting profanities on the front windows of the business and called the cops," she told him. "They showed up, caught him in the act, and arrested him for being drunk and disorderly, as well as for vandalism. When they got him back to the station and booked him, they saw that I had a restraining order against Jason, and cross-referenced that to me also being the owner of The Big Event."

The guy was beginning to be a real pain in the ass, Ben thought, and wondered if Jason's actions were in any way related to the snakes that had been sent the day before, or the blackmail attempts against Nathan Delacroix. It all tied together and made sense, with Christine's ex-fiancé having the strongest motivation for terrorizing her, but so

far there was no concrete evidence that Jason was responsible for anything that had happened so far.

He released a frustrated sigh. "So, that was a courtesy
call, so to speak."

She nodded. "Yes, which I appreciate. At least I know
what to expect when I get to the office in the morning. I'll
have to get someone out right away to take care of the
spray paint on the windows."

"I'll take care of that for you," he said, alleviating that
burden. It was just a matter of using a razor and some
acetone to remove the offensive words, and that would
give him something to do tomorrow. "Did they say what
would happen with Jason?"

"The officer said he'll most likely be arraigned in the
morning and released on bail if he can get it posted." She
sighed heavily. "I just wish he'd leave me alone and get
on with his life."

That was easier said than done, Ben suspected. "He's
obviously still bitter about a lot of things and blames you
for his downfall. The guy needs help with his anger and
drinking problems."

"I can't argue with you there." She flopped back on her
pillow and stared at the ceiling. "Tomorrow is certainly
going to be a fun-filled day," she said, an edge of sarcasm
to her voice. "If this vandalism isn't enough to deal with, I
have a lunch date with my mother."

And she didn't sound happy about it, either. Neither
was he, considering he'd be subjected to Audrey's impe-
rious attitude, as well. "I didn't know you were meeting
your mother for lunch."

Christine rolled her head on the pillow so she could look
at him. "She called me today at the office, right before the
snake incident, and she said we needed to 'do lunch,' which
translates into she needs to talk to me about something."

"She couldn't do it over the phone?"

She rolled her eyes. "Oh, she could, but she likes the whole 'see and be seen' aspect of lunch in a nice, expensive restaurant."

"Okay, then we'll go and 'see and be seen,' " he said, his teasing comment coaxing a smile out of her.

Lifting a hand, she cupped his cheek in her palm, her thumb scratching over the light stubble on his jaw. "Ahhh, you're such a trouper."

"You forget, as your bodyguard, I don't have much of a choice."

She laughed. "Regardless, I appreciate the buffer. Having you there will hopefully make the lunch, and the conversation, more pleasant."

Ben wasn't sure about that, but kept the comment to himself as she switched off the light.

He lay back down, and she automatically snuggled up against his side, her cheek resting on his chest and one arm slung across his stomach. It had been forever since he'd actually *slept* with a woman all night long, let alone cuddled with one. But after living a solitary life for so long, he couldn't deny that he liked the intimacy of holding Christine close throughout the night, and waking up to her in the morning.

Unfortunately, he knew better than to get used to the feeling. By this same time next week, he'd be back in his own bed in his stark apartment. Alone once again.

AT noon the next day, Ben and Christine walked into The Capital Grille and were led toward a private area of the restaurant where Audrey Delacroix was already seated and had already consumed half a glass of wine. Instead of wearing his normal jeans and shirt, today Ben had opted for a pair of nice brown trousers and a collared shirt. Considering that most everyone was decked out in business attire, he was glad that he'd dressed up for the occasion.

The host stopped at Audrey's table, and Ben waited while Christine greeted her mother and bent down to give her a kiss on the cheek before saying hello himself.

"Good afternoon, Mrs. Delacroix," he said politely.

She didn't even glance his way. "Hello." Her tone was rigid and forced, as she'd replied only because etiquette demanded she do so.

The host pulled out a chair for Christine, and once she was seated, Ben moved to sit down beside her.

"You'll be sitting with Dominic over in the other room." She waved a dismissive hand in that direction, still not meeting his gaze, making him feel once again like the lowly hired help.

Christine leaned forward in her seat and shot Audrey a mortified look. *"Mother!"*

"It's okay." Ben settled a hand on Christine's shoulder to reassure her. "As long as I can see you at all times, I don't have a problem with that."

Christine glanced up at him apologetically, and he let her know with an easygoing smile that she had absolutely nothing to be sorry for. It wasn't her fault that her mother felt compelled to be so rude to him, or anyone else that didn't meet her prominent criteria.

So much for providing a buffer for Christine, Ben thought as he followed the host to a table in the adjoining room, where he said hello and shook hands with Audrey's security agent, Dominic, before sitting down. The two of them were seated in a way that they could see and watch Audrey and Christine, but were far enough away not to be associated with them while they ate lunch.

Ben went ahead and ordered the grilled swordfish with lemon herb butter, along with a soda, and while their entrees were being prepared he conversed with Dominic, who Ben knew from working as a part-time bodyguard for Nathan. The other man used to be an undercover agent before going into the security business, so between the two of them they had plenty to talk about to keep them occupied during lunch.

Over the next hour, while Ben enjoyed his tender, flavorful swordfish and kept up a steady stream of conversation with Dominic, he also watched Christine and Audrey interact and came to the conclusion that the other woman was as cold as ice. After learning from Christine just how glacial Audrey actually was, physically and emotionally, he couldn't help but feel sorry for her being so caustic all the time—and wanting everyone else around her to be just as miserable.

He also found it interesting that Audrey never smiled at Christine, and she never displayed any warmth or outward affection for her only child. She sat in her chair with her back straight and her hands folded in her lap, immaculately dressed in her long-sleeved silk top and not a blond hair out of place as she finished off four full glasses of wine.

They could have been two strangers having a meal together, if not for the myriad emotions he witnessed passing over Christine's features that told him their conversation was very personal. He was seated too far away to hear what they were discussing, but whatever was on Audrey's mind caused a look of disdain to pinch her features, and made Christine increasingly upset—to the point that she cut the lunch short and didn't even finish her salad. Even more telling was the fact that Christine pushed back her chair and left her furious-looking mother sitting at the table by herself as she headed straight for him in the other room.

She stopped at his table and managed a sweet and genuine hello to Dominic before turning to Ben. She glanced from his empty plate to his face. "I'm glad to see you at least enjoyed *your* meal," she said pointedly, making it clear that her lunch hadn't settled as well as his had. "I'm ready to go."

Oh, boy. Christine looked like a woman scorned, and Ben decided it wasn't a pretty sight.

Since the meal was expensed to the Delacroix account and he didn't have to wait for a check, Ben scooted back his chair and escorted Christine out of the restaurant. The valet brought her Lexus around to the carport, and after opening the passenger side door for her, he slid behind the wheel and directed the vehicle back to The Big Event.

He spent the first half of the drive watching Christine fume and stew as she stared out the side window, waiting patiently for her to either tell him what was wrong, or explode from the tension building within her.

When she did neither, he decided to see what he could wheedle out of her. "What happened back there at the restaurant with your mother?"

"Nothing," she replied succinctly.

He wanted to laugh, but opted for another form of humor instead. "The food was that bad, huh? Or was it the service? That waiter did seem a little slow getting your salad to the table."

She shot him a bewildered look. "*What* are you talking about?"

After making a left-hand turn on the street where her business was located, he shrugged casually. "Something has you a little irked. I figured if it wasn't something your mother said or did, it had to be something related to your lunch."

She sighed, releasing some of the stiffness from her shoulders, as well as softening the taut line of her lips. "The lunch was fine. My mother, however, was in rare form today."

He parked the car in Christine's designated spot behind the business, cut the engine, but didn't make any move to get out of the vehicle. Instead, he turned toward her and rested his arm along the back of her seat.

"Care to talk about it?" he asked gently. Honestly, he was damn curious what had gone on between the two women to make a normally carefree and cheerful Christine so antagonized.

She released a long "arrgghhh!" of frustration that seemed to deflate most of her anger, then met his gaze, her expression taking on that impish quality he adored. "Sorry, I just had to let that out."

He grinned. "I completely understand." He grew silent again, leaving the decision to talk up to her. She was quiet for so long, he almost thought that she was going to keep everything to herself.

But then she finally spoke. "My mother received a phone call from one of her friends who told her that she'd heard that I was dating my bodyguard. So, she asked me if it was true."

Ben winced, belatedly realizing how Christine's little scheme had come around to bite her in the butt as far as her mother was concerned. No doubt, Audrey hadn't been pleased to hear that her daughter might be dating someone far beneath their social stature. Not when Audrey expected far better for Christine—even if that meant marrying a man who didn't love and cherish her, as Jason clearly had not.

He wrapped a silky strand of her hair around his finger, feeling just ensnared by the woman herself. "What did you tell your mother?"

"That my personal life was no longer any of her business," she said with a mutinous lift of her chin. "But she wouldn't leave it alone and kept pushing for an answer, so I told her the truth, that I *was* dating you, and it shouldn't be an issue with her since I'm an adult, I'm single, and it wasn't her choice to make. And that, of course, led to a heated argument about . . ."

She let the rest of her sentence trail off as she shook her head and looked away, giving Ben the distinct feeling that the unpleasant verbal exchange had been all about him, and not in a positive way, either. And knowing that made him all the more aware of the many differences between them when it came to living in the Delacroix's world of wealth, politics, and high-society precedence.

Christine rubbed her fingers across her forehead. "Anyway, she made me so mad that I had to put an end to the lunch or I knew I'd end up making a scene she wouldn't have appreciated."

With his fingers still tangled in her hair, he caressed his thumb along her soft cheek. "Well, in a few more days, she'll have nothing to worry about." The election was in five days, and once that was over and Christine's safety was secured, they'd revert back to being friends and acquaintances, which would undoubtedly thrill her mother.

Christine's cell phone rang, interrupting the moment between them. She dug into her purse for the unit, checked the caller ID, and grimaced. "It's Craig. He's been trying to get a hold of me for the past two days to talk about something regarding my party next week. I should take his call."

She answered the phone, and Ben listened as she discussed a few last party details with Craig. As much as he despised the man for various reasons, Ben was beginning to think that he was fairly harmless—especially in comparison to Jason, whose bitter antics were starting to get more personal and public. Craig definitely liked Christine and had no qualms about making his attraction known, and even though those intimate feelings weren't

reciprocated, there was no crime in a man being interested in a woman.

Even if Ben didn't like it one bit.

AFTER the crazy, stressful week Christine'd had, Ben
was glad that she'd agreed to accompany him to Joel and
Lora's wedding—a small, casual affair equivalent to a
warm, family gathering that everyone felt a part of. The
Saturday outing provided them both with the much-
needed opportunity to get out of the house, and gave
Christine a welcome distraction from her mother's silent
treatment after their lunch a few days ago, as well as the
fact that Jason was out on bail and her father had received
yet another threat to drop out of the upcoming election.

It was a perfect cool and sunny day for an afternoon,
outdoor wedding. The guests sat on padded folding chairs
as Joel and Lora stood beneath an archway decorated
with bright, colorful flowers and exchanged their vows in
front of family and friends. Their expressions were full
of the kind of love and adoration a person couldn't help
but envy, and as Ben cast a quick glance at Christine sitting beside him, he could see that she was just as caught
up in the ceremony, and the genuine emotion between the
couple, as most of the women there were.

Joel and Lora were flanked by Lora's best friend, Syd-
ney, who was standing in as the bridesmaid, and Lora's
brother, Zach, as the best man. Considering everything
that Zach Marshall had been through—in the Iraq War
and then dealing with the aftermath by burying his
painful past with addictions to gambling and alcohol that
nearly ruined his life—he finally looked clean and sober.
Zach had spent a good amount of time in rehab and was
still working through his personal demons, but thanks
to Joel and Lora's unwavering support, as well as his

becoming a security agent at ESS, which offered him a strong comradery with his ex-Marine buddies, the man was finally making a stable life for himself. And because of that, Ben was very happy for Zach.

As the minister read an intimate poem to the guests that spoke about love and friendship and the kind of eternal promises made between a husband and wife, Ben felt Christine's hand slide into his, gentle and warm. Palm to palm, their fingers intertwined, and something within Ben filled with a longing so strong, it nearly overwhelmed him. It amazed him that this woman, who was no doubt used to elaborate weddings, was so touched by such a simple ceremony.

Then the minister introduced Lora and Joel as a married couple, and the moment between Ben and Christine dissipated as they stood up with the rest of the guests and cheered as Joel kissed his blushing bride with enthusiasm.

A casual reception followed in the backyard, with a buffet of food, upbeat music for dancing, and an abundance of babies and toddlers courtesy of all the Wilde family members that had gotten married over the past few years. With his hand resting on the base of Christine's spine, he led her toward where Joel and Lora were standing off to the side, mingling with guests.

As soon as Ben reached Joel, he shook the other man's hand and gave him a firm slap on the back. "Congratulations, Wilde Man," he said, then turned his attention to Lora, who was wearing a flowing white wedding dress and a very happy smile. "You look absolutely beautiful." He kissed her on the cheek. "I'm glad to see that Joel found someone who can keep him in line."

"All that military training has come in handy." Lora's eyes sparkled with female humor as she hooked her arm through her groom's. "He knows how to take orders very well."

Joel rolled his eyes, silently conceding to his wife's comment. Ben laughed, then went on to introduce the woman by his side. "I'd like you both to meet Christy."

Lora's eyes widened in delight. "Oh, you brought a date!"

She seemed so excited, mainly because Lora had spent the past year trying to find a suitable woman for him. He almost hated to burst her bubble. "Actually, she's a current client of ESS." Ben explained her relation to Nathan Delacroix, which garnered Christine a round of promises from the newly married couple to vote for the man.

"It's a pleasure to meet both of you," Christine said sincerely. "It was a beautiful ceremony."

"Thank you." Lora beamed. "I hope you two plan to stay awhile and enjoy the reception."

"Absolutely," Ben replied. "We were just heading over to the buffet for something to eat."

A young boy ran by them, but before he could pass Joel, the other man reached out and caught him up in his arms. Ben recognized the cute, energetic four-year-old as Cody, Steve Wilde's son.

"Whoa, partner!" Joel exclaimed in an animated voice. "Where do you think you're going at the speed of light?"

Cody squirmed in his embrace and pointed to a table near the buffet. "I wanna see the cake!"

Joel glanced in that direction. The confection the boy was interested in was a double-tiered chocolate-frosted cake that looked rich and delicious. "Just keep your fingers out of it, okay?"

The boy grinned impishly. " 'Kay!" As soon as Joel set him back down, Cody took off once again, with another one of Joel's little relatives following behind to see the cake, too.

Joel chuckled and shook his head. "Talk about double trouble."

"And you and your two brothers weren't triple trouble at that age?" Ben asked, certain the Wilde siblings had been an equal handful. "Besides, I'm sure you and Lora will be adding to the brood in a year or so."

"I'm looking forward to it," Lora chimed in. "Maybe a little girl who'll wrap Joel around her finger."

A half-grin curved Joel's lips as he met Lora's gaze. "Oh, man, you know I won't stand a chance against that."

She gently touched his cheek, the abundance of love between them so evident. "That's what I'm counting on."

The photographer came up to the new couple and pulled Joel and Lora away for some wedding photos with Joel's parents. Ben guided Christine toward the patio area where the food was located, and introduced her to a few other people on the way. They said a quick hello to Scott and Ashley, whom Christine had met at the charity event the previous weekend, and Adrian— one of Joel's cousins– and his wife, Chayse, stopped to chat with them, too.

After loading their plates with finger sandwiches, potato salad, fruit, and a few other appetizers, then picking up drinks at the bar, they made their way back to a table where Ben's buddies and coworkers, Kevin, Jon, and Zach, were sitting with their own meals. Christine sat down next to Kevin, the most familiar face of the group, and Ben took the chair next to her.

After introducing her to Jon and Zach, Kevin leaned toward her and said with a charming smile, "I think it's only fair that I should warn you that I wanted you here today so I could steal you away from Ben."

Christine suppressed a grin, but couldn't disguise the amusement dancing in her eyes. "A man with ulterior motives, huh?"

"You bet. Especially when it comes to beautiful women." Kevin winked at her.

"Be careful," Jon piped in from across the table. "Kevin's a player."

The other man snorted in reply. "Oh, and you're not?"

"I'm just not so obvious about it," Jon said with a smug look, and took a big bite of his potato salad.

Kevin dismissed his comment with a wave of his hand. "Yeah, whatever, Jon Boy."

Zach, the quiet one of the group, finally spoke up. "Geez, do you guys *ever* quit?"

"No." Kevin and Jon answered at the same time.

Christine laughed, then took a sip of her champagne. "You all sound like you could be brothers. Argumentative and very competitive."

"We're as close to being brothers as you can get," Ben said, knowing everyone else at the table felt the same exact way.

"Hey, Zach," Ben said, garnering the other man's attention. "How's things going for you at ESS?" He'd only been with the firm for a few months and hadn't been assigned any outside jobs yet. They all wanted to be sure that Zach would be ready, mentally and emotionally, to tackle the stress and pressures of an actual security job.

Zach finished taking a drink of his soda—his choice of beverage since alcohol was off-limits for him—then shrugged. "I'm becoming quite the computer geek," he said, a slight bit of humor in his tone as he referred to his current office position of using the computer and Internet to research specific information on some of their cases. "By the way, that reminds me. Kevin gave me that return address on the box that was delivered to Christine's office earlier this week, and it led to a dead end."

Ben noticed that Zach's comment had piqued Christine's curiosity, as well. "What do you mean?"

"The address led to one of those postal stores where you

can rent a postbox for a fee." Finished eating, Zach pushed his empty plate aside. "Except whoever sent the package just used the postal store as a bogus return address, since the box number he listed didn't even exist."

Ben wasn't surprised that the person had covered their tracks. "Thanks for checking it out. We have a pretty good idea who sent the snakes. It would have just been nice to get some solid evidence so we could press charges against the guy."

For the next half an hour, the conversation turned to more inconsequential topics that led to either Kevin and Jon ribbing one another, or Kevin flirting with Christine— no doubt to annoy Ben. There was a whole lot of laughter at their table, and once the DJ started spinning fun, upbeat tunes and encouraged guests to get up and dance, Kevin didn't hesitate to do so.

He stood up and grinned at Christine as Pink's "Get the Party Started" blasted from the speakers. "Since all the women here today are either married, engaged, or in a serious relationship, and you're not," he added, just to annoy Ben, "how about you and I go and dance?"

Kevin held his hand out to Christine, and she let him pull her up from her chair. "I'd love to dance," she said, and let him lead her toward the far end of the patio that had been designated as the dance floor.

Ben watched the two of them go, his gaze drawn to Christine's slender backside and the way her long-sleeved knit dress clung to all her soft curves. The dress was simple in design, but it was the jewel-toned purple hue of the material that made her look so vibrant, and those high heels that made her legs look so damned long and sexy.

"Are you going to let him make a move on your date like that?" Jon asked, clearly hoping for a tussle between the two men.

"Christy is free to dance with whoever she'd like."

Christy. Now the name slipped from his lips much too easily. Much too intimately. And that so was not a good thing.

"Then why are you glaring at Kevin?" Zach asked.

Ben didn't bother denying the truth. "Because he's deliberately provoking me and he knows it."

Jon chuckled much too knowingly. "You wouldn't feel provoked if you didn't have a thing for her, now would you?"

Ben transferred his dark scowl to Jon. "Shut up, already, will ya?"

"Sure thing, Benjamin." Grinning, and obviously done tormenting him, Jon stood up. "I think I'll go and put in a request with the DJ. 'Great Balls of Fire' ought to do it."

It was one of those songs they'd sang together in the military during down time when they were trying to find things to amuse themselves, and Ben knew it would bring back a lot of fun memories for all of them.

"While you're there, make a request for me, too," Ben said. "Garth Brooks's 'Friends in Low Places.' "

Jon laughed. "You got it."

Ben nursed the last of his beer and returned his attention to Christine, who was having a great time out on the dance floor with Kevin, and a lot of the other guests. After putting in a few song requests, Jon joined the party revelers and did his best to try to steal Christine from Kevin so he'd have a dance partner, too.

He couldn't help but notice how well she fit in with everyone. She was classy, yet so approachable. So likeable and accepting. Compared to her mother, a person would never have known that Christine came from a very prominent, wealthy family.

Nearly a dozen songs later, and after being dipped, twirled, and generally worn out from the energetic dances, Christine returned to the table looking happy and relaxed. She sat down next to him, her face flushed as she tried to catch her breath.

She swiped away a damp strand of hair clinging to her cheek, her eyes a bright, sparkling shade of blue. "Those two sure know how to wear a girl out."

Since the two of them were currently alone at the table, Ben decided to stake his claim where he could. He placed a hand on her bare knee beneath the table, and leaned in close. "Lucky for me, I know how to wear you out in the way that matters most."

"Mmmm." She touched her fingers beneath his chin, her gaze brimming with desire and heat—all for him. "That you do. And you don't have to worry, I have plenty of energy left for later."

"Christine?"

Both Ben and Christine turned at the sound of a female voice calling her name. Ben instantly recognized Mia Wilde with her unique gray-silver eyes, who was holding a bundled-up baby in her arms as she approached.

"You're Christine Delacroix, the one who owns The Big Event, right?" she asked, smiling warmly as she extended her hand toward Christine. "I'm Mia Wilde."

"Oh!" Christine's eyes widened with genuine delight as she shook the other woman's hand. "After talking on the phone so many times, it's a pleasure to finally meet you in person. This gives me the opportunity to thank you face-to-face for your donation to the Children's AIDS Foundation auction. And call me Christy, please."

"I was happy to be a part of the charity auction," Mia said as she shifted the squirming baby in her arms. "The high bidder for the stained glass design contacted me this week, so I'll be starting their design pretty soon."

"That's wonderful." Christine smiled at the little dark-haired baby peeking from the pink blanket she was wrapped up in. "And who is that?"

Mia beamed like the proud new mother she was. "This is my three-month-old daughter, Sophie, the latest addition to the ever-growing Wilde family."

"She's beautiful," Christine said softly. "Do you mind if I hold her?"

"Are you kidding me?" Mia laughed and happily handed over the little girl. "I'd love the break. She's like carrying around a thirteen-pound weight."

Christine gazed down at the cherubic face staring back up at her. "She's a very lucky girl to be surrounded by so much family."

"Yes, though having a very large family can be a curse, too," Mia said wryly, and Ben knew she was referring to her very overprotective brothers and cousins. "But mostly it is a blessing."

"Hey, I've been looking for you." Cameron, Mia's husband, came up behind her and wrapped his arms around her waist. "The DJ is playing our song."

Mia tipped her head and listened to the tune, then frowned at Cameron. "This isn't our song. I don't even think we *have* a song."

"Then consider this one it." He gave her an irresistible grin. "It's a slow song, someone else is holding the baby, and I want to dance with my wife."

Christine waved her free hand at the couple. "Go right ahead. I'll watch Sophie."

"Are you sure?" Mia asked, though it was clear to see that she'd welcome the opportunity to enjoy a slow dance with her husband.

"I'm absolutely sure," Christine said, encouraging her to go. "I love babies and she's very sweet."

"Come on, let's go before she realizes that Sophie is just fooling her." Cameron grabbed Mia's hand and pulled her toward the patio.

"She *is* a good baby," Mia said from over her shoulder as her husband dragged her away.

Once the couple was gone, Christine pulled the blanket a bit looser to see more of the baby. Sophie was wearing a frilly pink dress for the occasion of seeing her uncle Joel get married, and her little arms flailed wildly as they were freed from the covers. Christine laughed and pressed her pinky into the baby's palm, and Sophie latched on to the finger and cooed.

An affectionate smile curved Christine's lips as she glanced up at him. "Would you like to hold her?"

Ben held up both of his hands, not sure how to handle such a little wriggling thing like Sophie. "No, it's okay. You're doing a great job with her."

Christine went back to talking to the baby in a low, gentle tone, and the infant girl stared up at her in mesmerized awe. There was something about seeing Christine like this—the tender look on her face, the maternal, nurturing instincts in play—that struck a chord deep inside of Ben.

Marriage. Family. Babies. A sense of complete and utter contentment. He'd almost had that once with Kim. They'd talked about all those things, along with envisioning a future that had seemed so hopeful and promising, and filled with all the things that had been missing from his own life for so long.

Those bright, aspiring dreams had died with Kim. And so had a big part of him. His heart and emotions hadn't been the same since that fateful day in Iraq when he'd held his dying fiancee in his arms.

But as he watched Christine bond with the tiny baby in her arms, he knew that someday, when the right person came along, this woman would make some lucky guy a wonderful wife and mother.

Unfortunately, that man wouldn't be him.

Fourteen

HOURS later, Ben followed Christine into her house and switched on the light in the living room. She turned around to face him, her high-heeled shoes dangling from her fingertips, and a soft, contented smile on her lips.

"I really had a nice time today . . . and tonight," she added, since the reception and celebration had lasted until nearly ten.

"So did Jon and Kevin," he replied good-naturedly as he slipped his hands into his pants' pockets. "They sure kept you busy out on the dance floor."

She laughed and curled her bare toes into the carpet. "They're nice guys. All of them. And they don't do a thing for me," she assured him. Closing the distance between the two of them, she placed a hand on his chest, her eyes an extraordinary shade of blue. "Except they do make me laugh. A lot. And that's not a bad thing considering my life lately."

"I definitely agree with that."

"I hope you don't mind that I invited them to my

birthday party at Envy next week. They'll definitely keep the guests entertained."

He grinned. "I can't argue with that."

She tipped her head, causing her tousled hair to fall to one side. "How about you? Did you have a good time?"

"Yeah, I did." He'd spent most of the day watching Christine—mingling with his friends, interacting with the guests, holding Mia's daughter, Sophie. He thought about those high heels she'd worn for hours, her energy out on the dance floor, and the few yawns she'd tried to hide on the drive home, and knew she had to be worn out. "You must be exhausted."

"My feet are a bit sore, but I'm actually wide awake." She started toward her bedroom, then stopped and looked over her shoulder at him, a come-hither look in her eyes. "I need a little help getting my dress off. Care to help?"

Since the dress was made of a stretchy kind of material, and there was no zipper, taking it off was just a matter of pulling it over her head—and that certainly didn't require his assistance. But her sweet smile was filled with the kind of pure, shameless temptation that made him weak in the knees and unable to resist anything about her. Knowing he'd be a fool to refuse since he only had a few more nights to spend with her, he took Christine's hand and followed her back to her master bedroom.

After today, his emotions felt as though they were in an upheaval that he couldn't quite sort out. He knew and understood that their affair was a temporary deal—she'd made that clear from the beginning. Having just broken off an engagement and still dealing with the wrath of her mother, Christine wasn't looking for anything permanent. And now, she was getting a taste for being independent and out from under Audrey's thumb, and he knew she loved that newfound freedom.

As for him, he'd never fit into Christine's life long-term,

at least not comfortably considering their opposite lifestyles. Hell, he didn't even know if he could give her everything she deserved emotionally from a relationship— he wasn't sure he had it in him anymore. Between the wrenching realization that his mother had walked out on him when he was a boy, never to be heard from again, to losing Kim and even other comrades he'd befriended in the war, he felt all tapped out.

But he couldn't deny that he wanted her. Desired her. And ultimately, he cared deeply for her, and those were key elements when it came to being with Christine. The bedroom was the one place they were equal and com- pletely compatible, in every way. It was their own private world where no one existed but the two of them and a wealth of passion.

When they reached her room, she tossed her shoes aside and turned back toward him. With only the soft glow of the nightstand light illuminating them, she met his gaze and silently began unbuttoning his shirt. Need- ing to taste her, he delved his fingers into her hair and tipped her head back as he lowered his head until their lips meshed and their tongues mated.

Slowly, leisurely, they undressed one another. Cloth- ing fell to the floor in a haphazard mess, until they were both naked. Between soft, soulful kisses, hands wan- dered, touched and caressed bare flesh, increasing the level of arousal simmering between them. His fingers glided across her breasts, trailed down her belly, and eventually found their way between her supple thighs, where she was so soft and slick and sensitive. He stroked her, and she gasped into his mouth . . . moaned her ap- proval as he brought her close to orgasm . . . then she made a small, mewling sound of protest when he stopped short of giving her what her body ached for.

Needing to be inside of her when she climaxed, and

wanting to watch her expression as she came for him, he ended the kiss, pushed her down onto the bed, and settled to his knees between her spread legs. He glided his palms down her quivering thighs, and slid the pads of his thumbs through her weeping flesh.

Her hands fisted into the covers, and her hips moved against the feather-light touch of his fingers. "Stop teasing me," she said, half-laughing.

He grinned, loving how playful she could be, even when she was so aroused. As for him, his erection jutted out from his groin, hot and hard, more than ready to give her what she wanted.

"I need a condom," he said, and started to reach toward the nightstand, where she kept a supply.

She grabbed his arm, stopping him before he could pull the drawer open and retrieve one of the foil packets. "Not tonight."

He pulled back and stared down at her, confused. "What do you mean?"

"I'm on the pill," she said, and bit on her lower lip with a bit of uncertainty, and a whole lot of vulnerability that told Ben just how much she trusted him. "I know that using a condom is the safe way to go, but I'm good healthwise."

"Me, too," he said, and moved back to the spot between her legs, his gaze taking in the way she was laid out before him, his for the taking. "Are you sure about this?"

She nodded. "More sure than I've been about anything in a very long time. I want to feel you inside of me, *all* of you, without a condom to take away any of the sensation."

The thought of having all that wet heat wrapped around his cock, with absolutely nothing between them, made him shudder with anticipation, lust, and desire. Crawling up and over her body, he pushed her thighs farther apart as his hips nestled intimately against hers, and the tip of his shaft probed at her damp entrance.

When she realized what he intended, she splayed a hand on his chest to keep him from making that final downward thrust into her. "What are you doing?" she asked, her eyes wide.

He smiled. "I'm making love to you." The words slipped out of him without censor, but they felt more right than wrong.

She appeared startled for a moment because they'd always referred to what was between them as *sex*, but then she quickly recovered. "No missionary position, remember?"

"Yeah, I remember." He dropped a kiss on her nose, then took both of her hands, entwined their fingers, and pinned them next to her head so she couldn't use them at all. So that she'd have no choice but to just feel. "But sometimes, the missionary position can be good," he murmured huskily. "*Very* good."

Her lashes fell to half-mast, and her body softened beneath his. "Show me," she whispered.

He lowered himself completely over her, aligning them from chest to thighs. His jaw tensed as he slowly slid inside of her, then leisurely pulled out again, until just the head of his penis filled her. He entered her once more, this time all the way to the base of his shaft, and moaned as the slick friction dragging along his bare cock provided the most exquisite sensation—one that threatened to make him come way too quickly if he wasn't careful.

He dropped his head to the crook of her neck, his breath dampening her skin, and for the longest time he didn't move, enjoying the warmth surrounding him.

She squirmed restlessly, impatiently, beneath him, a silent plea for him to move.

"Wrap your legs around my waist, Christy," he rasped into her ear.

She did as he asked, and he groaned when he felt her soft, slender thighs hugging his hips. The intimate position lifted her pelvis higher, allowed for a deeper penetration that made her gasp. He tried to savor everything about being inside of her this way, but the temptation was just too great, and when she arched beneath him so that he rubbed against her clitoris, which heightened her pleasure, he couldn't stop the instinctive need to push harder, deeper. He eased back, almost to the point of withdrawal, then tunneled his way back inside with a purposeful stroke.

Their rhythm was slow at first, and he concentrated on the scent of her hair, the heated vanilla fragrance still clinging to her skin, the feel of her fingers curling tight against his. Anything but the building, pulsing pressure in his groin.

Hungry for the taste of her, he lowered his mouth to hers and kissed her with aggression and greed. God, she was so sweet, he thought. So beautiful, and generous, and responsive. He rolled his hips hard against hers, then plunged faster, then faster still, until she was moaning beneath the crush of his lips and he knew she was close to climaxing.

He lifted his head, and as he continued to drive into her tight, moist flesh, he watched her. Pleasure suffused her expression and she looked up at him through passion-glazed eyes, her lips pink and swollen from his kisses. She sucked in a breath, and her eyes rolled back as her orgasm began rippling through her, the feel of her tensing and fluttering around his cock more than enough to finally push him over the edge.

With a hoarse shout, he came inside of her in a blinding rush of heat that sizzled along his nerve endings. His body shook as his orgasm peaked and then subsided. When it was over, he dropped his head to her shoulder, unable to discount the overwhelming sense of completion washing over him.

"That was good," she said on a breathy sigh. "*Very* good."

Smiling, he turned his head, and pressed his lips to her hair, her cheek, then kissed her slow and deep. He wanted to hold onto this moment, and her, forever . . . but knew, and accepted, that it wasn't meant to be.

CHRISTINE was roused from a deep sleep by the violent twitching of Ben's body next to hers, and the awful, guttural sounds coming from the back of his throat. Momentarily confused, she came up on her arm and stared down at him, and when he jerked again and cried out in his sleep, she knew he was in the throes of some kind of nightmare.

She touched his bare chest and found it damp with perspiration. Feeling his heart racing beneath her palm, she gave him a gentle shake. "Ben, wake up," she said, trying not to jostle him too badly.

He awoke with a start, anyway. Eyes wild with terror, he bolted upright in bed, his breathing ragged. His entire body was tense and his fists clenched at his sides, as if he was ready to confront some unknown evil.

She stroked a hand down his back in an attempt to soothe him. "Hey, are you okay?" she asked softly.

It took him a moment to realize where he was, and then he raked a hand through his tousled hair and exhaled a harsh stream of breath. "It was a bad dream. It happens sometimes." He shook his head, as if that gesture would dispel the internal demons still lingering in his mind.

He was trying to remain calm and casual about the entire situation, but she instinctively knew what the dream had been about—something that had happened in the war, most likely pertaining to his fiancée, Kim. And Christine was more than willing to listen if Ben needed to vent and get those bad memories out in the open, instead of keeping them bottled up inside where they could only fester and breed horrific nightmares.

It was nearly seven in the morning on Sunday, almost time for them to get up anyway. "Do you want to talk about it?"

His expression turned grim. "Trust me, those night-mares are something I have to live with, but the details of those dreams aren't something you want to hear about."

"How do you know that?" She wasn't a weak and fragile female who couldn't withstand to hear a few har-rowing stories.

"Because the details are shocking, ugly, and vile," he said, an angry, bitter edge to his voice. "And worst of all, what I dream about is *real* and something I had to live through and will never, ever forget, no matter how hard I try. There's no sense dragging someone else into my own personal hell."

There was so much pain and heartache in his gaze, and it hurt her to see him hurting so much. He was doing his best to push her away emotionally, and she just wasn't go-ing to let him shut her out that way. Hopefully, if he talked about those awful memories, maybe he could begin to heal inside and those nightmares would finally leave him alone.

"What happened to your fiancée, Ben?" she asked softly, persistently.

Sighing heavily, he lay back down on the pillow and draped his arm over his eyes. "Let it go, Christine."

He sounded tired and weary—no doubt tired of carry-ing so many painful burdens and weary from years of holding it all inside.

"I don't want to let it go." She recalled the picture she'd seen in his apartment of Ben and his fiancée—once very happy and in love. "Tell me about Kim, please?"

When he remained quiet, she tried to think of a way to draw him out, to get him to talk, and decided to start at the beginning. "How did the two of you meet?"

He moved his arm to let one dark brown eye glower at her. "You really aren't going to leave it alone, are you?" he asked gruffly.

She smiled at him, not the least put off by his scowl. She'd learned enough about this man to know that his growl was much worse than his bite. "I'm afraid not, so you might as well start talking."

A deep breath unraveled out of him, and then he spoke. "We met when we were both deployed to Iraq and were stationed at the same Marine base near Fallujah," he said, staring at the ceiling. "We started out as friends, and things progressed from there. We'd planned on getting married as soon as each of our tours in Iraq was over."

Knowing how that had turned out, Christine's heart twisted with anguish for Ben and what he'd endured. "So, she was a Marine, too?"

He nodded. "She was a first lieutenant, and was part of the female search force that was used to pat down the Iraqi women for contraband when they came through checkpoints." Turning his head on the pillow, he met her gaze. "It was a job that had to be handled with sensitivity, and since many Muslim women cover themselves from head to toe to avoid contact with males who aren't close relatives, male Marines aren't allowed to touch them, but they still had to be searched to make sure they weren't concealing any weapons beneath their loose garb."

A small smile touched the corner of his mouth as he remembered, and continued. "She was small compared to a lot of the other female Marines, but Kim was strong and tough when the situation warranted. She dealt with the Iraqi women politely, but firmly, and didn't put up with any shit from anybody."

Christine settled more comfortably beside him on the bed. "You included?" she teased.

"Yeah, me included. She definitely kept me in line, but she was also such a kind and caring person, and as soft as a marshmallow inside. She loved giving candy and school supplies to the Iraqi children we often came into contact with, and she taught the young girls to play hopscotch and recruited us guys to show them how to do double Dutch jump rope. *That* was not a pretty sight," he said wryly.

She laughed, imagining these big strapping Marines attempting to be light on their feet as they tried to stay in sync with the two turning ropes.

"Anyway, Kim and I came from small towns and shared the same values and similar family situations that bonded us on a deeper level. Her father was an alcoholic that abused her, and she joined the military right after graduating high school as a way to make a better life for herself. And for the time that she was in the military, she did just that."

Christine swallowed hard, trying hard not to think about how big the contrast was between Kim's background and lifestyle, and her own. It reminded her too much of the differences between herself and Ben. "She sounds like a wonderful woman," she said, a bit envious of what the two of them had shared.

"She was my best friend." Shadows of anguish etched his features right before he looked away again. "One night, we were in a convoy of Humvees carrying members of a female search team back to base when we were ambushed. A suicide car bomber drove his vehicle into the second Humvee right in front of ours, which was carrying Kim. The bomb ignited a huge blast that killed the driver and set the vehicle on fire. But that wasn't all. There were about a dozen Iraqi gunmen who joined in on the ambush, too."

His voice had grown thick with excess emotion and he paused, then cleared his throat before continuing. "Kim and the other women in the Humvee immediately jumped out to get away from the fiery explosion, but as she ran toward our vehicle to take cover while we returned fire, she was shot in the back."

As she listened to his story, Christine's chest grew tight with sorrow and she ached deep inside for the pain and loss he'd endured. She knew he wasn't finished, so she remained quiet, waiting for him to go on.

"I saw it all happen, and as soon as she was shot and dropped to the ground, I went after her, right into open fire," he said hoarsely as he relived the harrowing past. "She was so vulnerable and defenseless out there, and I picked her up and ran with her in my arms until we were behind our Humvee while the rest of my unit fought off the gunmen."

He exhaled a shuddering breath and met her gaze again. "I kept telling her to hang on, that she was going to be okay, that I just needed her to hold on until I could get her to a medic. By the time the fight ended, two of the men from my unit, and three of the women, were dead. Including Kim."

The torment and haunting grief in his eyes was a tangible thing. "It should have been *me*. I should have died that day, not her! I was there in the convoy to protect her, and instead I failed her," he said angrily, then pressed the heels of his palms against his eyes, his bitterness and resentment obviously causing him so much inner turmoil. "She didn't deserve to be murdered in cold blood like that and I would have done *anything* to give my life for hers."

Christine hated that he felt responsible for Kim's death, that four years after the fact he was still blaming himself for what had happened—for not protecting as he'd been trained to do. But she also knew that there was absolutely nothing she could say that would make him feel differently about the situation. It was his burden to bear, until he was ready to let it go on his own.

She blinked and felt a trickle of moisture roll down her cheek. A tear for the woman he'd loved with such devotion, and had lost in such a devastating way. And sadness for the jaded man he'd become deep inside.

He reached out and gently wiped away the wetness on her cheek, his touch lingering on her face. "Not a pretty story, is it?"

"War is never easy or pretty," she whispered, and even though she knew her next words weren't much in the way of easing his internal misery, they were genuine and she felt compelled to say them anyway. "I'm sorry, Ben. So sorry."

"Me, too." Sliding his fingers around to the nape of her neck, he drew her down so that her head was resting on his chest and she was lying next to his warm, hard body once again.

She could hear the heavy beating of his heart against her ear, and she closed her eyes, wrapped her arms around him, and held him close. It was the only thing she could do to offer him a little comfort, to ease his suffering. To let him know that she cared and was there for him.

And then she wondered who was going to soothe *her* heartache when he was gone.

Fifteen

THREE weeks with Christine had gone much faster than Ben had anticipated. Tomorrow, Tuesday, voters would decide who they wanted for a new governor—Nathan Delacroix or Charles Lambert—and depending on who won the election, Ben's job as Christine's bodyguard would possibly be over. If Nathan won, he was certain that his assignment would be extended a few extra weeks, just to ensure Christine's safety and to make sure there were no other threats issued against her or Nathan.

Ben shifted on the couch in the reception area of The Big Event as he continued his game of FreeCell while waiting for Christine to finish a phone call so they could leave for the night. He honestly wasn't sure how he felt about the possibility of spending more time with Christine beyond this next week, any more than he knew how he felt about leaving her tomorrow—if that's what happened.

Professionally, she was an assignment and an ESS client, and he'd protect her for as long as necessary because that was his job. But on a personal level, he was torn inside. In such a short span of time things had gotten so intense between them—sexually *and* emotionally. He'd not only crossed a physical line with this woman when that went against his code of mixing business with pleasure, but somewhere along the way his emotions had gotten all tangled up in the mess, too.

And that was something he never saw coming until it was too late—when he'd bared his soul to Christine, along with his deepest, darkest anguish, and the guilt and remorse that had consumed him since Kim's death. The night that he'd lost Kim was something he never talked about with anyone—the guys he worked with were well aware of what happened that fateful night, but they understood it was an off-limits topic for him—yet he'd trusted Christine with the nightmares that haunted him on a regular basis.

But that wasn't all. While he usually kept any kind of personal discussions with a client to a minimum, those kinds of revealing, intimate conversations with Christine had become a common source of pillow talk with them. They'd talked much too openly about their pasts, their family issues, and shared other painful secrets that had given him a glimpse into who Christine was deep inside—a woman with a huge, generous heart who was finally embracing the independent spirit her mother had spent too many years stifling.

God, he was in way over his head when it came to Christine, and Ben knew he had to take a huge step back emotionally, as well as physically. He'd promised Christine he'd go with her to Envy the night after the election to help her celebrate her twenty-seventh birthday, and he decided that would be it for the two of them. In fact, if she did need extended security, he was seriously considering having Kevin or Jon take over for the duration of the assignment in order to make a clean break, instead of drawing out the inevitable.

The sound of two female voices heading toward the reception area pulled Ben from his thoughts. Madison and Christine came into view as they discussed some details on an upcoming retirement party they'd been commissioned to organize and plan, and as soon as they finished their conversation, Christine set a file folder on the front desk and glanced over at him.

"Are you about ready to go?"

It was nearly five thirty in the evening, and it wasn't like it would take him very long at all to pack up for the night. It was just a matter of shutting down his laptop, putting it in its case, and grabbing the novel he was nearly done with. "I'm ready when you are."

"I'm good," she said, and unlocked the cabinet where she and Madison kept their purses during the day. "How about you?" Christine asked her assistant.

"I have a few more things to finish up before I leave for the evening," Madison said.

Christine nodded in understanding. "Don't forget to vote before coming into work in the morning," she reminded her friend.

Madison laughed. "Don't worry, I won't. Your father is going to kick Charles Lambert's ass tomorrow."

Christine grinned. "God, I hope so! Someone has to stand up for the underdog, and it's clear that Lambert is chomping at the bit to tear down the neighborhoods on the lower west side so he can build to accommodate and appease a lot of the wealthier residents of Chicago." Her voice rang with disgust.

"They're already saying it's going to be a very close race," Ben chimed in as he stood, his computer case in hand. He had endless time during the day to read through news reports, and everyone was gearing up for the big race tomorrow and speculating on the outcome.

Nodding in agreement, Christine slid the strap of her

purse over her shoulder and picked up her briefcase. "Which is why every single vote counts in this election."

They started for the front door, and just before walking out Christine glanced back at Madison. "Lock the door behind us when we leave."

Madison rolled her eyes at Christine's overprotective reminder, which really wasn't necessary since Ben had made it a rule that the door remained securely locked when he wasn't around to look after Madison, too. "Yes, *Mom*."

The glass door swung shut behind them, and Madison turned the lock and gave them a quick wave. Car keys in hand, Ben walked with Christine toward his truck, which he'd parked a few stores down from her business after lunch. But before they reached his vehicle, Madison called out to Christine, stopping them both on the sidewalk.

"Christy!" Standing with the door propped open with one hand, Madison lifted a file folder for her to see. "You forgot the contract on the Lewis account that you wanted to take home and review tonight."

"Oh, thanks!" Christine started back toward The Big Event, but Ben stopped her before she could go.

Pressing a button on his remote, he unlocked the truck, which was only a few yards away from where they were standing. "You get into the truck and I'll get the folder for you."

Ben waited and watched as Christine headed to the vehicle, wanting to make sure she was securely inside before going back for the file. Out of the corner of his eye he saw a white car stop in the middle of traffic, causing horns to blare from other irate drivers. Ben glanced in that direction, noting that it was a white BMW coupe seconds before he realized that Jason Forrester was behind the wheel and he was pointing what looked to be an assault rifle out the passenger window directly at Christine.

Son of a bitch! He didn't have time to pull his own con-

cealed weapon. Instead, finely honed military instincts
took over, along with a rush of adrenaline, and he dropped
his laptop bag and bolted back toward Christine, his only
thought to protect her as he yelled, "Christy, *get down*!"

Oblivious as to what was going on, she turned around
with a look of bewilderment on her face, just as Ben
heard an eery *phftt* coming from Jason's car, then another
shot. Unable to reach Christine in time, he watched in
horror as her body jerked from the impact, and then she
glanced down to see two vivid red spots forming on her
cream silk blouse—one near her left shoulder, and another on the right side of her abdomen.

Clearly in shock at the realization that she'd been shot,
she swayed on her high-heeled shoes, tried to step back,
but instead collapsed to the sidewalk, her purse and briefcase scattering around her as she lay there, staring up at
the sky with wide, startled eyes.

The squeal of tires told Ben that Jason had taken off,
and he dropped to his knees beside Christine to assess the
situation, his mind reeling and his chest tightening with
the effort to keep his own panic at bay.

"Oh, my God, oh, my God!" Madison said hysterically as she ran up to them. "Is she all right?"

Ben didn't know, and his stomach cramped at the
thought of anything happening to Christine. Of losing yet
another person he'd come to care for. "Call nine-one-
one!" he barked out, trying to shake some sense into
Madison. "Get an ambulance here *now*!"

"Already done!" someone else said from nearby, making Ben vaguely aware that a small crowd was starting to
form around Christine on the sidewalk.

"Stay with me, sweetheart. You're going to be just
fine." It wasn't a promise he had the right to make, but he
refused to think differently.

She glanced up at him with pain-filled eyes, then

opened her mouth to speak, but only a croak of sound escaped her.

"Don't talk," he said softly, though his own voice shook with fear. "You've been shot." *Twice.* But that wasn't something she needed to know or hear at the moment.

Because one of the bullets had hit her so close to the stomach, which could prove to be a life-threatening injury if she bled out, he knew he had to staunch the flow of blood until medical help arrived. With hands that were less than steady, he managed to unbutton her blouse and pull it away from the right side of her waist. He gently ran his fingers over the spot that was covered in bright red blood, searching for a wound . . . but couldn't find one.

What the hell?

Christine winced and moaned as he probed the welt forming on her skin, assuring him that she had been struck with *something*. Frowning in confusion, he pulled his hand away and rubbed the thick, sticky substance between his fingers. It didn't feel thin and slick like fresh blood, and as he took a whiff of the wetness on his fingers, he inhaled the distinct chemical scent of *paint*.

Un-fucking-believable. Jason had shot her with a paintball gun, not a real, authentic assault rifle. The relief that poured through Ben was so profound, he felt a well of emotion rise up into his throat and he dropped his head forward to give himself a private moment to gather his composure. Other than being sore and bruised, *she was going to be okay*.

He exhaled a deep breath and met Christine's gaze. "Jason shot you with a paintball gun," he said once he was back in control again.

Her eyes flashed with fire and anger, letting Ben know that she really was okay. "It hurts."

"It'll definitely hurt like hell for a while and you'll be bruised in those areas, but there doesn't appear to be any

242   JANELLE DENISON

permanent damage. But I'm still going to have you
checked out just to make sure." He grabbed her hand and
gently pulled her upright. "Come on, let's get you back
into your office until the paramedics and police arrive."

He helped her up the rest of the way, wrapped an arm
around her waist, and led her back to The Big Event. Madison grabbed Christine's purse and briefcase, along with
Ben's computer bag, and just as they stepped back into the
reception area, the sound of multiple sirens in the distance
grew louder, until an ambulance and two squad cars arrived.

Moments later, the paramedics were hovering over
Christine by the couch, taking her vitals and checking the
welts on her abdomen and shoulder. Three police officers
took Ben aside, and after he explained what had happened, and who had assaulted Christine, two of the po-
licemen went back outside to take statements from the
people who'd witnessed the attack.

The officer who'd stayed behind assured Ben that there
would be an immediate warrant issued for Jason's arrest.
Combined with his recent transgressions against Christine, Ben knew that there would be no chance of bail for
Jason this time around, and that he was looking at some
serious jail time down the road for this latest attack and for
breaking the terms of the restraining order once again.

Knowing that Jason would be behind bars for a while
was fine with Ben. Between his blackmail attempts toward Nathan Delacroix and his aggression toward Christine, the man was a menace and a threat and needed some
serious help.

Ben was just glad to know that once Jason was arrested, Christine would be safe on her own again.

BUNDLED up in her favorite fleece robe and hands
wrapped around a warm mug of chamomile tea, Christine

glanced over at Ben, who was sitting in the single chair in her living room, which was too far away from where she sat, as they listened to the evening news speculate on the outcome of tomorrow's election.

Ever since they'd arrived back home after the paramedics had released her and the police had finished questioning her about Jason, Ben had been quiet and even a bit distant. After making a call to her parents to give them the latest news and reassuring them that she truly was okay, she and Ben had eaten dinner, and she'd taken a long, hot shower to help ease the soreness in her shoulder and abdomen where bruises were already forming. Then they'd settled in the living room to watch a few shows together, and any attempt at conversation with Ben resulted in a go-nowhere kind of answer from him.

It was frustrating and aggravating, and she was pretty certain she knew where his isolated mood was stemming from. Now that she was privy to what had happened to Kim, and how Ben blamed himself for not being able to keep her safe, she had a feeling that he was berating himself for letting Jason get close enough to hurt *her*.

And that mentality of Ben's frustrated the heck out of her. "What happened today wasn't your fault," she said, figuring they were better off getting it all out in the open, instead of letting him stew on it all night long.

He glanced at her, his eyes revealing nothing. "I know that. I didn't pull the trigger on that paintball gun."

There was the slightest edge of sarcasm to his voice, which she didn't appreciate. "Let me rephrase my comment. It wasn't your fault that you weren't able to get me out of the way before Jason shot me."

His jaw clenched. "I'm your bodyguard, Christine. My job is to protect you at all costs. I should have taken both of those shots *for* you. What if it had been a bullet instead of just paint in that rifle?"

"There are no 'what ifs,' Ben," she said, her annoyance mounting. "It wasn't a bullet. I'm okay. You're good at what you do, but shit happens sometimes."

He had no reply to that. Instead he rubbed at his forehead, looking tired and weary. "The good news is, the police have Jason back in custody, so at least that's one less thing for you to worry about."

She took a sip of her tea, letting it warm her all the way down to her belly. "You really think he was the one behind the threats and blackmail attempts toward my father?"

"He had every motive," Ben said confidently. "He had an irrational grudge against you, and he obviously wanted to ruin your father's chance at winning the election since your dad killed Jason's political career—not that Jason didn't deserve to be ostracized for embezzling campaign funds. Hopefully, they'll nail his ass and he'll be spending enough time in prison to sober him up and make him reassess the direction of his life."

"Yeah, that would be nice," she agreed, and finished off her tea. "By the way, I think I'm going to take it easy tomorrow and work from home after I go out and vote. My shoulder and stomach feel really tender, and I'd rather be here for the day than at the office."

He nodded. "That's a good idea."

Exhausted after the day she'd had, she stood up and took her empty mug to the kitchen, then returned to the living room, switching off lights as she went.

"Are you ready to call it a night?" she asked Ben.

He looked at her, his gaze uncertain, and still way too withdrawn. "I really don't think it's a good idea for us to do anything tonight."

She rolled her eyes. "The last thing on my mind right now is sex," she fibbed, knowing she could be persuaded very easily when it came to Ben. "I want to go to bed and *sleep*. With you. I promise not to take advantage of you in any way whatsoever, if that's what you're worried about."

That prompted a smile to quirk the corners of his mouth. "Now that's a relief," he teased, a semblance of his old self emerging once again. Standing, he took her hand and led the way back to her bedroom.

Christine was grateful that he'd given in to her request. With their days together numbered, she didn't want to be alone tonight. She wanted to feel the warmth of his body against hers all night long, and wake up cuddled in his arms. She wanted to enjoy all the special intimacies she'd grown used to sharing with him over the course of the past few weeks.

Because too soon, she knew she'd be back to being alone and on her own, and that was something her heart wasn't ready to face just yet.

THE day seemed to fly by in a flash. Between watching news reports on the election, fielding calls from Madison at the office, finalizing details on an upcoming sports banquet she'd been hired to plan and coordinate, and numerous calls from her annoyed mother, six o'clock in the evening arrived much sooner than Christine realized.

After yesterday's incident with Jason, her shoulder and side felt battered and bruised, and it was difficult to lift her arm or twist at the waist without groaning or wincing from the aching pain. She might not have been shot with a real bullet, but Jason had definitely left a lasting impression on her body.

Done working for the day, she shut down her computer and cleaned up her home office, then made her way into the living room where Ben was sitting in the armchair watching the evening news. She glanced at the TV screen, saw the percentages of votes between each candidate, and felt her stomach tumble anxiously. Considering that there was no clear-cut winner yet, she could only imagine how her father was doing at the moment.

"Good Lord, this has become a nail-biting election," she said, and sat down on the side of the couch that was closest to Ben's chair.

"We did our part," Ben replied, and smiled at her. "Now it's up to the rest of the state to vote for the right guy. And that would be your father."

She crossed her fingers and held them up for Ben to see. "Here's hoping."

Ben was quiet for a moment, then asked, "Is everything okay between you and your mother?"

He must have overheard her many conversations with her mother today, not all of them pleasant, unfortunately. "Is it ever?"

Laughter glimmered in his golden brown eyes. "Not from what I've seen."

She settled more comfortably into the corner of the couch, and curled her jean-clad legs up under her. "According to my mother, I'm going to make some man a horrible wife."

He lifted a dark brow. "Why? Because you're not at the campaign office, physically supporting your father?"

"Yes." Boy, he knew her mother better than she'd realized. Then again, she'd shared enough with Ben for him to easily nail Audrey's controlling, demanding personality. "I've talked to my father a few times today, and I sent him some flowers to let him know I'm thinking of him, but my mother insists that I should be there, that we show a united front as a family, especially when my father makes his acceptance speech."

"And?" Ben asked, obviously knowing there was more.

She bit her bottom lip, still unable to believe just how bold she'd been in her response—or how good it had felt to stand up for herself. "I don't think she appreciated me telling her it's her job to stand beside my father and pretend to be the doting wife. I don't need to be there, and considering what happened yesterday with Jason, my father completely understands why I'm not."

"*Pretend* to be the doting wife?" he repeated, his incredulous tone telling her that he couldn't believe that she'd actually said those exact words.

"Well, it's the truth," she said softly, wishing that things were different between her mother and father—that their marriage was based on love and respect instead of what her father's political career did for her mother's social standing in Chicago. "The voting public might not have a clue, but I know it, she knows it, and my father knows it."

He nodded in understanding, let the topic go, and so did she.

As they continued to watch the news in silence, her stomach rumbled hungrily, reminding her that they needed to eat dinner. "What do you say we order in pizza tonight?" she asked. She wasn't in the mood to cook or leave the house to go to a restaurant.

"Sounds good to me."

She went to the kitchen, looked up the number for pizza delivery, and ordered a pepperoni with extra cheese. As she walked back into the living room, she remembered something she'd meant to tell Ben.

"Craig called earlier to see if I needed a ride to my party at Envy tomorrow night," she said as she sat back down on the couch.

A spark of irritation lit Ben's gaze at the mention of the other man's name. "And what did you tell him?" he asked gruffly.

She wanted to smile at the territorial look in his eyes, as well as point out to Ben that bit of possessiveness he'd just displayed, but knew it wasn't something he wanted to hear when he'd spent the past twenty-four hours trying to establish new boundaries between them that leaned more toward friends than lovers. Still, she couldn't help but harbor a shred of hope that he'd give them a chance beyond this assignment of his.

She tucked a stray strand of hair behind her ear and put Ben out of his misery. "I told Craig that *you'd* be taking me."

Ben smirked. "I'll bet that thrilled the pants off of him."

He'd definitely been disappointed, and had even admitted to her that he'd been secretly hoping that things wouldn't work out with Ben so she'd be free for the birthday bash *he'd* planned for her. She wasn't quite sure how to take that comment, and had chalked it up to male jealousy on Craig's part. His curt remark was also the deciding factor for her to break as many ties to Craig as possible after tomorrow night. As much as she appreciated his contacts, she didn't need them, and she didn't want to feel obligated to him in any way whatsoever when she knew Craig had feelings for her—feelings that she didn't, and wouldn't ever, reciprocate.

"You know," Ben said casually, drawing her attention back to him. "I still find it odd that Craig is so intent on pursuing you when his father is so in favor of backing Charles Lambert for governor. It just feels like such a conflict of interest to me. Does Craig not share his father's political views, especially on the whole gentrification issue?"

The subject had been brought up between her and Craig, and she knew his thoughts on the matter. "Actually, Craig *is* in favor of tearing down the lower west side and rebuilding the area, especially since his father's development company would be hired for the project if Lambert wins. But Craig's relationship with his dad has been strained for years because Craig didn't go to work for Crosby's development company, and Craig's been trying to get back into his father's good graces ever since."

Ben shook his head. "Another dysfunctional family saga, huh?"

"Every family has their issues," she said, certain it was true.

Their dinner arrived, and they ate their pizza while watching the election coverage on TV. By nine o'clock that evening it was announced that Charles Lambert had won the election by a 6 percent margin and would be the new governor of Chicago.

Shocked and disappointed, Christine immediately picked up the phone and called her father, who was doing okay despite the loss. He'd fought a good, fair fight, and that was all he could do.

Then came Nathan Delacroix's concession speech, which was aired on a local channel. He congratulated Lambert on his win, but also promised to continue his fight to help the lower west side of Chicago on other political levels. Audrey stood not by his side, but behind him, clearly unhappy over the loss.

When the news switched over to Charles Lambert's campaign office where his staff was celebrating his victory, Ben stood up and headed down the hallway toward the back rooms. Christine watched him go, an uneasy sense of foreboding settling in the pit of her belly.

Quietly, she followed him and came to a stop in the doorway of the guest bedroom, where Ben had his duffle on the bed and was putting his personal things into the bag. Her heart seemed to lodge in her throat and it took her a moment to speak.

"What are you doing?" she asked, hating the thought of him leaving. Over the past few weeks, he'd become such a daily part of her life—one she'd come to anticipate and enjoy.

"I'm just packing up the bulk of my things," he said, not looking at her.

She watched him pull out a small stack of neatly folded T-shirts from one of the dresser drawers and tuck them into his duffle bag. Then he finally turned around to face her, looking so sexy and gorgeous and closed off that her chest hurt.

"I still have to talk to your father in the morning, but considering that Jason is behind bars, and unfortunately your father just lost the election, I'm sure Nathan will release me from this security assignment and I'll be leaving soon."

There were so many more reasons for him to stay, but she could see by his determined expression, along with the reserved behavior he'd exhibited all day long, that his feelings on the issue were already made up. She'd learned enough about Ben to know that arguing those points with him when he was in such a stubborn frame of mind would be futile.

Knowing she still had tomorrow night with him, for now she let it go. He'd promised to take her to Envy to celebrate her twenty-seventh birthday, and afterward, there was only one gift she wanted from Ben—and she planned to ask for it.

A real relationship.

A future.

His love.

She truly didn't know if any of that was possible for him, but she knew she'd have to tell him the truth tomorrow night. He had her heart. Now, she wanted his.

Forever.

Sixteen

BEN parked his truck in Christine's driveway at seven the following evening to pick her up for her birthday party at Envy. After talking to Nathan earlier that morning and being relieved of duty as Christine's security agent, he'd headed back to his apartment while she'd gone off to work—on her own and without him as a bodyguard. As it should be. As it would be from now on.

Switching off the engine, he closed his eyes for a moment and released a long, deep breath in hopes of bolstering his fortitude—along with the willpower to keep things between them fun and casual and amicable—and not letting himself cross that line into emotional, intimate territory once again.

It was just a matter of getting through tonight, then bringing Christine back home and putting an end to their relationship, instead of dragging out an unavoidable breakup down the road. Which was why he'd never made her any promises he knew he wouldn't be able to keep. Not only was he unwilling to risk his heart again, they were just too different to make it work for the long haul, their lifestyles so vastly opposite, and he refused to put them both through that kind of emotional upheaval.

With his plan firmly in mind, Ben headed up to the front of Christine's house and knocked on the door. When she answered and he took one look at her alluring, head-turning outfit, he knew he was in for a long night of fighting the urge to touch and caress all that creamy, bared flesh.

She was wearing a bright red, form-fitting cocktail dress with only two thin rhinestone straps holding up the sexy ensemble. While the slinky material clung to her curves, the hem of the dress ended in a flirty bit of ruffle that showcased her toned thighs and long, slender legs. He dared to look down at her feet and had to swallow back a groan when he saw the leopard print high-heeled shoes she'd worn that first night she'd seduced him.

He glanced back up, saw the sinful smile on her lips, and knew she'd deliberately worn those pumps to tempt and tease him and make him think about all the ways he'd taken her while she'd worn those provocative shoes.

Then there were her glossy red lips he ached to taste, the upper swell of her breasts pushed up by the tight bodice of her dress, and all that thick, blond hair of hers that she'd worn down tonight. The silky strands had been curled into soft waves and were tousled into a provocative disarray around her shoulders—once again making him recall how she looked after a night of sex, with her hair all disheveled from his hands and fingers. His groin throbbed at the erotic memories floating through his mind.

"So, what do you think?" She executed a little twirl on her high heels, presenting him with a front and back view of her sexy little dress. "Do I look like the birthday girl?"

He thought she looked gorgeous, classy, and so incredibly sophisticated compared to the casual black jeans and button-down shirt he'd worn. He had no doubt that she would be the most beautiful, sensual woman at Envy tonight, and he had no idea how he was going to keep his hands off of her all evening long.

"I think that I'm going to have to keep a close eye on you tonight," he replied with a grin, keeping things light between them. "You forget that Kevin and Jon are going to be there, and looking as hot as you do, I have no doubt that they'll try to steal you away."

"They can try, but it's not going to happen." Eyes sparkling happily, she splayed her hand on his chest and leaned in to softly, warmly, kiss his lips. "I'm all yours to-night, Ben. I wore this dress and these shoes for you, and you can just imagine what I'm wearing, or *not* wearing, beneath it all," she said wickedly.

Ben didn't allow his thoughts to travel down that path, because if he did he knew they'd never make it to Envy, and that went against the lecture he'd just given himself in his truck about keeping things platonic, and his hands to himself.

So, instead, he said, "We need to get going so we don't arrive late."

"Arriving late is fashionable. Didn't you know that?" Laughing, she stepped back into the foyer, grabbed a small purse and a sweater that matched her dress, then locked the front door behind her.

Minutes later, they were in his truck, headed toward the nightclub and the birthday bash Craig had planned for her.

During the drive, Christine kept up a steady stream of conversation. She gave him an update on how her father was doing a day after losing the election, and assured him that Nathan was holding up much better than her mother was. She told him about her day at the office and her lunch with a client. She was clearly happy and excited and ready to celebrate her birthday with him and her friends.

When they arrived, the two of them were ushered to the VIP section of the nightclub, where the large, private room had been decorated with festive balloons and streamers, fragrant floral arrangements, and a huge banner wishing Christine a happy birthday. Already, a huge crowd of people were milling around, nearly filling the place to capacity.

As they walked inside, Craig came up to them and greeted Christine with a hello and an intimate smile. Ben was lucky enough to get a curt nod of acknowledgment that made it clear that the other man was annoyed that he was still around. Then, without asking, Craig pulled Christine into the center of the room to make an announcement, putting the spotlight on the two of them and leaving Ben standing alone on the sidelines.

"The birthday girl has arrived," Craig announced into a cordless microphone, then cued the band to start playing the happy birthday song.

Everyone sang along, and after the tune ended, a shower of colorful, sparkling confetti rained down on everyone from above, causing the guests to clap and cheer, and the festivities to begin.

Craig pulled Christine into a hug that lasted longer than necessary, and Ben watched from across the room as she stiffened, then put her hand on Craig's chest to push away from him as nicely as possible. It was clear that the other man's embrace made Christine uncomfortable, but she'd handled the situation on her own, and seemingly without offending Craig.

"Who the hell is he?" a deep male voice asked.

Ben had been so intent on keeping an eye on Craig and Christine that he hadn't seen Jon and Kevin walk up to him. It was nice to see a few familiar faces in a huge sea of people he didn't recognize. "That's Craig Crosby. He's the one who's throwing the party for Christine."

Kevin crossed his arms over his chest and glared at the other man. "Yeah, well, I don't like him."

Ben chuckled at his friend's intuitive reply. "Join the club."

The three of them continued to watch Craig and Christine from afar. Every time she attempted to excuse herself and walk away from Craig, he grabbed her arm and pulled her back, trying to draw her into another round of conversation. As much as Ben wanted to go over to Craig and stake a claim on Christine, it just wasn't his place to do so anymore. As long as Craig wasn't hurting her in any way physically, he'd let her handle the situation on her own.

"Do you want us to take care of him for you?" Kevin asked, sounding like an overprotective brother just itching to pound some flesh. "Rough him up a bit and make sure he understands that Christine is off-limits?"

Unfortunately, that was part of the problem. "She's not off-limits," Ben managed to say. As much as he hated to admit it, Christine was free to see and date whoever she wanted. Even if he didn't like her choice.

Jon slanted him an incredulous look. "Oh, so you don't mind if that slimeball puts his hands all over her?" he asked, doing nothing to disguise the sarcasm in his voice.

Oh, Ben minded all right. More than was prudent or wise. Especially when it came to Craig. "Christine is handling herself just fine."

In fact, she'd finally managed to extricate herself from Craig's grasp and was heading back toward them, that provocative red dress and those leopard print high heels making his gut clench with desire. Her eyes lit up when she saw Jon and Kevin, and she greeted them with a warm, affectionate hug that his friends enjoyed way too much—mainly to provoke him, Ben knew.

"I'm so glad you guys came," she said sincerely. "Where's Zach?"

"He had something else he needed to do tonight," Kevin said vaguely. "But he did tell me to wish you a happy birthday."

Christine smiled. "That was sweet of him."

Ben guessed that Zach had decided not to come to the party because he still wasn't ready to be around the temptation of alcohol that flowed so endlessly at a nightclub like this one. The man was still struggling with his addictions, and Ben understood and respected Zach's decision.

"Well, well, well," a familiar female voice drawled mockingly. "If it isn't the birthday girl holding court with her own little entourage of hunky males."

Ben turned to see Leanne, who was wearing a pink strapless dress the color of Pepto-Bismol, and was carrying a frothy, froufrou cocktail in the same matching hue. By the glazed look in her eyes, she'd gotten an early start on her drinking and was more than a little buzzed.

"Hi, Ben," she said, giving him a sultry smile before turning her attention to Jon and Kevin. "I don't think we've ever met. Are you tonight's entertainment?"

A comical look passed over Jon's expression. "Excuse me?"

"Strippers," she said, the word slurring ever-so-slightly as she eyed them appreciatively. "You two look like you could be strippers. You should know that I tip *really* well."

Kevin laughed in amusement. "Honey, I only strip when I really, really like a woman. Not when one pays me to."

"Oh." Not certain what to make of his comment,

Leanne scrunched up her nose, took a drink of the pink stuff in her glass, then moved on to someone else she knew.

As soon as the other woman was out of hearing range, Ben looked at Christine. "You invited her?"

"Good God, no!" Christine looked at him as if he'd lost his mind. "I'm sure she invited herself. It's fine, as long as she behaves herself and doesn't cause a scene like she did the last time when she dumped her drink on me."

Ben stared after Leanne, watching the way she worked the crowd at Christine's party. "Yeah, well, I wouldn't put it past her, so watch yourself around her."

"Don't worry," Kevin chimed in. "Jon and I will keep Christine so busy out on the dance floor that there won't be an opportunity for anyone to cause a scene but us." He winked at her.

Christine laughed. "I can tell it's going to be a fun night." Her gaze slid to something behind Ben, then she smiled and waved. "There's Madison, Ronnie, and Mark. Let's go join them."

Once they reached the trio, introductions were made for Kevin and Jon. They dragged over a few more chairs, and the seven of them talked and laughed while enjoying the appetizers that were being served. Before long, Craig came up to their group, specifically to Christine, and told her there were some people he wanted her to meet—as in very important contacts for her business.

It was clear to Ben that she really didn't want to go with Craig, but she wasn't one to be rude, and she scooted back her chair and stood. "I'll be right back."

Except she didn't return right away. Ben watched for the next half an hour as Craig monopolized her time, taking her from one person to the next to introduce her, and acting as though *he* were her date for the evening. Ben kept the two in sight, but now that he was no longer her bodyguard, there was no need to stay glued to her side, and he wasn't going to intrude on what Craig had referred to as "business."

Kevin had no such qualms. "I need a dance partner, and Christy looks like she could use a break from all that *business* stuff," he said, and headed in her direction.

Seconds later, Kevin was leading Christine toward the dance floor. She looked relieved at the interruption and the chance to enjoy the music, while Craig glared at Kevin in annoyance for stealing Christine away. Leanne came up to Craig, clearly eager to pick up where Christine left off, but Crosby wasn't interested and left her standing there with a pout on her face.

Knowing that he had nothing to worry about with Kevin dancing with Christine, Ben returned his attention to the conversation at the table.

The next few hours passed quickly. When Kevin and Jon weren't keeping Christine busy out on the dance floor, a slew of friends stopped by the table they were sitting at to wish her a happy birthday. Craig managed to pull her away once more to blow out the candles on her birthday cake and to cut the first slice, but she returned right after with a plate holding a large piece of her cake.

Instead of taking the seat next to his, she surprised him by sitting down on his lap, the flirty hem of her dress rising much too high on her thighs. If that wasn't enough to overload his senses and set him on fire, then the way she licked her glossy bottom lip did the trick.

Her eyes widened in mock innocence. "Oops. I forgot a fork."

He recognized that shameless look in her eyes and knew he was in big trouble. After being good all night, Christine was suddenly turning bad. Very bad.

"I guess he'll just have to feed it to you with his fingers," Ronnie suggested, laughter in her voice.

Christine touched her fingers to his cheek, her oh-so-sweet smile concealing a more brazen plan. "You would do that for me, wouldn't you, Ben?"

He hesitated, knowing where something like this could lead. Knowing, too, that she was deliberately taunting him, daring him to give into the desire arching between them. If he wasn't trying so damned hard to keep things platonic tonight, it would have been fun to give in to her request. He was just about to tell her he'd go and get her a fork, but then Jon spoke and changed his mind.

"I'll feed the cake to you, Christy," Jon offered willingly, a gregarious smile on his lips.

"Like hell you will," Ben muttered, just loud enough for his friend to hear, and laugh. Ben decided he could do this and *not* let it turn into a seductive game between them.

Breaking off a small corner of the cake, he brought it up to Christine's parted lips, and she took the morsel from him, her tongue barely grazing the tips of his fingers. Another piece, and she ate it with delicate little bites in between moaning her appreciation for the taste. She even fed him a small portion of the moist, yellow cake.

The process was all very sweet and chaste . . . until he reached for a napkin to wipe the frosting off his fingers.

She grabbed his wrist to stop him. "You can't waste the frosting," she said, chastising him. "It's the best part of the cake."

Then she proceeded to lick the sticky buttercream from his fingers. Slowly. Leisurely. Using her tongue to swipe the sweetness from his skin, and her teeth to scrape the confection from the pad of his thumb. By the time she was done, he was grateful that she was sitting on his lap, because her brazen display had made him as hard as stone and he was certain she could feel his erection pressing against her hip.

As if Christine hadn't just turned him inside out with wanting her, she struck up a conversation with her friends, giving his libido time to cool.

The upbeat song that the band was playing came to an end, and a slower melody began to fill the room. "I think we'll wind things down for a little bit," one of the band members said into the microphone as the lights were dimmed. "Let's have the birthday girl pick someone special to dance with during this song, which is titled 'Someone Like You'."

Christine looked down at him, her gaze adoring and filled with an emotion he refused to name. "That special person would be you," she said, and stood, extending her hand toward him.

Ben didn't dance. It just wasn't his thing, which was why he didn't mind when Kevin and Jon had fun with Christine as a partner. But this was different. This was more about a good-bye for him, and he just couldn't pass up the chance to hold her close one last time.

Taking her hand, he led her to the dance floor and pulled her into his arms as the slow song played and the singer's voice crooned the romantic lyrics. He placed a hand at the base of her spine, and she twined her arms around his neck, aligning their bodies so that they were touching intimately from chest to thighs, and igniting sparks of heat with the slightest move they made. She rested her head on his shoulder with her lips grazing his neck, and he pressed his cheek to her soft, fragrant hair. Closing his eyes, he inhaled deeply, memorizing the scent of her skin, the soft, yielding press of her curves against him, and the way she curled into him so trustingly.

Letting her go tonight was going to kill him, even if it was the right thing to do.

After a while, she pulled back and looked into his eyes, her fingers threading through the hair at the nape of his neck. Her beautiful expression was soft with reverence . . . and the undeniable glow of love. It was the latter emotion that completely and utterly slayed him. Uncaring of the fact that they were standing in the middle of a crowded dance floor, he lowered his head and kissed her.

One . . . last . . . time.

Her lips automatically parted beneath his, so soft and giving, just like the woman herself. Their tongues touched, mated seductively, and he tasted her desire, her escalating need. By the time the kiss ended, she was breathing hard, and he was already withdrawing emotionally, from her and their relationship.

"Take me home, Ben," she whispered, wearing her own heart on her sleeve. "I want to be alone with you."

He swallowed hard, unsure what to say to her but, "Okay," because he *would* be taking her home.

And then he was going to walk away.

STILL out on the dance floor, Christine could feel Ben pulling back, retreating from all the feelings swirling between them, and knew that tonight she'd be fighting for the one thing she wanted most in her life.

Ben.

She understood the past pain that scarred him and kept him from taking a chance with her. His mother's abandonment. The loss of his fiancée in the most horrific way. The guilt and remorse he'd buried in the deepest recesses of his soul over the fact that he hadn't been able to save Kim from an ambush when it had been his job to protect her. And now, he believed that there was nothing left in his heart to give to another woman.

Christine knew differently.

She knew the fears he harbored. That he believed their background and lifestyles made them too incompatible and they'd never mesh for a long-term relationship. That he'd never be able to live up to certain expectations, and that he'd never have her mother's approval.

As if she cared about any of that.

Christine figured she had enough ammunition to blow every single one of his excuses into smithereens. And as soon as they arrived back at her place, she planned to do just that.

The slow song ended, and she stepped out of his embrace. "I need to use the ladies' room before we go," she said, suddenly realizing just how full her bladder was. "I'll meet you back at the table."

"All right."

He went in one direction, and she headed the opposite way toward the restrooms. By the time she walked back out, her mind was already forming every defense it could to any possible excuse Ben tossed her way. She was so wrapped up in her thoughts that she nearly collided into Jodie, one of the bar waitresses, who was standing in front of her.

"I'm sorry, Jodie," Christine said, giving the other woman a friendly smile. "I wasn't watching where I was going."

"Actually, I was waiting for you." The other woman returned Christine's smile with one of her own. "Mr. Crosby said he promised you a bottle of champagne from his private collection for your birthday. He asked me to take you down to the cellar so you can pick out what you'd like."

Earlier, when she'd been with Craig while cutting her cake, he'd told her he wanted to give her a bottle of champagne to celebrate her birthday. At the time, Christine told him that any kind of gift really wasn't necessary, even though he'd insisted. But now that she was leaving with Ben and heading back to her place, the thought of having a bottle of champagne to share with him sounded like a nice idea to complement her planned seduction.

"The cellar is this way," Jodie said, then led Christine down a private corridor behind the main bar.

They passed a few closed doors, then stopped at the very last one at the end of the hallway. Jodie took a ring of keys from her pocket, unlocked the wooden door, and opened it wide. After switching on a light that illuminated the lower portion of the room, she started down the wooden stairs and Christine followed behind.

As they descended into the cellar, Christine shivered and rubbed her bare arms as cold, refrigerated air cascaded over her skin. "Wow, if I'd known how freezing it was down here, I would have worn my sweater."

Jodie laughed. "I know it's a bit on the chilly side, but we have to keep the cellar set at about fifty-seven degrees to keep the various wines at their peak."

The bar waitress strolled across the surprisingly large room, which looked as though it was a basement that had been recently renovated with hardwood floors and customized ground-to-ceiling racks that could easily accommodate hundreds of bottles of wine. Most of the cubbyholes were filled, and Jodie came to a stop in front of an area that had been sectioned off from the rest of the room.

"Here is Craig's private collection, and those are the champagnes right over there," she said, pointing a finger in that direction. "He said for you to help yourself to whatever one you'd like. If you want something really nice, I'd say go for the Krug."

"Thanks. I'll take a look and see what he has." Christine wasn't interested in picking the most expensive bottle, just something she and Ben would enjoy.

Jodie shifted anxiously on her feet. "I've got to get back to my drink orders before they pile up, but you can take your time down here. When you leave, just shut the door behind you. It automatically locks from the outside."

"Great. Thanks, Jodie."

Once the other woman was gone, Christine scanned the wooden racks and pulled out a few of the foil-topped bottles to read the labels. After a few minutes of perusing Craig's very expansive collection, and shivering from the cold, she came across a Dom Perignon Rosé. Remembering once having that particular champagne at a wedding and liking the taste, she decided to choose that bottle.

Just as she turned around, she heard the cellar door at the top the stairs close with a soft "click," then slow, steady footsteps coming down the wooden stairs until Craig appeared in the chamber below, looking impeccably dressed in a black suit and crisp white shirt. His hair looked mussed, as though he'd run his fingers through the strands, but it was the eerily calm yet calculated look in his eyes that sparked a sense of unease deep inside her stomach.

"Hey," she said, forcing a cheerful note to her voice and acting as though nothing was wrong. "I just finished picking a bottle of champagne and was coming back up to thank you."

With his hands tucked into the front pockets of his dress pants, he slowly, gradually, strolled toward her, a wholly sexual smile curving the corners of his mouth. "You can thank me just as well down here." His dark gaze raked down the length of her, not bothering to disguise the fact that he wanted her.

His meaning was clear, and as frantic as her heart was beating beneath her breast, she refused to panic or allow him to get the upper hand in the situation if she could help it. She had to get out of there and away from him, pronto.

"It's a bit cold in here, and the party is upstairs." She

smiled and visibly shivered for effect. "How about we take this champagne with us and celebrate where it's nice and warm and my teeth aren't chattering?"

She moved to the right to go around him and bolt for the stairs, but he countered the move and blocked the way with his body.

His stare turned hot and predatory. "I thought we could have our own private party down here in the cellar, where it's nice and quiet and we can be all by ourselves."

Oh, God. She couldn't believe this was happening to her. She hugged the chilled champagne to her chest, her fingers gripping the neck just in case she had to use the bottle as a weapon. It was the only protection she had.

"I really need to go, Craig," she said, asserting a firm, confident tone to her voice, despite the fear nearly strangling her. "Ben is waiting for me."

As he moved even closer, he casually ran his finger along a rack holding bottles of wine. "Well, he can wait a bit longer, now can't he?"

Christine lifted her chin, wishing she were taller. Craig was a big, substantial man, and as he neared, he made her feel too damned small and vulnerable, which she hated. Finally, Craig stopped, leaving only a few feet between the two of them. Behind her was a rack of wines, and in front of her, much too far away, were the stairs leading to her freedom. She knew she had to distract him in order to get there.

"Ben will come looking for me if I don't get back to him," she said, knowing it was true.

"He can look for you all he wants, but the cellar door is locked from the outside, and he doesn't have a key." He smiled in a way that made her skin crawl. "According to Jodie, nobody knows you're down here but her, and me, and I made sure she's much too busy to bother us."

Then that meant she was on her own, and she figured

the direct approach was all she had left in her favor. "But that doesn't stop *me* from leaving."

Curling her fingers even more tightly around the neck of the bottle, she stepped around him and headed for the stairs, but he grabbed her upper arm to stop her. Just as he pulled her back around, she swung the bottle of champagne at his head.

He saw it coming and ducked, then came back up just as she aimed it at his head from the other direction. He caught her wrist before the bottle could connect with the side of his face and squeezed tight, until the crushing pain he exerted was too unbearable and she dropped the champagne. The bottle crashed to the floor, exploding in a spray of bubbly liquid and shards of glass that pricked and cut at her bare legs.

He shoved her against a nearby wall, so hard that her head hit the concrete surface and she swore she saw stars. When her vision came back into focus, she realized that he'd braced his hands on either side of her shoulders and had wedged a thigh between hers to keep her trapped against the wall and his body. His face was right in front of hers, and he looked pissed.

His jaw clenched tight, and anger flashed in his eyes. "That was a *very* expensive bottle of champagne."

If he expected her to apologize, he had another thing coming. "Go to hell," she hissed.

She struggled against him to get away, aiming her nails at his face and eyes, but he was so much stronger than she was, and he managed to subdue her much too easily. He caught both of her hands in one of his, then reached toward a nearby shelf and grabbed a long, thin piece of rope he must have left there earlier. He yanked her arms behind her back and within seconds had the rope wrapped around her wrists and her hands tightly secured.

He was breathing hard by the time he was done, a quiet kind of fury brewing within him. "You really shouldn't be so rude and unappreciative, Christine." He pressed her up against the wall once again, then framed her jaw with one of his big hands so that she couldn't move her head at all, making her all too aware of just how truly helpless she was. "I planned this little surprise birthday party down here just for you and me, and you're not going anywhere until we're done celebrating. So, you might as well relax and enjoy yourself."

She shuddered, and it had nothing to do with the chill in the air, and everything to do with what his words implied. "If you don't let me go, I'll scream so loud your eardrums will break."

He laughed, the sound arrogant. "You go right ahead. It won't do you much good. Between the cellar being soundproof, and how loud it is upstairs with the band playing, you can scream all you want and no one will hear you." The pressure of his hand on her face eased as he trailed his fingers down her chest to the slope of her breasts. "In fact, I'm fairly certain that by the time I'm done with you, your throat will be raw from screaming."

Bile seemed to fill her mouth. "You're sick."

Her words didn't affect him at all. He was too caught up in his own madness to care. "I've waited patiently for you to come around. For months, I dealt with your rejections. For weeks, I've watched you with Ben, waiting for you to tire of him and come to your senses about me." His voice rose with anger. "I'm tired of waiting, Christy. I'm tired of you fucking another guy and being a whore when you should be mine." In his rage, he grabbed one of the thin rhinestone straps holding up her dress and yanked it hard, ripping it off and sending those small crystals bouncing to the floor.

Terror spiked through her. She could see what was

coming, knew that if she didn't keep him talking and distracted that he was going to rape her. Or worse. "Why are
you doing this, Craig?" she asked, her calm question belying the fear clawing inside her. "I thought we were
friends."

"Friends?" His voice rose incredulously as he pushed
away from her, his expression filled with disgust. "You
used me, Christy. I've helped you with your business and
given you contacts. I was there for you after your nasty
breakup with Jason, ready and willing to be the man you
needed in your life. But all you did was take and take and
take, then discard me like a piece of trash when you no
longer needed me."

His bitter words broadsided her, and she suspected
that they stemmed from a whole lot more than just her.
She was most likely just the catalyst that had sent him
over the edge. "You know that's not true," she said, trying
to reason with him. "I've appreciated everything you've
done for me."

He reached out and caressed the backs of his fingers
along her cheek, and she tried not to cringe in revulsion
at his touch. "Maybe you'd like to show me just how appreciative you are."

She desperately tried to wrack her brain for some kind
of stall tactic. "Not here."

"We're not going anywhere else. We're going to stay
right here until I'm done with you." That depraved light
in his gaze shone brighter. "Until I've used you the way
you've used me. Do you know how long I've waited to get
you alone and have you all to myself like this?"

She shook her head. "How long?"

"Months." His mouth twisted with rancor. "A few
weeks ago I had you alone in my office, half-naked in my
private bathroom. If it hadn't been for Ben, you would
have been mine then. Then, I tried to get you alone the

night of the charity event. God, I was so close, too. You were drugged and you were so willing to do whatever I wanted."

Thank God Ben had come to her rescue. "What else?" she asked, needing to know everything.

"Those snakes you received in the mail? I sent them to you." He looked very pleased with himself. "I had it timed for me to arrive when you opened your mail that day. I sat out in my car and watched through the windows of your business as you took the package to your office. I was going to walk inside The Big Event as you opened the box and discovered the snakes." His expression turned irate. "*I* was supposed to be the one you ran to for protection. *I* was the one who was supposed to save you, but Ben was there. Always Ben!"

Christine couldn't believe what she was hearing.

"Nobody appreciates what I do," Craig ranted angrily as he paced in front of her. "Not you. Not my family. Not even my father! I'm the one who helped Charles Lambert win the election so that my father's development company could get the contract to rebuild the lower west side. I'm the one who sent those threats to your father to drop out of the race so Lambert and my father would benefit from all the extra income that new development would generate. But nobody appreciated what I tried to do. Especially not my father. Instead, he told me I was an idiot for doing something so stupid." His rage over his father's slur was tangible.

Christine had to agree with Jonathan Crosby about his son's state of mind, but there was one thing that didn't make sense to her. "But *my* father didn't drop out of the race."

"I know." Craig shook his head in mock sadness. "And I did warn him that if he didn't step down that he'd lose what was most precious to him. And here you are now."

His smile was pure evil.

"You don't want to do this, Craig," she said, doing and saying whatever it took to change his mind. Because right now, she had no leverage other than her words that could save her.

"I'm so tired of everyone taking and taking and taking from me," he said spitefully. "Now I'm going to take what I want, and nobody is going to stop me. Not even your precious Ben. Tonight, you're all mine."

"I'll *never* be yours, Craig," she said, her voice strong and sure in her conviction. "I love Ben, and nothing you do to me will ever change that."

"Shut up!" he yelled, then backhanded her across the face, the force of it causing her head to snap to the side. "Shut the fuck up!"

He knotted her hair in his fist, yanked back her head, and brought his mouth down on hers. She fought the kiss, the invasion of his tongue, refusing to give even a small part of herself to him. And that only infuriated him more.

His hands pulled at her dress and groped her, making her physically ill at the thought of what was about to happen down here in this isolated, secluded cellar. With her hands tied behind her back, struggling against him was futile. All she could do was close her eyes, detach herself from the situation, and pray that it was over quickly.

Seventeen

BEN glanced at his watch for the fifth time in so many minutes. It had been nearly twenty minutes since Christine told him she needed to go to the ladies' room, and he was still waiting on her. He shifted restlessly in his seat and glanced back in the direction of the ladies' room, but still, nothing.

"You know how women can be when they go to the restroom," Kevin said, obviously sensing his impatience. "She's probably fussing with her hair and makeup."

Primping just wasn't Christine's thing. Sure, she always looked like a million bucks, but she wasn't one to spend a whole lot of time in front of a mirror. Something just wasn't settling right with him.

"Either that, or one of the guests waylaid her to wish her a happy birthday," Ronnie suggested.

"Could be." He knew it was possible that she'd gotten sidetracked, but something was gnawing at those instincts within him, and he wasn't about to ignore them. "I'm going to go look for her."

He strolled back toward the restrooms and glanced around the general area. He circled the dance floor and then went into the main bar area to check there, too. Still, there was no sign of Christine, and he blew out a frustrated stream of breath in order to keep his growing anxiety at bay.

One of the bar waitresses passed by him with a tray full of drinks. He recognized the woman as Jodie, who'd delivered cocktails to their table a few times tonight. Pretty much everyone at Envy thought that he was Christine's boyfriend, and he used that to his advantage now.

He stopped the young woman, who looked up at him with a harried smile. "Hi, Jodie. Have you seen Christine?" he asked hopefully.

"Actually, yes I have," she replied. "Mr. Crosby had me take her down to the wine cellar to pick out a bottle of champagne for her birthday. That was a while ago, so I can't imagine that she'd still be there, though."

Just the mention of Craig's name had Ben's stomach twisting into huge, gigantic knots. "Was Craig with her?"

"Not when I left her there, though I did see Craig go in that direction soon after, probably to help her pick out one of the champagne's from his private collection."

It was clear to Ben that Jodie was oblivious to Craig's nefarious side. "Look, I need you to take me to wherever the wine cellar is."

"Can it wait a few minutes?" She indicated her tray, brimming with bottles of beers and other cocktails. "I've got to get this drink order delivered."

"No, it can't." Ben didn't have a few minutes to wait, or to waste. "I need you to take me there, *now*," he said urgently. "Christy might be in trouble."

A startled look passed over Jodie's features, but thankfully she didn't argue, or try to assure him that Christine was okay. Instead, she caught the attention of another bar waitress and asked the other woman to deliver the drinks for her. Then she led the way down a private corridor behind the main bar. They came to a stop at the last door at the end of the hallway.

"Here's the cellar. I left the door open. I really do doubt they're here," she said, even as she fished a key ring from her front apron pocket. "But if it makes you feel better, we can double-check to be sure."

"Thanks." Ben wasn't going anywhere until he knew for certain that Christine wasn't down in that cellar.

She unlocked the door, and as soon as it opened Ben heard a woman's muffled attempt at yelling, some scuffling, then Craig spoke.

"Who's up there?" he demanded harshly, making Ben realize that he couldn't see all the way up the stairs to the door, which worked to his advantage.

Jodie was staring at Ben with wide, startled eyes. Apparently, she had come to the realization that Craig had set her up to get Christine down in the cellar alone. Ben nodded his head, indicating for her to reply.

"It's Jodie, Mr. Crosby," she said, her voice steady despite the look of dismay on her face. "Is Christine down there with you?"

"No, she's not," Craig replied in a crisp tone, and again there was another noise that sounded like he was trying to restrain or subdue someone. "She left a while ago. Now, I'd like some privacy down here and I don't want to be bothered or interrupted. Make sure everyone upstairs knows that."

"Yes, Mr. Crosby."

Jodie drew the door closed, but left it so that it didn't shut tightly and Ben could easily push it back open. When she glanced back at him, her panic increased when she saw that he'd withdrawn the gun he'd had concealed.

"Oh, my God," she whispered as tears welled in her

eyes. "I honestly had no idea Mr. Crosby would do something like this."

Ben just prayed that the other man hadn't hurt Christine in any way, because if he had, then Ben wouldn't be responsible for his actions. A slow, painful death wouldn't be near good enough for Craig.

"Look, I'm a security agent," he said in a low voice, trying to keep Jodie calm so that she wouldn't go into hysterics, even as his own heart was beating frantically in his chest. "I need you to go to call the police. Tell them that there's a hostage situation at Envy, and you need them here immediately."

She nodded in understanding, then headed back out to the main area. Ben waited until she was gone, then inhaled a deep, steady breath before quietly nudging the door back open again, his weapon poised and ready. It took every ounce of restraint he possessed not to just rush in, guns blazing, but he didn't know what the situation was like, or if Craig was armed. So, he cautiously made his way down the stairs, his entire body tensing at the sound of Christine pleading with Craig to stop whatever he was doing to her.

Another step, and they came into view. Rage surged through Ben at the sickening sight of Craig's face buried against Christine neck, and his hands in places they had no business being. Craig's back was to Ben, so he couldn't shoot the other man because there was too great of a chance that the bullet would go straight through him to Christine, who he had pinned against the wall.

He knew the exact moment that Christine saw him. Her eyes grew round, but she didn't say a word to give his presence away. Her hands looked as though they'd been restrained behind her back, rendering her helpless when it came to Craig's superior strength. She struggled against him, even tried to kick him, but it did her no good.

Silently, he made his way down the rest of the stairs, his gun trained on Craig's back, right in the vicinity of his heart. He still didn't know if he had any kind of weapon, and that was the only thing that kept Ben from not charging over to the other man and ripping him away from Christine—then beating the living shit out of him.

"Let her go, Crosby," Ben demanded.

Craig moved quicker than Ben anticipated. He spun around, and at the same time he pulled Christine around too, so that she was standing in front of him like a human shield. Then he wrapped an arm around her waist to keep her secured in place.

As far as Ben could see, Craig didn't have a weapon, but now Christine was in his direct line of fire. Her expression was terrified, and he noticed that the side of her face near her eye was red and puffy, and the straps of her dress had been torn off. Other than Craig putting his hands all over Christine, it appeared she was okay and unharmed. *Thank God.*

"Ahhh, your knight in shining armor has arrived," Craig drawled sarcastically, his face nestled close to Christine's cheek. "Just in the nick of time, as always." Then his eyes narrowed into menacing slits as he glared at Ben. "God, I hate you!" he spat venomously. "Everything was going my way until you came along, stole Christy away, and screwed everything up!"

The man was obviously a mental case, and Ben treaded lightly so that he didn't do or say something to send Craig over the edge. "It's over Craig. Let her go."

"It's not over until I say it's over!" he yelled like a crazed man. Then he bent down, pulling Christine with him, and reached for something on the floor. When he straightened again, he held a sharp piece of broken glass in his hand. He touched the serrated edge to her cheek and pressed just enough to make Christine whimper from the sting of pain.

"Put your gun down," Craig ordered, and dragged the blade down to the pulse beating in Christine's throat.

Despite the threat, Ben refused to release the gun—it was the only leverage he had in this power play between them and he wasn't about to put Christine in such a vulnerable position. He refused to let anything bad happen to her, knowing he'd never be able to live with himself if Craig harmed her in any way.

Images of Kim in Iraq during the ambush flashed in his head. In his mind's eye he saw her getting shot, then dying in his arms all over again. His throat started to close up with guilt, and he swallowed it back. He couldn't change the past or bring Kim back, but he was determined that his situation with Christine would end much differently . . . if only he could get a clear shot at Craig.

Ben looked into Christine's eyes, seeing the fear there, but also a strength and fortitude that made him proud, as well as an innate faith in his ability to defend her, to protect and save her. She believed in him, trusted in him, and it was those undiluted emotions that were nearly his undoing.

But then she closed her eyes and he watched her relax just the slightest bit, just enough to let him know without words what she was about to do—give him the clearance he needed to take Craig down.

In the meantime, Ben tried to reason with Craig until the opportunity presented itself. "Look, you let her go, and you can walk a free man," he lied, knowing he would do everything within his power to make sure that Craig spent decades behind bars, where he belonged. "There's no reason to hurt Christine."

"I'm not giving her up! She's *mine*," Craig ranted furiously. "And if I can't have her, no one will. Especially not you!"

During Craig's bitter outburst, he waved the sharp

piece of glass in the air, using it to punctuate the resentment and vehemence of his words and leaving Christine
free to complete her maneuver. In that unguarded moment,
she unexpectedly went limp in Craig's arms, dropping like
a lead weight and throwing him off balance—mentally and
physically. She slipped from his grasp and fell to the floor,
and as soon as she was out of the way, and before Craig
could comprehend what had just happened, Ben pulled the
trigger and shot the other man in the left shoulder.

Craig dropped the shard of glass in his hand and
howled in pain as the bullet penetrated flesh and bone.
Christine scrambled away the best she could with her
hands tied behind her back, and when Craig took a step
toward her once again, Ben stopped him cold before he
could touch her.

"That was just a warning shot, asshole," Ben said,
keeping his gun aimed high and pointed right between
Craig's eyes. "You go anywhere near Christine before the
cops arrive and I'll blow your fucking head off." And he
meant it, too.

Obviously not wanting to test Ben's threat, Craig
pressed a hand over his wound and slid along the wall to
the floor, a defeated, broken man.

IT was nearly two hours later before Christine could finally go home. Soon after Ben shot Craig the police arrived and took him into custody. Statements had to be
taken, reports had to be filled out, and because the cops
had piqued the curiosity of her friends, she stopped to explain what had happened and assure them that she was
okay.

As soon as she and Ben arrived back at her house, she
asked him to wait while she took a shower and changed
into something more comfortable. Her legs were sticky

from the champagne she'd dropped, and she had a few minor cuts from the shattered glass that she needed to wash. Overall, she just wanted to scrub away the over-whelming unpleasantness of the entire night and start out fresh and clean with Ben.

She no longer needed a bodyguard or a pretend boyfriend. What she wanted now with Ben was the real deal and something she'd never had with any other man before him. A best friend she loved spending time with and could confide her deepest secrets to, knowing they'd be safe with him. A generous lover who complemented her on so many sexual, intimate levels. A committed rela-tionship based on love, respect, and trust.

But it was clear as she walked back into the kitchen and saw his businesslike stance against the far counter, and the impassive look in his eyes, that he'd already re-treated from her and any of the feelings that had taken root and blossomed between them in their time together. This distant man in front of her with his emotional walls erected sky-high was not the warm, attentive, accessible man she'd just spent the past three weeks with. Instead, this was a man who was running scared and refused to face his past in order to have a future . . . with her.

Still, she was determined that he wasn't going to leave tonight without her giving him the two things he needed most in his life—her heart and her unconditional love. Whether he accepted her gift or not was entirely up to him.

With that in mind, she walked toward him and stopped a few feet away. She'd put on a pair of old sweatpants and an equally ancient pullover hoodie for warmth. Her hair was still damp and she'd washed all her makeup off her face in the shower. All traces of the sophisticated woman he was used to seeing were gone, and in her place was the person she was beneath all the exterior trappings: a plain and simple girl who ached to be loved and cared for by this man.

His gaze roamed over her face and came to a stop on the swollen, bluish-purple mark on the right side of her cheek where Craig had hit her, which would eventually match the bruises still on her shoulder and stomach, courtesy of Jason.

Ben gave her a lopsided grin, but didn't reach out and touch her as she wished he would. "What is it about you that turns men into psychopaths?" he teased, obviously trying to keep things light and easy between them.

"Must be my sparkling personality," she said with equal amounts of humor. "But don't worry, as far as I know, there's no more jilted men lurking out there."

"Good thing." His expression turned much too serious. "Are you going to be okay?"

Physically, she knew she'd heal. Emotionally, though, she had a feeling that it was going to take her a very long time to recover from the pain tightening like a visc around her heart.

"I'm fine," she assured him. "It'll take more than a shiner or a couple of shots with a paintball gun to do me in. I'm not all fluff, you know."

A low, rough rumble of laughter escaped him. "Yeah, you're one tough cookie."

She realized how strong she'd become over the past few weeks—internally and mentally—and knew she had Ben and his support and encouragement to thank for a lot of her transformation. "I guess I'm just done with letting people walk all over me. I've had enough and I'm not taking it anymore," she said playfully.

He didn't smile as she'd expected him to. "It's a good mentality to have." He paused, and she knew what was coming even before the words left his mouth. "I should go."

She crossed her arms over her chest, mirroring his stubborn attitude. "What if I want you to stay?"

A muscle in his jaw ticked. "Another night together isn't going to make ending this any easier."

She shook her head, wondering if he was being deliberately obtuse to avoid the real underlying issues between them. If so, she was about to put everything out there so there would be no mistaking what she wanted, or how she felt about him.

"The thing is, I don't want just one last night with you, Ben. I want, and need, a whole lot more."

"That's part of the problem, Christine," he said gruffly, his eyes flashing with gold flecks of anger. "I just don't have it in me to give you everything you need and deserve. You've known that all along."

Yes, he'd made it abundantly clear that he didn't fit into her life, and that his emotions had been stripped raw from past experiences, but she just didn't believe that he was dead inside, that he didn't have the ability to care for another woman, because she'd seen and felt evidence to the contrary.

"I love you, Ben," she said, risking it all for him. "With all my heart, with all my soul, with everything I am." She swallowed hard, hating that dark look of denial pinching his gorgeous features. "And whether you can admit it to yourself, or not, I *know* you feel something for me, too."

He groaned, sounding like a man who'd been mortally wounded. "I can't do this again, Christine."

Okay, that hurt—that she didn't mean enough to him for him to take a chance, that she wasn't worth the risk to his already battered heart. It also made her angry enough to confront him with what she knew to be true.

"You haven't said the words, but I know you love me, too," she said ruthlessly. "I've seen the emotion in your eyes. I *felt* it with every fiber of my being the night you told me that we were making *love*."

He took a step toward her. "Christine—"

She held up a hand to keep him at a distance. "Don't say anything. I don't what to hear you deny the truth, to me or yourself. I *know* what's real and true. You obviously don't and I can't force you to see or feel something that you won't allow to touch your heart or emotions."

He released a harsh stream of breath and looked away.

But she wasn't done with him just yet. Her throat filled with frustrated tears, and she swallowed them back, refusing to let them fall free in front of Ben. There would be plenty of time for crying later, when she was alone.

"After my mother's controlling influence, then everything that happened with Jason, I thought what I wanted was freedom and independence and being on my own for a good long while," she told him, knowing he was listening even if he wasn't looking at her. "But you know what? I realized during these past few weeks of being with you that it's a matter of finding the right man who completes me in ways that no other person ever has. A man I can talk to about anything, and trust with the most private aspects of my life, and my past. A man who makes me feel sexy, and desirable, and has shown me that I'm fully capable of experiencing and enjoying passion and lust and the kind of intense pleasure I'd only fantasized about."

Finally, she reached out and touched him, because that physical connection was absolutely necessary. Caressing her fingertips along his jaw, she turned his head back toward her so he was forced to meet her gaze again. "If you don't already know, that man is *you*, Ben. You're everything I want and need in my life, and if you're ever ready to stop using your past and the guilt you've allowed to consume you as an excuse to deny your true feelings for me, you know where I am and how to find me."

She took a step back, then another, feeling the chasm between them growing ever wider in so many ways. "You can let yourself out," she said, then turned and headed back to her bedroom, knowing she wouldn't be able to bear watching him walk out of her life for the final time.

"THOSE of us guys who aren't wearing a ball and chain like Joel are heading over to Nick's Sports Bar for some beer and a few games of pool," Kevin said to Ben after his playful dig to the newly married partner at Elite Security Specialists. "Care to join us for a round or two?"

"Hey, don't knock it until you've tried it," Joel said in defense of what he'd referred to as wedded bliss since returning from his honeymoon a few days ago. "There's something to be said about going home every night to a woman who loves and adores you." He grinned like the besotted fool that he was.

Kevin rolled his eyes as he pushed away from the conference table and stood. "Okay. Whatever. That whole one-woman thing just isn't for me."

"Hey, to each his own," Joel said in understanding, since he'd felt the same way not too long ago. "But being in love with the right woman and having a wife does tend to change a guy's priorities."

"Gawd, it's getting sickeningly sweet in here," Kevin said with an exaggerated shudder, then glanced at Ben. "You in or you out, Cabrera?"

Ben shook his head as he picked up a file folder that held the details of his next assignment. "Sorry, I won't be able to make it," he said brusquely.

Kevin jammed his hands on his hips impatiently. "Okay, look, we've got Joel who has his head in the clouds, which I can understand considering he just spent the past week getting laid on a regular basis, and then there's you, the exact opposite. Ever since the Delacroix case ended, you've been one moody son of a bitch."

Ben's lips tightened in annoyance. "For your information, I have an appointment with Nathan Delacroix in about an hour, not that I owe you an explanation for not wanting to go and hang out with you guys at a singles' bar."

Kevin held his hands up in a sign of backing off, his expression contrite for pushing Ben a bit too far. "Okay, you go and tend to business. If you change your mind and want to join Jon, Zach, and I, you know where to find us."

Once Kevin left with Jon and Zach, Ben walked out of the ESS offices with Joel. Before they parted ways to their different vehicles, Joel stopped and faced Ben, his features filled with concern.

"Seriously, are you okay?" Joel asked. "I hate to admit it, but Kevin's right. You haven't been yourself."

Ben sighed and rubbed at the constant ache in his temples. "It'll pass."

Joel eyed him with too much foresight. "You sure about that?"

Honestly, Ben wasn't sure about anything anymore. He'd spent the past week and a half trying to bury himself in work in an attempt to forget about everything that had transpired between them that last night. All the things she'd said to him before he'd walked out of her house—the hope shining in her blue eyes when she'd told him she loved him, and how well she knew what was in his heart and soul when he didn't even know himself anymore.

He truly believed that ending their relationship had been the right thing to do—that Christine deserved a man who was whole in every way, and one that didn't come with the kind of excess emotional baggage such as guilt and regrets that would keep him from giving her everything she needed in her life. Instead, leaving her behind had only increased the awful, desolate, empty feeling deep inside of him.

"You gotta let it go, Ben," Joel said quietly, pulling him from his internal thoughts.

"What are you talking about?" Ben asked gruffly, even though he knew exactly where this conversation was heading.

"I'm talking about what happened to Kim," Joel said bluntly, reading him much too well. "It wasn't your fault, man. You gotta believe that, and you have to stop blaming yourself for her death or it's going to eat you alive and make the rest of your life miserable and lonely as hell."

Ben looked away, because he was beginning to suspect that was true.

"We all went through shit in Iraq, and we all handled the fallout in our own way," Joel went on ruthlessly, as only a good friend could do. "Just don't let it stop you from going after the best thing that has come into your life in a very long time. And that would be Christine Delacroix."

"What do you know about it?" Ben asked, wondering how Joel had come to such an insightful conclusion.

Joel grinned. "It was so obvious not only to me, but to Lora, that you have feelings for Christine. We saw you at the wedding together, and Lora commented on the way you watched Christine the entire night. She told me she recognized that look of longing in your eyes, because she'd seen the same thing with me—wanting something, but believing you didn't deserve it."

Ben shook his head, unable to hide the smile lifting the corners of his mouth. "Lora's a smart woman."

"They all are, Ben." Joel slapped him on the back, sharing a moment of comradery. "And trust me, I've learned that they usually know what's best for us, even when we don't have a clue. You can't change the past, or

the horrors we endured in the war. We all know that because we each lived through our own personal nightmares
in Iraq and we've dealt with it in our own ways. But
there's no reason why you can't live life to the fullest
now. And let me tell you, living life with a good woman,
the *right* woman, has a way of making the past not so
painful and difficult."

"You're a lucky man," Ben said, knowing it was true.

"You would be, too, if you'd just stop denying the
truth." Joel's direct gaze spoke volumes. "What you feel
for Christine is real. It's the present and your future.
Don't be an ass and turn your back on a woman who
loves you the way she obviously does, or else you'll regret it for the rest of your miserable life."

Ben took his friend's advice to heart. "Thanks, Joel."

"Hey, I'm just returning the favor," he said, reminding
Ben of how he'd done the same thing for him not too long
ago. "I've been there, so I completely understand that
sometimes it takes someone else kicking you in the ass to
make you realize what an idiot you're being."

"Gee, thanks." Ben grinned, then glanced at his watch.
"I've got to get going. Delacroix is waiting on me."

"What's going on?" Joel asked curiously. "I thought
that case was wrapped up and closed."

"As far as I know, it is. All he said was that he wanted
to talk to me about certain aspects of the case that he
didn't quite understand."

"That's odd." Joel frowned, looking just as confused
as Ben felt about the call he'd received earlier from
Nathan. "I can't imagine what's left to discuss."

"Me, neither." Ben shrugged. "I'm sure he just has a
few questions about the night of Craig's arrest."

"Probably," Joel agreed, then shifted anxiously on his
feet. "Now, every minute I waste here with you is a
minute less I have with Lora. I'm outta here."

Ben grinned as he walked to his truck, a part of him envying what Joel had with Lora. Yet he knew if he took a chance on Christine, he could have the same exact thing. He spent the drive to Nathan Delacroix's house recalling everything she'd said to him on that last night with her—and mulling over Joel's advice today, too. By the time he arrived at Nathan's and rang the doorbell that echoed throughout the massive home, Ben felt a glimmer of optimism that maybe things could work between him and Christine . . . until Maggie let him inside the house and he was slapped with an in-your-face reminder of how the Delacroixs lived, along with the realization of what Christine was, and everything Ben was not—classy, refined, and well-bred.

"Hi, Mr. Cabrera," Maggie said, greeting him with a genuine smile. "It's nice to see you again."

"You, too, Maggie. I'm here to see Mr. Delacroix."

Maggie nodded. "He's waiting for you in his office."

Even though Ben knew where Nathan's office was located, Maggie led the way, and as Ben walked through the huge house that was decorated with such lavish elegance, those doubts and insecurities settled deep in his gut, chasing away the confidence that Joel had just instilled in him, making him wonder if he could ever really mesh into Christine's life. Or would he be an outcast and scorned by her mother at every opportunity for not being good enough for her daughter?

Maggie opened the door to Nathan's office, and Ben stepped inside, greeting the other man with a firm handshake and friendly hello. For someone who'd just lost the election for governor, Nathan looked more casual and relaxed than Ben could ever remember seeing him, and oddly enough, content, too.

Nathan waved a hand toward one of the leather chairs in front of his desk. "Have a seat, Ben."

He did as the other man asked, and as soon as he was settled in the chair, Ben jumped right into business. "You wanted to discuss the case with me?"

"I did." Nathan leaned back in his chair, his gaze candid and direct. "I'd like you to tell me what, exactly, happened to Christine. She hasn't been the same since you left."

That bit of information took Ben by surprise. "You know everything that happened. It was all in the report. Is she not doing okay?"

Nathan steepled his hands in front of him, his expression reflecting his concern. "No, and quite frankly, I'm worried about her."

Unease rippled through Ben at the thought of Christine having some kind of delayed reaction to what had happened to her, first with Jason, then with Craig. "What's wrong with her?"

"Actually, I was hoping *you'd* be able to tell *me*."

Ben shook his head in confusion. "I have no idea. I haven't spoken to her since that last night with Craig."

Nathan digested that, then said, "I'm thinking that's part of the problem."

Ben frowned. This conversation made no real sense to him, and even though he knew there was some kind of point to this discussion, he couldn't grasp what the other man was trying to say. "Mr. Delacroix, I mean no disrespect, but I have no idea what you're talking about."

Nathan sighed. "You're a smart man, Ben, but I'm thinking you have a lot to learn when it comes to my daughter. She loves you, you know."

Ben caught his jaw before it fell open in shock. "She told you that?"

"She didn't have to. I've seen her and I've talked to her, and I don't think I've ever seen Christine so miserable. And, unfortunately, I've had firsthand experience with that kind of misery so I know exactly what she's going through. And seeing her so upset and hurting makes me *very* unhappy, because my daughter's happiness and well-being means everything to me."

Ben was so stunned by Nathan's intuition, he didn't know how to respond. But obviously, Nathan had plenty to say to him, and all he expected Ben to do was sit there and listen.

"I've always liked you, Ben. You're trustworthy and dependable, and have the kind of integrity that most men lack these days," Nathan said, and Ben knew he was referring to the previous men in Christine's life. "When my daughter needed a bodyguard, I picked you for the job for two very distinct reasons. One, I knew I could trust you with my daughter, to protect her and keep her safe. And two, I saw the way you and Christine were with one another. There was a certain kind of attraction and chemistry between you, and I thought maybe, hopefully, you two would hit it off and something deeper would develop."

Ben couldn't believe what he was hearing, and he certainly didn't know what to say.

"Judging by how emotional Christine has been lately, I'm guessing that you two more than just hit it off."

"Yes, we did," Ben admitted, but didn't reveal any details to the other man, because what he felt for Christine was a personal, private thing, and she deserved to hear it from him first—that he did love her, and wanted a future with her. And he'd tell her all that and more, just as soon as this meeting with her father was over.

"You know, Christine told me what happened in Iraq, and I'm very sorry for what you lost there."

"Thank you, sir."

The anguish he always felt when he thought about Kim and her horrific death was still there, but not nearly as strong and overwhelming as it always had been. People told him that time would heal all wounds, but he was beginning to believe that Christine, with her gentle heart and tender way of understanding him, had been the one to soothe his pain, assuage his grief, and make him whole once again.

"She also mentioned how uncomfortable you are with the differences in your background and how Audrey feels about you."

Ben winced, feeling a rush of embarrassment heat his face. He wished that Christine hadn't divulged that bit of information, but since she had and it was all out in the open, he was just as honest. "Mrs. Delacroix has never made a secret of the fact that she doesn't care for me, especially when it comes to her daughter."

"I'm very sorry about that," Nathan said, apologizing for his wife's crass behavior. "But despite Audrey's negative and judgmental attitude when it comes to some people, I've always raised Christine to accept people at face value, and that's exactly what she's done with you. Luckily, she takes after me more than her mother in that regard," he added with a proud grin.

"One more thing," Nathan said, growing serious once again. "Losing this election was the best thing that ever happened to me."

The other man was full of surprises tonight, and Ben couldn't even begin to guess how this discussion would end. "How so?"

"It's allowed me to have a life of my own. To be true to myself and finally do what I should have done many years ago," Nathan said with conviction. "I'm divorcing Audrey, and I'm making sure that she gets help for her drinking problem that has grown increasingly worse over the years, and hopefully she'll be able to work through her bitterness at life in general. As for me, I'm tired of putting on a front and perpetrating a lie in public of being a happily married man when I'm not. I've wasted too many years being alone and lonely and I'm getting too damned old to live life that way. Don't make the same mistake I did by not going after the one thing that matters most in life."

Because Christine had confided in him, Ben knew that Nathan was referring to the woman he'd been having an affair with all these years. The woman he loved. The woman who'd waited patiently for him while he remained married to a spiteful wife and pursued a political career.

And now, Ben was going to go after the *only* thing that mattered in his life—the unconditional love of a tender-hearted, sensitive, beautiful woman.

Nathan sat forward in his chair, his gaze softening with genuine esteem. "I know how hard it is to face failure, or admit defeat, but sometimes it's best to put the past behind us where it belongs, and move forward with our lives."

"That's great advice." Ben stood, anxious to see Christine and hoping like hell that he still had a chance with her. "Is there anything else I need to know before I go and talk to Christy?" he asked the other man.

Nathan grinned. "Yeah. Just take care of her, cherish her, and make her happy for the rest of her life."

Ben nodded, knowing he'd do all that, and much more. "Consider it done."

Eighteen

CHRISTINE wasn't home from work for even ten minutes before someone knocked loudly on the front door. She was tired and cranky and all she wanted to do was pull off her blouse, skirt, and shoes and soak in a hot tub of water with big bubbles and a glass of wine, and soothe the heartache that had been her constant companion since Ben had walked out of her life.

She planned to indulge in that nightly ritual, just as soon as she got rid of whoever was on her front porch.

Figuring it was a solicitor trying to sell something she didn't want, she opened the door intending to give them a polite "thanks, but no thanks," but the words died on her lips—because even if this particular man wanted to sweet-talk her into buying oceanfront property in Arizona, there was no way she'd ever be able to refuse the offer.

Ben stood in front of her, solid and real, and not a dream or figment of her imagination. He looked just as gorgeous as ever, and he was watching her intently, waiting for a reaction, and she had to resist the urge to launch herself into his arms. Considering the way things had ended between them, and the current apprehension emanating from him, she didn't know why he was there, or what to expect.

When she said nothing at all, he finally spoke. "Can I come in and talk to you?"

"Sure." She opened the door wide, and after he entered, she led the way into the living room.

Turning to face him, she crossed her arms over her chest and met his gaze. An awkward silence settled between them, which she absolutely hated because it had never been like that with them before. They'd always been able to talk about everything and anything, and that was no longer the case.

"Would you like something to drink?" she asked, for lack of something better to say.

"No, thanks," he replied, his tone low and rough . . . and just a bit uncertain, which matched the vulnerability and underlying fear shining in his eyes.

And that's when she realized the reason for his visit. Ben was a man who was strong and steady and sure. A man who'd learned to safeguard his emotions, and protect the heart that had been shattered more than just once. First, when his mother had walked out on him, and then when Kim had died in his arms.

But now, there were no walls, no defenses, and nothing to hide the wealth of feelings that she knew was all for her. But knowing was not enough. She had to hear the words from him.

"What do you want, Ben?" she asked, her soft whisper imploring him to open up and trust her, to believe in what they had together.

He exhaled a deep breath that unraveled into a groan. "The only thing I want, the only thing I need, is *you*."

Everything within her rejoiced, but outwardly she remained calm. "What changed?" She had to know.

"Me, hopefully." Sincerity rang true in his voice. His expression held no shutters, nothing closed off from her. "You're the first woman who has ever cared enough to pry out every painful secret I have, and force me to face some of my greatest fears, one of which is to take a chance and love someone again."

She held her breath, waiting and hoping . . .

"I love you, Christy," he said, his voice filled with such overwhelming confidence, such amazing certainty, that it brought tears to her eyes.

Finally, he closed the distance between them. He framed her face in his big, warm hands and stared deeply, adoringly, into her eyes, making her feel like the most precious thing in his life. And she believed it, too.

"I love the strong, generous, independent woman you are," he said, continuing his litany of fealty and devotion. "I love the way you make me laugh and smile. I love arguing with you and I love making love to you. And, I even love when you kick my ass in basketball," he added with a touch of humor.

She laughed around the emotion clogging her throat.

"But mostly, I love the way you make me *feel* when I thought I was dead inside, and that's something I can't, and don't, want to live without."

She bit her bottom lip, and when she blinked, a tear rolled down her cheek.

He gently wiped away the moisture with his thumb, looking dismayed. "Why in the world are you crying?"

"Because I'm so happy," she said, knowing that as a guy, he wouldn't understand unless she explained. "With all the bad luck I've had with the men in my past, I never thought I'd ever get this lucky."

"I'm the lucky one," he insisted.

Okay, she wasn't going to argue with that. "I never knew what true love was, or what it felt like, until you. And I don't ever want the feeling to end."

"I won't let it. I promise." He brushed his lips across hers in a soft, featherlight kiss. "Marry me, Christy."

She pulled back, her eyes wide and hopeful. "Do you mean it?"

He released a long-suffering sigh. "For only about ten seconds, then the offer is off the table, so you need to decide fast," he teased.

"Yes," she said quickly, and threw her arms around his neck to hug him tight. "Yes, Ben, I'll marry you!"

She kissed him, deeply, her desire and love for this man knowing no boundaries. When they finally came up for air, she knew exactly how she wanted to get married— and it didn't include the kind of circus her mother would no doubt plan, given the chance.

"I want to elope," she told him, certain that would make him happy, too. "I want to go somewhere with you, just the two of us. I'm thinking somewhere sultry and romantic like Hawaii."

A grin quirked one corner of his sexy mouth. "Your mother would never forgive you."

"I'm okay with that." She threaded her fingers through his hair and pressed her body closer to his, rubbing her thighs sinuously against his, and generating a whole lotta heat in the process. "I don't want a big, huge, elaborate wedding, and I know you don't, either."

"But I would, for you."

She knew he meant it, and that was enough for her. "Thank you, but there's no need for either of us to go through eight months of planning *hell*." The thought made her shudder. She might plan other people's events for a living, but she'd been there, done that for herself, and it just wasn't for her personally. "And I really don't want to wait that long to get married."

"I'm ready anytime you are."

She wondered if next week was too soon for him. Now that she had Ben back in her life, she never wanted to let him go.

Then she thought of something she needed to tell him. "By the way, my parents are getting a divorce." For her, it was a huge relief, even though she knew her mother had a very rocky road ahead of her. And a lot of personal issues to deal with, as well.

"I know," he said quietly.

"You do?" She stared at him in shock. "How?"

He shrugged, and slid his hands around to her bottom as he walked her backward toward the long, wide couch, his intentions clear. "Your father told me."

She came to a stop before he could distract her further. "Wait a minute. You talked to my father?"

"Yeah," he admitted sheepishly. "Between him and Joel, they knocked some sense into me and made me realize what a fool I was for letting you go."

She grinned, making a mental note to thank both men when she got the chance. "They were both right, you know."

"Stop your gloating," he said in a playful growl.

He urged her back another step, then tumbled her onto the couch. She gasped as he came down on top of her, nestling his hips between her thighs until she could feel the press of his erection against the very heart of her. They were both still completely dressed, but she knew that wouldn't last much longer.

Face-to-face, he stared down at her, the love in his eyes nearly stealing her breath from her lungs. "How do you feel about having babies?"

She thought of two little boys that looked just like Ben, and maybe a girl to help balance out all that male testosterone. She wanted to give Ben the family he never had. "I want at least three."

"That works for me." He slid his hand beneath her skirt and trailed his fingers along her thigh. "In fact, I'm thinking we'd better start practicing, because it might take us a while to get it right."

She laughed, unable to contain the joy and happiness filling her to overflowing. "I couldn't agree with you more," she said, and pulled his mouth down to hers, ready to sacrifice herself to the cause, and more than willing to spend the rest of her life proving just how much she loved this man.

Turn the page for a special preview of

Sea Witch

by Virginia Kantra
Coming soon from Berkley Sensation!

IF she didn't have sex with something soon, she would burst out of her skin.

She plunged through the blue-shot water, driven by a whisper on the wind, a pulse in her blood that carried her along like a warm current. The lavender sky was brindled pink and daubed with indigo clouds. On the beach, fire leaped from the rocks, glowing with the heat of the dying sun.

Her mate was dead. Dead so long ago that the tearing pain, the fresh, bright welling of fury and grief, had ebbed and healed, leaving only a scar on her heart. She barely missed him anymore. She did not allow herself to miss him.

But she missed sex.

Her craving flayed her, hollowed her from the inside out. Lately she'd felt as if she were being slowly scraped to a pelt, a shell, lifeless and empty. She wanted to be touched. She yearned to be filled again, to feel someone move inside her, deep inside her, hard and urgent inside her.

The memory quickened her blood.

She rode the waves to shore, drawn by the warmth of the flames and the heat of the young bodies clustered there. Healthy human bodies, male and female.

Mostly male.

SOME damn fool had built a fire on the point. Police Chief Caleb Hunter spotted the glow from the road.

Mainers welcomed most visitors to their shore. But Bruce Whittaker had made it clear when he called that the islanders' tolerance didn't extend to bonfires on the beach.

Caleb had no particular objection to beach fires, as long as whoever set the fire used the designated picnic areas or obtained a permit. At the point, the wind was likely to carry sparks to the trees. The volunteers at the fire department, fishermen mostly, didn't like to be pulled out of bed to deal with somebody else's carelessness.

Caleb pulled his marked Jeep behind the litter of vehicles parked on the shoulder of the road: a tricked-out Wrangler, a ticket-me red Firebird, and a late-model Lexus with New York plates. Two weeks shy of Memorial Day, and already the island population was swelling with folks from Away. Caleb didn't mind. The annual influx of summer people paid his salary. Besides, compared to Mosul or Sadr City or even Portland down the coast, World's End was a walk on the beach. Even at the height of the season.

Caleb could have gone back to the Portland PD. Hell, after his medical discharge from the National Guard, he could have gone anywhere. Since 9/11, with the call-up of the reserves and the demands of homeland security, most big city police departments were understaffed and overwhelmed. A decorated combat veteran—even one with his left leg cobbled together with enough screws, plates, and assorted hardware to set off the metal detector

every time he walked through the police station doors—
was a sure hire.

The minute Caleb heard old Roy Miller was retiring,
he had put in for the chief's job on World's End, struggling upright in his hospital bed to update his résumé. He
didn't want to make busts or headlines anymore. He just
wanted to keep the peace, to find some peace, to walk pa-
trol without getting shot at. To feel the wind on his face
again and smell the salt in the air.

To drive along a road without the world blowing up
around him.

He eased from the vehicle, maneuvering his stiff knee
around the steering wheel. He left his lights on. Going
without backup into an isolated area after dark, he felt a
familiar prickle between his shoulder blades. Sweat slid
down his spine.

*Get over it. You're in World's End. Nothing ever happens
here.*

Which was about all he could handle now.

Nothing.

He crossed the strip of trees, thankful this particular
stretch of beach wasn't all slippery rock, and stepped
silently onto sand.

SHE came ashore downwind behind an outcrop of rock
that reared from the surrounding beach like the standing
stones of Orkney.

Water lapped on sand and shale. An evening breeze
caressed her damp skin, teasing every nerve to quivering
life. Her senses strained for the whiff of smoke, the rumble of male laughter, drifting on the wind. Her nipples
hardened.

She shivered.

Not with cold. With anticipation.

She combed her wet hair with her fingers and arranged it over her bare shoulders. First things first. She needed clothes.

Even in this body, her blood kept her warm. But she knew from past encounters that her nakedness would be . . . unexpected. She did not want to raise questions or waste time and energy in explanations.

She had not come ashore to talk.

Desire swelled inside her like a child, weighting her breasts and her loins.

She picked her way around the base of the rock on tender, unprotected feet. There, clumped like seaweed above the tide line, was that a . . . *blanket*? She shook it from the sand—*a towel*—and tucked it around her waist, delighting in the bright orange color. A few feet farther on, in the shadows outside the bonfire, she discovered a gray fleece garment with long sleeves and some kind of hood. Drab. Very drab. But it would serve to disguise her. She pulled the garment over her head, fumbling her arms through the sleeves, and smiled ruefully when the cuffs flopped over her hands.

The unfamiliar friction of the clothing chafed and excited her. She slid through twilight, her pulse quick and hot. Still in the shadows, she paused, her widened gaze sweeping the group of six—*seven, eight*—figures sprawled or standing in the circle of the firelight. Two females. Six males. She eyed them avidly.

They were very young.

Sexually mature, perhaps, but their faces were soft and unformed and their eyes shallow. The girls were shrill. The boys were loud. Raw and unconfident, they jostled and nudged, laying claim to the air around them with large, uncoordinated gestures.

Disappointment seeped through her.

"Hey! Watch it!"

Something spilled on the sand. Her sensitive nostrils caught the reek of alcohol.

Not only young, but drunk. Perhaps that explained the clumsiness.

She sighed. She did not prey on drunks. Or children.

Light stabbed at her pupils, twin white beams and flashing blue lights from the ridge above the beach. She blinked, momentarily disoriented.

A girl yelped.

A boy groaned.

"Run," someone shouted.

Sand spurted as the humans darted and shifted like fish in the path of a shark. They were caught between the rock and the strand, with the light in their eyes and the sea at their backs. She followed their panicked glances, squinting toward the tree line.

Silhouetted against the high white beams and dark, narrow tree trunks stood a tall, broad figure.

Her blood rushed like the ocean in her ears. Her heart pounded. Even allowing for the distortion of the light, he looked big. Strong. Male. His silly, constraining clothes only emphasized the breadth and power of his chest and shoulders, the thick muscles of his legs and arms.

He moved stiffly down the beach, his face in shadow. As he neared the fire, red light slid greedily over his wide, clear forehead and narrow nose. His mouth was firm and unsmiling.

Her gaze expanded to take him in. Her pulse kicked up again. She felt the vibration to the soles of her feet and the tips of her fingers.

This was a man.

KIDS.

Caleb shook his head and pulled out his ticket book.

Back when he was in high school, you got busted drinking on the beach, you poured your cans on the sand and maybe endured a lecture from your parents. Not that his old man had cared what Caleb did. After Caleb's mom decamped with his older brother, Bart Hunter hadn't cared about much of anything except his boat, his bottle, and the tides.

But times—and statutes—had changed.

Caleb confiscated the cooler full of beer.

"You can't take that," one punk objected. "I'm twenty-one. It's mine."

Caleb arched an eyebrow. "You found it?"

"I bought it."

Which meant he could be charged with furnishing liquor to minors.

Caleb nodded. "And you are . . . ?"

The kid's jaw stuck out. "Robert Stowe."

"Can I see your license, Mr. Stowe?"

He made them put out the fire while he wrote them up: seven citations for possession and—in the case of twenty-one-year-old Robert Stowe—a summons to district court.

He handed back their driver's licenses along with the citations. "You boys walk the girls home now. Your cars will still be here in the morning."

"It's too far to walk," a pretty, sulky brunette complained. "And it's dark."

Caleb glanced from the last tinge of pink in the sky to the girl. Jessica Dalton, her driver's license read. Eighteen years old. Her daddy was a colorectal surgeon from Boston with a house right on the water, about a mile down the road.

"I'd be happy to call your parents to pick you up," he offered, straight-faced.

"Screw that," announced the nineteen-year-old owner of the Jeep. "I'm driving."

"If I start giving Breathalyzer tests for OUIs, it's going to be a long night," Caleb said evenly. "Especially when I impound your vehicle."

"You can't do that," Stowe said.

Caleb leveled a look at him.

"Come on, Robbie." The other girl tugged his arm. "We can go to my place."

Caleb watched them gather their gear and stumble across the sand.

"I can't find my sweatshirt."

"Who cares? It's ugly."

"You're ugly."

"Come on."

Their voices drifted through the dusk. Caleb waited for them to make a move toward their cars, but something— his threat to tell their parents, maybe, or his shiny new shield or his checkpoint glare—had convinced them to abandon their vehicles for the night.

He dragged his hand over his forehead, dismayed to notice both were sweating.

That was okay.

He was okay.

He was fine, damn it.

He stood with the sound of the surf in his ears, breathing in the fresh salt air, until his skin cooled and his heartbeat slowed. When he couldn't feel the twitch between his shoulder blades anymore, he hefted the cooler and lumbered to the Jeep. His knee shifted and adjusted to take his weight on the soft sand. He'd passed the 1.5 mile run required by the state of Maine to prove his fitness for duty. But that had been on a level track, not struggling to stabilize on uneven ground in the dark.

He stowed the evidence in back, slammed the hatch, and glanced toward the beach.

A woman shone at the water's edge, wrapped in twilight

and a towel. The sea foamed around her bare, pale feet. Her long, dark hair lifted in the breeze. Her face was pale and perfect as the moon.

For one second, the sight caught him like a wave smack in the chest, robbing him of speech. Of breath. Yearning rushed through his soul like the wind over the water, stirring him to the depths. His hands curled into fists at his sides.

Not okay. He throttled back his roaring imagination. She was just a kid. A girl. An underage girl in an oversize sweatshirt with—his gaze dipped again, briefly—a really nice rack.

And he was a cop. Time to think like a cop. Mystery Girl hadn't been with the group around the fire. So where had she been hiding?

Caleb stomped back through the trees. The girl stood with her bare feet planted in the sand, watching him approach. At least he didn't have to chase her.

He stopped a few yards away. "Your friends are gone. You missed them."

She tilted her head, regarding him with large, dark, wide-set eyes. "They are not my friends."

"Guess not," he agreed. "Since they left without you."

She smiled. Her lips were soft and full, her teeth white and slightly pointed. "I meant I do not know them. They are very . . . young, are they not?"

He narrowed his gaze on her face, mentally reassessing her age. Her skin was baby fine, smooth and well cared for. No makeup. No visible piercings or tattoos. Not even a tan.

"How old are you?"

Her smile broadened. "Older than I look."

He resisted the urge to smile back. She could be over the legal drinking age—not jailbait, after all. Those eyes held a purely adult awareness, and her smile was knowing. But he'd pounded Portland's pavements long enough to know the kind of trouble a cop invited giving a pretty woman a break. "Can I see your license, please?"

She blinked slowly. "My . . ."

"ID," he snapped. "Do you have it?"

"Ah. No. I did not realize I would need any."

He took in her damp hair, the towel tucked around her waist. If she'd come down to the beach to swim . . . Okay, nobody swam in May but fools or tourists. But even if she was simply taking a walk, her story made sense. "You staying near here?"

Her dark gaze traveled over him. She nodded. "Yes, I believe I will. Am," she corrected.

He was sweating again, and not from nerves. His emotions had been on ice a long time, but he still recognized the slow burn of desire.

"Address?" he asked harshly.

"I don't remember." She smiled again, charmingly, looking him full in the eyes. "I only recently arrived."

He refused to be charmed. But he couldn't deny the tug of attraction, deep in his belly. "Name?"

"Margred."

Margred. Sounded foreign. He kind of liked it.

He raised his brows. "Just Margred?"

"Margaret, I think you would say."

"Last name?"

She took a step closer, making everything under the sweatshirt sway. *Hell-o, breasts.* "Do you need one?"

He couldn't think. He couldn't remember being this distracted and turned on since he'd sat behind Susanna Colburn in seventh grade English and spent most of second period with a hard-on. Something about her voice . . . her eyes . . . It was weird.

"In case I need to get in touch with you," he explained.

"That would be nice."

He was staring at her mouth. Her wide, wet, full-lipped mouth. "What?"

"If you got in touch with me. I want you to touch me."

He jerked himself back. "What?"

She looked surprised. "Isn't that what you want?"

Yes.

"No."

Fuck.

Caleb was frustrated, savagely disappointed with himself and with her. He knew plenty of women—badge bunnies—went for cops. Some figured sex would get them out of trouble or a ticket. Some were simply into uniforms or guns or handcuffs.

He hadn't taken her for one of them.

"Oh." She regarded him thoughtfully.

His stomach muscles tightened.

And then she smiled. "You are lying," she said.

Yeah, he was.

He shrugged. "Just because I'm—" *horny, hot, hard* "—attracted doesn't mean I have to act on it."

She tilted her head. "Why not?"

He exhaled, a gust between a laugh and a groan. "For starters, I'm a cop."

"Cops don't have sex?"

He couldn't believe they were having this discussion. "Not on duty."

Which was mostly true. True for him, anyway. He hadn't seen any horizontal action since . . . God, since the last time he was home on leave, over eighteen months ago. His brief marriage hadn't survived his first deployment, and nobody since had cared enough to be waiting when he got out.

"When are you not on duty?" she asked.

He shook his head. "What, you want a date?"

Even sarcasm didn't throw this chick. "I would meet you again, yes. I am . . . attracted, too."

She wanted him.

Not that it mattered.

He cleared his throat. "I'm never off duty. Until Memorial Day, I'm the only cop on the island."

"I don't live on your island. I am only . . ." Again with the pause, like English was her second language or something. ". . . visiting," she concluded with a smile.

Like fucking a tourist would be perfectly okay.

Well, wouldn't it?

The thought popped unbidden into his head. It wasn't like he was arresting her. He didn't even suspect her of anything except wanting to have sex with him, and he wasn't a big enough hypocrite to hold that against her.

But he didn't understand this alleged attraction she felt. He felt.

And Caleb did not trust what he did not understand.

"Where are you staying?" he asked. "I'll walk you home."

"Are you trying to get rid of me?"

"I'm trying to keep you safe."

"That's very kind of you. And quite unnecessary."

He stuck his hands in his pockets, rocking back on his heels. "You getting rid of me now?"

She smiled, her teeth white in the moonlight. "No."

"So?"

She turned away, her footprints creating small, reflective pools in the sand. "So I will see you."

He was oddly reluctant to let her go. "Where?"

"Around. On the beach. I walk on the beach in the evening." She looked at him over her shoulder. "Come find me sometime . . . when you're not on duty."

Janelle Denison is the *USA Today* bestselling author of many contemporary romances. She lives in Rialto, California, with her family.